Praise for *Night Bites*

"Sixteen original queer, bi- and hetero tales of blood and lust: the first vampiric sheaf ever solely by women, with a feminine and feminist view of the genre. . . . Strong and satisfying."
— *Kirkus Reviews*

"Wonderfully broad-ranging, this anthology will find an appreciative audience among both vampire aficionados and just plain adventurous readers." — *Booklist*

"The tales in *Night Bites* will delight vampire lovers, horror readers and anyone looking for something new, different and exciting to read." — *Cricket in the Corner*

"*Night Bites* contains 16 excellent stories, all unique in their portrayal of the vampire myth. . . . The women of *Night Bites* will take you on a journey through a sometimes sinister, chilling and realistic world of vampires. . . . These vampire stories breathe fresh new life into a genre that has been known by its stereotypes. . . . Our only complaint about the book is that we want more: Let's hope a sequel comes along or we'll be out for blood."
— *Amazon City Library*

"Unique offerings for those who enjoy offbeat literature."
— *Library Journal*

Other Books by Victoria A. Brownworth

Night Bites: Vampire Tales by Women (ed.)
Out for Blood: Tales of Mystery and Suspense by Women (ed.)
Too Queer: Essays from a Radical Life
Thirteen by Seven: Collected Short Stories (ed.)
Sometime in June: Collected Stories
Sweet Olive
Quatorze: Collected Poems
Equinox and Other Poems

Books by Victoria A. Brownworth and Judith M. Redding

Film Fatales: Independent Women Directors
Out for More Blood: Tales of Malice and Retaliation by Women (eds.)

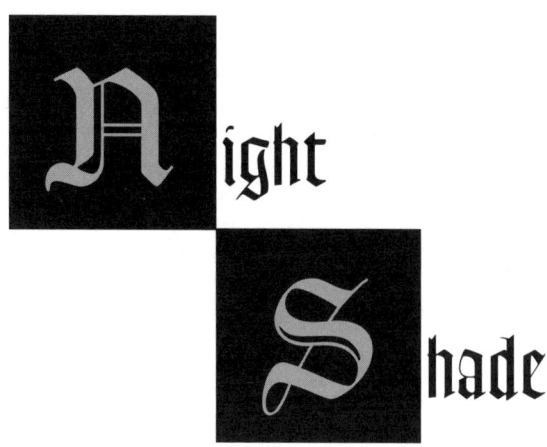

Gothic Tales by Women

Edited by Victoria A. Brownworth
and Judith M. Redding

Copyright © 1999 by Victoria A. Brownworth and Judith M. Redding

All rights reserved. No portion of this book may be reproduced in any form, with the exception of brief passages in reviews, without prior written permission from Seal Press.

Seal Press
3131 Western Avenue, Suite 410
Seattle, WA 98121
206-283-7844
sealprss@scn.org

This book is a collection of fiction. Any resemblance to actual individuals or events is entirely coincidental and unintentional.

"Silkie" is reprinted with permission of Alyson Publications © 1999 by Barbara Wilson.

Cover design: Patrick David Barber
Cover photo: Kajetan Kandler/Tony Stone Images
Text design: Laura Gronewold

Library of Congress Cataloging-in-Publication Data
Night shade: Gothic tales by women / edited by Victoria A. Brownworth and Judith M. Redding.
1. Horror tales, American. 2. Gothic revival (Literature)
3. Short stories, American—Women authors.
I. Brownworth, Victoria A. II. Redding, Judith M.
PS648.H6N496   1999   823'.08729089287—dc21   99-13306
ISBN 1-58005-024-7

Printed in the United States of America
First printing, April 1999

10   9   8   7   6   5   4   3   2   1

Distributed to the trade by Publishers Group West
In Canada: Publishers Group West Canada, Toronto, Ontario
In the U.K. and Europe: Airlift Book Company, Middlesex, England
In Australia: Banyan Tree Book Distributors, Kent Town, South Australia

For Fiona Islington, who perfected the art of legerdemain

Acknowledgments

Anthologies are the proverbial blessing and curse: It is always exciting to read a host of writing by a range of writers, but inevitably not every story can be included. So thanks to all the writers, women and men, who submitted stories, those included here and those we could not include.

Contributions to an anthology go well beyond the writing, editing and submissions. Thus we especially wish to thank Joan Poole, Carolyn Phillips, Edmund Kaminsky, Constance Kaminsky, Jennifer Goldenberg, Theodore Brownworth, Meredith Kane, Roz Warren, Beverly Robertson, Marcia Brown, Roberta Hacker and Jane Shaw for their varied and sundry help in the preparation of this book. As ever, thanks go out to Ruthann Robson and Mabel Maney for their sage advice, attentive ears and keen sense of irony. Thanks also to Story Clapp, Dr. Tish Fabens and Dr. Jonathan Gomberg.

Our continued thanks to Seal Press for their unflagging efforts in the publication of edgy feminist writing. Our appreciation to Faith Conlon, Lee Damsky, Ingrid Emerick, Laura Gronewold, Kate Loeb, Lisa Okey and Lynn Siniscalchi. Finally, our editor Jennie Goode provided excellent editorial advice and good humor throughout, making this project as enjoyable as work is ever meant to be.

Table of Contents

Introduction
Victoria A. Brownworth — ix

The Existential Housewife
Lisa D. Williamson — 3

Femme Coverte
Diane DeKelb-Rittenhouse — 21

Creepers
Joanne Dahme — 54

Luella Miller
Mary E. Wilkins-Freeman — 81

The Birthday Present
Roz Warren — 96

La Noche
Terri de la Peña — 104

Newtime Cowboy
Joyce Wagner — 122

Apéritif
Susan Raffo — 137

Feeding the Dark
Jean Stewart — 143

The Acolyte
Toni Brown — 172

Pierced
Linda K. Wright — 177

Silkie
Barbara Wilson — 185

Mud
Judith M. Redding — 200

Keys
Ruthann Robson — 210

Vengeance of Epona
Susanna Sturgis — 221

Breech Birth
Meredith S. Baird — 240

Day of the Dead
Victoria A. Brownworth — 257

About the Contributors — 277

Introduction

From ghoulies and ghosties and long-legged beasties and things that go bump in the night, good Lord deliver us. — Old Scottish prayer

ince the proverbial dawn of time, humans have been both haunted by and attracted to things supernatural, things beyond our human ability to conceptualize. We have always conjured images of a world—call it a parallel universe, another dimension, heaven or hell—beyond our own, but with a similar configuration to our own. We believe in gods and goddesses or a singular God, supernatural beings who order the universe as we know it and as we have yet to know it. Many of us also believe in other supernatural beings, those who create chaos—demons. And we believe that these beings—Good and Evil—orchestrate their agendas from a place we cannot see or really even imagine.

Inherent in the acceptance of a supernatural world is the concomitant belief that within the dimensions of this "other side" things happen that influence us on *this* side; those on the other side can traverse the chasm that separates both worlds in order to facilitate their plans. So beyond a belief that god/God influences our daily lives is another series of beliefs: that other supernatural creatures move from that world to ours, infiltrating the mundane in extraordinary ways. Most cultures and religions, for example, believe the dead can help the living with their travails. Shintoists pray to the ancestral dead; Catholics seek intercession with Christ from their dead, most especially the saints. In culture and myth the ghosts or shades of the dead frequently pass through that scrim to visit the living—either to impart information or to exact revenge.

In this parallel world, possibilities exist that do not exist in our own—semblances of ourselves in the form of ghosts, demons, succubi, incubi, tricksters, vampires, lycanthropes and other supernatural entities. Our imaginations and beliefs put a human—or semihuman—face on these beings that are both more and less than human. We imbue these creatures with powers we may wish to have, or believe one day we will have.

Chief among these supernatural abilities is the power to shift our mortal, human shape: to alter our physical being, and become that which we are not but may want to be—if only briefly—in order to accomplish a goal or acquire experience inaccessible to us in our ordinary—that is human—form. Shapeshifting has long been a tenet of most cultures and belief systems, from the ancient Far East to the modern West, from ancient polytheistic and animistic religions to the Judeo-Christian. All civilizations, including those from which modern societies devolved—Indian, African, Asian, Norse, Egyptian, Greek, Roman, Celtic, Mayan and North American—have their shapeshifting myths. This power has numerous advantages that are often used to alter or save lives and sometimes employed for frivolous or even malicious purposes.

The Greek god Zeus changed shape to disguise himself from his wife Hera so he could engage in dalliances with women; Zeus turned Europa into a cow and himself into a bull to hide from Hera during a tryst. Other gods and goddesses have been known to shift shape in order to escape danger, like Loki, the Norse god who changed into a fox to elude a plethora of enemies. Still others have been shapeshifted against their will as punishment for their bad behavior.

Shapeshifting with more spiritual consequence also occurred. The god Yahweh spoke to Moses through the guise of a burning bush. Another compelling tale of mystical shapeshifting in the modern era is the transubstantiation during the Catholic Mass: The bread and wine are transformed into Christ's body and blood.

Most commonly, shapeshifting facilitates actions and exchanges between the supernatural world and our own. Our fascination with supernatural beings stems in part from our desire to achieve powers beyond our own limited human potential—not merely to fly in a plane, for example, but to fly as a bird, to see the world as the eagle of Native American or Mayan myth. And what of the tricksters and shamans who change not only their own shape but the shapes of others?

The intensity of our desire to experience the realm of the supernatural also arises from our very human need to understand our mortal limits and what happens to us when our human shapes die. Mythology and other supernatural lore often focus on the exchange between mortals and those who have passed from the human realm into the next world. Can we return from the dead, from the world (if such a world exists) beyond the grave? And if we come back, will we be in our human form or in some altered shape? Reincarnation in Hinduism, for example, posits that humans can be—and frequently are—reincarnated as animals or even insects; among Hindus the cow is sacred and the god Ganesh is himself half-man, half-elephant. In Native American myths the great gods are all animals; returning from the dead as an animal is not unusual.

Ghosts inevitably differ from their former, human selves. They are ethereal, ectoplasmic, no longer human, but with a guise of humanity still clinging to them. This ephemeral humanity can enhance their once-human emotions of compassion and concern; they then exhibit such feelings for those still on this side who must pass into the next world. In Norse myth ghosts from the hereafter come by ship to guide the newly dead home to Valhalla, while in Egyptian myth humans with the heads of jackals come to guide the dead into the spirit world. But ghosts can also, as in Japanese myth, be vengeful, imbued with an otherworldly strength that allows them to wreak vengeance and reprisal on those who did them ill in the corporeal world. And among the supernatural are vampires—neither ghosts nor humans but something in between—the *undead* who shift shape as easily as they move from the dead to the living.

The soul, the spiritual essence of humans, plays a significant role in all things mystical. In Chinese myth a body must be buried within a certain period of time after death or the horseman of death will claim the soul for eternity, regardless of whether the dead person lived a good or bad life. In Orthodox Judaism the dead must be buried before sundown; the body must be intact, and no autopsies or other violations of the body can be performed. In most fundamentalist Christian religions a body must also be buried intact in order to be resurrected at the Second Coming of Christ.

Inevitably this issue of the human soul limns all myth and literature of the supernatural. Because while the human shape—the body—defines us in the mortal realm and is the literal *corpus* of the corporeal world, it is our souls that ultimately allow us the power to traverse between this realm and the next, to become one with the supernatural being or beings in whom we believe. Thus protection of the soul from the demonic on the other side remains an elemental aspect of myth and the literature of the supernatural.

The concept of the soul and its immortality has lured storytellers for centuries. What becomes of our souls when the human body no longer exists? Can the soul be stolen from the body while we are still living? Are there creatures who pass between the supernatural world and our own who feed on souls or steal souls? In Haiti and other Caribbean nations where voodoo religions are practiced, it is believed the dead can stalk the living and steal souls; zombies are in fact the soulless, used by shamans to seek out yet more souls for capture. For it is the soul that holds the greatest power in humans and is therefore seductive to those in the nonmortal realm.

These questions of mortality and immortality, of body and soul, plague, madden and intrigue us—and thus throughout the millennia have become the stuff of spoken and written myth, legend and lore. In the West, gothic tales of the supernatural were written predominantly for and by women, particularly in the nineteenth century. While male writers focused on the more academic and theological aspects of discourse on the supernatural, women explored the supernatural from the vantage point of the ordinary person by writing stories—some light, some lurid, some literary.

The unofficial birth of this literary tradition of gothic writing by women happened in 1816 on a dark and stormy night much like the ones that have become staples of the genre. The nineteen-year-old Mary Wollstonecraft Godwin engaged in a storytelling contest with her fiancé, the Romantic poet Percy Bysshe Shelley; their close friend and Romantic poet George Gordon, Lord Byron; Mary's stepsister, Claire; and a physician friend, Dr. John Polidori.

When the storm-streaked sky began to lighten as dawn approached, Mary Shelley had, unbeknownst to her, executed one of the most enduring gothic tales in literary history. Her story, of a fiendishly egomaniacal doctor and his desire to create life from bits and pieces of the dead in a ghoulish reconception of Christ's resurrection, has become the quintessential tale of the fine line between this world and the next, between Good and Evil. In what later was published as a novella entitled *Frankenstein: or the Modern Prometheus*, Mary Shelley explores that murky space between the natural world and the supernatural dimension. Because her story echoes resoundingly with questions about mortality and immortality, body and soul, because we are both drawn to and revulsed by the "monster"—created by a monster in his own right, the misguided scientist Dr. Victor Frankenstein—we continue to find the tale as compelling as it was to those four who first heard it amidst the thunder and lightning of the summer storm at Byron's country home.

The variety of tales in *Night Shade* exemplifies the scope of women writers' approaches to the supernatural. Mary Shelley's remains the only tale from that stormy long-ago night to not merely survive in a dusty archive, but to become a classic; few have not heard of *Frankenstein*, though many have forgotten the young female creator of the tale. *Frankenstein* endures in part because Mary Shelley's place as a woman in a male-dominated society (the larger society as well as the literary milieu of which she was only a titular member; her mother, Mary Wollstonecraft, authored the seminal eighteenth-century feminist treatise, *Vindication of the Rights of Woman*) gave her a unique understanding of both the hubris of men and the intensely female nature of her "monster"—her monster being a metaphor for all those who are "other" in society.

Such otherness has long been the purview of female storytellers, and the tale we now know as *Frankenstein* defines otherness. The monster, Frankenstein's creation, has sensibilities at odds with both the man who created him and the (male) society into which he is unwittingly and unwillingly thrust. His most compelling connections to humans with souls (which Shelley makes clear he does not have, as only God can impart humans with a soul) are his adversarial and almost slavelike relationship with Frankenstein and his brief encounter with the young child whom he inadvertently kills. The other humans in the story hound him, raising the question anew of what a soul actually imparts to those who have one. In fact, it is the monster himself who realizes he can never become truly human and that Frankenstein must also be destroyed so as not to repeat his ghastly experiment. In the end the monster proves his humanity by chasing Frankenstein literally to the ends of the earth—the Arctic—killing his evil creator and himself, thereby protecting the world from further soulless transgressions.

Another foray into the gothic is Emily Brontë's classic novel *Wuthering Heights*. A tale of love that endures to and beyond the grave, *Wuthering Heights* is but one of many novels and stories to explore the theme of immortal love that transcends even death. Ghost stories and other tales of visitations from the other side, like Brontë's novel, were prevalent in the literature of the nineteenth century, particularly in popular women's magazines.

Compelling social factors, particularly poverty and disease, may have contributed to the expansion of this literary genre. Death—and thus concerns about what happened after death—stalked women throughout the past two centuries (and before). The average life expectancy for women in the nineteenth century was thirty years. Many women died in childbirth or soon after from complications such as infection or hemorrhage (as did Mary Shelley's mother). Tuberculosis, commonly referred to as consumption, was rampant and killed many women (including Emily Brontë). The disease emaciated and exhausted its victims, who became virtual wraiths—literally living ghosts.

These real-life wraiths—sapped of vital energy, dying over a protracted period of time—gave rise to literary counterparts. It is more than coincidence that the premier vampire story of all time, Bram Stoker's *Dracula*, was written during the height of the worldwide tuberculosis epidemic. But the foundation for gothic tales and stories of the supernatural wasn't solely epidemiological. Religion, particularly Christianity, also strongly influenced discourse on the role of the corporeal and the realm of the supernatural; only humans could have a soul, thus the ultimate punishment for humans could be a transformation into animal form. Such religious beliefs also spawned theories of biblical retribution. For example, those who carried the proverbial mark of Cain were cursed by God to become, like the lycanthrope, nonhuman and, consequently, soulless.

Demonic possessions could also cause a shift in the natural world as vengeful beings from the other side wreaked havoc among humans. Behavior that was out of the ordinary was often perceived as demonic, because the Devil was as real an entity as God, and the barriers between this world and the next were easily breached.

Women were often seen as the purveyors of Evil; they were the cause of the Great Fall, the loss of heaven when Eve allowed herself to be tempted by the shapeshifting Devil in serpent form. Witchcraft, with its ritual magic and the conjuring of entities from the other side, including spirits, demons and the Devil himself, was the established purview of women. And witchcraft made women suspect. Through witchcraft women could shift their shapes as well as the shapes of others; they could fly. Witches were seen as demonic forces among humans and as a consequence were considered extremely dangerous. Witches could endanger not only one's mortal life but one's *immortal* life; in their guises as erotic succubi they were known to steal souls.

Thus the systematic annihilation of witches was orchestrated by various Christian religions, most notably Catholicism during the Spanish Inquisition, over a period of four centuries. In Europe alone an estimated nine million witches were killed during the height of the witch hunts. But the fear of demonic women traveled with the early settlers to the colonies in North America. In 1692 twenty-three people were hanged, pressed to death and drowned as witches, and another 150 people imprisoned, in Salem, Massachusetts, after a series of witch trials ordered by the local government. The youngest "witch" was only five years old.

The events in Salem elucidate how religious belief often combined with superstition. And superstition remained deeply ingrained among women (and men) of every class well into the twentieth century. In turn these superstitions, overlaid with an often fanatic religiosity, served to create new myths. In the eighteenth and nineteenth centuries, talking to the dead via séances, Ouija boards, hypnosis and other rituals became a regular social event in the parlors of the middle and upper classes, while folklore and legends about the presence of the dead among the living prevailed among the lower classes. Such superstitions led naturally to twice-told tales of visitors from a world other than our own. And although throughout history women had—except as purveyors of witchcraft—seemed largely exempt from the full range of demonic possession by virtue of what was perceived as their inherent innocence, this began to change in the late eighteenth century. Suddenly women were as likely as men to travel between both worlds and to transform themselves in order to achieve their supernatural intent.

But such supernatural transformation had a basis in real life. Vampires, lycanthropes and all manner of ghosts and ghouls were more than mere legend to many. Some gothic tale-telling was predicated on simple facts of the times. A child born with a birth defect, or who developed oddly or became disabled through accident or disease, could easily become the stuff of gossip and speculation, which might also lead to new myths. The boy with a condition that caused hair to grow over much of his face was easily transformed through rumor into the village werewolf; the young woman paralyzed in a fall whose father took her swimming after dark at the local lake was whispered into a mermaid; the pale, wraithlike consumptive rarely seen by her neighbors before nightfall evolved into a vampire.

Gossip played its own role in the development of the gothic tale and, as explained above, sometimes in the "act" of transformation itself. Gothic tales were often grounded in the everyday, using the well-defined barriers of class or economic status to heighten the mystery of difference between those worlds. Class difference was mysterious in itself. Thus the young servant girl who caught the eye of the scion of the estate might have found true love—or might have been inveigled by a demon disguised as an attractive and wealthy young man. Our heroine might be fighting to preserve her virtue against the forces of money and social status—or she might be up against something far more sinister, like a battle for her very soul.

These metaphors abound in the gothic romances that remain a popular literary genre to this day. The seductive and sometimes demonic power of the hidden secret fuels many a gothic tale, whether that secret is as simple as a first wife gone mad and kept prisoner in the attic or whether it is exposed each time the moon waxes full and villagers are found murdered on the moor. Writers like Daphne du Maurier, Victoria Holt, Phyllis Whitney, Dorothy Eden and many others wove the elements of the supernatural into the daily lives of their young heroines, just as Anne Rice and Stephen King do today. The battle between Good and Evil will forever make compelling storytelling.

Shapeshifting—the literal transformation of the body—is rooted in a host of cultural, religious and social beliefs. And that other transformation, from the living to the dead and sometimes back again, continues to be explored as the veil separating the corporeal from the supernatural becomes more and more diaphanous. Women continue to chart the territory between these two worlds, traveling into the realm of the supernatural through the vehicle of the ordinary. Some of the writers in *Night Shade* pay homage to legends of centuries past, but with a distinctly modern twist, while others harken back to timeless tales of gothic lore. Still others create wholly new metaphors of transformation.

Mary E. Wilkins-Freeman's story, "Luella Miller," written nearly a century and a half ago for a women's magazine, incorporates much of the mythologizing explained here. Yet "Luella Miller" remains fresh, luring the reader with its mesmerizing tale and delineating the role of gossip in a village where whispers conjure fear.

Barbara Wilson's "Silkie" and Toni Brown's "The Acolyte" take well-known legends and transpose them to modern times; their skilled reconfiguring of familiar children's stories create new, very adult, myths. Conversely, in "Creepers," Joanne Dahme illustrates what happens when the shadow in the closet or the thing under the bed is far more than just the febrile imaginings of a young girl. And the love of horses common to young girls takes on mythic qualities in "Vengeance of Epona," Susanna Sturgis's tale of transformation and revenge.

Vengeance has many guises, and as many rationales. The

ancient and modern converge to exact vengeance—or is it justice?—in "Mud," Judith M. Redding's eerie murder mystery and Diane DeKelb-Rittenhouse's tale of nineteenth-century sibling rivalry and gender and class conflict, *"Femme Coverte."*

Healing broken hearts, seeking what we have lost, righting wrongs, redeeming ourselves—all can become the stuff of transformative change. When the realities of the world seem far more disturbing than the mysteries that lie on the other side, borrowing from the supernatural may be the only means to survival. In Linda K. Wright's "Pierced," an African-American mother tries to heal the unbearable pain of loss through ancient rituals. The protagonists in Victoria A. Brownworth's "Day of the Dead" face visitors from the spirit world and demons from the corporeal with voodoo. Spirits and an eroticism heightened by magic also intervene to avert disaster in Jean Stewart's "Feeding the Dark" and Terri de la Peña's "La Noche."

Class consciousness, social hypocrisy and greed underscore the necessity for transformation in Lisa D. Williamson's "The Existential Housewife," Ruthann Robson's "Keys," Meredith S. Baird's "Breech Birth" and Joyce Wagner's "Newtime Cowboy," where each tale subtly reconfigures the physical world, bringing the reader deftly in touch with the altered states of the protagonists.

Finally, tales of transformation—as Zeus knew well—are not without their lighter side. True love isn't always what it seems in Roz Warren's "The Birthday Present," and lust has many exciting dimensions in Susan Raffo's "Apéritif."

From the traditionally gothic to the uniquely modern, the stories in *Night Shade* both reinforce the consummate role of women in the gothic genre and redefine it. These are exciting, engaging tales that will impart just the right *frisson*, whether read, like Mary Shelley's *Frankenstein*, in the dark of a stormy night fraught with atmosphere or while basking in the warmth of a cheery, sunlit day. These stories will raise anew all those age-old questions about the hazy space between what is and what might be. Was that creak on the stair merely the housecat—and is the housecat indeed just an ordinary housecat? And that keening outside the window—an owl perhaps? Or the cry of a lone wolf, a wolf who on nights with no full moon can be found demurely shelving books in the children's department of the local library where she has worked for many years. Read on and wonder next time the hostess puts her hand on your shoulder at a party or that neighborhood dog stares a little too intently, if all is what it seems—or if the veil between this world and another has dropped, just a bit, to reveal mysteries both ancient and new.

Victoria A. Brownworth
Philadelphia, Pennsylvania
January 1999

Night Shade

The Existential Housewife

Lisa D. Williamson

> *Existentialism: A philosophy that emphasizes the uniqueness and isolation of the individual experience in a hostile or indifferent universe, regards human existence as unexplainable, and stresses freedom of choice and responsibility for the consequences of one's acts.*
> — The American Heritage Dictionary

elinda sat on the dusty attic floor, her jean-clad legs tucked beneath her. She read the dictionary quotation one last time and closed the notebook, a relic from college days. Stroking the burgundy faux-leather cover with the barest touch of her fingertips, Mel hugged the book to her chest.

The one window in this section of the attic was covered securely with opaque plastic sheeting, allowing only a diffused yellow light to filter through. Melinda stared toward the small window, not really noticing it or the swirl of dust motes caught dancing in the dim illumination. She had long since stopped sneezing; the greater part of the filth she had disturbed when she had first come up had subsided again, settling over her like a veil, sifting into her hair, smudging her cheek, leaving streaks on her jeans. The unfinished floorboards and the rough-hewn rafters that met in a severely cramped, inverted V made the attic appear rustic, not at all like the immaculate, elegant house beneath. It was, instead, the untidy graveyard of buried memories and past lives. There were precarious stacks of cardboard and plastic storage boxes piled up to the insulation-blanketed beams, holding clothes that were no longer in style and had years ago ceased to fit, books that no one had read in more than ten years, broken tables and lamps that still waited patiently to be fixed—all the detritus of lives lived too long in one spot. The notebook Melinda now held was taken from a box crammed into the back corner, an old, dilapidated cardboard storage crate that contained her college work from long ago: her term papers, her creative writing assignments, her class notes.

Melinda didn't know what obscure impulse had drawn her up here. The attic was a place where no one ever came, except to deposit another box of unwanted junk. She ran a dusty hand through her wavy brown hair. She would have to get moving soon. Although the house was ready, she was not. She still had to shower and shave her legs. She still had to dry and pull and spray her unruly hair into some semblance of casual chic. She still had to stand in front of her open closet and decide what she liked, what would fit, what would be impressive to the people Bailey had invited over to impress. It was an effortless type of evening; God knew she had done it often enough before. But for some reason, it seemed hard today. The thought of standing for one more night, gazing with incredulous admiration at some fool half her height and a third her intelligence, brought the same strange mist to her eyes that had been appearing unbidden all day. If she didn't move soon, and move quickly, she would not be ready by the time Bailey came home. Bailey would be annoyed.

But somehow, even that thought was not enough to propel her to her feet and back down to her life.

Melinda again opened the old notebook, opened it to the page still marked by her finger. Words seemed to jump out at her, hitting her with the impact of a slap to the face. *Isolated. Hostile.*

Indifferent. How true.

Was she suffering a midlife crisis? Bailey would be angry that it came on the night of his most important party. He hated whiners. Why her? Why now? It was all very inconvenient, a feeling she neither wanted nor could do anything about.

Melinda bent her head over the open notebook, inhaling the fusty scent of old paper, as if by immersing herself in the smell of school and independent thought and the still-new promise of things to come, she could make herself forget that twenty years had passed, and that she had grown middle-aged and fat and gray and boring like all those dull people she had vowed never to be like.

What had happened? Was it that her kids were close to leaving home and leading their own lives? She barely saw them anymore—now that Bailey had gotten Jamie and Stephen their own car so they wouldn't be borrowing hers all the time, she didn't even get their urgent calls from school: "Mom, I forgot my lacrosse stick," or "Mom, if you don't bring in a note, I won't be able to go on the class trip." Her children had turned into itinerant boarders who never seemed to need her anymore. Was it just a preview of empty-nest syndrome? Was that it?

Or was it Bailey? Was it that he seemed to resent her staying home, when for twenty years, it had been her job? Was it that he looked at her now as if she were just some extra mouth to feed, someone who wasn't pulling her own weight? Perhaps he thought that after twenty years she could just slip into a high-paying executive job, when the only entry on her resume was "Wife and Mom."

The indifference from her kids, the hostility from her husband—it all added up to Melinda's sense of isolation. She rose abruptly, tossing the notebook back into its box.

"I'm an existential housewife," she said aloud and, with a soft noise that could have been a laugh, went downstairs to change.

The change first happened when Melinda was getting ready for the party. She had stayed a long time in the shower, letting water almost hotter than she could bear beat on her, washing out both the dirt from the attic and, she hoped, the strange feeling of melancholy. Perhaps, she thought, the perfumed soaps and conditioners and lotions would mask the rancid taste of despondency she could neither explain nor shake.

Melinda stood naked, steamy and still red from the shower, feeling the nubby texture of the bathroom mat underfoot. Although with the modern ventilation system in the bathroom, the large and well-lit mirror was steam-free, it had become her habit in the last few years to perform her ablutions without looking at herself, at the old stretch marks, the drooping breasts, the rounded stomach. Mel picked up a plastic bottle of styling gel from the patterned blue, red and yellow handmade Italian tiles that covered the sink shelf and poured a small amount into her hand. She had performed this beauty ritual hundreds, perhaps thousands of times in the past, and was comforted by the thought that following this routine would allow her to slip back into her normal frame of mind. Slap some gel in her hair, rub it through and tame her mane into something elegant. *Click your heels together three times and you'll be home.*

But this time routine did not save her. She poured the gel into a small circle on her hand and casually looked down. Mel blinked and her breath caught in her throat with a strangled gasp. She shook her head violently and looked again. Her heart faltered. Melinda could not tell where the gel ended and her hands began. Even as she again blinked hard to clear her vision, wondering what was wrong with her, the fingers on her left hand turned translucent and gooey, like the gel, and began drooping toward the floor, as if they were made of the same viscous liquid and were going to drip off her arm.

Mel cried out and leapt sideways, as if to escape her own body. In her terror, her hand flailed over the counter, sweeping bottles and jars to the floor in a horrific crash. She pressed her right hand to her face in an automatic reflex of panic, then jerked it away again in equal hysteria. She could not tell, in that moment, if she had felt firm flesh or not. Her thoughts were a jumble, a sane and calm "Thank God no one's home" punctuated by a darker, insistent "Oh my God, oh my God," overlying a deep, thudding dread that was echoed by the pounding of her heart. Mel stumbled backward, hitting the toilet with the back of her legs, collapsing onto the commode. She had her eyes squeezed tightly shut, afraid to look at her hands. Afraid not to. Unable to prolong the moment further, she opened her eyes slowly—just a slit—her forehead knit into rows of horror. Her two hands were spread open, palm edge to palm edge, as if to receive communion, the small quarter-size blob of lotion sitting intact on her perfectly normal left palm. Melinda stared at her hands in disbelief, and began to shake uncontrollably.

As Melinda saw it, when Bailey found her sitting, still naked, shivering on the commode countless minutes later, there were a couple of possible scenarios, neither of which was very comforting. Either her eyes were going, another reminder that she had passed the forty-year-old borderline and was in the wasteland of failing organs, or she was going mad, whether because of midlife crisis or empty-nest syndrome or pre-menopause, it hardly mattered.

And yet... Mel kept playing back the scene in the bathroom in her mind. Much as she would have liked to persuade herself it had never happened, as much as she knew delusions were real to the delusional, she couldn't shake her gut feeling that something had happened. She inspected her hands for the hundredth time since the incident. They were well-cared-for, manicured hands. Nothing *outré*. An appointment with the doctor, she thought, rising abruptly and moving toward her bedroom to stand in front of the closet. An eye exam. Then maybe Prozac, or Valium. That should help.

And when Bailey, from across the vast, Waverly-decorated

room, asked if anything were the matter, while pointedly tapping on his watch, she calmly told him, "No, I'm fine. I'll be ready soon." And he accepted that, ignoring the state he had found her in, confident, as always, in her ability to make things right.

"Melinda, I don't know how you do it." Melinda stared down at the three strands of hair trying to pretend they were a hundred stretching across the top of Bob's head as he crammed another miniature quiche into his mouth. They stood in her elegant living room, surrounded by all the other guests, ankle deep in wall-to-wall, overlaid with an intricate oriental. "My wife doesn't even know where the kitchen is. But I bet she could tell you how to get to the tennis courts fast enough."

Bob laughed. Melinda moved a corner of her mouth up in a tepid imitation of a smile. She had spent the evening avoiding looking at her hands, and instead looked at the blob of cream cheese dough adhering to Bob's chin and at his shirt straining to cover his executive paunch. Melinda resisted the impulse to pat Bob's stomach, much like she would have touched a pregnant woman's, feeling for the kick.

"Well at least someone in the house knows where the kitchen is," she thought as she moved through the party noises of animated conversation and tinkling ice on glass to offer hors d'oeuvres to her other guests. But she didn't say it; she had long ago excised such acerbic comments from her conversation.

What had happened to her? In her youth, she would have skewered Bob, and the dozens more like him in the room, with barely a thought. She had been militant, freethinking and outspoken. Mel could precisely trace her path from the college-day Melinda to the present-day matron, and she could not put her finger on exactly where things had changed. She had learned, slowly, step by step, that life was a compromise. That if she wanted to get to point C, she had to pass through point B. The fact that she now—at this late point in her life—found point C inadequate completely confused her.

She hadn't particularly wanted to get married. But she was madly, passionately in love with Bailey, who was strong, ambitious and full of his own vision of the future. Mel had thought it fantastic that two people with such radically different views of the world could come together, almost an affirmation of the vision of world peace that had been sweeping the nation's campuses back in the sixties and seventies. What did it matter to her, a little scrap of paper that said they were married? She would have him, paper or not. Although he was equally passionate about Mel, he would have her only with the paper. So, right out of college, they got married. It was a compromise, but in Mel's view, not a big one: She was monogamous by nature and, married or living in sin, would have stuck to Bailey till the end of her days anyway.

Mel had been working in a publishing house when she got pregnant, more than a year later. Her job was strictly grunt work, reading unsolicited manuscripts that were mostly boring tripe. The pay was dreadful, but both the job and the salary were the requisite dues that would enable her to move higher up the ladder. Bailey was floundering around for a purpose. He had tried repping, then sales, and at the time of Mel's pregnancy, had just started at a brokerage house. As with Mel's job, the hours were horrific and the pay was pitiful. Mel and Bailey discussed their goals for the baby endlessly. They both agreed that they didn't want to have their baby just to shove it into daycare. They both agreed that Bailey's potential for a high salary was greater than Mel's. They both agreed that Mel could get freelance jobs from her editors and work out of their small one-bedroom apartment.

So Mel became a housewife. It was a choice she had been comfortable with. When she saw the strain on the families where both parents worked, when she saw the illnesses daycare children came home with, when she saw the children who grew up brash and cocky because of their proximity to older children at the daycare, she knew she had made a good compromise. It was only when she was dismissed after the dreaded "Do you work?" question that she felt deficient. But really, what could be more important than successfully launching her own contribution to the next generation? Mel still couldn't answer that question. Even when she found out that not having more than two consecutive hours of sleep a night prevented her from being able to accept freelance jobs; even when washing diapers, making baby food, doing all the millions of little, insignificant things that she felt it necessary to do first for Jamie, then for Stephen, took up every waking hour; even then Melinda couldn't say what she would have done differently.

"Mel!" Bailey called her from the door of the kitchen, breaking into her reverie. It was that neutral-sounding voice an angry spouse uses in front of other people. She let her guests take the tray of food from her and wove her way over to him. She stood before him and raised an eyebrow in question.

He grabbed her arm—not so it hurt, but so that he had her full attention.

"Mel, you *knew* Frank Haldeman was coming tonight. You *know* he likes his martinis with three olives. Where the *hell* are the olives?" He waved a naked martini in front of her face, slopping the liquid from side to side in the wedge-shaped glass.

Mel looked at him and thought, *I can't look at my hands because I'm afraid of what I'll see, and you're worried about Frank Haldeman's olives?*

Instead of saying this, though, she calmly took the glass from him, said, "I'll check," and went to the refrigerator. But she knew there'd be nothing there. She'd been in the attic all afternoon and had completely forgotten the olives. She bent over and looked into the well-stocked fridge anyway.

"I knew Mellie would fix me up." A loud and cheery voice attacked her from behind. She turned. Frank Haldeman crowded up to her, virtually pushing her into the refrigerator, and gave her a kiss on the cheek. "I told that husband of yours, Mellie, that you always take care of me."

Mel hated Frank. She hated the power he exuded, she hated the easy familiarity he assumed with her, she hated that he called her "Mellie," a perfectly revolting name that she somehow suspected he knew and used for that reason. But Bailey needed Frank—Bailey damn near worshipped Frank—so Mel always kept a lid on her true feelings. She thought, though, as with her name, Frank knew what was unsaid and reveled in the power it gave him.

But now she had no idea what he was talking about. Was it a joke? Was he just underscoring that Mel had indeed *not* taken care of him? Melinda looked down. The glass she was holding was a piece of Waterford she had picked out when she and Bailey had gone to Ireland. She had always loved the way the hand-cut facets sparkled in the light. Frank's martini looked like a transparent oil slick in the elegant glass. And there, impossibly, nestled in the bottom, refracted through the liquor, were three perfect green olives, impaled on a toothpick. Mel sucked in her breath and looked up in panic at Frank's face. What the hell was going on? Where had the olives come from? Frank didn't notice Mel's reaction. He plucked the glass from her hand and moved on to his next contact. As he pulled the martini from her, Mel watched her fingers in horror. She only had three. The fourth gradually, almost imperceptibly, transformed from three green spheres run through with a toothpick to a two-jointed finger topped with a perfect mauve, manicured nail.

Mel thought, *It's not enough that a few hours ago my fingers were dripping off my hand. Now they're beginning to turn into condiments.* Mel watched, bereft of speech, as Frank retreated from her, waving his now unadorned martini around, greeting friends, enjoying himself, oblivious to what had just happened.

"Sorry, hon," whispered an equally ignorant Bailey in Mel's ear as she stood frozen, looking at her hand. "I panicked. How could I ever doubt you?" He kissed her lightly and moved off himself, to trawl the party.

Mel fled to the powder room. She did not turn on the light,

and stood in the room lit only by a small scented candle at the sink, looking at herself in the mirror. She knew now she wasn't losing her mind—Bailey and Frank had seen the olives as clearly as she had. No one had yet noticed that she was morphing, but surely that was only a matter of time. How would her family react? What would they do when they found out she was dissolving away?

Mel looked hard at herself. Slowly, she picked up the small glass bowl with the lit votive candle from the vanity. Concentrating, Mel held her hand over the flame. She could see a thumb and four distinct fingers, the bone structure, the faint glow of the translucent veins and cartilage and flesh. Everything normal. But still, something had changed.

She thought back to her original theory, that she was either losing her sight or her grip on reality. That one way or another, this was all in her mind. But now she knew that was not true, not unless Frank and Bailey were sharing her own, personal delusion. Now a third alternative occurred to her, one that was patently bizarre, although no more so than her day so far.

Melinda had spent a lifetime blending in, being invisible, a barely discernible support to her family that her body was now emulating. She was ceasing to exist as her own entity and, as she had for most of her adult life, was taking on the character and shading of those around her. Only now it wasn't just the important executives or the needy children she was reflecting. It was everyday things, things of no importance, things all about her.

Melinda found this thought almost laughable. Almost. Maybe the fact that she would entertain it at all was a sign that the second choice—she was losing her mind—was the real answer to her dilemma. But that wouldn't explain Frank and Bailey.

Mel had no idea what to do next. She had an obscure desire to run to the attic and huddle in the darkest corner until everything went back to the way it had been. But the party was going to go on, whether she wanted it to or not. Her absence would be noticed. Bailey would miss her. She would just have to go out and keep pretending nothing was happening.

A soft knock came at the door. Mel started, then said, "I'll be right out," and washed her hands in stingingly cold water as if that might keep them from changing again. She turned the light on so no one would realize she'd been locked in the bathroom in the near dark, and left.

The rest of the party took on a surreal aspect. Melinda found, as she drank another glass of chardonnay, that if she looked at things in a slightly skewed way, she might actually be able to enjoy her predicament, considering she had no control over it.

A brief moment of lightness came when Bailey approached her saying, "Frank's lost his olives, and I can't find any more."

Mel found herself answering, "If he didn't swill down so much gin, he probably wouldn't have that problem." It was a touch, a faint shadow of her former self, and although Bailey backed off in consternation, she finally found something that night to smile about.

After that small surge of self-assertiveness, Mel's episodes increased in frequency. Or maybe it was her drinking. She had tossed back a couple of glasses of wine in quick succession after she had emerged from the powder room. The alcohol had hit her empty stomach and shot through her veins, allowing her a small measure of detachment. The wine had also detached Mel from her judgment. People that just yesterday she had merely found mildly offensive or somewhat annoying, she suddenly found completely intolerable. While one small part of her brain—the last of her sobriety, perhaps—was aghast at her disloyalty to Bailey, the suddenly expansive, drunken part of her rejoiced.

No more compromises, Mel thought.

Carol Wordsworth was the epitome of the corporate wife. It was amazing, Mel had often thought, how such a small package—five feet, three inches and oh-so-slender—could be crammed with so much hypocrisy, self-absorption and downright meanness. But, as with most of the people in her house this evening, Mel was always meticulously polite to Carol, for Bailey's sake.

Carol was not only petite (Melinda's private nickname for her was "The Stump"), not only slender, but her complexion was flawless and her clothes were from the best shops. Her children went to private schools, and she drove a small white Mercedes convertible. It had always irked Melinda that someone with the personality of a pit viper could slither through life untouched by reality.

Melinda vividly remembered the day she had met Carol. It was years ago, at one of those many women's functions she attended—sports, church, school; she couldn't recall now. A mutual friend had introduced them. Carol was identified as the woman down the road who'd moved into the old Bolger mansion. Mel had been presented as the local bohemian—she made her own baby food, sewed her own home furnishings and wrote stories for her children. Eccentric, but harmless.

Carol had somehow managed to look down at the taller Melinda, had stretched close to Mel so that they were almost nose-to-nose, and had said, "I hate people like that."

Now, at the party, Mel greeted Carol, ready to do her hostess duty, ready to ask how she was, what her children were up to—the usual questions. Carol, dressed to kill in a size one cerise silk dress, was effusive: how nice of you to invite me, how pretty your house is, all the correct things to say that Mel knew she didn't mean in the least. As the two of them walked from the front door in to the party, Carol sneezed a couple of times, small, high chirps.

"Oh, excuse me," Carol held a hand to her chest. Her voice raised almost imperceptibly. "I have a terrible dust allergy." And she looked around the room, as if she could just see the particles of grime and dirt suspended in the air. As if Mel hadn't spent the last week cleaning and scouring the house in preparation for this party. As if Mel wouldn't care, or wouldn't understand, that she had just been subtly insulted. As if the other guests surrounding them hadn't heard her loud observation.

Mel could feel her face freeze into a polite smile. Ignoring

Carol's remark, she laid a hand on her shoulder and gently urged her forward. "There are some people here I'd like you to meet," Mel said to Carol, thinking she'd dump Carol on Bob and his group.

Bob was predictably taken with Carol. He playfully kissed her hand when Mel introduced them. Carol kept sneezing—*chirp, chirp, chirp*—then waving her hand around vaguely. "It's the dust."

Mel's hand still rested on Carol's shoulder. She wanted to dig her fingers into Carol's flesh. Instead, she watched, curiously without panic now, as her fingers slowly morphed once again. Only this time her fingers didn't melt into hair gel or olives. On Carol's bright, cherry-red silk dress appeared a long greenish-yellow trail of phlegm. While Carol sneezed, Bob's eyes flickered from her face to her shoulder, and back. Bob's friends' eyes did likewise. It was almost, Mel thought, like observing an audience watch a tennis match, the way all of their heads darted back and forth. She could see that some of them were wondering how to tell Carol about the offensive stain, and that the others had decided they weren't going to.

Bob suddenly sniffed the air. "I think I smell some more of your quiches, Mel," he said, as he and his entourage left in a mass retreat.

Mel gave one last pat to Carol's shoulder, as her fingers shimmered and re-formed into firm flesh.

"I should go help them," Mel said. Carol sneezed again, looking puzzled that her previously appreciative audience had suddenly left.

Maynard Johnson had always irked Melinda. He was a forceful right-to-lifer, a holier-than-thou neoconservative. Mel had many friends who held some of the same beliefs in varying degrees, but what irked her about Maynard was his absolute conviction that he and God conferred daily. Perhaps, Mel thought tonight, he thinks he *is* God. She sat in the same conversational circle as Maynard, sipping from her wine, listening to Maynard hold forth in his rational, even tones and gritted her teeth. Maynard had gotten so wound up during the evening, he had at some point thrown off his jacket, loosened his tie and rolled up his sleeves. While he gesticulated with his left hand, his right was wrapped around his scotch and water, resting on the end table that separated him from Mel. Without really thinking about it, Mel gently rested her hand on his forearm. He started, interrupting himself for a moment, then when he saw it was only Mel, went on with his story. Mel watched, as if from a distance, as her fingers again morphed and blended and disappeared. A stark blue tattoo appeared on Maynard's forearm. One of the people around Maynard, listening intently to his political talk, noticed the tattoo and shot a startled glance at him, her face suddenly stone cold. After a few moments, she whispered something to her husband, who looked at Maynard's arm and was equally stricken. Melinda watched in silence as the domino effect took place all around Maynard. Since he was used to holding the floor, he didn't realize no one else was talking until one by one, everybody had turned away and gone. Melinda was the only one left. Maynard leaned over to her and asked, "What was that all about?" Melinda slid her hand off Maynard's arm, patted him lightly and said, "Who knows? They probably just needed refills." Mel watched her fingers revert back from the blue-black swastika and went off to get another refill herself.

Sometime during the evening, the doorbell rang. Mel wouldn't have heard it above the din of the party, which was getting louder as the liquor supply was dwindling, but she happened to be passing through the foyer at the time. Opening the front door, she found Jamie's girlfriend, Amelia, standing on the stoop.

"Oh, hi, Mrs. Millhouse," Amelia said, twisting a strand of her long hair around a finger. "I don't mean to disturb your party. I'm just picking up Jamie."

Jamie at that moment bounded down the stairs and stood next to his mother.

"We're going out for a movie, Mom," he said, planting a quick peck somewhere near her cheek. "Don't wait up."

Melinda put a hand against her son's chest, holding gently to his windbreaker. "Wouldn't you like to bring Amelia in for a moment? You could both grab a soda, and there are some great hors d'oeuvres, if I do say so myself." She turned to Amelia and said, "You like shrimp, don't you?"

Amelia started to automatically say, "Yes, Mrs. Millhouse," while Jamie looked at his mother with a teenage mixture of dismay and disgust.

"*Mom*," he said, the inflection of his voice saying everything that needed to be said. Amelia glanced at Mel and shrugged apologetically, then turned back to Jamie.

"Oh Jamie, that's so sweet," Amelia said, out of the blue. She took Jamie's hand and ran down the sidewalk with him.

Mel closed the door, but not before she heard Jamie say, "*What's* so sweet? Amy, what're you *talking* about?"—and Amelia's return laughter. Mel had also seen it, though, and watched as her fingers changed back from a round pinlike shape that had said, "My Mom's #1."

The party was finally over. As usual, the house looked like a major storm front had moved through, glasses and beer bottles and canapé plates everywhere, under furniture, in potted plants, behind bric-a-brac. Melinda would be finding them for days. Normally she would start cleaning up immediately, getting the first few loads in the dishwasher out of the way. But tonight she could hardly stand, and thought she would probably end up breaking more than she cleaned.

Fortunately, her behavior—her morphing—had passed by unnoticed. Bailey was unaware of the little waves of disturbance that had periodically passed through his party. Except for Carol Wordsworth's abrupt departure fairly early in the evening, Bailey counted the party a success. He was, however, aware that his wife had had more to drink than usual.

"Didn't the party go well?" he said, hands on hips, looking around the messy rooms with satisfaction. Then he noticed her standing there, swaying. "A little too well for some of us," he told Mel with laughter in his voice. "Off to bed with you. I'll do a bit of picking up and be right behind you." When he saw that Melinda was having difficulty navigating the stairs, however, he swept her upstairs himself, leaving the dishes behind.

Mel knew what was on Bailey's mind—Bailey was always amorous when he was pleased with himself. Despite warning herself ahead of time, as she got caught up in the passion, Mel forgot to be cautious where she placed her hands. Her morphing caught them both unawares. When Bailey looked down and said, "It's funny, I *feel* fine," it was too late for her to remove her hand. But then he said, "Oh, Mel, I haven't been so good to you tonight all the way around, have I?" and she felt a small, guilty twinge of satisfaction. And as Bailey kissed her behind her ear and began stroking her in a genuine feeling of contrition, she couldn't think of a way to admit her own contribution. Later, as they both drifted off in a close, companionable sleep, Mel wasn't sure if it wasn't for the best, anyway.

Mel came downstairs late the next morning in an incredibly buoyant mood, considering the deep, pounding headache her excess drinking of the night before had occasioned. Still dressed in her big fluffy robe and slippers, she descended the stairs gingerly, almost bursting with the feeling that she was a new person. An odd—a very odd—thing had happened to her yesterday. She had changed, and because of that, her life had changed.

But then she glanced down into the living room below and stopped. She sat, falling onto the step with a jarring bump that traveled from her tailbone up into her hangover.

Bailey and the boys had gone out for their usual Saturday morning round of golf, which she had been grateful for because it left the house quiet and peaceful. But all the detritus of the night before still lay spread before her, like a party wasteland. Glasses, bottles, crumpled napkins, half-eaten food, all overlaid with the smell of old beer and tobacco ash.

You'd think they could have managed to take out one lousy trash bag, Mel thought. The sight below—and what it meant—hit her hard because she hadn't expected it. Her differentness had been so obvious to her, her new power so evident at the party, she had thought everyone would now see how completely things had changed.

How could they? Mel thought, her teeth clenched. How did you walk past a half-ton of trash without noticing it? A reasonable question that she had been ignoring for over fifteen years. *What am I, chopped liver?* And she looked quickly down at her hands. But rather than what she expected, Mel saw instead that her fingers, partially hidden in the folds of her chenille robe, had morphed into sharp, curved blades, deadly looking files and long, pointed knives. She hurriedly buried her hands deeper into her robe, refusing to look again. *They don't realize what I am,* she thought. But then she wasn't exactly sure, either.

Mel wandered through the empty, silent rooms, picking up dirty dishes, retrieving trash from behind seat cushions and wiping damp circles off of the furniture, thinking about the odd direction her life had taken. It was, she thought, like a kaleidoscope: All the pieces were the same, yet with one twist, everything appeared somehow different. But apparently, only to her.

Mel put the dishes in the sink and automatically started to rinse them. She thought better of it, however, and made herself some tea instead. She sank down into the big chair in the TV room and held her steaming mug, leaning her head back and closing her eyes.

Although on the surface, everything was the same, she thought perhaps she knew what was different. The balance of power—such an amorphous, indefinable thing—had somehow tilted back her way. And she was going to be very, very careful she didn't lose it again.

Bailey had been so loving and attentive last night, then this morning had reverted to his old behavior. She was going to have to do something about that. And the boys, well, they were still young enough to learn.

After she finished her tea, Mel got up for another mug. She looked at the crystal, and thought she'd at least fill the sink with hot, sudsy water.

Mel heard the distant rumble of the garage door opening, the slamming of car doors, the loud laughing and joking of her three men. The kitchen door burst open, and Bailey and her sons greeted her with the boisterous good humor of a morning gone well.

Mel lifted her hands from the soapy water, shaking the suds from them and drying them on the dishtowel. In the face of such exuberance, it was impossible for her not to smile in return. Yes, things were different now. Bailey and the boys just didn't know it yet. With her hands still glistening slightly from the dishwater, Mel reached out to them.

Femme Coverte

Diane DeKelb-Rittenhouse

As always, it was an accident of birth: eight crucial minutes between first-born and twin, between heir and younger sibling. Had their natal order been reversed, perhaps she would have been content. But the second accident transcended the first, and it was this circumstance that gave rise to all that followed. For Lorena Rivington had been born female on the plantation Rivington's Rest in the Year of Our Lord 1815, and thus had no title to the lands, the slaves, the stock or the fortune that were destined to pass into the hands of her eight-minutes-younger brother.

This critical difference was made plain to her from childhood in the very tone of her mother's voice, when she presented "my daughter, Lorena" and "my son, Raymond" to guests. Oh yes, Lorena could hear the vague reproach in the one, the satisfaction in the other, and knew who counted with their mother. Perhaps, had her father taken the same pride in her that her mother took in her brother, Lorena would never have pursued her desperate course. But while Francis Rivington called her "Lally" with affection, by her thirteenth year she understood that there would never be more than that simple, callous affection. Francis had abandoned the diminutive "Ray" long before the twins turned twelve, but he would never dignify Lorena's newfound maturity with any appellation other than the one he had attached to her during her babyhood.

Not long after, she discovered that this eternal relegation to the role of child was blessed by society and codified by law.

"*Femme coverte,*" her grandfather's lawyer said patiently. "That is the term under the English common law which obtains in the rest of the Republic. Our own fair state, of course, still upholds the civil law derived from France. In this matter, however, both codes are, if not identical, similar enough in the pertinent issues." He meant, Lorena realized, that under either system, women were held to be better ruled by men.

The lawyer delivered his lecture while they sat, not in Francis Rivington's oak-paneled study, but in the sitting room from which Eugenie Rivington conducted the day-to-day business of plantation life. Like all else in the manor house, the room was exquisitely appointed. Rivingtons had come to Louisiana with the British in the mid-eighteenth century, enduring after Britain had ceded its territorial claims, prospering in the era of statehood. Rivington's Rest, erected on the ruins of the family's earlier farmstead, was a tribute to that prosperity. Rising from the fertile black Louisiana soil like a Corinthian temple to a forgotten god, the manor house had been built in the classic mode shortly after the War for Independence. Eugenie—whose father, the Comte du Verre, had fled the Revolution in France to land, penniless, in New Orleans (and perforce into marriage with the only child of a wealthy planter)— had lately refurnished Rivington's Rest with an eye more to the Imperial styles of the French court than the Federalist styles of the American republic. The plantation's mistress, her yet-slender form fetchingly draped in a rose-silk tea gown, sat in a gilded lyre-backed chair, a liveried slave diligently wielding his palmetto fan to ensure her comfort. Lorena's mother had been the toast of New

Orleans little more than a dozen years before. Barely past thirty now, should she return to the Crescent City she was likely to enjoy a similar success. Lawyer Jackson, fortified with a glass of port, reflected that the same was not true of Lorena. The elderly lawyer rested his ample bulk upon an elegant but suitably sturdy divan, and considered the young girl seated before him. It was a pity for Lorena, and a blessing for Raymond, that both twins had inherited their mother's raven-haired, white-skinned coloring and their father's strong features. For where Eugenie had the delicate form and heart-shaped face bequeathed by generations of French aristocracy, her children flaunted the large robust frames of the English yeomen from whom Francis Rivington's line had sprung. Lorena Rivington, Lawyer Jackson concluded, would more likely grow into a handsome woman than a pretty one, and it was perhaps fortunate that her dowry would now be very handsome indeed. Putting aside those thoughts, he cleared his throat and took up the matter at hand.

"Now, I don't expect you to understand the details, Miss Lorena, what you might call the fine points. But the plain truth is that the *femme coverte* is the reason your Great-Aunt Celeste's property in Georgia could not be left to you directly." Another refugee from France, Great-Aunt Celeste had also married a wealthy American, and proceeded to survive both her husband and the few children she had borne him. There being no other heirs, she was free to dispose of her late husband's estate as she chose. She had, apparently, chosen to leave it to Lorena, or at least in trust for her with the Comte, whose own death had followed within a year of hers, and whose lawyer now pontificated upon the ramifications of the bequest. "Young as you are, I imagine the meaning of the *coverte* requires some explanation," he began.

"I imagine it's rather like the meaning of 'covert,' Mr. Jackson," Lorena responded. "Something hidden, or under cover."

"Don't be pert, Lally," Eugenie Rivington warned her daughter.

"That's all right, Miz Rivington," Lawyer Jackson said easily.

"Miss Lorena is doing just splendidly. I'm sure she'd much rather be picking out new dress patterns or purchasing some ribbons for those pretty curls than listening to me go on about bequests and codicils." Unnoticed by the adults, Lorena's hands tightened in her lap. "And indeed, she's hit the nail on the head, so to speak. *Femme coverte* properly applies to a married lady; in law, she is one with her husband, her possessions becoming his, her rights veiled, or covered, by his. The thing is, Miss Lorena, while your great-aunt's bequest was well intentioned, it wasn't, perhaps, terribly practical. Most especially, a clause in her will prevents your guardians from selling the plantation before you attain your majority. I'm not quite sure why Miz Celeste wanted to encumber your affairs that way, seeing as how the maintenance of a property two states distant from your own presents no small difficulty. Certainly, your granddaddy disposed of his own remote estate most advantageously." Fleeing Royalists had been awarded estates on the Mississippi at the end of the previous century, but the Comte found his property too far removed from the amenities of New Orleans for his comfort. He quickly sold it, investing the money in a profitable shipping partnership headquartered in the city. The du Verre interest in the partnership would now pass to Francis, and eventually from him to Raymond, a model Lawyer Jackson evidently felt would have been advantageous if applied to Lorena's Georgian property.

"Whatever Miz Celeste had planned, perhaps there is some explanation in the letter she has left you." He withdrew a heavy cream-colored envelope from his portfolio of legal documents, and handed it to Lorena. It was addressed in a florid hand, and the faint scent of violets yet clung to it. Lorena made no move to open the letter, and after a moment, the lawyer cleared his throat and continued. "Be that as it may, your granddaddy had matters well in hand," he said. "He understood the importance of seeing that you be properly guarded and protected. Under the laws of Georgia, your property will be owned, effectively, by your husband. It is essential, for your own well-being, that he be the sort of honorable man who can be relied upon to see that you have the comforts to which you are entitled. To ensure this, your property has been placed in trust. You'll enjoy a comfortable allowance therefrom until your marriage. Then, so long as you choose a man approved by your father—or in the unhappy and unlikely event of his death, by such legal guardian as he may appoint—your property will pass into your husband's hands, and he can manage your affairs."

"And if I never marry?"

"Why, Miss Lorena, a gal as pretty as you could no more help finding a husband than clover can help finding the bee," the lawyer responded with what he hoped was a credible assurance. "Not every young lady is so fortunate, to be sure, and must retain the legal status of *femme sole*."

"A woman who can act on her own?" Lorena inquired politely.

"To an extent," the lawyer said dismissively. "But women need the protection and guidance of responsible male relatives." Lorena correctly understood this to mean that, civil law or common, as an unmarried woman over twenty-one she would be able to act on her own behalf in only the most limited ways, her rights and abilities circumscribed and curtailed by the same accident of birth that dictated her brother's ascendancy over her own.

Lawyer Jackson and his sheaf of legal papers, with its bequests and codicils, soon departed. Lorena was left to ponder their meaning. The missive from her great-aunt proved to be quite succinct, two words in fact: *Never marry*. The advice was clearly heartfelt, but Lorena wasn't sure she ought to take it.

Her future, she realized, had been settled from the first. Until now there had been no formal plan for her inheritance. She had always known that if she married a man of her parents' choosing, she would be given a dowry agreed upon by her father and her groom; most likely slaves, as they, rather than land, were the customary endowment for daughters in the South. Marrying against parental wishes might mean disinheritance. Not marrying at all meant, ultimately, living at her brother's sufferance.

It took very little thought for Lorena to decide that, despite Great-Aunt Celeste's warning, marriage to a suitable partner would be her most pleasant option. As mistress of her own home, with all the entitlements and prerogatives that station entailed, Lorena would have a greater degree of freedom than she enjoyed as a daughter or could hope to achieve as a burdensome spinster cast—allowance or no—on the charity of her brother . . . and his wife. The justice of these arrangements was not to be argued: Women were, as everyone knew, more delicate, more sensitive; their brains were smaller, their understanding more limited. God Himself had decreed that woman should look to her mate for guidance and correction. Lorena's family, her faith, her every experience taught her the wisdom of these arrangements. But they rankled. And corroded. And, inevitably, they forced change.

Change was long in coming. It began three years later, on the day of the Matthews's barbecue. Raymond rode his new bay gelding—a gift for his sixteenth birthday—beside their father on his roan. Lorena rode in the carriage across from her mother and beside Alice, the thin, worn, middle-aged slave who had been her "mammy" and was now her personal servant—when she could be spared from her duties as nurse and midwife to the other slaves.

"*I* should have had a new horse, too!" Lorena complained to her mother.

"Only hoydens ride horseback, Lally," her mother replied disinterestedly. "Ladies are too delicate."

"Eleanor and Margaret Collins ride," Lorena pointed out.

"And Maybelle Collins is a fool to let them," Eugenie responded disparagingly. "Dark as Indians they are, and freckled to boot. But then, that is no more than what one expects from the *Américains.*"

Lorena forbore to mention that she was herself half American, but did not abandon the argument. "It isn't fair! I can ride better than Raymond, any day. Leastways, when I'm not stuffed into a whalebone cage, I can."

"Don't be vulgar," Eugenie said, her tone and look deadly cold.

Lorena swallowed her words, and spent the rest of the ride looking out at the ripening fields of the Louisiana countryside. The voices of her father and brother, raised in laughter or friendly argument, drifted back to her on the summer breeze.

Louisiana did not have the established plantation aristocracy known in other parts of the South. Much of the state was still a wilderness, and little beyond the banks of the Mississippi and Red Rivers, or the areas near the bayous, had been settled for any length of time. But in the parish where Rivington's Rest lay, a few families had achieved a level of comfortable prosperity. Now, with the influx of Americans growing stronger each year since statehood had been granted, there were a number of families in the area who would, with those already established, become the state's aristocracy within a generation. Lorena knew many of the young men attending the Matthews's barbecue quite well. Up until this year, she had been too young to catch their interest, or return it, but at sixteen she was marriageable—marriage at twenty was the average for a belle, but brides of fifteen were not uncommon—and discreet, speculative glances began to come her way. Of these, Billy Collins's glances were the most acceptable to Lorena, and the least to her mother. The tall young man with hair as red as her father's roan gelding swept them a courtly bow, blue eyes glinting humor as he begged the honor of escorting Miss Rivington out to the lawn. Eugenie informed him coolly that Lorena's brother would be given that honor, and deftly maneuvered her disappointed offspring out of the way of an unsuitable attachment.

Eugenie's maneuverings of Raymond were at once more subtle and more blatant. Sarah Matthews, petite and blonde and not quite sixteen herself, seemed to have caught Raymond's eye. There was nothing for Eugenie to dislike in such a match; the Matthews plantation was close enough to Rivington's Rest that land might become involved in any consideration of dowry, certainly to Francis's and ultimately Raymond's advantage. And Sarah was a lady from her rosebud-twined curls to her pink satin slippers. Lorena was sure Sarah would have vapors at the mention of whalebone corsets and faint outright at the prospect of riding a horse.

Yet, unaccountably, Eugenie *did* dislike the match. Lorena recognized the faint narrowing of her mother's eyes, the slight pinch around her already thin mouth, as tokens of disapproval. As the sight evoking these reactions was the innocuous one of Raymond bringing Sarah a cup of punch or standing up with her for one of the reels, Lorena concluded that *Maman* must simply think the twins too young for serious courting.

Eugenie Rivington's actions a week later proved that conclusion wrong.

Her name was Cassiopeia, and she was fourteen. Eugenie thought the name too pretentious, and called her Pansy. Eugenie did not want the new slave getting ideas above her station, not with the plans she had for her. Pansy was of mixed blood, begotten by a white overseer on a half-African, half-Chickasaw slave. Though no greater than her Indian blood, and half that of her white heritage, her African ancestry determined her fate. Far from mitigating her circumstances, the fact that she was descended from the Chickasaw caused her to be despised in some quarters for a red nigger as well as a black one. In other quarters her background excited a different response.

Pansy had the high cheekbones and almond eyes of her red forebears, who had also bequeathed her skin the color of wildflower honey and the texture of unfurled rose petals. Eugenie claimed to have purchased her to be trained as an upstairs maid, but Lorena knew they had several candidates for that post among their own people. But none of those candidates moved as smoothly as mist on meadows or spoke with voices like Eugenie's best plum cordial: intoxicating fire distilled to beguiling mildness. Raymond's gaze followed the new slave as she moved about her putative tasks; he looked as if he wanted to wrap himself in mist and drown in plum cordial. The virtues of Miss Sarah Matthews ceased to be his only topic of conversation, and he seemed less inclined to leave Rivington's Rest for jaunts to visit any of the neighboring plantations.

Ever the gentleman, Raymond waited the three months until Pansy turned fifteen before he raped her.

These events were supposed to be beyond Lorena's knowledge; a gently bred young lady was to be kept in ignorance of the base appetites that plagued young men. But Lorena had, in innocence, passed by her brother's room at the critical moment, and had seen Pansy weeping not long after. Lorena, as much a product of her time as was her brother and, indeed, Pansy herself, knew better than to acknowledge that she had the slightest idea of what might be wrong. And yet, this supposed ignorance of the darker appetites was to go against her female nature; for it was also taught by her church and her culture that woman was eternally the temptress, Eve's daughter, seducing innocent men away from the paths of virtue. It was this philosophy that allowed Eugenie to believe that Pansy was no better than she should be, and made it acceptable to her that the girl slake lusts aroused by the willful Miss Matthews. At least with Pansy there was no question of Raymond's attentions being diverted away from their proper focus: choosing the mistress of Rivington's Rest.

As attested by the annual swelling of Pansy's belly—though each event resulted in a stillbirth rather than a living child—Raymond's attentions did not stray from home for the next two years. Sarah Matthews entertained a number of beaus, but rejected all serious proposals. Her indulgent parents were not pressing her to make a choice, and she declared she was enjoying her time as a belle too much to settle down quite yet. But if Raymond were about when she made such a statement, a languishing look beneath her lashes accompanied her words, and Lorena understood that if her brother ever took it in mind to come to the point, Sarah might consider relinquishing her freedom.

For her own part, Lorena had not formed a strong attachment to any of the young men who came, ostensibly to visit her brother, and spent hours at Rivington's Rest. Billy Collins—Eugenie had never warmed to him, but she was at least civil—maintained his edge over the other swains, because he was the best dancer, had the broadest shoulders, the nicest smile. But as Lorena turned eighteen, he had not yet declared himself. She thought nothing of the matter, because she was even less eager than Sarah Matthews to exchange the carefree status of belle for the careworn status of matron; but at the beginning of the new year, matters changed for Lorena, and everyone else at Rivington's Rest.

Francis ignored the cold. He had never been seriously ill and was impatient with his wife's fussing about something so minor. But it was not a simple ailment, and within a week he was unable to move from his bed for the coughing and congestion that filled his lungs.

Within a week of that, he was dead; Raymond inherited all that had been his father's. Until he attained his majority, Lawyer Jackson would handle legal matters, as much for Eugenie as for Raymond himself. And, of course, for Lorena. But in practice if not in law, Raymond ruled the plantation—and everyone on it.

There could be no formal courtship during the required year of mourning, but otherwise life went on much as it had before. Pansy's belly swelled for a third time, as unproductively as ever. For the third time, the mistress did not deign to notice the state of her "upstairs maid," and Lorena, who did notice, did not dare to comment upon it. Meanwhile, Lorena's beaus kept their visits— still purportedly to Raymond—brief and circumspect, never crossing the fine line between neighborly support and unseemly socializing. As the obligatory year of grieving came to a close, however, Raymond decided that it was time to fulfill his dynastic obligations.

"Nonsense," Eugenie said bluntly when he informed his family that he would be asking Sarah Matthews to marry him, "you've years before you need do anything of the sort."

"Well, *Maman*, if I had younger brothers, and if Father were still alive, that would be true. But I can't endanger Rivington's Rest and everything our family has built here. I need sons to carry on after me. You should understand that, if anyone does." Lorena saw her mother stiffen at the last remark. Eugenie had been the only child of her parents to survive infancy, as had her mother before her. While those circumstances had made her an heiress, they had also endangered the family fortunes. The lines of Clairmont and of du Verre had come to an end for lack of the crucial male heir. All her life, Eugenie had been made keenly aware of the necessity for sons; Raymond's birth and his survival past infancy were her enduring triumph.

Now that triumph turned bitter, as Raymond coolly outlined his plans for bringing home the woman—the chit of a girl!—who would, perforce, be the new mistress of Rivington's Rest. After he left the room, Lorena, who did not understand why her mother opposed Raymond's marriage, offered consolation.

"I'm sure you needn't worry over Raymond unduly, *Maman*. Sarah is too much a lady to accept a gentleman on his very first proposal. Why, I'm sure it will be another year or two before she agrees to wed him. Of course, the engagement shouldn't really last more than two months, but it might stretch another year if Sarah is determined; you know she has always claimed she's in no hurry to marry. All in all, Raymond is bound to wait until he's twenty-two before they actually marry, and that is not so very young for a gentleman, you know."

"What I know, Lally, is that you are a fool," was the scathing reply. "Raymond is my son, *mine!* I know how it will be. If he wants Sarah, he will have her, and before six months are out. Well, he may make her his wife, but he will *not* place her above *me!*"

To Lorena's shocked protests that Raymond would never be so unfeeling as to displace his fond parent, Eugenie did not respond.

"It does not matter," her mother said coldly. "I know how to hold what is mine."

Eugenie Rivington was as good as her word. She had been correct about Raymond; Sarah was wedded and bedded before spring turned to summer, her stomach swelling at almost the same time as Pansy's, a fact genteelly ignored by all. And Eugenie had been correct about herself; Sarah's efforts to take the reins at Rivington's Rest were gently, subtly, implacably rebuffed. Sarah was not to bother with planting the garden; her skin was too delicate to withstand the southern sun. Her recipe for the sausages so plentiful during hog-slaughtering season was appreciated, but the spices were too mild for the more robust Rivington palates; Eugenie would continue to use her own. And, of course, Sarah needn't bother about the disciplining of the slaves. Or their management. Eugenie had everything well in hand. Eventually, Sarah stopped trying to do anything more demanding than her needlework, or fitting her nursery out for the newest Rivington heir.

While Sarah lethargically waited out the term of her pregnancy, Lorena grew increasingly restless. She was nearly twenty, and it was high time her own affairs were settled. Yet they seemed further from resolution than ever. From his broadly delivered hints and the florid nature of his addresses, she thought Billy Collins was about to make the long-anticipated declaration. One day, indeed, he came to the manor without the usual accompaniment of rival swains, and after an affectionate—and pointed—greeting to "my dearest girl," went directly to speak to Raymond in his study. Lorena rushed upstairs to her bedroom, changing into a morning gown that was a bit more elegant than her day dress, wanting to give the occasion its due. But as she stood near her window, holding to a bedpost while Alice tightened the strings of her hated corset the extra half-inch necessary for the new ensemble, Lorena saw Billy stride from the house quickly, calling for his horse. He mounted swiftly and spurred the beast to a gallop, riding down the avenue of oaks without a single look back at the manor house.

A few weeks later, at a ball celebrating the engagement of another couple, Lorena saw Billy with his head bent attentively over that of seventeen-year-old Lucy Whitby. Lorena smiled politely, acknowledging his correct bow—and noting the inability of his eyes to meet her own—then flirted outrageously with Percy Harrington and Dalton Trelawny. Both young men subsequently joined the crowd of suitors who still descended upon Rivington's Rest, but Lorena couldn't summon enough interest to keep them there for long. In fact, Lorena found herself more restless than ever. The meaningless banter she was expected to exchange with her swains no longer amused her; the few tasks her mother had assigned her on the plantation no longer seemed too burdensome, but rather too trivial. She abandoned her needlework to the complacent Sarah and, despite her mother's disapproval, took to riding farther and farther afield on the plantation.

Lorena was not fool enough to leave her own—her brother's—property. The safety of a woman alone was only assured when she kept to her appointed boundaries. But there were parts of the land that had not been quite successfully reclaimed from the wild, areas where a woman reconsidering her life might find a bit of privacy.

On one such ride, Lorena instead found Pansy retching in the woods.

Lorena dismounted her horse and ran to the fallen slave. Pansy was again near her time, and Lorena feared that a fourth stillbirth was about to occur.

"You fool gal," Lorena chastised the stricken woman even as she assisted her to sit up. "Aren't you too near your time to go running off into the woods?" In fact, neither Pansy nor Sarah was due for two more months, but Pansy had never carried to term yet. "Rest against this tree," Lorena told her. "There's a stream nearby. I'll fetch some water." Shockingly, Pansy dared accost the young mistress, snatching Lorena's arm to detain her.

"Don't need water," she gasped. "Need Mam Regine." Lorena frowned. She knew, of course, that the old freedwoman was rumored to live in the woods. Colorful tales of the former Santa Domingan slave woman's history—her lovers, her rebellions, her purported magic powers—had been told for years. But the idea that Mam Regine was anywhere near her own home was a disconcerting one. And why would Pansy need an old voodoo woman now? Surely Alice, the slave midwife, was the person for whom Pansy should be crying out. She was about to tell Pansy to stop her foolishness and let her fetch Alice, when Pansy seemed to clench in on herself, the force of her grip bruising the tender flesh of Lorena's arm. "Mam Regine!" Pansy gasped again, as whatever transport of pain she endured crested, then loosed its hold on her. Lorena capitulated.

"All right then. But where on earth will I find her around here?" Pansy whispered directions. Lorena ran back to her horse and rode off the track she had been following, deeper into the woods.

The place was a lean-to, surely not meant for a permanent dwelling. Indeed, it was empty when Lorena approached it. The shack contained only a rope-cord bed and a rough wooden table, near which were two rickety chairs. No fire had burned in the hearth for some time, and the one iron pot hanging within it was empty of all save dust. Lorena thought she had erred, and was considering fetching Alice despite Pansy's protests, when a voice spoke behind her.

"Ah, mam'selle, things never be quite what they seem." Lorena whirled. The woman behind her—how had she entered the shack so soundlessly?—could not be Mam Regine, not the ancient crone of childhood tales. This woman had the unmarked skin of a girl scarcely older than Lorena herself, even though that skin was black as a moonless night. Her form, too, though draped in voluminous skirts and a simple bodice of plain black cotton, was slender and unbent, surely too straight for anyone who had suffered the lash as often as the rebellious slave was said to have done. True, the chamois bag fastened to her waist with a knotted cord might hold some fetish of supposedly mystic power, and the polished beads at her throat might have magic of their own. But she did not look to be a witch. And yet, in the curve of those so-full lips, in the glint of those ink-dark eyes, there seemed something intriguing, something that might have accounted for the absolute obsession of her last master, the one who had given her her freedom on his deathbed. And perhaps the hair, hidden beneath a kerchief of patterned silk, might prove grizzled silver rather than shining onyx. Whoever—whatever—she was, she was the only possible source of help for Pansy in this place.

Lorena drew her own form up to its tallest, remembering her

dignity. "I've a slave girl about to give birth in the woods. She's calling for Mam Regine, so if you know where she can be found, fetch her to me at once."

"Pansy knows the cost of Mam Regine's help. She be paying that now."

"What she's paying is the cost of her own sin, and my brother's," Lorena retorted.

"*Vraiment?*" the strange woman said politely with a lift of her brow.

"If you don't want to help me—" Lorena began in some heat.

"Ah, but that is for you to decide," the woman said cryptically with a hint of mocking laughter. "Come, mam'selle, let us find Pansy."

They heard her before they found her, gripped in another contraction. Lorena helped the freedwoman down from the horse before dismounting herself. Mam Regine knelt beside the moaning girl and spoke to her softly in a rhythmic patois that was just beyond the edge of Lorena's comprehension. The words seemed familiar, she felt she ought to know them. But whatever meaning they suggested to her mind faded before she could quite grasp and comprehend it. A ridiculous supposition, that Mam Regine—if it was indeed she—had cast a spell to keep Lorena from understanding the conversation, occurred to her and she frowned at the voodaun. Out in the sunlight, what had appeared black cotton in the gloom of the lean-to proved instead a very deep purple, the necklace of cheap beads really a strand of amethysts. The scarf was still silk, and the bag still chamois, and Mam Regine loosened the drawstring to find something inside. Lorena could not see what the woman handed Pansy, but the girl took it eagerly, and swallowed at once whatever herb or potion she had been given. With a sigh, Pansy leaned back against the tree, her eyes closing, her body relaxed.

"That won't stop matters long. She be needing a cart to take her back to the big house. Then your Alice can do what remains to be done."

"She's miscarrying again, isn't she?" Oddly, the woman laughed.

"Oh, mam'selle. You know better than that, yes, you do." Lorena stared at her in confusion, but the woman shook her head. "It don't make no never mind. You'll know where to come, now. But take that horse and send the cart. I'll stay with this child till it gets here." Lorena found herself obeying, but it was the only practical course, after all.

At length, the cart fetched Pansy to the big house, and to the bare attic room where she slept when Raymond did not require her, where she had labored similarly three times before. Within a few hours, Pansy was delivered of her fourth stillborn burden. Lorena entered the room as Alice wrapped the wizened, twisted thing in the rags intended for swaddling. As the old woman departed she shook her head sadly. "Would have been a boy," she said.

"They would all have been boys," Pansy said softly. Alice shook her head again and left.

"Do you regret it?" Lorena asked quietly. "Killing them?" During the hours of waiting, she had worked out what Mam Regine's words must mean. Pansy looked at her directly, without lowering her glance as behooved a slave.

"If you know I killed them, then you should know why."

Lorena shook her head. "But I don't. If you bore my brother sons, he would have been pleased with you. He might have set aside a cabin for you and your children."

The slave sighed wearily. "Never," she said. "He wants me where I am convenient. And my children would have interfered with his convenience."

"You can't imagine he would have sold them away! It's downright illegal to sell a child under ten in this state."

Pansy's laughter was a harsh, grating sound with no humor to it. "Miss Lorena, are you yet in ignorance of what your brother will dare? Did he not spoil your engagement to Mr. Billy?"

"Why, whatever do you mean?" Lorena said slowly.

In a few stark sentences, Pansy related what one of the other slaves had overheard on the afternoon when Billy had formally asked Raymond for Lorena's hand. Raymond had refused to approve him, thus denying him not only Lorena, but access to her Georgian properties. Lorena did not want to believe Pansy's words, but the account rang true: Raymond's ruthlessness, Billy's ineffectiveness. No wonder he could no longer meet her eyes. Lorena fled the room.

Her night was sleepless, but the next morning her restlessness was worse than ever. She slipped from the house just after dawn, once more riding out to the woods. Lorena had no conscious destination in mind, but gave her mare its head. Still, when she recognized where she was, she smiled grimly to herself and dismounted.

This time, the shack was not empty. A fire burned in the hearth, the cauldron steamed on the fire and a tantalizing scent rose from the cauldron.

"Shouldn't go riding without eating first," Mam Regine said. Although her voice was the same, the voodaun gave a vastly different appearance from the day before. Today, a wrinkled crone with stooped back and swollen ankles bent over the bubbling cauldron. Her skirts were tawny gold, and the amethyst beads had been changed for amber and copper. The kerchief had been abandoned, leaving her cotton-white hair to straggle down her back. She was stirring the pot, sniffing gingerly and reaching into her chamois bag for a pinch of herbs. Any sensible, rational person would have concluded that this was a different woman than the one who appeared the day before. Lorena knew better.

"I had no appetite. A fact of which, I am sure, you were quite aware," Lorena told her coolly. "Is that meant for my breakfast?"

"Might be meant for all kinds of things, mam'selle," Mam Regine allowed. "Question is, what do you be meaning?" Lorena seated herself on the nearest of the two battered chairs and considered her answer.

"I mean to marry," she said thoughtfully. "Or I had meant to do so. Certainly, I mean to leave my brother's house and remove my property from his administration. There aren't any relatives I can go to, though." She sighed. "Marriage would have made everything neat and simple."

Laughter greeted her last remark. "There be nothing neat or simple about marriage. Still, it has its advantages. What you need to know is, are they the right advantages?"

"Why wouldn't they be?" Lorena asked.

"You be thinking you need someone to stand up to your brother, so that he don't interfere in your life, or drain the funds from your accounts to spend on his own plantation. But will a husband be any better? Worse, maybe. Maybe you need to find your own strength, and your own way. Then, perhaps, you can find the right husband, not just any boy with a nice smile and skill on the dance floor."

Lorena cocked an eyebrow, and stared speculatively at the voodaun. "And how do I begin to find my strength?" she asked.

"Strength be found in the most unlikely places. Take my soup, now. Nothing more strengthening than a good soup." Mam Regine ladled some of the cauldron's contents into a pottery mug, and handed it to Lorena. The girl sniffed it curiously, found it smelled even better at close quarters and took a cautious sip. It was hot and spicy, tasty as a creole gumbo. The soup went down smoothly, warming her belly and spreading a welcome heat through all her limbs. Lorena drained the mug. Mam Regine smiled broadly.

"Will it kill me?" Lorena asked.

"Eventually, mam'selle, life will kill us all."

Lorena's ride home, and, indeed, the rest of the day, proved uneventful. She ignored her mother's scolding, listened patiently to Sarah's fretting, smiled politely at her brother's declamations and, after a brief visit with the recovering Pansy, retired early to her room.

She slept deeply, for hours, until the full moon, newly risen, shone through the curtains of her room. Only a few rays found their way through the heavy draperies of the window and the netted hangings of her bed. But they were enough. Lorena woke quickly and threw off her covers. She felt the pull of the moon and, opening her bedroom window, leaned out to admire its silver beauty. The night was warm, and after a few minutes, she decided to go out into the garden.

She didn't bother with shoes, or with a candle. Lorena found she could see perfectly well by moonlight. She did not stop to consider how odd her actions were, how likely to incite parental rage if discovered. Lorena simply moved quietly and quickly down the stairs and went into the garden. No fear was on her of night prowling creatures, or of discovery. Lorena felt, instead, oddly vital, alive and energetic.

As she paced beneath the magnolia and camphor trees, though, she began to feel something akin to her bedeviling restlessness, but somehow more purposeful.

One of the many things a well-brought-up belle was not supposed to know about was the voodoo ceremonies that were held in secret by the slaves. She was not supposed to know about the dancing, about the wild rhythms as the slaves appealed to the spirits they venerated, the dance itself pagan worship, unseemly, exotic, forbidden. Oh no, Lorena was not supposed to know about that dancing, and maybe she hadn't known much before. But the knowledge had somehow sprung up inside her, coursing through her blood, pounding in rhythm with her heart, tingling along her bones. Lorena closed her eyes and began to dance beneath the moon, her heartbeat the reverberation of drums, her feet stamping the garden soil as if she could release the power of the very earth into her own flesh. Pagan, certainly. Father Etienne would be scandalized, her brother might take a whip to her, her mother would never live down the shame. Lorena smiled and danced on.

Eventually, she stopped beneath one of the larger trees. She opened her eyes. The world seemed newly made to her. It was as if whatever had been there before, the house and garden she had seen every day of her life, and which held no surprises, had been torn down and rebuilt in her dancing. The new might mimic the old, but she knew there would be differences, differences she only had to look to see. Lorena lifted her arm, noting how the moonlight shone through the thin batiste of her nightgown and illuminated the rounded limb within. Odd how light she felt, how supple and yet how powerful. Suddenly, the delicate weight of her nightgown seemed cumbersome, as restrictive as the hated corset. She should discard it. Yes, why not? Who was there to see beyond the protective screening of the blooming magnolias? Lorena shed the garment and stood, naked in the moonlight, her arms raised to heaven, her face turned toward the moon. How wonderful, she thought, to be a woman. Despite the indignities, the circumvention of her rights, how lovely to have firm young breasts, a feminine, rounded belly and long, shapely legs. How powerful to have the ability to create life from her own flesh. How amazing to be, after all, source and surcease, eternally, emphatically female. She stretched as sensuously as any cat, a panther in a jungle, and then, in the most natural movement in the world, dropped to four limbs.

There was a moment's agony, but it was welcome. Bone compressed and reshaped, muscle expanded and contracted into new forms, her skin stretched to cover all. From that skin, a new growth, midnight black as her hair, curled luxuriantly. Lorena opened her eyes to find all colors washed away in the moonlight, all objects standing out in stark relief, in tones of white and black and gray. Her senses were suddenly sharper, clearer, the scent of magnolia and camphor now underscored by the earthy damp of the nearby bayou, night sounds of small hunting things coming clear to her ears. Filled with power and wonder, Lorena lifted her muzzle to the sky and howled.

She ran for hours, loping swiftly into the woods, disdainful of any merely natural nocturnal predators abiding there. A lone bobcat dared show itself. Her bared fangs and warning growl were sufficient deterrent to its curiosity. Later, there was hunger, and a small wakeful thing died in a welter of bloody fur. Appeased, she loped swiftly home.

Lorena's restlessness was done for good and for all. Her next morning's ride was taken with due deliberation. There was a bad moment when her mare, ears flat to her skull, snorted fearfully and backed away, but Lorena had no patience for such tricks. A firm word—underscored by a soft growl heard only by the horse—settled matters.

"I thought you had to be bitten by the *loup-garou* in order to become one," she said when she found Mam Regine, today a pubescent girl in magenta and rubies.

"Perhaps the legends are wrong. Maybe you have to do the biting."

"Well, I've bitten, and swallowed the lot. But it seems all too easy. Surely you haven't given me this power out of the goodness of your heart? What payment are you expecting?"

"That be the foolishest thing you've said yet," Mam Regine said with a laugh. "Your power is my power; the more you have, the more I gain. But you're right. There is always a price to pay, though not to me. Don't worry. When you find your strength—your *true* strength; this is just a taste—you'll know what the price is, and how to meet it."

But the price of Lorena's new powers did not immediately reveal itself. Instead, more power came to the fore. It began in small, simple ways. Returning home from her ride, Lorena caught her reflection in a hallway mirror and, frowning, moved closer. She realized, for the first time, how unsuitable were the pastel muslins she dressed in. The colors were proper for an unmarried girl, but they did not complement her bold coloring, and the cut of her day gown did not flatter her womanly, rather than girlish, shape. Too, the ringlets into which her maid perpetually coaxed Lorena's thick hair were too frivolous for her strong features. Oh, she looked well enough, but not as well as she suddenly realized she could look.

The curling tongs and rags were most easily dispensed with, and Raymond raised no objection to the feminine amusement of a shopping trip in the city. Nor, surprisingly, did he object when Lorena declared her intention of taking the now recovered Pansy with her instead of Alice. The long ride in the carriage, its top raised to protect them from the omnipresent Louisiana dust, provided them with an opportunity for private conversation.

"You can't keep destroying your babies, Pansy."

"I can't bear them, either."

"Then prevent their conception. Surely Mam Regine can help with that."

"Perhaps. But at least when I am heavily pregnant, your brother leaves me alone."

"You pay too steep a price for your relief."

"Still, mam'selle, it is mine to pay."

"There must be something else that can be done." But short of freeing Pansy, which Raymond would never agree to do, they could not think what. Shopping proved a distraction for Lorena. She looked at fabrics and pattern cards with new eyes, suddenly aware of subtle nuances of shade and shape that would mean the difference between a flattering garment and a useless rag. She decided that nothing less than a completely new wardrobe would suit her, and set about replacing everything, down to her stockings and shoes.

Ultimately, several trips back and forth to the city were made, and on one occasion Lorena stayed overnight in the townhouse her grandparents had owned and which Raymond still maintained. The next morning, as she and Pansy walked back to the modiste, they encountered Billy Collins escorting his sister Margaret. Lorena wore a new walking dress, green as new grass, the ribbon sash snug against her waist. She noticed that, if Billy's eyes no longer met her own, his gaze remained upon her. She felt his regard all the while she chattered gaily with Margaret. Bidding them a laughing *adieu* after a few moments, she realized that she had little regret at the encounter, and nothing of pain. If she had ever loved Billy, she was well and truly cured.

Unfortunately, she was also well and truly cured of whatever fond regard she had ever held for any of her other swains. The boys still flocking to her home seemed just that: a gaggle of spirited boys, of no more interest than a bevy of small children to whom one is not related can be, and certainly none of them suitable as matrimonial prospects. Lorena found more and more excuses to avoid them, to their grief and despair. This pleased her brother, but Lorena was no longer concerned with Raymond's pleasures or dislikes. As long as he allowed her to go her own road, she managed well enough. Sooner or later, though, she would want what he would not yield, and they would come to grief over it. Lorena was determined, however, that this time matters would fall out as she intended, not as her brother willed.

Meanwhile, except when she spent nights in the city, Lorena continued her nocturnal runs as a *loup-garou*. Avoiding human contact while in wolf-shape was an easy enough thing to accomplish; she could smell humans long before they could see her. But as the weeks went by, it occurred to her that, pleasant as her new powers were, they could not be everything Mam Regine intended. Lorena considered seeking her benefactress out, but realized that she should puzzle the matter through for herself. Eventually, she came back to the old legends which said that the danger was in allowing yourself to be bitten by the monster. But that wasn't true, she realized. In fact, the power came from what she had taken into herself. And then she understood what to do.

A few nights later, Raymond had an unpleasant shock as he rode over his estates.

"Damned brute looked like a wolf," he swore as Alice cut away his trousers and bathed the blood from his calf. Even the thick leather of his riding boots had not been proof against the strong jaws and sharp teeth of the "stray cur" who had attacked him. Lorena murmured soothingly, more to reassure the very gravid and easily upset Sarah and even the distraught Eugenie than to comfort Raymond. He disdained her pity. She did not waste it upon him.

Naturally, there was a hunt. Of course, it was fruitless.

"Probably maddened by starvation," Raymond concluded. "Most likely dead by now." That was, he thought, the end of the matter. But it was, instead, the beginning.

It wasn't hard to duplicate Mam Regine's recipe for soup, not now that her powers had sharpened every sense. Finding the needed herbs was the work of one evening's run, spicing it with the merest trifle of her own blood. The kitchen slaves were too wise to voice aloud any surprise that Miss Lorena, who had never lifted a kettle in her life and hardly knew mint from parsley, should suddenly prove adept with stock and savory. That the simmering pot was to be left strictly alone surprised none of them and, certainly, despite the mouth-watering smells that rose from it, dismayed them not at all. The only difficulty Lorena foresaw would be in getting Raymond to take a dish while keeping Eugenie and Sarah from so much as a taste. Pansy's aid proved indispensable; she could, when she exerted herself, persuade Raymond to a great deal. It was done privately, so that neither the old mistress nor the young was endangered.

After moonrise, Raymond fell alive into an odd slumber. The night was hot, and grew gradually more so, the very air thickening in his lungs. He could not draw breath with his customary freedom. Bands of steel circled his ribs, compressed his waist, seeming to draw tighter with every struggling inhalation. A voice whispered in his ear—Pansy?—telling him that it was late, and that he needed to rise and dress. He rose unsteadily, and it was Pansy, not his manservant, who helped him dress. Stranger still, the shoes into which his feet were thrust were not his comfortable riding boots, but something smaller, more cramped, devices that forced his weight up on the balls of his feet, straining his calf muscles into unnatural tension, applying unaccustomed pressure to the small of his back. Raymond tried to protest, but Pansy was helping him into the next garment, and he found his mouth momentarily choked by a froth of lace. The restriction about his waist grew tighter, as Pansy busied herself behind him, murmuring soothingly that he should just hold on to the bedpost and take deep breaths. Raymond indeed drew breath, to bellow in rage, but as Pansy tugged viciously on the laces, he found himself gasping instead, lungs starved for air. And now came another muffling roll of fabric as

Pansy fitted him into a final garment, this one requiring her to fasten dozens of tiny buttons along his spine. But if he thought this peculiar torture would end with that, he was wrong. Pansy somehow got him to sit, and now his hair was being pulled and twisted. Hot metal came too near his scalp, small sharp pins were jabbed into his head. Finally, Pansy said he was ready. He tottered to his feet as she coaxed him forward. Each step was painful: His toes pinched, the arches of his feet ached and now, each stride he took was constrained and hobbled by yards of hampering fabric. Ultimately, he stood before a large looking glass that he knew graced Lorena's bedroom. Pansy, smiling approval, moved away from the glass, and Raymond stared at his reflection . . . the reflection of a young woman of fashion, handsome rather than beautiful: Lorena, who opened her mouth to scream . . .

The plantation was in turmoil: Miz Sarah had gone into labor, and Miss Lorena was suffering from some sort of fever that had her raving, confined to her bed. Miz Eugenie was more concerned with the coming Rivington heir than with the current Rivington spinster, but Mr. Raymond kindly sent Pansy to help Alice attend his sister.

When Sarah was informed that the product of her effort was a very healthy girl, she wept in disappointment. Eugenie grudgingly offered the comfort that as her labor had been relatively easy and as she was young, she should not despair of giving Raymond a son next time.

Raymond's pronouncement—that he was quite pleased with his daughter and unconcerned about the prospect of sons—brought a gasp from Eugenie and tears of relief from Sarah. Pansy, who heard of it later, smiled.

Nothing seemed to ruffle Mr. Raymond's cheerful disposition over the next few days; even his sister's lingering illness did not unduly distress him. He claimed he had complete faith in Pansy's assurances that Miss Lorena's fever was waning, and that the patient's periodic lucidity—only in Mr. Raymond's presence, but then, they *were* twins—was a sure sign that she was improving nicely. Still, nights were the worst for Miss Lorena.

She had obeyed the overseer's every order, had not dared indicate by a resentful glance or a querulous tone that she was too tired, too weak, too overburdened to complete the work as quickly as he wished. The coarsely woven cotton of her dress was soaked in sweat. Although she had worn such garments all her life, her tender skin had never become accustomed to such rough fabric, and was constantly abraded. Finally, it was quitting time and she stumbled into her cabin, about to drop to her corn-husk-filled pallet in exhaustion.

There was a noise at the door. She turned to find the overseer entering her cabin, whip in hand. He smiled as, walking toward her, he unbuttoned his trousers with his free hand . . .

"Do you think it has been enough?" Pansy asked when the sufferer had shrieked her throat raw and grown quiet at last.

"Not at all."

Sarah recovered her strength rapidly, as her baby, little Sarah, thrived. When Raymond inquired if his wife would feel deserted if he rode into the city for a day or so, she laughingly assured him that she had no desire to curtail his pleasures, and bade him enjoy himself.

Raymond was greeted with great conviviality when he made his appearance in the city at the club where gentlemen of his class usually gathered to discuss the business of the day. Commiseration on the birth of a daughter was met with the hearty assurance that a daughter was as welcome as a son. After the social amenities were met, Raymond drew aside one of the other planters, a man who had made the shift from cotton to sugar ten years before, and began to discuss the advantages of such a move. Rivington's Rest was ideally situated for sugar, with a swamp near enough to the fields to provide the necessary drainage.

"Tried to convince your daddy to make the change when I did. Of course, it requires a powerful outlay of ready money."

Raymond, smiling, told his neighbor that the matter could be arranged, and they parted company.

Miss Lorena tossed on her bed in fever dreams.

Her husband was disappointed, she knew. Otherwise, he would not have deserted her bed to couple with every slave woman below the age of forty on their plantation. God knew what company he kept in town. She had made every effort to please him, trying to overcome the dictates of modesty, trying to give him the pleasure he demanded. But it was difficult: She herself found no pleasure in their marriage bed, only duty. And humiliation. And pain . . .

"How long will you continue this?" Pansy asked.

"Do *you* think it has been enough?"

The slave looked her in the eye. "No," she said. "Not nearly enough."

Miss Lorena's odd fever continued for several weeks. Even Miz Eugenie grew concerned enough to think the doctor should be summoned. That gentleman gave as his considered opinion that Miss Lorena had most likely acquired some inflammation of the lungs from her habit of riding too near the bayous. Some miasma from the swamp must have infected her. He advised a tisane which Pansy dutifully prepared each night. However, Lorena had taken one disdainful sniff of the brew and declared it likely to kill her brother in his weakened state. So the tisane was allowed to cool before being dumped into the soil of the potted plants on the balcony outside Lorena's chamber. Whatever its effect on humans, it proved salutary for the plants.

Her adventures were varied, but all equally horrible. She was always utterly powerless, always set about with strictures and rules that demanded she express no opinions, have no thoughts of her own. She had not even the power to decide her own fate; a master, a father, a husband, a brother, a male cousin must act for her. And yet, it seemed to her that she knew what it might be like to be autonomous, independent. In a dream she had known herself to be, and was seen by the world as, a person whose opinions mattered, who was not to be condescended to: a person whose decisions must be honored and not dismissed, or overset by someone else who supposedly knew better what was best for her but might merely be acting for his own convenience. And it seemed to her as well, that in that dream, she had acted as thoughtlessly, as callously, as meanly as others now acted toward her. However, why ever, even in a dream, had she been so cruel? Bitterly regretful, she began to weep.

"I do not think I can continue this, after all," Lorena told Pansy the next morning. The slave had soaked two handkerchiefs through because of the tears shed by the dreaming figure on the bed. "I ought to be content. I can do as I will with what is mine, express my opinions without fear that they will be dismissed as trivialities. But the charade has paled. I find it as thankless to give up my femininity to achieve my rights as it was to find my rights curtailed because of my femininity. On the whole, I prefer to live as female."

"But not as a dependent."

"Never, ever again."

Miss Lorena rebounded from her fever more quickly than any would have suspected: bedridden one day, up and out riding the next.

"I think I understand the price, now."

"Well, mam'selle, I never doubted that you would."

Alarmingly, Mr. Raymond seemed to have caught a touch of the fever himself, but a day's bed rest seemed to cure him, as well.

Or so it seemed at first.

Not all the changes were bad, of course. Raymond Rivington became not merely a besotted father, but the most attentive of husbands. And certainly, the most indulgent of brothers. The neighborhood looked askance at some of his early ideas; not only did he make his sister his legal partner in the sugar plantation she helped finance by selling her Georgian property, but also in the shipping company his grandfather had helped found. A year or two later, he raised more than a few eyebrows, not because he freed his slave Pansy—faithful slaves were manumitted on occasion—but because sending both her and her mother north with a sizable amount of money gleaned from the substantial profits of his sugar plantation was a flamboyant extravagance. Pansy's mother, a plump middle-aged woman in bright green skirts with a string of beads about her neck that looked for all the world like uncut emeralds, was herself a flamboyant extravagance. And what did it mean that Miss Lorena was with them at the station, hugging the older woman whom no one remembered ever seeing at Rivington's Rest, and promising to visit? Worse, an inebriated and distraught Lawyer Jackson let slip the information that little Sarah was going to inherit equally from her father with little Raymond (born a year after his elder sister) and little Francis (born the year after that).

Not long after, Eugenie gave up on her madcap offspring, taking a house in town with a few favored slaves. The slaves in question were not particularly happy at being so favored, but contented themselves with certain promises made privately to them by Master Raymond. Master Raymond was not the master he had been before his daughter's birth. Somehow, fatherhood had softened a strict man and turned him into a generous one. The whipping post at Rivington's Rest had gone years without usage, and the overseer who had reigned unquestioned for twenty years quit rather than lower himself to "coddling the darkies." He was not replaced.

Lorena was reasonably happy. Raymond had become as decent, as caring and thoughtful a man as could be hoped for. Of course, life was not perfect. Pansy had been freed, but Raymond, she knew, would never be able to take the ultimate step of manumitting all his slaves. Lorena, initially content merely to better the lot of her slaves, found she was no longer comfortable owning them. She moved her profits from the sugar plantation into the shipping firm. The investments her brother made for them both under her direction soon offset whatever loss was incurred.

At twenty-four, then, Lorena was as much her own mistress as she could be, and with the passage of the first Married Women's Property Act in the neighboring state of Mississippi, she had every expectation that even marriage could not interfere with her new freedom. True, the dedicated swains who had haunted the plantation from the time she was sixteen had all fallen away not long after she began to bother herself with trade, but she did not regret them. Billy Collins made an attempt to get back in her good graces, but she had gently yet firmly rebuffed him. A few months later, she had attended his wedding to Lucy Whitby with a great deal of enjoyment. Watching him lead his new bride about the dance floor, she wondered how she ever thought she could have settled for a nice pair of shoulders and an ability to waltz. All in all, both her human life and her hours as the *loup-garou* were very pleasant.

But they were not quite enough.

And then, one night as she sped through the forest, she came across strange spoor.

The smell was acrid man-scent mixed with something more feral. Lorena howled in rage. This was *her* territory, how dare another *loup-garou* invade it! She hunted along the trail, but caught no more than a glint of tawny pelt in the trees ahead of her. Moments later came a full-throated baying howl, which stopped her pursuit, raising her hackles. Perhaps this was a challenge best left unanswered. Snarling, she rejected the thought. Still, the moon was by now low on the horizon, and she needed to head home. There would be other nights, she promised herself.

The next, however, found her in New Orleans at a ball being given to honor the return of Billy Collins and his bride from their wedding trip. Sarah and Lorena were left to their own devices when Raymond excused himself to meet with some of the other planters. He did not remain away long.

Lorena had her back to the doorway, but her heightened senses told her who it was—what it was—before she turned at her brother's hail.

His hair was tawny, his eyes moonlight silver. He was taller than Billy Collins, and his shoulders were broader, too. She did not know how well he danced, but he moved with the controlled grace of some wild, arrogant predator. She allowed her territorial snarl to become a polite social smile. He bared his own teeth in answer.

"Lorena, may I present Mr. Lucas Burton of New York? You'll remember that his firm has become one of our biggest customers in that city. He claims you have a friend in common."

"Madam Regine Hunter," Mr. Lucas Burton of New York said in a voice like honeyed whiskey. Lorena shivered in response, and allowed him to take her hand. The fingers clasping her own were warm and strong and vital.

"But of course, Mr. Burton. How is dear Madam Hunter?" she said as, bowing to her brother, Burton led her toward the dance floor.

"Better when I tell her I have seen you," he said as he swept her into a waltz.

"And when *I* tell her that you were so rude as to hunt my territory without my permission?" she said sweetly, the growl in her throat too low-pitched for any ears but his.

"Ah, but I wasn't hunting, my dear," his tone was all innocence. She knew better than to believe it, but as he intended, it amused her. "I was, in fact, hoping to introduce myself. Although I suppose you could say I was hunting for you."

"And why, Mr. Burton, should I let you catch me?" she asked archly, not willing to be *too* amused, just yet.

"Because you will never be satisfied with a man who cannot run with you beneath the moon," he said, teeth flashing in another charming, deadly smile. She bristled at this, but before she could protest, he continued, "As I could never be happy with such a lack in a spouse of my own. It is our nature."

"You know so much about our nature then?" she replied, still unconvinced, although despite herself, she was enjoying the dance. He moved smoothly, assuredly on the floor, turning her gracefully, their bodies moving as one. She grudgingly acknowledged to herself that she had never been as well matched.

"I know enough," he said. "I know what the wolf in us demands of our mates. Despite everything you have been taught about a woman's obligations and a man's prerogatives, you will never suffer a husband who thinks to amuse himself in a bed other than your own. At his first infidelity, you will reveal what you are and tear his throat with your naked fangs."

"Whereas if you were my husband, you could defend yourself from such an—unladylike?—assault on your male prerogative?" She allowed herself a touch of anger.

"Never think so." A hint of anger colored his own tone. The dance ended, but if she thought to make her curtsy and take her leave she was disappointed. Burton showed his teeth in what others might take for an appreciative smile. She revealed her own in what would be counted a flirtatious response. Undaunted, he drew her arm through his and walked her not back toward her family, but to the opposite end of the ballroom where the punch bowl had been placed. She respected his refusal to back down. She wasn't about to back down herself.

"Such an exhilarating dance, the waltz. Allow me to fetch you a glass of punch, Miss Rivington. It will, I am sure, refresh you."

"Why, however could I turn down such a *gentlemanly* offer?" she replied mockingly. His faint growl rewarded her. She laughed softly in response.

The promised punch was insipid, or perhaps she was too concerned with other matters to properly enjoy it. It was, of course, merely diversion: The true attraction of the punch bowl was that it had been placed on a table a few feet away from the French doors, which led out to a broad terrace and down to a garden where few, if any, of the guests had decided to go.

"Understand me, Miss Rivington: When a wolf mates, it mates for life," he said as he guided her out beneath the stars.

"In that case, Mr. Burton, I should not, perhaps, be in any hurry to find a mate."

His next words surprised her more than anything that had gone before. "No. Decidedly, you should not." His tone was absolutely sincere, his expression solemn, the look in his silvery eyes grave. "There are damned few of us in the world, Miss Rivington, but enough that you have choices." The smile returned, and this time she allowed herself to succumb, a little, to its intended charm. "Although, when you have met the others, I am sure you will bestow yourself . . . upon the most suitable candidate." She couldn't help herself, she allowed her own smile to answer his.

"And how am I to meet these . . . candidates?"

"Why, you have merely to accept the invitation Madam Hunter has entrusted to me. She would like you to visit her in New York, and perhaps join her on a trip abroad."

"With you, of course, as my escort?" she queried. He bowed.

"Your obedient servant, ma'am." The strains of another waltz drifted out to them from the open doors of the ballroom.

"Abominable wretch," she purred, taking a step toward him.

"Contrary vixen," he grinned back, pulling her into his arms. He kissed her. Soundly. Expertly. Satisfyingly. It was an appalling liberty to take. She realized that she would have left him to his own devices had he not. She wondered if she would find the other candidates as enjoyable.

"You have the right of it, you know," she said, deciding he deserved a final warning. "I am not a biddable woman, Mr. Burton."

"Had I wanted a biddable wife, Miss Rivington," he said with another lupine grin, "I would never have sought you out."

Her delighted laughter drifted over the garden like moonlight over forest paths, as he whirled her to the rhythm of the dance.

Creepers

Joanne Dahme

The baby died last summer, about a month after my thirteenth birthday. It was just about the time the ivy had finally reached all the way up the side of the house to the baby's window. My mother calls it "English ivy" because it reminds her of the ivy that grows all over the English castles and cathedrals, but she said that its official name is *Hedera helix,* which is Latin for "Climbing Spindle." She has plenty of pictures of castles and churches from a trip she and my dad took two years ago. And she's right. From the looks of it, there's tons of ivy in England. And even though our house isn't a castle or cathedral, the ivy is everywhere.

Caitlin—that was my sister's name—died in her sleep. My mom said that it happens sometimes, for reasons that the doctors still don't understand real well. I can still remember my mom and dad standing over her empty crib, holding on to each other and crying. I felt so cold and empty—sort of like how I felt when I was five and lost my favorite teddy bear at the grocery store. Without Teddy in my arms, I had trouble remembering quite what he had looked like. It was the same feeling with Caitlin. I remember looking out Caitlin's window and seeing the pointed leaves of the ivy blowing lightly in the breeze, like they were rocking back and forth, imitating the sorrow of my parents. I hate the way the ivy clings to our house. I hate the way it looked, holding on for dear life at Caitlin's window.

I didn't always hate the ivy. I really hardly even noticed it until Caitlin was gone. It was then that I started having the dreams—nightmares about ivy creeping along the side of the house, grabbing hold of the rain pipe and wrapping around it, like it was shimmying its way up along the stones and crevices, till it finally reaches my window. But in my dreams, the ivy never stops there. In my dreams, the ivy actually thrusts its tiny tendrils, too green and small to have leaves, between the bottom of the window pane and sill, and pushes the window up just enough to give it room to slither in. I always wake up when it reaches the bottom of my bed. So far anyway.

At first my parents thought my nightmares were because of Caitlin's death. But when I started freaking out about the ivy, I think that got them a little angry, and scared too. And I have to admit, it did seem a little strange. I mean, it got to a point where I didn't want to go out our front door because the ivy was wrapped all around the white columns and arches at the top of the front steps. It was all over our house, and at night sometimes, I felt like I was suffocating beneath it.

"Sam, what do you think is bothering Courtney?" I overheard my mother say to my father one night as they were clearing the dinner dishes. They thought that I had already gone upstairs to do my homework, but I was still in the hallway, getting my knapsack out of the hallway closet, where I tossed it every afternoon when I got home from school.

"I don't know, Claire," my dad answered in his most serious voice. "I think we forget, because Courtney sometimes acts much older, that she's only thirteen. Maybe we could have done a better job of explaining Caitlin's death to her. Maybe it scared her more than we know. It's only been a few months."

Boy, you could have heard a pin drop. You couldn't talk about Caitlin's death without driving my mom over the edge. I could hear the tears in her voice. For years, my mom used to say that having another baby was at the top of her prayers. She wanted so badly to give me a brother or sister. The doctors weren't so sure. So when Caitlin was born, it seemed like a real miracle. I think that's why Caitlin's death seemed to hit my mom the hardest.

"How can we explain something that we can't understand ourselves?" I heard my mom ask. Even though I couldn't see her, I could picture her answering my dad. One of her bony hands would be grasping the edge of the walnut dining table to steady herself, and the other hand would be slamming the table hard in frustration. I could almost feel my hand sting thinking about it. Then she would look at my dad like she was just daring him to answer.

My dad mumbled something back. But I did hear him say that maybe I just needed more time for my life to get back to normal.

"Normal!" my mom repeated, kind of sarcastically. "Normal," she said again, with less excitement. And then I heard the water running in the kitchen sink, and the soft clink of the dishes being washed. Now that sounded normal to me.

I used to love our house. My mom said it is an old greystone and that it is probably almost one hundred years old. When I was younger, I used to sit down on the roots of the big old oak tree that stands on the other side of our driveway and lean back into the jagged bark of the tree, making a rough seat. The view from the tree makes our house look enormous. Our house is a two-story stone building, with lots of wood trim; my dad hired a bunch of painters to repaint it a shiny white not too long ago. A few steps lead up to our front door, which has some really cool columns on both sides of it, with a rounded arch sitting on top of the columns, just like the kids' building blocks. Lots of windows, with the windows on the second floor "gabled," as my mom likes to say. And a big chimney on the left side of the house, which is from the fireplace in our family room. The ivy covers our house like a blanket, like a dark green rippling curtain that is never pulled back.

And our house has tons of big, leafy trees growing all around it, so that if you didn't know our driveway led to a road, you might think that our house was in the middle of the woods. Actually, woods surround our house on two sides—in the back of our house, and to the left of our house, if your back is to the road. Facing the road, on the other side, are cornfields. I love looking across the way at the long, neat rows that seem to stretch into forever—or at least as far as I can see. We really are kind of far from other people. I think our closest neighbor is about two miles away by car.

We have a big yard—about two acres, my dad says in a grumbling way when he's sitting on top of the riding mower cutting the grass. The trees that he has to wind around when he's mowing are the same huge trees that make up the woods—big maples and oaks, typical Pennsylvania trees. The ones in our yard look like they broke rank with their buddies, daring to go beyond the woods' borders. We don't have any fences or anything, but you can tell where the woods end and where our yard begins just by looking at where the thick line of trees suddenly stops, as if my dad drew a line, daring them to cross it. The old cemetery is on the right side of our house. An old stone wall runs along the cemetery border, thank God. I know I wouldn't like the idea of those old gravestones not having anything to butt up against to contain them.

My mom knows a lot about the local history, since she's a librarian and can get her hands on all kinds of books real easy. Actually, she is Bucks County's unofficial historian, and sometimes fills in for the Delaware Canal tourist guides in New Hope. As a volunteer, of course, she's always quick to add. She's my greatest resource when I'm doing a school paper. I ask a few questions and then the next day she comes home carting tons of books. She doesn't look like a librarian though. I think she looks more like an artist. She's medium height, and thin and bony. I sometimes tease her that her bones at her elbows and wrists look like they're about to pop out, and that they can be lethal weapons if she elbows someone too hard. Her hair is full and straight, parted in the middle, and stops just at her chin. And it's the coolest light brown, kind of blonde color. It's my mom's face that makes her look like an artist, though. She's very serious looking, just naturally I guess, because although she doesn't smile automatically, she has a great sense of humor. Being thirty-eight, she looks a lot younger than the mothers of my friends. But it's her big brown eyes, which look even bigger behind her wire-rimmed glasses, that when they train on you, make you think, "artist."

Now my dad is the opposite of my mom. He's sort of tall, but he's hardly skinny. He's more what people would call "chubby," probably because the most exercise he gets is picking up branches and stuff in the yard before he hops on the mower. He looks younger too, though, with his freckled face and skin and light reddish hair. Dad laughs easily, practically all the time, unless he's really nervous or upset about something. His blue eyes always look crinkly. Dad is vice president of a computer marketing company in Newtown. He's what people call a "natural born salesman." I'm glad I look like my mom.

I've got the same dark blonde hair, but mine is long and once was long enough to touch my butt. But now it's just halfway down my back, and I like to tie it back. Otherwise it's always getting in my way. I'm not as thin as my mom is. My dad says I'm built more like an athlete, probably from all the years I've played soccer. I'm in eighth grade and on the varsity team, so I must have inherited my dad's love of sports. My mom can't stand them, although she does come to my games. She says that's different.

Caitlin was too little for me to say who she looked like for sure. She was only six months old. I feel like I didn't get enough time to really look at her—to figure her out. Her eyes were brown though, my mom used to be fond of pointing out. And boy, did you have to work to make her smile. It's weird, but in all the pictures we have of her, she reminds me now of a ghost baby. No smile, no real expression. She's never really looking at you, but past you. Like there's something more interesting going on behind your back.

Caitlin is buried in the cemetery next door. I used to joke to my friends that my closest neighbors are all deadheads, or deadbeats, or something like that. But now that Caitlin is buried there, I never joke about it anymore.

The cemetery is old, and not the best kept. Many of the gravestones have been knocked over, or are cracking, or are so worn out that you can barely make out an inscription on them. There's an old guy, Jim, who works as the groundskeeper there. He looks like he's about eighty years old, and has a wild bush of white hair on his head, and isn't the fastest person alive. But my dad swears that Jim is only about sixty. Jim mows the grass, on a mower like Dad's, thank God, and pulls some weeds and tries to keep the grave sites tidy. But he told me that the cemetery is mostly full, so they don't get a whole lot of new "guests." That's what *he* called them. And there isn't a whole lot of money to keep the place looking great. Jim does his best, though. He said that the cemetery people made an exception for Caitlin, being as she was so small and that my mom and dad live next door. They could understand my parents wanting her so close. Jim says he takes extra good care of Caitlin's grave. He even planted some daisies around it last month, but they haven't come up yet.

It was a hot, cloudy day last July when Caitlin was buried. I remember looking up and thinking how moody the sky looked—huge black clouds, fat and bursting at their seams, seemed to be flying by. They looked angry about the funeral, and that made me feel good. Mom looked so tiny, almost shrunken, in the black summer dress she wore. My dad didn't want her to wear black, probably because it made it feel like an official funeral. But she's always such a traditionalist. I wore my favorite white-flowered print dress. Thank God I didn't have a black dress. Mom mentioned something about buying one but thought better of it after Dad gave her a look.

Mom and Dad stood clinging to one another beside the tiny white casket. The nice young priest from our church stood on the other side, whispering soft prayers. I think he was afraid of disturbing my parents, and was hoping to get through the prayers without a scene. Somebody said it was his first child's funeral. Mom had both her arms around Dad's waist, and her head against his shoulder. I think she was propping herself up against him. Dad looked as if he had had all the joy punched out of him. He had grabbed hold of my hand. I held his gently, feeling like if I held it too tightly, he might crumple. But Dad did pretty well. He had to thank about fifty people—some friends and relatives, some people from where my parents worked—on behalf of both of them. My mom stayed propped up by his side, though, and nodded to everyone as he spoke.

I had been in the cemetery before, a lot of times really, on exploring trips with my friends when we were younger and, more recently, on Hallowe'en nights. And I never noticed the ivy in the cemetery. Not along the walls, not on the trunks of the trees that were here way before the cemetery. But at the funeral, there was the ivy, draped over the gravestone next to where Caitlin would be, like it was listening patiently to the whole service. I walked over to the gravestone, to see where the ivy had come from. Its trail actually cut over a bunch of graves, went up and over the stone wall, and then into our yard. I looked at the gravestone next to Caitlin's again, out of curiosity. It was worn but still readable. The stone said, "Sally James, beloved daughter of Martha and Andrew. 1925–1930." How sad, I remember thinking. Now there would be two little girls buried here. It was then that my dad called my name, telling me it was time to toss my carnation onto Caitlin's casket. I walked over, trying my best not to cry, but my throat felt like it was about to burst. As I leaned over to let my carnation drop, I looked down to see a vine of that ivy at my feet, practically peeking into the grave. I tried to grind that piece of ivy with the heel of my sandal the best I could. Then Dad told me it was time to go back to the house.

The first few months after Caitlin's funeral were sort of quiet and numb. Mom cried a lot, and Dad tried to gently coax her into going back to work and stuff. The only thing he didn't have to talk her into was coming to my soccer games. That fall, she didn't miss one, and she kind of drove me crazy 'cause she worried all the time that I was going to get hurt. Dad asked me to be patient. He said it was normal for parents to feel that way, and that Mom was just saying it out loud, when for a long time she learned to keep it to herself. But with Caitlin, he said, and then sort of trailed off. I know, I nodded.

Actually, everyone was treating me like I might break. My teacher, my parents' friends, people at church—they all spoke to me in these hushed voices like my ears were hurting or something. If it weren't for my friends and Jim, I would have gone crazy. I missed Caitlin, and I wanted people to say her name, not to pretend that she never existed. But Dad would point out that they meant well.

It was right around this time, in the late fall, that I began noticing the ivy more. I guess it was the way it stood out suddenly. All of the trees surrounding our house had lost their leaves. I hated to see them so naked and bony. Only the ivy was still thick and green, so green that it looked like it stole all of the color from the woods, as if it were the ivy's fault that the trees were all bare. But what struck me more was that the ivy looked like it had literally flung itself all over our house. Its vines, like thousands of long spindly arms, were wrapped around our house in a bear hug.

I mentioned my concern about the ivy to my parents that night at dinner. I think I started the conversation with a question like, "What would happen if we burned the ivy off our house? Would our house be okay?" At first my mom and dad just sort of looked at me. Then my mom quickly wiped her mouth with her napkin and fixed her big brown eyes right on me, as if she were looking to see if I had a temperature.

"Why would you want to kill the ivy, Courtney?" She sounded just a little surprised. "It's our only reminder of warm weather. Aren't you glad to see a bit of green still around?"

"No, I think it's ugly," I answered. "You can't even see our house. It's like an octopus, with thousands of ugly green tentacles." This was before I started having the dreams. They started soon after this, right before Christmas.

"Just pretend we're in an English castle, Courtney. You know how drafty those old castles were. The ivy will keep us warm." Then my dad winked at me from across the table. I tried to smile back at him, but I wasn't so sure. Behind my dad, I could see some of that ivy peeking in the dining room window. Vines of ivy hung over and blew in the wind, like they were rappelling across the glass. If the ivy were wire, it would have made awful scratching sounds as it blew back and forth across the window. The ivy made me shiver. It didn't keep *me* warm.

On the afternoon of Christmas Eve, the three of us went over to visit Caitlin. My mom brought some holly and red ribbons to make a little wreath. My dad brought one of those little pine trees that you see in the supermarket, with tiny Christmas balls on it. He wanted Caitlin to have a Christmas tree. I brought one of my old baby dolls, one of my favorites when I was little. She looked weatherproof, so I thought she'd be okay out there. I felt mad that Caitlin never had a Christmas, so I wanted to give her a toy. Mom and Dad said it was the perfect gift.

It was cloudy and cold in the cemetery, so we didn't stay too long. But there were other people visiting grave sites, and people were waving back and forth, so it seemed less lonely than usual. After we placed our gifts around Caitlin's grave, I made sure that there wasn't any ivy creeping around. I didn't see any this time. I looked back to our house, which was of course blanketed in the stuff. It was so thick it reminded me of green felt. Our house could have been a giant Christmas ornament. But before I had a chance to get mad about it, I heard Jim call my name.

Jim and I had become friends, mostly I guess because he saw me practically every day, even on the days I didn't go into the cemetery. He usually arrived for work around the same time I was waiting outside for the school bus. Sometimes he'd stop his car and park it outside the cemetery gate to keep me company if the bus was late. Especially when it started to get cold. He said his company would keep my mind off the chill, which it did. At first this practice made my mom a little nervous, but Dad convinced Mom that Jim was just a lonely old man who worked in the cemetery and needed a little contact with the living. Jim was always especially careful in taking care of Caitlin's grave, too, which eventually softened my mom toward him.

He was sitting in his pickup truck on the dirt road that snaked through the cemetery; with the window down and the motor still running, he waved to me to come over. "Merry Christmas," he called gently to my mom and dad. I looked at my parents to see if it was all right, and they both nodded. They were both crying a little and probably wanted some privacy. I ran over to Jim. It felt good to get my cold muscles moving. I climbed up onto the running board on the driver's side.

"Merry Christmas, Courtney," Jim said as he leaned through the open window and brushed a kiss on my forehead. He smelled of mothballs. "I got you a little present." He held in his hand a small red box with a green ribbon. I was a little embarrassed. I didn't have anything for Jim.

"Oh Jim, I don't have a present for you," I said. "That's not fair."

"Don't worry about it. It's just a little thing. Open it." The look in Jim's eyes caused me to hesitate for a minute. They looked concerned. "Go ahead," he said, this time more lightly.

"Okay." First I rubbed my hands together, to get them warm. I pulled off the wrapping and opened the box. Inside lay a small silver bracelet, made to look like vines of ivy wrapping around each other in a circle. I must have looked surprised. I didn't say anything. I had told Jim about my nightmares.

"It will protect you," Jim said, quickly answering my unspoken question. "Friends of my mother's gave it to her many years ago when they moved away from here. They had a daughter—who had the same fear of ivy as you."

I still wasn't too sure about that bracelet. "Who was the girl? Did you know her, Jim?"

Jim looked off toward our house. "No," he answered slowly. "I never knew her. But she was one of the James girls. Her sister is buried next to Caitlin." He paused and looked in the direction of Caitlin's grave. "They moved from here when I was a little boy. I guess the girl didn't need the bracelet anymore."

"She was Sally James's sister?" I asked, excited about this revelation. "But where did she live?"

Again, Jim took his time answering. Actually, all he did was look in the direction of our house. Dad and Mom called to me then, so he never really had to officially answer me.

I wore Jim's bracelet all the time, which Mom thought was very odd since I hated the ivy so much. At first she freaked out when I showed her the bracelet. She told my dad that it wasn't normal for a man Jim's age to be giving young girls gifts if they weren't family. But my dad likes Jim. Jim is the only other person, outside of family, that my dad feels comfortable talking to about Caitlin. I could tell because I would sometimes look out my bedroom window and see Dad standing by Caitlin's grave after he came home from work. Jim would be standing beside him, with his arm thrown across my dad's shoulders. I think my dad liked having Jim with him there more than he liked my mom's company. With my mom, Dad had to be the strong one. With Jim, he could just be Dad. Again, Dad convinced my mom that Jim was alone and thought of us as family.

For a while, the bracelet seemed to work. Through all of January and February I didn't have a nightmare. I even felt braver coming in and out of our front door, almost taking my time passing under the ivy hanging from the arch and columns. I began to believe that the bracelet was to the ivy like garlic was to a vampire. I was almost able to stop thinking about the ivy all the time until that night in March, when I saw the girl.

The moon was especially bright that night, full and beautiful. Although the lights were out in my bedroom, and my bedroom door was closed, the light from the moon seemed to cast a magical glow. I could see everything in my room—my bureau, my bookcases, my desk, my closet and its door which was only partially closed. That surprised me 'cause usually I made sure it was fully closed. Seeing it open, I hopped out of bed to close it, and then decided to get a better look at the moon through my window. I pulled back the curtain and drew a breath, surprised at the bright shadows that the moon was creating. Everything seemed softly lit, so that the woods and road and cemetery were visible. I was staring down into our yard, looking to see if the trees had shadows, when I saw the girl.

She was running along the stone wall which divided the cemetery and our house, heading toward the road, when she stopped and looked right up at me. My heart was pounding like crazy suddenly and I almost yelled to my mom and dad. But I was afraid, too, that if I yelled, she might disappear. She looked so small and pale, like she was only in kindergarten. And even though it was freezing outside, all she had on was a long dark dress, old-fashioned looking, like the ones I saw in my mom's history of fashion from the Roaring Twenties. The two of us were frozen in place like statues staring at one another. Because of the moonlight, I could even see her large round eyes and her dark hair, which was whipping about her face almost like it was standing up in all directions, sort of like mine does when I first get up in the morning.

I couldn't believe that for such a little kid, she didn't even look scared, what with being outside all by herself in the middle of the night. She didn't even look surprised to see me looking at her. She just kept staring straight up at me, like she was curious to see what I might do. While I was debating if I should get my mom and dad, I saw something suddenly creep over the cemetery wall. It was the ivy.

Vines of it seemed to spill over the wall right behind the girl. All the while, she kept standing straight as an arrow as the ivy dropped to the ground and began twirling about her feet, like garden snakes piling coil upon coil. I wanted to scream out to her, "Watch out for the ivy! Run!" But nothing seemed to come out of me. Instead, I saw the girl turn toward the ivy and crouch down, extending her arms as if she were calling to a shy kitten. But it wasn't a kitten that came prancing to her. It was more ivy, streams of it, flowing from our house in tiny rivulets to her hands.

I did scream then. And I began banging on my window. But while my hands were pressed up against the glass, my room suddenly went dark as if a thick curtain had been quickly drawn. Except it wasn't a curtain. It was the ivy, stretching itself across my window, blocking my view.

I blew out of my room, screaming for my parents, and practically tackled them in the hallway as they came running. I know that what I was yelling at them didn't make much sense, but as my mom pulled me close to her and drew me under her warm terry cloth robe, my dad ran down the stairs to the front door. In a few minutes he was back, and gently pulled me from my mother to hold me close.

"It's alright, Courtney. Nothing is out there. It's just another bad dream." He sounded even less convincing to me when he said, "You're safe now."

Over the next few weeks, I searched for the girl, always during the day of course. I was suddenly very much afraid of the dark. I insisted that my mom and dad pull out some old night-lights to put in the hallway. I even borrowed the one in Caitlin's bedroom and stuck it into the socket right beneath one of my bedroom windows. My dad said it was because of my nightmares, and that my request was certainly understandable. My mom, though, was getting more and more worried about me. She began bringing home books from the library on dreams and adolescent psychology. I didn't know how to convince either of them that the girl wasn't a dream, except maybe to get a picture of her. That's why I went looking for her, as soon as I got home from school, with my camera packed in my knapsack. I skipped volleyball practice a few times, telling my coach that I wasn't feeling too well.

Sometimes I even searched for the girl after we ate dinner. There was still some daylight left now, till about seven o'clock, so by the time we finished eating and cleaning up, I had about a half-hour to look around. I'd walk around our yard, following the perimeter of trees. I always made sure that I walked on our side of the border, and not the woods' side, because it was close to getting dark. I even walked along the stone wall that separated our yard from the cemetery, standing in the same exact spot where the little girl stood as she peered up at my bedroom window. The new spring grass looked the same in this spot as it did in the rest of the yard. I guess I was hoping to see footprints or something.

I looked up at my bedroom window to see how I might have looked to the girl. My window was easy to see from here, but you really couldn't see anything inside the window. And the night that I saw her, I didn't have my bedroom lights on, so I wondered if she really saw me at all. I looked at the entire house then, which was of course still covered with the ivy. In the light April breeze, the ivy gently fluttered on its vines, looking relaxed and at home. I wanted to walk up to a wall and tear it off, but of course I couldn't do that. But I did have my bracelet on, so I held out my arm to the ivy, to be sure that I was protected. I swore that the ivy shuddered, as if a sudden strong breeze had rifled its army of leaves. I lowered my arm, and just as quickly, the ivy settled down. I knew that this was no ordinary ivy. But how could I convince my parents?

When I told Jim about the girl, about how I saw her running around in the middle of the night, he didn't say anything at first. He just sort of frowned, his forehead scrunching into the folds that I figured had been created by a thousand frowns before this one. He pulled a white handkerchief from his jeans pocket and wiped his face, as if he were sweating already. I think it's a nervous habit of Jim's. He then ran his freckled hand through his wavy white hair, and asked me softly, "What did she look like?"

I told Jim about her clothes, her wild hair, about how she didn't seem afraid standing outside in the middle of the night all by herself. But when I told Jim about the ivy, I could tell he was real upset because he didn't wait for the bus to come. He just told me to stay away from her if I ever saw her again, and to never take my bracelet off. Of course, that hardly made me feel any better. I didn't even get the chance to ask him any more questions because he quickly turned and hurried off to his car, to get right to the cemetery. Hurrying like that was unusual for Jim.

About a week later, I finally saw her again. It was just after dinner, and I was standing at our kitchen window, which looks out into our backyard. I was rinsing the dishes when I saw the girl running from the direction of the cemetery into the woods in back of the house. It wasn't quite dusk yet; we had recently turned the clocks ahead. I practically dropped the dishes into the sink and ran to the hall closet to grab my knapsack. My camera was still in there.

"Courtney!" my mom yelled. "Where are you going?" From the closet I yelled something about seeing a deer and wanting to get its picture. In a moment I was running out the kitchen door. "Well, come right back after you get your picture! It will be dark soon!" she reminded me.

When I was in the yard, I could see the girl standing on the edge of the trees, by the foot of one of the many dirt hiking trails that cut in and out of the woods. It was as if she had stood there, waiting for me, as if she knew that I would come running after her. She was wearing the same old-fashioned dress she wore before, and her hair still looked like it badly needed brushing. She waved to me, sort of shyly, like she wanted me to follow her. I noticed she was wearing something around her tiny wrist. And then she took off down the path.

I looked back at the house first, at the ivy, which was barely moving now, despite the soft April breeze. It seemed to be holding its breath, like every last leaf wanted to see what I would do next. Boy I hated that ivy. Everytime I looked at it I felt so angry. I knew that it was always watching me, waiting for me to take my bracelet off. So it could do what? Get me like it somehow got Caitlin? I believed that—and I think that's what scared me the most. I realized what Jim had been saying all along without using the words. The ivy was after me.

I looked back to the girl. She was already a good way down the path. Beneath the canopy of trees, which were all blooming now with fuzzy green leaves, she looked so tiny. I started running after her.

I'm a pretty fast runner, so it only took me about a minute to catch up to her. "Wait!" I yelled to her. "I just want to talk to you! I won't hurt you!"

She slowed down, turning to look back at me. And then she stopped by the big old oak tree that marked the spot where the path forked. The old oak has a trunk about three feet wide, and seems as tall as the sky. Its branches stretch way above any of the other trees near our house. It also has about a hundred names carved into its trunk. Mine was there somewhere, and Caitlin's too. I had carved Caitlin's in there a few days after the funeral. We were only about a few hundred yards from the house. I couldn't see our house from here, but I could see where the path spilled into the openness of our yard.

The girl was standing, facing the tree, and was running her hand across the rough bark, feeling the curves and lines of some of the names dug into it. I stood a few feet away from her, not sure how close I could come, so as not to scare her. For the first time, I noticed she wasn't wearing shoes. Her toes were sticking out from beneath the hem of her dress. They were very white and dirty.

"Is my name on here?" she asked, her voice very tiny and soft. She sounded like many of the kindergartners on my bus, which surprised me, though I'm not quite sure why.

"Uh, I don't know," I answered carefully. "What is your name?"

She turned to face me now, her small feet balanced on top of one of the thick roots of the tree that bulged above the soil. Now that I saw her up close, she looked like an honest-to-God little girl, not someone who I needed to be afraid of, as Jim had warned me. She was paler than anyone I knew. And she looked awfully skinny. Her eyes were huge and brown, real sad looking and too big for her tiny face. Her lips had no color; neither did her skin. Maybe she was like a wild child of the forest, like those stories I had read where children were raised by animals in the jungle after their parents were killed in some horrible accident.

"You say your name first," she answered shyly, without a smile. She stared at me with those hypnotic eyes.

"My name is Courtney, and I live in that house, over there," I said, pointing toward the end of the path we had just run up. Looking down the path, I noticed that the sunlight was getting weaker.

"I know," she answered quietly. "You live in the house with the ivy. I like your house." She was looking down at her bare toes. She had something in her hands, a twig or something, that she was twisting. It was then that I noticed the bracelet on her wrist. It was an ivy bracelet, just like mine, except hers was tarnished and dark.

"Your bracelet!" I blurted out in surprise. "Where did you get it? It's just like mine!" I held my wrist out to her, so that she could see it.

Suddenly she was very excited. She was smiling at me as she grabbed my hands. She grabbed them so quickly that I dropped my camera. I noticed that she was missing some teeth, and her hands felt ice cold. "Are you my sister?" she asked hopefully.

It was then that I felt very cold. The sunlight was all but gone, and the path was filled with dark shadows. I knew I should be back home by now. I could see the soft lights from our house. I didn't want to be out in the dark—in the woods—with this girl.

"Who is your sister?" I asked slowly. I suddenly felt the fear in my stomach.

"Could you put my name on the tree?" she asked brightly instead. "I want my name on there too. I like my name on things. Please?" She was still holding my hands. They were beginning to feel numb.

"I'm sorry," I said. "But I've got to get home." I tried pulling my hands from hers, but she was strong for such a little girl. Her fingers dug into my wrists. Her hands looked so white in the shadows, and she held on to me as if she were really scared that I might leave her. I couldn't leave her out here in the woods by herself, I realized. I'd have to bring her home and have Mom or Dad call the police.

It was then that I felt the ivy wrapping itself around my ankles, its vines trying to squeeze themselves past the cuffs of my jeans. I looked down to see the ivy swirling about my feet, as if I were standing on the shore in a wave pulled back to the ocean. But this wave wasn't washing back. I screamed. I could feel the vines groping around my calves.

"Don't be afraid, Courtney," the girl tried to yell above my screaming. She had let go of my wrists by now. "The ivy is good." Even in my frenzy to rip the ivy from my ankles, I could see that the ivy was also wrapping itself around the girl's ankles. "See," she said, pointing down toward the ivy, "it won't hurt you." I tore at the vines with such force, ripping it from my legs, that I sent myself flying backward, landing on my butt on the path. The path felt alive. I could hear the leaves of the ivy rustling, its vines crawling all over the path like hundreds of snakes slithering beneath me. They were all grasping at me, trying to get a good hold on my hands and legs.

I shot up, though, my feet dancing, stomping at the leaves. My hands were searching my arms, my body, my legs for the clinging ivy. I felt like the ivy was sticking to my body as if I had passed through a giant spider's web.

"Courtney, please. Stop fighting it. Stop hurting the ivy," the girl yelled. She sounded a little angry now, as if she were scolding me.

I broke away from the last green tentacle and ran. I never looked back, but only ran toward the lights of my house, stumbling a few times on the dark dirt path. But despite my terror, I could still hear the girl yell after me, "It won't hurt you!"

A few weeks had passed since that night in the woods, and I didn't see the girl. It's not like I wanted to see her either. I was really afraid. At first, all I wanted to do was tell Jim what happened. I was sure now that it was the ivy that had taken Caitlin. And I knew Jim knew more than he was telling me.

The ivy seemed to be acting differently too. At the end of April, we had a lot of rain—so much rain that one of the roads into town lost a bridge to Mill Creek. The rain seemed to wash out everything, so that our lawn, which just a few weeks ago was covered with soft green grass, was suddenly just sloppy, slippery mud. Only the ivy seemed to flourish under the downpour. I swore it covered our house twice as thick as it did before. And it had turned a lush, deep green color, its leaves all but covering up any of the brown vines that anchored it to our walls. But worst of all, the ivy didn't seem to be afraid of my bracelet anymore. When I ran from the bus to the steps of my front door, it sometimes suddenly dropped in front of me, dangling before me, as if daring me to come in. At the dinner table, I would look out our window to see it drooping there, staring in and just watching me. I didn't know what to do.

I told my parents about the girl, about how I met her in the woods. I skipped the part about the ivy, because I knew that they would just try to explain it as the darkness playing tricks on me. But the dark couldn't make up the girl. My dad had gone into the woods that night. I had wanted him to wait until morning, but of course he didn't want to wait—said it wouldn't be right to let a little girl just wander around the woods. "She's not a normal little girl," I had yelled. But it didn't matter. He never found her.

When I finally caught up with Jim, I found him at Caitlin's grave, scrubbing off something from her tombstone. He was very upset. He was dipping a scrub brush into a bucket of something, and was working so fast that he kept spilling water out of the bucket every time he dipped his hand and brush into it. He hadn't even heard me coming, didn't notice me standing behind him for a few minutes. It's only now that I can remember seeing a name scrawled in black across the tombstone. The writing looked like the writing of a little kid. The name began with a "C" and was long enough to spell "Courtney." But I couldn't make it out because Jim had already washed a lot of it away.

When I called Jim's name he nearly jumped out of his skin. "Jesus Christ, Courtney! Don't sneak up on me like that!" I knew he was upset because I never heard him curse. And then he went right back to scrubbing, all the faster.

"I'm sorry, Jim. I didn't mean to startle you," I apologized. I slowly walked toward him until I was squatting by his side. I had to tell him about the little girl and the ivy. And I did. And this time, I didn't leave anything out. I told Jim about how the ivy tried to wrap itself around my legs, how it tried to pull me down onto the ground and cover me.

At first Jim didn't say anything. It was so quiet we could hear all the spring birds chirping in the trees. It was warm for April that day and very sunny, so anything bad seemed impossible. Jim was digging his fingers into his forehead like he was trying to rub his mind clear. When he finally looked me in the eye, I noticed how red and bloodshot his own eyes were. He was perspiring from all the scrubbing. The flannel shirt he always wore was probably too hot for the day.

"I don't understand it," he finally said. "That bracelet should be protecting you. It should keep the ivy away from you. That's what my mother told me." Then Jim took my wrist in his hand, inspecting the bracelet suspiciously. He continued to frown, which didn't make me feel at all better.

"Your parents must take you away from here. I don't know what else to do—after what happened to you in the woods, and what happened here last night." And then he just shook his head. There was no joy left in him from the Jim I knew.

"But Jim, what about the girl?" I asked. "Do you think she's Sally James? The girl who is supposed to be buried next to Caitlin?"

But Jim wouldn't answer me. "Nobody will believe that, Courtney," was all Jim would say. "But somehow I'm going to have to talk to your parents."

I think Jim did speak with my parents because a few days later, my mother was furious, mumbling to my dad about that "old man" feeding my fears and filling my head with these wild ideas. Now they both wanted me to stay away from Jim. My dad said that sometimes when people get old, they get confused about things and act a little strange. But I knew that Jim was the only one who could save me now.

It was getting warm. By May, it was even warm enough at night to open the windows. But I refused to open mine. When my mother went to my window one night to open it, I practically screamed at her to keep it shut and locked. I wanted to yell at her that I didn't want the ivy to get in, to push itself through the tiny holes in the screen so that it could slither to my bed and take me away—the way it did in my dreams. I had trouble sleeping just knowing it was out there, patiently waiting outside my window. My mother didn't insist. She would just stand by the window and look out, blind to the ivy staring right back in at her.

It was the Friday before Memorial Day when the ivy finally made its move. Mom and Dad and I were excited about the big barbecue we were planning for Monday. It would be the first party that we'd had since Caitlin died. My dad thought it would do us all good to have some fun. I was even allowed to invite my friends.

By the time the school bus dropped me off, the sky was dark with rain clouds. They had been kind of hanging around all day, making the day hot and sticky, only threatening rain. Now they looked really nasty, as if they meant business.

I ran up our driveway, unlocked our front door and yelled that I was home. But there was no one there. There was a note by the phone on the desk in the atrium. It was from my mom. It said that she and Dad would be out shopping for the party till about 8 P.M.

This should have really been no big deal. I am thirteen, I reminded myself. But since Caitlin's death—and the ivy—I didn't like being home all by myself.

I tried to keep myself busy. I cleaned my room, watched some TV. I even thought about doing some homework, but quickly changed my mind. That's when the thunderstorm started. It was about 7:30 P.M.

Pelting rain quickly followed loud angry claps. I ran around the house downstairs turning all the lights on and closing all the curtains. It was already dark because of the storm, but I still knew that the ivy was out there and didn't want to imagine it looking in at me. At a few of the windows, the ivy was plastered against the glass by the rain. Its leaves were wet, and they glistened in the flashes of lightning.

By eight o'clock no one was home yet and I started to panic. Then the phone rang. It was my mom. "Is everything all right?" she asked me. She wanted to let me know that she and Dad would be a little late. A tree had fallen across Route 263, which was the quickest road to our house from town. They would have to go to Center Bridge, the next town over, and get on Route 413, which looped you the long way back on to 263.

I tried to sound brave, even though I was terrified now. I didn't know how to explain it to myself. Everything seemed okay, but I felt that something awful was going to happen. Maybe I could call Jim, I thought, even though I'm not allowed to talk to him. But maybe Jim could stay here with me until my parents get home. Maybe I could sneak him out before they saw him. I held out for maybe twenty minutes and then decided to call him.

But that was as far as I got with Jim. There was a soft knock at the door. Mom and Dad! I thought. The tree was probably moved and the road reopened. They didn't have to go the long way home after all!

But it was the girl. She stood there, still barefoot, on the top step of the landing. She was soaked—her dress was plastered to her tiny body, her hair clung to her wet face and neck.

"Courtney, can I come in? I'm so cold," she half whispered to me.

I backed up. I didn't know what to do. I could feel that awful panic tumbling around in my stomach. She didn't look cold—she wasn't shivering or anything. Should I shove her out the door and push her down the steps, I asked myself. She couldn't be cold because she's always cold. I knew what she was.

But before I could do anything, the ivy got in. It suddenly flowed across the door's threshold, parting at the girl's feet to form two separate streams. The ivy on her right side washed into the living room, the ivy on her left made a course into the dining room. The ivy was thick and green and shimmering with wet and was pouring in the front door like an endless wave.

"Sally!" I screamed. "Shut the door! Stop the ivy!" For I knew she was Sally—I knew for sure that she was the little girl who Caitlin had been buried next to.

"No, Courtney. I can't do that. The ivy needs you," she said calmly. "Besides, this was my house first, you know. You can't tell me what to do here." She then turned to check the progress of the ivy, which was now thick enough to create a living, green carpet on the floors of both rooms. Actually, there was so much ivy that it was tumbling over itself, searching the walls and the furniture for anything to give it a foothold to wrap itself around and climb. And then the lights went out. I knew the ivy had disconnected the outside wires.

That's when the phone rang on the desk behind me. I almost lunged for it, but in one of the flashes of light, I saw that the ivy was draped all over the desk, quickly wrapping itself around the phone. It had already begun to climb the stairs and the banister, slithering one step at a time to reach the second floor.

I felt so weak from fear, I kept praying to God not to let me faint like the women in scary movies. I knew the ivy would surely get me then. I eyed the front door. It was still open. I could see the rain falling in thick, slanting lines. Thunder was grumbling in the distance with each flash of light.

"You can't run away!" Sally said, reading my thoughts. "The ivy will find you. You've got the bracelet." I had forgotten about the bracelet. I tried holding the bracelet out toward the ivy, like I did that day outside of the house. But the ivy didn't flinch or fall back. The ivy seemed to shudder, just like it did before. Except that now, the ivy seemed to shudder with excitement.

"You're one of us now, Courtney. First me, then Caitlin—now you." Sally talked patiently to me, like a teacher, as if she were trying to calm me down. "Look in the dining room," she said, raising her pale, skinny arm to point into the room.

I heard the baby before I saw it. I heard the soft crying, a little meowing cry as if the baby were tired and just wanted someone to hold her. It was hard to see anything in the dining room, with the darkness and the jungle of ivy that covered everything. The ivy was covering the table, was looped over the hutch. It had wound itself around the curtains and dangled from the chandelier.

But in the next flash of light I saw her—Caitlin—the baby—lying atop the dining room table, thrashing and kicking her legs at the air. A blanket of ivy churned beneath her.

I was so scared I couldn't move. I couldn't take my eyes off the table. But then, in the next flash of lightning, she was gone.

"Caitlin!" I screamed. "No!"

"She's still here, Courtney," Sally was now standing by my elbow, wrapping her arm around my waist. "She's a part of the ivy. Caitlin and I gave it life."

"No!" I yelled. "I don't want to give it life! I hate the ivy. It's evil!" I was crying now, I was so furious. But Sally had other ideas.

She gave her arms to the ivy. Instead of her skinny little arm

CREEPERS $ 77

wrapped around my waist, it was the ivy now coiling around my body like a snake. Sally's face was still next to me, and her body too, but her arms and legs were now shuddering, trembling stalks of green ivy. The ivy seemed to be growing from her body. I looked at Sally in horror. For the first time, she smiled at me. "See?" she said brightly.

"Don't be afraid, Courtney," she whispered into my ear, as the ivy continued to wrap me up like a mummy. Suddenly all I could see were tiny yellow spots dancing before my eyes. I couldn't breathe. The ivy was strangling me.

"Courtney!" I heard someone scream. It was a man's voice. It was Jim's voice. I wanted to yell back, "Yes! I'm here!" But the ivy was all over my face. I didn't want it getting into my mouth.

I smelled the gasoline first, and then heard Sally screaming "No! no! no!" Jim was holding me then, struggling to tear the ivy from me. He stopped for a second, and I felt a sudden burst of heat—smelled the awful sweet smell of the burning ivy—heard the fire crackling as it attacked the furniture and curtains.

Suddenly the ivy was falling away from me, dropping as if it were stunned. The fire was quickly filling up the living and dining rooms. Jim must have spilled a lot of gas. The light of the fire was blinding, but despite the brightness and the smoke I could see the burning vines—the green leaves already eaten by the flames—the vines smoldering, curling up like burnt pieces of paper.

Jim then carried me out the front door and laid me gently on the wet lawn. I didn't mind the rain, which felt cold and rough. With the rain, and with Jim pulling the now lifeless ivy from my clothes and hair, I felt clean. I could only stare at our burning house. Against the darkness it reminded me of the Chinese lanterns we hung up in our backyard for summer barbecues. Smoke was pouring through the front door. I could see Sally standing there—standing on the threshold—stubbornly, angrily looking out at us.

Again, I heard the baby cry—this time screaming, the way Caitlin did when she was angry for attention. I buried my face in

Jim's wet, smoky sweatshirt.

"It's okay, Courtney. That's not really Caitlin. That's the ivy yelling. We've beaten it," he said wearily.

The next sound I heard was the sound of my parents' jeep screeching into our driveway.

We're living in an apartment in town now, at least until we find a new house. My mom wants to stay in Bucks County, but she doesn't want our new house to be anywhere near the old one. She's even talking about moving Caitlin, but my dad's hoping she changes her mind once she has a chance to think about it.

My parents have been really upset since the fire. It's almost as if Caitlin died all over again. At first they didn't know what to believe. When they had called that night—the night Sally came to the house—and I didn't answer, my dad called Jim, against my mom's wishes. Jim was close by, he explained later, and he knew that I liked and trusted Jim. My dad knew that Jim would never hurt me.

At first, they thought that Jim had started the fire just because he was crazy, and not to save me from the ivy. But as I sat huddled in our car with them, watching the firemen work to save our house, I told them everything—about Sally, and the ivy, and about Caitlin, and the ivy taking her. They didn't know what to believe. I think they were in shock.

But the fire report talked about the ivy. It said that the fire investigators had never seen anything like it—ivy vines were found all over the house, lying twisted and charred. They found them curled around the banisters, around curtain rods and lighting fixtures. They even found the ivy in the air ducts. The report said that the ivy occupied the house as if the house had been abandoned for many years. I think it was the report that finally convinced my parents.

I asked Jim what to do about the bracelet. He kept blaming himself for assuming that the bracelet was made to protect against the ivy. When he had found the bracelet after rummaging through his mother's attic, he figured that since the older James girl had survived the house, that the bracelet must have protected her. He didn't know that Sally had worn the same bracelet. He didn't know where the bracelets came from, except that the James family had given it to his mother, along with some other belongings, after they fled the house. Jim said that instead, the bracelet almost killed me, and that we had to get rid of it.

I knew what to do with the bracelet. At first I thought about burying it, somewhere in the yard, by the woods. But then I thought—what if the ivy made the bracelet somehow? What if I buried it, and the ivy grew, as if the bracelet were a seed?

That's when I decided to throw it into the river—put it in a bag full of rocks and let it drown. And that's what I did. My dad drove me to the river and stood right behind me as I threw it in.

There's been no sign of Sally since the fire. My dad says that maybe she's at peace now, and Caitlin too. When we stopped at Caitlin's grave the other day, I checked the whole area for ivy, and there wasn't a sign of a vine anywhere. Maybe if we come back a few times and see that everything in the cemetery is okay, my mom might change her mind about moving Caitlin. I hope so. I feel bad about leaving Sally alone and cold in the cemetery. My dad just says, "We'll see," as he looks over, across the cemetery wall, to the burnt shell of the house that used to hold us all together.

Luella Miller

Mary E. Wilkins-Freeman

Close to the village street stood the one-story house in which Luella Miller, who had an evil name in the village, had dwelt. She had been dead for years, yet there were those in the village who, in spite of the clearer light which comes on a vantage-point from a long-past danger, half believed in the tale which they had heard from their childhood. In their hearts, although they scarcely would have owned it, was a survival of the wild horror and frenzied fear of their ancestors who had dwelt in the same age with Luella Miller. Young people even would stare with a shudder at the old house as they passed, and children never played around it as was their wont around an untenanted building. Not a window in the old Miller house was broken: the panes reflected the morning sunlight in patches of emerald and blue, and the latch of the sagging front door was never lifted, although no bolt secured it. Since Luella Miller had been carried out of it, the house had had no tenant except one friendless old soul who had no choice between that and the far-off shelter of the open sky. This old woman, who had survived her kindred and friends, lived in the house one week, then one morning no smoke came out of the chimney, and a body of neighbors, a score strong, entered and found her dead in her bed. There were dark whispers as to the cause of her death, and there were those who testified to an expression of fear so exalted that it showed forth the state of the departing soul upon the dead face. The old woman had been hale and hearty when she entered the house, and in seven days she was dead; it seemed that she had fallen a victim to some uncanny power. The minister talked in the pulpit with covert severity against the sin of superstition; still the belief prevailed. Not a soul in the village but would have chosen the almshouse rather than that dwelling. No vagrant, if he heard the tale, would seek shelter beneath that old roof, unhallowed by nearly half a century of superstitious fear.

There was only one person in the village who had actually known Luella Miller. That person was a woman well over eighty, but a marvel of vitality and unextinct youth. Straight as an arrow, with the spring of one recently let loose from the bow of life, she moved about the streets, and she always went to church, rain or shine. She had never married, and had lived alone for years in a house across the road from Luella Miller's.

This woman had none of the garrulousness of age, but never in all her life had she ever held her tongue for any will save her own, and she never spared the truth when she essayed to present it. She it was who bore testimony to the life, evil, though possibly wittingly or designedly so, of Luella Miller, and to her personal appearance. When this old woman spoke—and she had the gift of description, although her thoughts were clothed in the rude vernacular of her native village—one could seem to see Luella Miller as she had really looked. According to this woman, Lydia Anderson by name, Luella Miller had been a beauty of a type rather unusual in New England. She had been a slight, pliant sort of creature, as ready with a strong yielding to fate and as unbreakable as a willow. She had glimmering lengths of straight, fair hair, which she wore softly looped round a long, lovely face. She had blue eyes full of soft pleading, little slender, clinging hands, and a wonderful grace of motion and attitude.

"Luella Miller used to sit in a way nobody else could if they sat up and studied a week of Sundays," said Lydia Anderson, "and it was a sight to see her walk. If one of them willows over there on the edge of the brook could start up and get its roots free of the ground, and move off, it would go just the way Luella Miller used to. She had a green shot silk she used to wear, too, and a hat with green ribbon streamers, and a lace veil blowing across her face and out sideways, and a green ribbon flyin' from her waist. That was what she came out bride in when she married Erastus Miller. Her name before she married was Hill. There was always a sight of "l's" in her name, married or single. Erastus Miller was good lookin', too, better lookin' than Luella. Sometimes I used to think that Luella wa'n't so handsome after all. Erastus just about worshipped her. I used to know him pretty well. He lived next door to me, and we went to school together. Folks used to say he was waitin' on me, but he wa'n't. I never thought he was except once or twice when he said things that some girls might have suspected meant somethin'. That was before Luella came here to teach the district school. It was funny how she came to get it, for folks said she hadn't any education, and that one of the big girls, Lottie Henderson, used to do all the teachin' for her, while she sat back and did embroidery work on a cambric pocket-handkerchief. Lottie Henderson was a real smart girl, a splendid scholar, and she just set her eyes by Luella, as all the girls did. Lottie would have made a real smart woman, but she died when Luella had been here about a year—just faded away and died—nobody knew what ailed her. She dragged herself to that schoolhouse and helped Luella teach till the very last minute. The committee all knew how Luella didn't do much of the work herself, but they winked at it. It wa'n't long after Lottie died that Erastus married her. I always thought he hurried it up because she wa'n't fit to teach. One of the big boys used to help her after Lottie died, but he hadn't much government, and the school didn't do very well, and Luella might have had to give it up, for the committee couldn't have shut their eyes to things much longer. The boy that helped her was a real honest, innocent sort of fellow, and he was a good scholar, too. Folks said he overstudied, and that was the reason he was took crazy the year after Luella married, but I don't know. And I don't know what made Erastus Miller go into consumption of the blood the year after he was married: consumption wa'n't in his family. He just grew weaker and weaker, and went almost bent double when he tried to wait on Luella, and he spoke feeble, like an old man. He worked terrible hard till the last trying to save up a little to leave Luella. I've seen him out in the worst storms on a wood-sled—he used to cut and sell wood—and he was hunched up on top lookin' more dead than alive. Once I couldn't stand it: I went over and helped him pitch some wood on the cart—I was always strong in my arms. I wouldn't stop for all he told me to, and I guess he was glad enough for the help. That was only a week before he died. He fell on the kitchen floor while he was gettin' breakfast. He always got the breakfast and let Luella lay abed. He did all the sweepin' and the washin' and the ironin' and most of the cookin'. He couldn't bear to have Luella lift her finger, and she let him do for her. She lived like queen for all the work she did. She didn't even do her sewin'. She said it made her shoulder ache to sew, and poor Erastus's sister Lily used to do all her sewin'. She wa'n't able to, either; she was never strong in her back, but she did it beautifully. She had to, to suit Luella, she was so dreadful particular. I never saw anythin' like the faggottin' and hemstitchin' that Lily Miller did for Luella. She made all Luella's weddin' outfit, and that green silk dress, after Maria Babbit cut it. Maria she cut it for nothin', and she did a lot more cuttin' and fittin' for nothin' for Luella, too. Lily Miller went to live with Luella after Erastus died. She gave up her home, though she was real attached to it and wa'n't a mite afraid to stay alone. She rented it and she went to live with Luella right away after the funeral."

Then this old woman, Lydia Anderson, who remembered Luella Miller, would go on to relate the story of Lily Miller. It seemed that on the removal of Lily Miller to the house of her dead brother, to live with his widow, the village people first began to talk. This Lily Miller had been hardly past her first youth, and a most robust and blooming woman, rosy-cheeked, with curls of strong, black hair overshadowing round, candid temples and bright dark eyes. It was not six months after she had taken up residence with her sister-in-law that her rosy color faded and her pretty curves became wan hollows. White shadows began to show in the black rings of her hair, and the light died out of her eyes, her features sharpened, and there were pathetic lines at her mouth, which yet wore always an expression of utter sweetness and even happiness. She was devoted to her sister-in-law; there was no doubt that she loved her with her whole heart, and was perfectly content in her service. It was her sole anxiety lest she should die and leave her alone.

"The way Lily Miller used to talk about Luella was enough to make you mad and enough to make you cry," said Lydia Anderson. "I've been in there sometimes toward the last when she was too feeble to cook and carried her some blanc-mange or custard—somethin' I thought she might relish, and she'd thank me, and when I asked her how she was, say she felt better than she did yesterday, and asked me if I didn't think she looked better, dreadful pitiful, and say poor Luella had an awful time takin' care of her and doin' the work—she wa'n't strong enough to do anythin'—when all the time Luella wa'n't liftin' her finger and poor Lily didn't get any care except what the neighbors gave her, and Luella eat up everythin' that was carried in for Lily. I had it real straight that she did. Luella used to just sit and cry and do nothin'. She did act real fond of Lily, and she pined away considerable, too. There was those that thought she'd go into a decline herself. But after Lily died, her Aunt Abby Mixter came, and then Luella picked up and grew as fat and rosy as ever. But poor Aunt Abby begun to droop just the way Lily had, and I guess somebody wrote to her married daughter, Mrs. Sam Abbot, who lived in Barre, for she wrote her mother that she must leave right away and come and make her a visit, but Aunt Abby wouldn't go. I can see her now. She was a real good-lookin' woman, tall and large, with a big, square face and a high forehead that looked of itself kind of benevolent and good. She just tended out on Luella as if she had been a baby, and when her married daughter sent for her she wouldn't stir one inch. She'd always thought a lot of her daughter, too, but she said Luella needed her and her married daughter didn't. Her daughter kept writin' and writin', but it didn't do any good. Finally she came, and when she saw how bad her mother looked, she broke down and cried and all but went on her knees to have her come away. She spoke her mind out to Luella, too. She told her that she'd killed her husband and everybody that had anythin' to do with her, and she'd thank her to leave her mother alone. Luella went into hysterics, and Aunt Abby was so frightened that she called me after her daughter went. Mrs. Sam Abbot she went away fairly cryin' out loud in the buggy, the neighbors heard her, and well she might, for she never saw her mother again alive. I went in that night when Aunt Abby called for me, standin' in the door with her little green-checked shawl over her head. I can see her now. 'Do come over here, Miss Anderson,' she sung out, kind of gasping for breath. I didn't stop for anythin'. I put over as fast as I could, and when I got there, there was Luella laughin' and cryin' all together, and Aunt Abby trying to hush her, and all the time she herself was white as a sheet and shakin' so she could hardly stand. 'For the land sakes, Mrs. Mixter,' says I, 'you look worse than she does. You ain't fit to be up out of your bed.'

"'Oh, there ain't anythin' the matter with me,' says she. Then she went on talkin' to Luella. 'There, there, don't, don't, poor little lamb,' says she. 'Aunt Abby is here. She ain't goin' away and leave you. Don't, poor little lamb.'

"'Do leave her with me, Mrs. Mixter, and you get back to bed,' says I, for Aunt Abby had been layin' down considerable lately, though somehow she contrived to do the work.

"'I'm well enough,' says she. 'Don't you think she had better have the doctor, Miss Anderson?'

"'The doctor,' says I, 'I think *you* had better have the doctor. I think you need him much worse than some folks I could mention.' And I looked straight at Luella Miller laughin' and cryin' and goin' on as if she was the center of all creation. All the time she was actin' so—seemed as if she was too sick to sense anythin'—she was keepin' a sharp lookout as to how we took it out of the corner of one eye. I see her. You could never cheat me about Luella Miller. Finally I got real mad and I run home and I got a bottle of valerian I had, and I poured some boilin' hot water on a handful of catnip, and I mixed up that catnip tea with most half a wineglass of valerian, and I went with it over to Luella's. I marched right up to Luella, a-holdin' out of that cup, all smokin'. 'Now,' says I, 'Luella Miller, *you swaller this!*'

"'What is—what is it, oh, what is it?' she sort of screeches out. Then she goes off a-laughin' enough to kill.

"'Poor lamb, poor little lamb,' says Aunt Abby, standin' over her, all kind of tottery, and tryin' to bathe her head with camphor.

"'*You swaller this right down,*' says I. And I didn't waste any ceremony. I just took hold of Luella Miller's chin and I tipped her head back, and I caught her mouth open with laughin', and I clapped that cup to her lips and I fairly hollered at her: 'Swaller, swaller, swaller!' and she gulped it right down. She had to, and I guess it did her good. Anyhow, she stopped cryin' and laughin' and let me put her to bed, and she went to sleep like a baby inside of half an hour. That was more than poor Aunt Abby did. She lay awake all that night and I stayed with her, though she tried not to have me; said she wa'n't sick enough for watchers. But I stayed, and I made some good cornmeal gruel and I fed her a teaspoon every little while all night long. It seemed to me as if she was jest dyin' from bein' all wore out. In the mornin' as soon as it was light I run over to the Bisbees and sent Johnny Bisbee for the doctor. I told him to tell the doctor to hurry, and he come pretty quick. Poor Aunt Abby didn't seem to know much of anythin' when he got there. You couldn't hardly tell she breathed, she was so used up. When the doctor had gone, Luella came into the room lookin' like a baby in her ruffled nightgown. I can see her now. Her eyes were as blue and her face all pink and white like a blossom, and she looked at Aunt Abby in the bed sort of innocent and surprised. 'Why,' says she, 'Aunt Abby ain't got up yet?'

"'No, she ain't,' says I, pretty short.

"'I thought I didn't smell the coffee,' says Luella.

"'Coffee,' says I. 'I guess if you have coffee this mornin' you'll make it yourself.'

"'I never made the coffee in all my life,' says she, dreadful astonished. 'Erastus always made the coffee as long as he lived, and then Lily she made it, and then Aunt Abby made it. I don't believe I *can* make the coffee, Miss Anderson.'

"'You can make it or go without, jest as you please,' says I.

"'Ain't Aunt Abby goin' to get up?' says she.

"'I guess she won't get up,' says I, 'sick as she is.' I was gettin' madder and madder. There was somethin' about that little pink-and-white thing standin' there and talkin' about coffee, when she had killed so many better folks than she was, and had jest killed another, that made me feel 'most as if I wished somebody would up and kill her before she had a chance to do any more harm.

"'Is Aunt Abby sick?' says Luella, as if she was sort of aggrieved and injured.

"'Yes,' says I, 'she's sick, and she's goin' to die, and then you'll be left alone, and you'll have to do for yourself and wait on yourself, or do without things.' I don't know but I was sort of hard, but it was the truth, and if I was any harder than Luella Miller had been I'll give up. I ain't never been sorry that I said it. Well, Luella, she up and had hysterics again at that, and I jest let her have 'em. All I did was to bundle her into the room on the other side of the entry where Aunt Abby couldn't hear her, if she wa'n't past it—I don't know but she was—and set her down hard in a chair and told her not to come back into the other room, and she minded. She had her hysterics in there till she got tired. When she found out that nobody was comin' to coddle her and do for her she stopped. At least I suppose she did. I had all I could do with poor

Aunt Abby tryin' to keep the breath of life in her. The doctor had told me that she was dreadful low, and give me some very strong medicine to give to her in drops real often, and told me real particular about the nourishment. Well, I did as he told me real faithful till she wa'n't able to swaller any longer. Then I had her daughter sent for. I had begun to realize that she wouldn't last any time at all. I hadn't realized it before, though I spoke to Luella the way I did. The doctor he came, and Mrs. Sam Abbot, but when she got there it was too late; her mother was dead. Aunt Abby's daughter just give one look at her mother layin' there, then she turned sort of sharp and sudden and looked at me.

"'Where is she?' says she, and I knew she meant Luella.

"'She's out in the kitchen,' says I. 'She's too nervous to see folks die. She's afraid it will make her sick.'

"The Doctor he speaks up then. He was a young man. Old Doctor Park had died the year before, and this was a young fellow just out of college. 'Mrs. Miller is not strong,' says he, kind of severe, 'and she is quite right in not agitating herself.'

"'You are another, young man; she's got her pretty claw on you,' thinks I, but I didn't say anythin' to him. I just said over to Mrs. Sam Abbot that Luella was in the kitchen, and Mrs. Sam Abbot she went out there, and I went, too, and I never heard anythin' like the way she talked to Luella Miller. I felt pretty hard to Luella myself, but this was more than I ever would have dared to say. Luella she was too scared to go into hysterics. She jest flopped. She seemed to jest shrink away to nothin' in that kitchen chair, with Mrs. Sam Abbot standin' over her and talkin' and tellin' her the truth. I guess the truth was most too much for her and no mistake, because Luella presently actually did faint away, and there wa'n't any sham about it, the way I always suspected there was about them hysterics. She fainted dead away and we had to lay her flat on the floor, and the Doctor he came runnin' out and he said somethin' about a weak heart dreadful fierce to Mrs. Sam Abbot, but she wa'n't a mite scared. She faced him jest as white as even Luella was layin' there lookin' like death and the Doctor feelin' of her pulse.

"'Weak heart,' says she, 'weak heart; weak fiddlesticks! There ain't nothin' weak about that woman. She's got strength enough to hang onto other folks till she kills 'em. Weak? It was my poor mother that was weak: this woman killed her as sure as if she had taken a knife to her.'

"But the Doctor he didn't pay much attention. He was bendin' over Luella layin' there with her yellow hair all streamin' and her pretty pink-and-white face all pale, and her blue eyes like stars gone out, and he was holdin' onto her hand and smoothin' her forehead, and tellin' me to get the brandy in Aunt Abby's room, and I was as sure as I wanted to be that Luella had got somebody else to hang onto, now Aunt Abby was gone, and I thought of poor Erastus Miller, and I sort of pitied the poor young Doctor, led away by a pretty face, and I made up my mind I'd see what I could do.

"I waited till Aunt Abby had been dead and buried about a month, and the Doctor was goin' to see Luella steady and folks were beginnin' to talk; then one evenin', when I knew the Doctor had been called out of town and wouldn't be round, I went over to Luella's. I found her all dressed up in a blue muslin with white polka dots on it, and her hair curled jest as pretty, and there wa'n't a young girl in the place could compare with her. There was somethin' about Luella Miller seemed to draw the heart right out of you, but she didn't draw it out of *me*. She was settin' rocking in the chair by her sittin'-room window, and Maria Brown had gone home. Maria Brown had been in to help her, or rather to do the work, for Luella wa'n't helped when she didn't do anythin'. Maria Brown was real capable and she didn't have any ties; she wa'n't married, and lived alone, so she'd offered. I couldn't see why she should do the work any more than Luella; she wa'n't any too strong; but she seemed to think she could and Luella seeeemed to think so, too, so she went over and did all the work—washed, and ironed, and baked, while Luella sat and rocked. Maria didn't live long afterward. She began to fade away just the same fashion the others had. Well, she was warned, but she acted real mad when folks said anythin': said Luella was a poor, abused woman, too delicate to help herself, and they'd ought to be ashamed, and if she died helpin' them that couldn't help themselves she would—and she did.

"'I s'pose Maria has gone home,' says I to Luella, when I had gone in and sat down opposite her.

"'Yes, Maria went half an hour ago, after she had got supper and washed the dishes,' says Luella, in her pretty way.

"'I suppose she has got a lot of work to do in her own house to-night,' says I, kind of bitter, but that was all thrown away on Luella Miller. It seemed to her right that other folks that wa'n't any better able than she was herself should wait on her, and she couldn't get it through her head that anybody should think it *wa'n't* right.

"'Yes,' says Luella, real sweet and pretty, 'yes, she said she had to do her washin' to-night. She has let it go for a fortnight along of comin' over here.'

"'Why don't she stay at home and do her washin' instead of comin' over here and doin' *your* work, when you are just as well able, and enough sight more so, than she is to do it?' says I.

"Then Luella she looked at me like a baby who has a rattle shook at it. She sort of laughed as innocent as you please. 'Oh, I can't do the work myself, Miss Anderson,' says she. 'I never did. Maria *has* to do it.'

"Then I spoke out: 'Has to do it!' says I. 'Has to do it! She don't have to do it, either. Maria Brown has her own home and enough to live on. She ain't beholden to you to come over here and slave for you and kill herself.'

"Luella she jest set and stared at me for all the world like a doll-baby that was so abused that it was comin' to life.

"'Yes,' says I, 'she's killin' herself. She's goin' to die just the way Erastus did, and Lily, and your Aunt Abby. You're killin' her jest as you did them. I don't know what there is about you, but you seem to bring a curse,' says I. 'You kill everybody that is fool enough to care anythin' about you and do for you.'

"She stared at me and she was pretty pale.

"'And Maria ain't the only one you're goin' to kill,' says I. 'You're goin' to kill Doctor Malcom before you're done with him.'

"Then a red color came flamin' all over her face. 'I ain't goin' to kill him, either,' says she, and she begun to cry.

"'Yes, you *be!*' says I. Then I spoke as I had never spoke before. You see, I felt it on account of Erastus. I told her that she hadn't any business to think of another man after she'd been married to one that had died for her: that she was a dreadful woman; and she was, that's true enough, but sometimes I have wondered lately if she knew it—if she wa'n't like a baby with scissors in its hand cuttin' everybody without knowin' what it was doin'.

"Luella she kept gettin' paler and paler, and she never took her eyes off my face. There was somethin' awful about the way she looked at me and never spoke one word. After awhile I quit talkin' and I went home. I watched that night, but her lamp went out before nine o'clock, and when Doctor Malcom came drivin' past and sort of slowed up he see there wa'n't any light and he drove along. I saw her sort of shy out of meetin' the next Sunday, too, so he shouldn't go home with her, and I begun to think mebbe she did have some conscience after all. It was only a week after that that Maria Brown died—sort of sudden at the last, though everybody had seen it was comin'. Well, then there was a good deal of feelin' and pretty dark whispers. Folks said the days of witchcraft had come again, and they were pretty shy of Luella. She acted sort of offish to the Doctor and he didn't go there, and there wa'n't anybody to do anythin' for her. I don't know how she *did* get along. I wouldn't go in there and offer to help her—not because I was afraid of dyin' like the rest but I thought she was just as well able to do her own work as I was to do it for her, and I thought it was about time that she did it and stopped killin' other folks. But it wa'n't very long before folks began to say that Luella herself was goin' into a decline jest the way her husband, and Lily, and Aunt Abby and the others had, and I saw myself that she looked pretty bad. I used to see her goin' past from the store with a bundle as if she could hardly crawl, but I remembered how Erastus used to wait and 'tend when he couldn't hardly put one foot before the other, and I didn't go out to help her.

"But at last one afternoon I saw the Doctor come drivin' up like mad with his medicine chest, and Mrs. Babbit came in after supper and said that Luella was real sick.

"'I'd offer to go in and nurse her,' says she, 'but I've got my children to consider, and mebbe it ain't true what they say, but it's queer how many folks that have done for her have died.'

"I didn't say anythin', but I considered how she had been Erastus's wife and how he had set his eyes by her, and I made up my mind to go in the next mornin', unless she was better, and see what I could do; but the next mornin' I see her at the window, and pretty soon she come steppin' out as spry as you please, and a little while afterward Mrs. Babbit came in and told me that the Doctor had got a girl from out of town, a Sarah Jones, to come there, and she said she was pretty sure that the Doctor was goin' to marry Luella.

"I saw him kiss her in her door that night myself, and I knew it was true. The woman came that afternoon, and the way she flew around was a caution. I don't believe Luella had swept since Maria had died. She swept and dusted, and washed and ironed; wet clothes and dusters and carpets were flyin' over there all day, and every time Luella set her foot out when the Doctor wa'n't there there was Sarah Jones helpin' of her up and down the steps, as if she hadn't learned to walk.

"Well, everybody knew that Luella and the Doctor were goin' to be married, but it wa'n't long before they began to talk about his lookin' so poorly, jest as they had about the others; and they talked about Sarah Jones, too.

"Well, the Doctor did die, and he wanted to be married first, so as to leave what little he had to Luella, but he died before the minister could get there, and Sarah Jones died a week afterward.

"Well, that wound up everything for Luella Miller. Not

another soul in the whole town would lift a finger for her. There got to be a sort of panic. Then she began to droop in good earnest. She used to have to go to the store herself, for Mrs. Babbit was afraid to let Tommy go for her, and I've seen her goin' past and stoppin' every two or three steps to rest. Well, I stood it as long as I could, but one day I see her comin' with her arms full and stoppin' to lean against the Babbit fence, and I run out and took her bundles and carried them to her house. Then I went home and never spoke one word to her though she called after me dreadful kind of pitiful. Well, that night I was taken sick with a chill, and I was sick as I wanted to be for two weeks. Mrs. Babbit had seen me run out to help Luella and she came in and told me I was goin' to die on account of it. I didn't know whether I was or not, but I considered I had done right by Erastus's wife.

"That last two weeks Luella she had a dreadful hard time, I guess. She was pretty sick, and as near as I could make out nobody dared go near her. I don't know as she was really needin' anythin' very much, for there was enough to eat in her house and it was warm weather, and she made out to cook a little flour gruel every day, I know, but I guess she had a hard time, she that had been so petted and done for all her life.

"When I got so I could go out, I went over there one morning. Mrs. Babbit had just come in to say she hadn't seen any smoke and she didn't know but what it was somebody's duty to go in, but she couldn't help thinkin' of her children, and I got right up, though I hadn't been out of the house for two weeks, and I went in there, and Luella she was layin' on the bed, and she was dyin'.

"She lasted all that day and into the night. But I sat there after the new doctor had gone away. Nobody else dared to go there. It was about midnight that I left her for a minute to run home and get some medicine I had been takin', for I begun to feel rather bad.

"It was a full moon that night, and just as I started out of my door to cross the street back to Luella's, I stopped short, for I saw something."

Lydia Anderson at this juncture always said with a certain defiance that she did not expect to be believed, and then proceeded in a hushed voice:

"I saw what I saw, and I know what I saw, and I will swear on my death bed that I saw it. I saw Luella Miller and Erastus Miller, and Lily, and Aunt Abby, and Maria, and the Doctor, and Sarah, all goin' out of her door, and all but Luella shone white in the moonlight, and they were all helpin' her along till she seemed to fairly fly in the midst of them. Then it all disappeared. I stood a minute with my heart poundin', then I went over there. I thought of goin' for Mrs. Babbit, but I thought she'd be afraid. So I went alone, though I knew what had happened. Luella was layin' real peaceful, dead on her bed."

This was the story that the old woman, Lydia Anderson, told, but the sequel was told by the people who survived her, and this is the tale which has become folklore in the village.

Lydia Anderson died when she was eighty-seven. She had continued wonderfully hale and hearty for one of her years until about two weeks before her death.

One bright moonlight evening she was sitting beside a window in her parlour when she made a sudden exclamation, and was out of the house and across the street before the neighbor who was taking care of her could stop her. She followed as fast as possible and found Lydia Anderson stretched on the ground before the door of Luella Miller's deserted house, and she was quite dead.

The next night there was a red gleam of fire athwart the moonlight and the old house of Luella Miller was burned to the ground. Nothing is now left of it except a few old cellar stones and a lilac bush, and in summer a helpless trail of morning glories among the weeds, which might be considered emblematic of Luella herself.

The Birthday Present

Roz Warren

Liza came into her shapeshifting powers, as was customary in her family, on the morning of her twenty-fifth birthday. Her mother smiled fondly as Liza appeared in the breakfast room for her morning coffee.

"Happy birthday, darling," Ariel said. "At last, you can look like whomever you please. Why not celebrate by becoming a great beauty and seducing that fellow you've had the awful crush on for so long?"

"His name is Matt," said Liza, pouring herself a cup of coffee.

"Well, now you can become the woman of Matt's dreams," said her mother, who didn't look a day over twenty-five herself.

"He's already married to the woman of his dreams. Not only is she calm and loving, but she's a brilliant pediatric cardiologist."

"But you told me she was homely."

Liza sighed. "Emily has inner beauty."

"Inner beauty," scoffed her mother. "Women don't need inner beauty."

"Mother, that is so retro."

Ariel shrugged. "Being drop-dead gorgeous may be only skin deep, but it's always worked for me. Why have magical powers in the first place if you can't allow yourself to enjoy them?" She flashed Liza a mischievous grin. "C'mon. Go get him! I dare you. It's *fun* to be a seductress."

"No. Absolutely not. It wouldn't be right."

Ariel narrowed her eyes. "Are you sure you're my daughter?"

Liza, an animal-lover, worked at a cat hospital. Although she didn't plan to take her mother's advice and transform herself into a *femme fatale* for his benefit, she did look forward to seeing Matt, who would be at the hospital that morning to visit Georgia, his cat. Matt was a travel writer. Although he was married, his wife worked long and unpredictable hours, so whenever he left town he boarded Georgia at the hospital to make sure she'd have plenty of cat-lovers to play with. Today, however, Georgia was there not because Matt was traveling, but because she'd stopped eating and was seriously ill. She was being held for observation and tests, and Matt visited her daily.

Liza had met Matt almost a year ago. Looking for a quiet place to eat her lunch, Liza had ducked into one of the hospital waiting areas and come upon a tall, husky man with dark curly hair, cradling in his arms a beautiful orange tabby the color of marmalade and crooning to the cat with loving, silly words. Seeing Liza, he grinned, unembarrassed.

"I'm Matt," he said. "And this is my best girl, Georgia."

"Pleased to meet you," smiled Liza, both amused and impressed with Matt's obvious devotion to his cat. This kind of tenderness, routine in women cat-owners, was rare in men. As Matt continued stroking the cat, he and Liza chatted about Georgia, about how beautiful she was, and how good-natured, then about her likes and dislikes, her quirks and habits. Certain of Georgia's antics reminded Liza of cats she'd known and loved, and she described them to Matt. An hour flew by. The longer Matt held and stroked his cat, the more relaxed Georgia became, until, limp in his arms, her eyes closed, she was purring so loudly that Liza had to laugh.

"*She* doesn't have a bad life, does she?"

"I spoil her rotten," Matt agreed cheerfully. "I just wish I could bring her along when I travel." He smiled at Liza. "But you'll take good care of her for me, won't you?"

After that, Liza always spent extra time with Georgia when Matt boarded her, and found herself looking forward to their conversations upon his return, about his travels and about his cat. An intelligent and good-natured man, Matt was easy to talk to. Unlike some owners, who breezed in to collect a boarded cat with no more interest than if they were picking up a shirt from the cleaners, Matt always asked about Georgia's week and listened with interest to any stories Liza could share. Clearly, when he was out of town he missed his cat. And, though a large and not otherwise graceful man, Matt was so tender and gentle with Georgia that it was easy for Liza to understand why the cat, in turn, was blissfully happy in his arms. *Who wouldn't be?* she thought to herself from time to time, watching Georgia snuggle against Matt's chest, purring with pleasure.

It wasn't until the first time Matt brought his wife Emily along when he picked up Georgia—when Liza saw how attuned to each other they were, and realized that Matt was as devoted to his wife as he was to his cat—that Liza realized she was a little bit in love with him.

This morning, when Liza arrived at the clinic, both Emily and Matt were there. Matt was holding Georgia and murmuring soft words. Emily stood with him, her hand on his arm. Despite Matt's efforts, Georgia was fretful and obviously uncomfortable. The worst part of this job, for Liza, was seeing animals in pain. And watching their owners feeling helpless. Liza tried to soothe Georgia and distract Matt, as the three of them waited for the vet to arrive. As helpless as she herself felt, Liza still took guilty pleasure in Matt's company. *Get over it*, she told herself. *He's taken.*

It didn't make her feel any better to see that Emily was more of a comfort to Matt than Liza could hope to be. When Matt looked at his wife, his face softened. *If only he would look at me like that*, Liza thought.

But—she suddenly realized—he could.

That afternoon, Ariel, glancing out her front window, was surprised to see her daughter coming up the walk, accompanied by a woman she didn't recognize. The stranger, a short, plain woman with intelligent eyes, had a tight grip on Liza's arm. Liza seemed to be having difficulty walking. Ariel, alarmed, rushed out to greet them. "Liza—is everything all right?"

"Mom, *I'm* Liza," the stranger said.

Ariel frowned. "Of all the women you could look like, *this* drab little pigeon is what you chose? I just don't understand you."

Her daughter smiled. "You will."

The woman who looked like Liza, but wasn't, gazed impassively at Ariel for a moment, then began to lick her own arm.

"Who on earth is this?" Ariel asked.

"This is a cat," said her daughter, "moved—temporarily—into my body."

Ariel raised an eyebrow.

"I needed to do that so I could put Emily, Matt's wife, into the cat's body."

"Matt—the man you have a crush on?" Ariel laughed. "You've turned his wife into a cat? I can't wait to hear this."

"I would never try to seduce Matt away from his wife," Liza said. Her companion was now staring fixedly at a bird who'd lighted on a tree nearby, and making soft clicking noises. "To take Matt away from Emily would be wrong. But when I realized that I now had the power to *become* Emily, or at least to appear to be Emily, if only for one night—" Liza giggled. "I just couldn't resist."

"And why should you? After all, it *is* your birthday."

"And it's not as if I'm taking Matt away from Emily. I'm just *borrowing* him."

"Very creative," her mother said approvingly.

"I lured Emily into the ladies' room, then copied her. But having two different versions of Matt's wife running around wouldn't work. I thought about copying my body for her, but with my powers of human thought and speech she'd understand what was going on. So I swiped her soul and stashed it in one of the cats we're boarding at the clinic. Then I put the cat into my body and brought her here."

"You did a three-way, a soul swipe and an interspecies transfer on your very first day? I'm so proud. Wait till I tell your Aunt Amelia."

"Can you keep her for me overnight? I've got to get back to the hospital before Matt gets suspicious."

Matt was, in fact, leaving the hospital just as Liza returned. She felt a moment's panic—could she really pull this off? What if he suspected that something was wrong? Then Matt saw her and his face lit up.

"I wondered where you'd disappeared to," he said, giving her a hug. Liza felt faint with pleasure.

"Let's have dinner out tonight," he said. "The usual place?"

"Uh—sure," she croaked, so keyed up she could barely speak. This gave her an idea. "My throat is sore. I don't want to lose my voice. You'll have to do most of the talking." The less she said, the less likely it was she'd say something wrong.

Dinner at a nearby restaurant went well, except for one touchy moment when Liza, a vegetarian, ordered a dinner salad, only to realize from Matt's startled look that Emily would have ordered meat. But he seemed to accept Liza's explanation that, with a cold coming on, she wanted to eat light. Otherwise, everything was perfect. Matt talked—about Georgia, about local politics and about his recent trip to Bali. Liza listened, soaking up his fond touches and warm looks. For Matt to look at her like this was all she'd wanted for months.

She couldn't wait to get him into bed.

Emily and Matt lived in a large contemporary house about a mile from the cat hospital. As they walked through the front door, Matt said, "I know you've got paperwork you want to get to before bed. I'll be in the den, watching the game."

Before Liza could protest, he vanished.

With the faint sound of televised sports in the background, Liza found Emily's office, kicked off her shoes, sat down at Emily's desk, figured out how to work her computer, and spent the next hour playing computer solitaire, crazy with impatience and lust. She was beginning to fear that Matt had fallen asleep in front of the television when he appeared at the office door. Her heart soared. This was it!

"Goodnight," he said cheerfully. "See you in the morning."

"Morning?"

"I'm going up to my room now."

Wait a minute. Matt didn't sleep with his wife?

"I do miss Georgia. It's tough to get to sleep without her little head tucked under my chin."

Matt slept with the cat?

"I'd be happy to tuck *my* little head under your chin," Liza said.

Matt laughed. "Now I know you're coming down with something. Goodnight, dear heart." He came into the room to give her a brief hug. "See you in the morning."

Liza was too stunned to speak. But the moment Matt left, she began searching through Emily's desk for personal papers. What was going on here? There had to be an explanation. Normally she would never read another person's journal, but when Liza finally found the small brown book labeled "Diary" on the cover, she opened it without hesitation. Matt and Emily, she read, had met, fallen in love and married, quickly and impulsively, only to discover that after the first attraction wore off, they were sexually incompatible. There was abundant love between them, but no chemistry. Sex was awkward and unsatisfying. Physical intimacy made Emily uncomfortable, and Matt was, by nature, more affectionate than sexual. For months they considered breaking up, but they loved each other far too much. So they stayed together, quite comfortably, in a sexless marriage.

The things you didn't know about people, Liza thought, closing Emily's journal. *She* and Matt weren't sexually incompatible. She was sure there was a spark there. If there wasn't, she'd create one. All she had to do was go upstairs and find his bedroom.

She longed to. But she couldn't. It wouldn't be fair. To Emily, or to Matt.

"Happy birthday," she said to herself. "The joke's on you."

The next day, Liza returned to her original shape, then swapped Emily and the cat back. "Did I doze off?" Emily asked. "You wouldn't *believe* the dreams I had. I was dancing with birds and rodents. And fabulous little balls with bells inside them kept rolling by. I really ought to cut down on my hours. Is it morning or evening? I'm not even sure what day it is. Thursday? Oops—I've got surgery scheduled this morning." She left.

As if things weren't awful enough, in the night, Georgia's condition had worsened. "There's nothing we can do," the vet told Matt when he arrived for his morning visit. Matt stayed with Georgia all morning. Liza came in as often as she could to keep him company. Finally, when Matt had left the room briefly to phone Emily, Georgia died.

Liza held the cat, struggling to hold back tears. She couldn't bear the thought of being there when Matt found out.

One evening, a week later, Matt and Emily were at home together when the doorbell rang. Emily opened the door to a beautiful woman she didn't recognize. "I'm Liza's mother," she said. "May I come in?"

"Certainly," said Emily. "We wondered what happened to Liza."

"She moved," Ariel said. "Suddenly. On an impulse."

Emily invited her in. They went to the living room, where Matt was sitting, reading a book, with a cat, an orange tabby, curled up on his lap. "Liza wanted me to apologize for leaving without saying goodbye," Ariel told him. "And she asked me to see how your cat was doing."

Matt stroked the purring cat. "As you can see, she's thriving."

"It was a miracle," Emily said. "One moment she was dying. Then, suddenly, a full recovery. Now she's her old self again."

Matt smiled. "It's great to have her back."

"That's all I wanted to know," said Ariel, rising to leave. "Liza will be glad to hear how happy you are."

"I hope Liza is happy, too," said Matt. "Wherever she is."

"Oh, I know she is," said Ariel. "She's my daughter, after all. I'm sure she's doing just fine."

The orange tabby, who'd been contentedly cleaning her right front paw, paused, looked at Ariel, stretched languidly and winked.

La Noche

Terri de la Peña

Vibiana Ruíz stepped with care on the sloping lawn carpet at Woodlawn Cemetery. Traces of freshly mown grass tickled the girl's sandaled feet and lay like scattered green threads amid the flat tombstones. Groundskeepers removed wilting bouquets once a week prior to mowing, and nearby famílias had not yet had time to replenish them with floral offerings from their gardens. Vibiana knew by the end of the day clusters of daisies, geraniums, gladioli and roses would dot the cemetery.

The girl paused, recognizing a familiar name on a burial marker. Bending, she brushed aside the grassy remnants to reveal the etched carving of a crucifix entwined con rositas. Vibiana made the sign of the cross, whispered a quick prayer in memory of her grandmother's friend and continued to walk among the graves.

A sudden ocean breeze ruffled the huge heads of the sunflowers nestled in her arms. They seemed to rise of their own volition as if offering to help the girl in her concentrated search. She did not notice their abrupt movement and had no need for their assistance. Vibiana knew the source of her quest.

Near the gated entry to the stone mausoleum, beneath the shade of an ancient sycamore, the girl halted. A granite marker held her attention. La Virgen de Guadalupe decorated its left border. Adjacent was the inscription: Descansa en paz, Rosamaria Gómez Ruíz, beloved wife, daughter and mother, 1955–1993.

Vibiana knelt. The sycamore's shade kept the grass damp. The girl seemed oblivious to the moist spots already appearing on the worn knees of her Levi's. She put the newspaper-wrapped sunflowers aside and reached over to remove the sunken metal vase. She noticed how easily she could lift it from its concave holder. By observing the pristine condition of her mother's grave, its marker clean and legible, Vibiana realized her grandmother tended it regularly.

"Mami, I'm so glad Abuelita's close by," the girl murmured. "She can visit you all the time. And guess what? I'll be staying with her till summer's over."

For a moment, Vibiana hesitated. Then she kissed the tip of one finger and touched it to the tombstone. The coldness of the granite stunned her. She shuddered and stood in one swift motion. Without a backward glance, she carried the metal vase to the spigot near the mausoleum. There, as she let water flow into the vase, she allowed herself to cry.

She did not know how long she remained watching the vase fill, the water spill over. Her hands seemed frozen as she continued to hold the metal container beneath the faucet. Bent over, she contorted herself in sorrow as well. Her long hair fell forward, shielding her like a protective black curtain. Vibiana wept so much she was no longer cognizant of her surroundings. At last, a back-firing truck on Pico Boulevard broke her spell of grief. The violent sound wrenched the girl into reality.

She turned off the spigot, tipped some of the water to the already drenched grass and wiped her eyes with a thin brown arm. Tossing her hair from her wet face, she wondered if someone had seen her. Perhaps it was still too early for anyone to have entered the cemetery grounds. Yet, askance, she noticed a furtive movement near the sycamore.

"No!" she shouted. "Stay away from there!"

An enormous black dog gamboled near Vibiana's mother's grave. In a bold maneuver, it snatched one of the sunflowers in its jaws and scampered away.

"Hey, come back here!" Vibiana yelled.

Her sad-eyed expression soon turned into a grin. The big animal simply wanted to play. Approaching, the wolflike dog began to run around her in ever-diminishing circles, the sunflower already limp.

"Just wait a minute." Vibiana tried not to laugh at the dog's frolicsome actions. "Let me fix the flowers for Mami and then I'll play, you silly thing."

The dog seemed to understand. She wagged her plume of a tail, slowed down and trotted beside Vibiana. She even pressed a very moist nose into the girl's free hand.

Vibiana laughed. "Don't make me spill this water."

The dog snorted in response, ran ahead and dropped the sunflower on the grave.

"Thanks." Vibiana eyed the droopy flower ruefully, but nonetheless added it to the bundle. "You must be lonesome too, huh?"

Amber eyes alight, tongue lolling, the dog sat still while Vibiana knelt to arrange the flowers. The girl worked in silence, almost forgetting the dog's presence. When she finished, she prayed an Our Father and three Hail Marys.

Vibiana sighed. "Oh, Mami. I wish you were here to talk to for real. There's so much I want to tell you."

With a whine, the black dog edged closer. She poked her pointy nose into the teenager's shoulder. On the verge of tears again, Vibiana hugged the big animal. She buried her face in the dog's thick fur and sobbed anew. Squirming, the dog at first strove to lick the girl's face. Eventually, she remained quiet, as if comprehending Vibiana's sadness.

"I'm sorry," the girl mumbled a few minutes later. "I don't

even know you and here I am crying on your shoulder."

Leaning back on her haunches, Vibiana did not protest when the black dog licked her face dry.

"You're a very sweet perrita," the girl added, somewhat embarrassed by the animal's natural show of affection. "Who's lucky enough to own you?"

Tail waving madly, the dog barked.

In spite of herself, Vibiana giggled. "Not so loud, huh?"

At the change in the girl's tone, the dog seemed overjoyed. She became frivolous, rolling over, long legs flailing in the air, tongue dangling. She pretended to nip Vibiana's knees. The girl accepted the dog's impromptu invitation to revert to childhood. She made a grab for the big animal. They wound up wrestling on the damp grass. Vibiana tickled the dog's belly and laughed at her almost convulsive reaction. They tussled together, both becoming coated with slivers of grass. However, when Vibiana felt a warm wetness on her hand, she pulled away abruptly. Fresh blood covered her fingers.

"Oh, my God. Did I hurt you?"

The dog scrambled to her feet and shook herself. Ears alert, she sniffed at the blood on the girl's fingers. Worried, Vibiana inspected the animal's muscular body, running her hands over the dog's back and extremities. The black animal quivered at the girl's touch. When she tentatively stroked the dog's lower belly again, Vibiana gasped.

"You're in heat."

The dog's amber eyes glimmered, as if to verify Vibiana's statement. Nuzzling against her, the large animal aimed her pointy nose at the girl's crotch.

"Just 'cause I got personal doesn't mean *you* have to." With some roughness, Vibiana pushed the dog away. She wiped her fingers on the grass, brushed off her clothes and got up. "I have to go."

Though her yellow eyes seemed to memorize the girl, the wolflike dog did not attempt to follow. She remained by the grave while Vibiana began to leave. Turning once in curiosity, the girl was surprised to see no sign of the black animal. Only the golden flowers nodded their good-byes in the morning breeze.

A startling row of sunflowers stood parallel to the fence behind Doña Ines. The scrawny woman leaned on her garden rake and interrupted her chores when the girl entered the front yard.

"¿Donde estabas, muchacha?"

"I went to see Mami." Vibiana gave her grandmother a brief hug. "Hope you don't mind I took some flowers for her."

"Mijita, that's what they're for." Doña Ines kissed the girl with tenderness. "Rosa loved my sunflowers. Y en este barrio son muy popular. Pero some people take them without asking." Doña Ines aimed a disdainful glance southward. "No one takes *anything* from Doña Refugio Torres's jardín on the next block. She has beautiful rosas and that huge black wolf to guard her yard."

"Really?" Vibiana at once was mindful of her grass-stained T-shirt and Levi's. "In the cemetery, I saw a dog that looked like a wolf. Wonder if—"

Brow furrowed, Doña Ines adjusted her wide-brimmed straw hat. She appraised her granddaughter. "Were you playing with la Noche, mija?"

"Is *that* her name?" Vibiana felt a bit uneasy when confronted with her grandmother's concerned expression. "Abuelita, you know how I miss having a dog. This one is so pretty, so friendly."

"Stay away from *her*," Doña Ines warned. "People say her owner, Doña Refugio, is a bruja."

"A witch?" With a giggle, Vibiana sank to the wobbly porch steps.

"Maybe you think that's funny, but some people say Doña Refugio lives with a woman—except no one ever sees her, eh? At least not in the daytime. Other people say la Noche isn't really a dog, sabes?"

"Abuelita, you've been watching too much of *Unsolved*

Mysteries."

Still laughing, Vibiana went inside. She made sure to stand away from the front window. She raised one hand to her nose and sniffed her fingers. Though no traces remained, she could smell the blood.

Doña Ines knocked on the bathroom door. "Vibiana, your father's on the phone."

The teenager had been staring at her bare breasts in the steamy mirror. Hearing her grandmother's voice, she hurried to wind a towel around herself. "I'll be right out." Vibiana dabbed the terrycloth in strategic places before throwing on a cotton robe and opening the door.

Her grandmother handed her the telephone and went outside. Vibiana stood by the screen door, leaning against its jamb. "Daddy, I didn't expect you to call today."

"Miss my girl. Everything okay, honey?"

"Much cooler here than in Arizona." The girl's voice softened. "I visited Mami this morning."

Victor Ruíz's sigh was audible. "Don't know why I listened to your grandma. We should've buried Rosa here in Tucson."

"Abuelita needs to be close to her, too." Vibiana sensed her father's loneliness. "Her only daughter—"

"My wife, your mother," he added. He sighed again. "Look, Vibiana, if being there is going to make you depressed—"

"I'm fine, Dad. Really." She hoped she sounded convincing. "The beach is so close to Abuelita's. What more can I ask for?" She paused. "Is everything all right with *you?*"

"Busy as hell. I decided to phone before I got tied up with service calls. People can't be without air conditioners, you know." Victor cleared his throat. "In case you're wondering, no one's left you any messages."

Vibiana's voice cooled. "My friends know where I am."

"*All* of them?"

La Noche

"The ones that matter." The girl shivered. "Dad, I just got out of the shower and don't want to catch a chill. Can I—"

"I'll phone you tomorrow after Mass, kid."

"Talk to you then."

Vibiana stirred the albóndigas on the stove while her grandmother brought over two soup bowls.

"I passed by Doña Chole's grave this morning and said a little prayer for her."

"Gracias, mijita. Pobrecita Chole." Doña Ines handed Vibiana a ladle. "She was my dearest friend."

"I barely remember her." The girl served the tasty soup and carried both bowls to the kitchen table.

They murmured a blessing over the meal and began to eat. "When Chole was very ill," Vibiana's grandmother began between sips, "Refugio showed up on her doorstep and offered to cure her with herbs. Chole sent her away—and died two days later."

"That's why you think this Refugio's a witch?" Vibiana hoped her smile hid her fascination.

"Well, mijita, I was there when that happened. Refugio did not look happy to be told to leave. And—she was the nurse on duty the night Rosa died."

"What?" Vibiana stared at her grandmother.

"Refugio's an R.N. Muy convenient, eh?"

"Oh, Abuelita," the girl scoffed. "Mami had breast cancer. It spread very fast. How could Refugio have had anything to do with *that*?"

"Think what you want, muchacha. Pero, por favor, stay far away from esa bruja y su loba negra."

That night Vibiana could not sleep. She tossed and turned on the narrow bed that had once been her mother's. Her cool hands rubbed the rounded contours of her breasts, as if seeking to soothe herself to rest, to forget. Yet whenever she touched herself, she remembered Marcos—his smooth hands caressing her in the cramped back seat of his father's Ford, the paintbrush colors of the desert sunset reflected against his naked chest, her strong brown legs entwined with his, wanting him, needing him.

Summery gusts of wind rattled the bedroom windows. She was not in Arizona with Marcos, but in California in her grandmother's house. She was used to the desert silence, not to the endless traffic sounds from nearby Pico Boulevard. A distant *hoo, hoo-hoo-hoo, hoo* heralded the presence of an owl, most probably roosting in one of the many trees in the cemetery. The eerie hoot made Vibiana shudder.

She made herself lie still, curled on her side, one hand at her breast, the other on her belly. She began to grow drowsy. Yet for one frightening moment, she thought she heard faint scratches on the window pane, as if a nocturnal animal were clawing the glass, trying to come in.

"Mami, please help me," she whispered while clutching the rumpled sheets. "I don't know what to do all by myself."

When Doña Ines turned on her favorite telenovela early Sunday afternoon, Vibiana pushed aside the entertainment section of the newspaper and rose.

"I promised Daddy I wouldn't sit around the house all day. I'm going to the mall, Abuelita."

Her grandmother surveyed her over half-rimmed spectacles. "You know how to get there?"

"On the Pico bus, verdad?"

With a nod, Doña Ines watched her. "Ten cuidado, eh? Don't let any muchachos get fresh with you, Vibiana."

"I'll be fine." The girl kissed the top of her grandmother's gray head. "See you later."

The midday sun struggled to shine through the heavy clouds. Vibiana headed up hilly Seventeenth Street opposite Woodlawn Cemetery. While she walked, her black hair swung with a rhythm all its own.

On seeing the pretty teenager, two cholos in a passing Chevy shouted, "Ay, que chula!" The girl paid them no heed.

She riveted her eyes to her left—row after row of neatly tended gardens. Before one little home, a multitude of blood-red roses suspended themselves over a picket fence. Their hypnotic scent beckoned Vibiana.

"You must be Doña Ines's nieta," a husky voice announced. A small brown woman emerged from behind the rosebushes. Her braided gray hair wound around her head like a silver turban. She wore a shapeless housecoat and pink bedroom slippers.

"How did you know?" Vibiana uttered before she realized it.

"You look very much like Rosa," the old woman said. Above the picket fence, over the intoxicating roses, she offered a lean brown hand. "Yo soy Refugio Torres."

A bit hesitantly, Vibiana clasped it, surprised at its warmth. She had expected a bruja to have an ice-cold grip. "Mucho gusto, Doña Refugio. My name's—"

"Vibiana," Refugio concluded. Her obsidian eyes bored into the teenager's perplexed ones. "The name of the virgin laid out like bounty in the Cathedral downtown. Have you ever seen her? They open the curtains of her fancy tomb on certain feast days to show her lovely corpse. Qué barbaridad, eh?"

The girl felt a bit light-headed. "My mother took me to see St. Vibiana a few times. I remember she wore a velvet gown."

"Sí, the exact color of these rosas." Doña Refugio removed a pair of pruning shears from her housecoat pocket. She clipped off one blood-red rose and handed it to the girl.

The perfume of the rose was overpowering. Wary of its thorns, Vibiana held the lovely flower gingerly. "My mother was fascinated with St. Vibiana's story," she managed to reply. "That's why she named me after her."

"Who can blame Rosa for falling under the spell of the legend? And who would ever think Vibiana's body would be brought to Los Angeles, so far from her homeland? Now los cabrones want to destroy the Cathedral and build an enormous new one. Nothing ever changes, muchacha. *Nothing.*" As if to soften her remarks, Refugio smiled at once, teeth white and even. "Did you come by looking for la Noche?"

Vibiana wondered if Refugio could read her mind. "No. I'm on my way to the bus stop."

"Ay, qué pena. La Noche's probably in the cemetery chasing the squirrels." Refugio's eyes continued to linger on the teenager. "El tecolote hunts them after sunset."

"Last night when I couldn't sleep," the girl murmured, "I heard an owl."

"¿De veras? La Noche was out then, too. Many times she goes to the cemetery to help whoever needs her. ¿Y sabes que? She always finds out their secrets."

When the Pico Boulevard bus halted on Broadway and Fourth, Vibiana got off. She did not head into the enclosed Santa Monica Place shopping mall but went farther west. The day after her mother's funeral had been the last time she had seen the Pacific Ocean. She remembered what Abuelita had said that day—that Spanish explorers had named the bay Santa Monica because it reminded them of the ocean of tears St. Monica had shed over her wayward son Augustine. Before going home to Arizona, Vibiana had visited the beach one last time, to cry, to let her own tears mingle in the Pacific's serene waters.

This time she headed as far west as she could, to the edge of Santa Monica Pier. She stood at the steel railing, buffeted by the marine gusts. She thought, for a fleeting moment, about hurling herself over. But, no, she did not want to hurt Daddy and Abuelita—or herself, for that matter. She wanted to live—without being shackled to responsibility.

All around her, families strolled, pushing baby carriages, playing with little ones. Children surrounded her. Mothers pointed out the hovering gulls; fathers explained the pier's renovated structure. Vibiana did not want to listen to their conversations nor see their happiness. She did not want to be a mother. At sixteen, she was too young.

Her religion taught her that abortion is murder. Vibiana did not want to be a killer, but she did not want to nurture a life within her either. Marcos was long gone. He would never help her. She was too embarrassed to turn to her father and grandmother for advice. She was afraid of their rejection. Perhaps Doña Refugio and la Noche would offer their own methods of assistance. Gazing at the placid ocean, Vibiana wondered what price she would have to pay. She reached into her shoulder bag and removed the blood-red rose Doña Refugio had given her. Even with the marine breezes blowing, the hypnotic scent of the roses filled the air. Mindful of the thorns, Vibiana began to pluck the velvety petals. They fell like blood drops into the Pacific's embracing waves.

Sunset streaked the sky in vivid shades of purple, pink and magenta. Vibiana disembarked from the bus on Fourteenth and Pico. Crossing the boulevard, she noticed the cemetery gates remained open.

"I need to talk to Mami," she thought, hurrying into the deserted grounds. "She'll help me make up my mind."

The sunflowers bowed when she knelt beside them. They tilted their big heads in her direction, ready to eavesdrop. "Mami, I know it's crazy, but Abuelita thinks Doña Refugio could have made you die. That *can't* be true. You were so sick. But what if Doña Refugio and la Noche could have made you well somehow? Wouldn't you have given them that chance? To save yourself? Don't you think I should try to let them help me if they can? I made an awful mistake and now I don't know what to do. Mami, I don't have a lot of choices."

Vibiana touched the tip of one finger to her lips and pressed it to the granite. The stone was warm, vibrant, not cold and dead. The girl pressed both hands there, to be sure she had not imagined the heat emanating from the gray stone. The lingering scent of roses wafted through. "Oh, Mami," she whispered. "I love you so much. Thank you for listening to me."

Rising, Vibiana wiped her eyes. She scanned the sky. It was a pinkish purple, the sun a memory. She did not want Abuelita to worry. She had to leave.

At the cemetery gates, she beheld a shadowy figure. La Noche barked in greeting and loped toward her. When Vibiana approached, the big animal leaped in jubilation. On her hind legs, la Noche was taller than the girl. The wolflike dog placed her huge paws on the girl's slender shoulders and thoroughly licked her brown face. Though the dog's powerful body frightened her at first, Vibiana liked the strong feel of that rough tongue, its incipient possessiveness. She hugged la Noche tightly, feeling the animal's great heart thumping against hers.

"Doña Refugio says you come here to help people. Noche, will you help *me?*"

The dog's amber eyes studied hers. A rare intelligence shone through. She whined and licked Vibiana again.

"Please come to my window again. Tonight I'll be ready."

During dinner, Vibiana was quiet. She used fatigue as an excuse.

"I walked all over, Abuelita. Then I couldn't stop looking at the ocean and lost track of time."

"You've only been here two days. No wonder you're cansada." Doña Ines poured herself another glass of Carta Blanca, her Sunday evening treat. "Pues, take a hot bath, mijita. Go to bed early and you'll feel better in the morning."

The full moon's brilliance shone against the closed blinds. Vibiana lay between crisp white sheets. She recalled Doña Refugio's comments about the Roman virgin Vibiana, her untouched beauty on display in the cathedral. The saint's modern-day counterpart was no virgin, however; Vibiana Ruíz certainly did not want to become a martyr either. Although she was fearful of what the night might bring, she felt oddly at peace. She longed to hear la Noche's insistent claws at the window.

She sensed the big animal's presence before hearing her. Immediately, Vibiana sat up and put on her sandals. She lifted the blinds and observed the black dog's steady amber eyes on hers. With caution, the girl opened the window and without a sound stepped over its sill. In a white cotton huipil which her grandmother had embroidered with cross-stitched roses, Vibiana seemed luminous, the full moon glowing upon her. In silence, she followed the wolflike dog from the yard, down the block to Woodlawn Cemetery.

La Noche ambled slightly ahead. She slithered through a gap in the chain-link fence and paused to let Vibiana catch up. Senses keen, the girl squeezed through the hole. The edge of her sleeve caught and she fumbled to loosen the fabric from the fence. When she released herself, she glanced around. La Noche had vanished. El tecolote hooted, ominously close. Vibiana almost panicked. The moon shone like a spotlight through the trees. Still she could not glimpse to where her nocturnal guide had disappeared.

"Vibiana," urged a voice she had never heard before. "Over here."

Too afraid to answer, the girl squinted. A tree trunk seemed to come alive. Vibiana gasped. She realized someone stood next to the sycamore. The dark figure began to materialize in the moonlight.

"Don't you recognize me?" A tall, ebony-haired mestiza emerged into full view. Clad in a sleek satin shirt, black leather jeans and boots, she was exquisite, lithe yet sensual. Her amber eyes proved her identity. "Vibiana, don't be afraid. I am la Noche."

"You're so beautiful," the girl whispered.

La Noche smiled. "So they tell me." She held out a strong brown hand. "Ven conmigo."

Accompanying her, the girl murmured her own mantra, "Mami, Mami, Mami." She trembled yet felt baffled by a sudden excitement.

La Noche touched the locked mausoleum gates. They opened effortlessly.

Vibiana blurted, "We're going in *there?*"

La Noche moved closer and faced her. "Did Refugio give you her slant on Santa Vibiana, virgin and martyr?"

The girl nodded with some trepidation.

"Don't be scared. That old lady gets so damn melodramatic." La Noche was exasperated. "Mira, querida, this won't work unless you trust me. You asked for my help. I need *your* confianza."

"You won't hurt me?"

"It's going to be fun, all right?"

Vibiana blinked. When she spoke, her voice shook, despite its challenge. "Doña Refugio says you always find out secrets. Do you know mine?"

"You don't want that baby inside you."

With a silent sob, Vibiana nodded. More determined than she felt, she followed la Noche within the iron mausoleum gates.

Inside, the scent of roses overwhelmed Vibiana, though she saw no evidence of any floral displays. A sliver of the full moon for illumination, she sat beside la Noche on the marble tomb of one of the city's leading citizens. She felt somewhat groggy, simultaneously alert and vibrant. Vibiana was too absorbed with la Noche's sensual beauty, her firm tenderness, to notice anything but the mesmerizing mestiza next to her. The girl did not even question the multitude of emotions she felt for la Noche. She told herself this mysterious mestiza was different, unlike anyone she had ever met. Vibiana viewed her as friend, savior—

"And lover," la Noche interrupted the girl's thoughts. "You

were right, Vibiana, when we tussled on the grass. I'm in heat. *You* arouse me. I want you so much my desire will make whatever you want happen. ¿Entiendes? I'll make love to you and absorb your grief, your pain, your burden—whatever you want."

"Does that mean what I think it means?" Vibiana whispered. She grew ever more hypnotized by those unwavering amber eyes.

"It means this," la Noche responded. She leaned over, her tongue teasing the girl's smooth cheek. With the tip of her probing tongue, la Noche began to outline Vibiana's full lips. The girl melted at that rough sensation. She began to tingle. She lost all semblance of control. La Noche did not have to do anything else. Vibiana's hungry mouth was already on hers.

"I do want you, Noche," she murmured.

"I want what you can give me," la Noche panted. She pulled her satin shirt over her head, unzipped her leather jeans.

"Let me," Vibiana insisted.

When she saw la Noche's coppery body, her sinewy nudity, for the first time, she almost swooned. She hurled off her own huipil and drew la Noche down with her. Blood-red rose petals suddenly covered the entire surface of the tomb. The lovers' thick black hair commingled as they spread themselves on the warm petals, over the no-longer-cold marble.

La Noche began to suck Vibiana's breasts, slurping like an unrestrained animal. The earthy sound and la Noche's possessive mouth further aroused the girl. She had never behaved with such abandon, not even with Marcos. She wrapped her long legs around la Noche, keeping her even nearer. She clasped la mujer's coarse black hair, losing herself in it, rubbing the rose petals over her and la Noche. She closed her eyes in ecstasy.

"Mira. Leche."

Vibiana raised her head to see a few droplets of milk seep from her breast. La Noche touched her finger to Vibiana's nipple and brought it to the girl's mouth. "This is what you taste like. Tomorrow it'll be gone."

After savoring her own milk, Vibiana seemed overcome by an animalistic energy. She straddled la Noche, thrusting her wet pubis against hers, listening to their erotic gurgles. She crouched over her, mouth to la Noche's voluptuous breasts, licking and sucking those coppery globes, those chocolate nipples. Soon she tasted un poquito de leche. When it began to flow more, Vibiana could not get enough of it. She loved la Noche's delicious taste. She began to lick and suck every part of her, every fold, every crevice. The creamy flavor, the unceasing rose fragrance, the erotic sensations, made her dizzy.

La Noche groaned and grappled with her. They rolled on the marble tomb, wrapped around each other, licking, biting, eating, scratching. They were caked with rose petals, soaked with perspiration and desire. They made love over and over, all night.

Vibiana began to feel exhausted. La Noche was relentless. She lay over the girl, pinning her to the marble, pressing herself so close they seemed inseparable.

"Noche, you said you wouldn't hurt me."

"You don't want the baby, do you, Vibiana?"

The girl shook her head from side to side. "No baby."

"Then give her to me."

"Yes. Noche—please—take her."

No sooner had the girl uttered those words when a jolting pain shot through her, burning in its intensity. Her womb seemed to twist, to writhe. She thought she would faint. The searing agony lasted only a minute while la Noche doubled over, grimacing. Energy drained from Vibiana. She felt lifeless while la Noche lay prone over her.

"Noche, are you all right?" Vibiana whispered seconds later.

Panting, long hair rumpled, la Noche at last curled on her side. She shook herself, doglike, and sat up slowly. She licked her lips. They eased into a lupine grin. "Gracias, Vibiana. Now she's mine."

For hours Vibiana did not awaken. She had no recollection of coming back through her bedroom window. As if drugged, she slept most of the day. Her grandmother checked on her from time to time, but simply assumed the girl was tired from the Arizona-to-California trip. Doña Ines smelled the lingering scent of roses around her granddaughter's bed. She thought the fragrance came from the rosebush in her garden.

Later, in the bathroom, stiff and sore, Vibiana noticed blood in her urine. At first she was alarmed. When she glanced at her pocket calendar, however, she realized her period, delayed for three months, had reverted to its normal schedule.

As the weeks passed, Vibiana found part-time work at a Guatemalan import shop on the Third Street Promenade. She made friends with other teenagers who had jobs in neighboring stores. She began having lunch with them, going to movies after work. She attended church functions with her grandmother and baby-sat some of the neighborhood children. Though she often thought about la Noche and Refugio Torres, she did not encounter them in the barrio. Their little house seemed still, unnaturally quiet. Sometimes, she wondered if she had imagined all of it, including her erstwhile pregnancy.

One evening, when she stepped off the Pico bus, she noticed the black dog by the cemetery gates. In curiosity, Vibiana jogged over. Tail wagging, the big animal awaited her.

"Hi, Noche. Where have you been? Been eating a lot, huh?" She patted the dog's massive head. "You're getting real fat."

With a low growl, la Noche nudged her. The dog circled Vibiana, as if flaunting her weight gain.

"So I didn't dream it. It *really* happened."

Satisfied, la Noche sat by the gates. Her pink tongue lolled and her lazy posture emphasized her round belly. Vibiana squatted beside her. She pressed a tentative hand to the dog's warm abdomen. She felt life thriving there, pulsating. With some reluctance, Vibiana moved her hand away.

"What one night of love can do." She sighed. "Gracias, Noche."

The ebony dog's amber eyes glimmered. She put a huge paw on Vibiana's shoulder and smothered her with very wet kisses.

Newtime Cowboy

Joyce Wagner

In the final winks of sleep, during the last close-to-the-surface dream of the morning, Tie Baker changed from a flesh-and-blood Hollywood superstar into a strip of film. Surprisingly—amazingly—it was his sister Jeannie who eventually set him free. It would be the last truly significant mistake she would make in her life.

The first had been fifteen years ago when she had allowed her brother to usurp control of her and her parents' lives by uprooting them from their postwar bungalow in Youngstown, Ohio. Jeannie had abandoned a position in customer service with the local phone company—a job that promised more security than glamour—to become Tie's personal secretary. A trifling curiosity about Movieland and a niggling suspicion that her parents needed protection from the same coerced her into packing up and joining the family exodus across the continent.

The move came about because Jeannie and Tie's mother, Dorothy Baczyk, now Dory Baker, had granted a Mother's Day interview to *Good Housekeeping* magazine. "Moms of Celebs," the story was called. So excited was she at being asked, it never occurred to her that she should get Tie's permission. She thought it would be a wonderful surprise. Within the month after Dorothy's wrinkled face and shoe-polish black hair graced the stands, the Tie Baker Family Relocation Program went into effect and he installed them all in his sprawling mission ranch home in the Hollywood Hills. Tie disliked surprises.

Tie's transformation took place on a cool but sunny California morning. The more oppressive heat that would strip the trees of their bodily fluids, making each a match waiting to be struck, was still weeks away. Tie awoke, floating on the light breeze coming into the bedroom through the sliding doors facing the pool. The gentleness of his drifting state almost lulled him back to sleep. An alert sentry in the far recesses of his brain sent forward the message: *Something's wrong here.* Tie's eyes popped open as he landed with a hiss on his priceless Ispahan Persian rug.

Most of Tie's home accouterments were expensive—and uncomfortable. Like waiters, decorators can be dealt with rudely only at considerable risk. The decorator who designed Tie's house sat at the summit of his celebrity and eschewed any second guessing at his art. Tie was left with a showplace that *Architectural Digest* described as "the ultimate in style and function." In truth, the living and working rooms were unlivable and unworkable. Not one chair or sofa could be inhabited for more than ten minutes, nor risen from with any degree of grace.

The studio! Oh, shit! I'll bet I'm late. Tie turned to where his alarm clock would have sat if he were still on the bed. He was just beginning to wonder why he was lying on the floor, when Jeannie's knock startled him. His new, flat form rippled like a ribbon.

"Tie? You awake? The limo's here."

Yeah. I'm up. Tell him to wait. Tie was sure he had said that out loud. In fact, it felt as if he had shouted it.

"Tie? You in there? The limo's here."

I'm coming, dammit! Once again, Tie's mouth moved to no avail. Tie clutched his throat, swallowing hard, feeling for difficulty. *Jeannie?* Nothing.

"Tie! The driver's here!"

Yes! Yes! I'm coming! Tie's hand flew to cover his mouth as if he had screamed something unutterable. Jeannie mumbled a word Tie was unaware she ever used, then her bare footslaps retreated down the custom-tiled hallway.

Shit. Now what? Tie raised his head, causing his feet to curl up. As he leaned in closer to examine this phenomenon, he rolled up completely and bowled across the room, bumping his cellulose nitrate butt on the dresser. *Shit.*

"So? Is he up, hey?" Dorothy Baczyk's fingers rapidly worked mint and cream and white acrylic yarn into a rippled afghan. This one was nearly ready for her weekly anonymous donation to charity. Tie wouldn't allow her finished coverlets in the house once they were completed. Ted Baczyk, Tie's father, would sneak off to the thrift shop the day following Dorothy's donation and buy back the afghan. He kept them secreted away in the closet of the room he claimed for his den, formerly the maid's room.

Dorothy's hair, now professionally colored in black and steely grays, was pulled back from her surgically tightened face. Tie had insisted on the surgery. The doctor had done what he could with skin that had lain fallow for so long and grew on a woman who liked to garden without a hat. The result was that the thousand fine lines that should have swooped in gentle curves were now stretched into unnatural angles. Contact lenses tinted her faded brown eyes to amber and a personal trainer cajoled her into shedding fat. Although her appearance suggested she controlled a large estate in the Hamptons, Dorothy couldn't seem to get a grasp on the role. No highly paid professional could remove good old Youngstown from her interior. Dory Baker was occasionally photographed, but never quoted. After the Mother's Day fiasco, Tie would never again allow it.

Jeannie raked her fingers through her short-cropped Hollywood hairdo of the week. This month, Tie had decreed it be dyed the yellow of sunflowers, but that color was already fading on her head and in popularity. It would soon be a different shade. Her eyes, sincerely the amber her mother's purported to be, peered out the kitchen window but focused within.

"So? What? Is he up? Answer your mother." Ted Baczyk lifted his eyes from the newspaper spread out on the table before him.

"I don't know. There wasn't any sound coming from his bedroom. Is that driver still out there?" Jeannie stood on tiptoe and leaned over the sink to get closer to the window.

Ted stared at his daughter's bony frame. He wondered when she would start eating right. "Maybe he's still in the shower, huh?"

"Don't think so, Pop. Think I would've heard it."

"You checked on the pool side, hey?"

"No, but thanks, Mother. Good idea." Jeannie bounded out the kitchen slider and danced in bare feet on hot cement past her bedroom slider, her parents' bedroom slider, the dining room slider, and the two living room sliders, all winking back sun to the pool. As she approached the L-wing that encompassed Tie's bedroom, she thanked the door gods that one of Tie's sliders was open. She hesitantly poked her head in. "Tie? You in there?"

Tie had heard the *ooches* and *ouches* of Jeannie's barefoot journey and instinctively coiled himself up tighter. After a few wobbly attempts he was able to roll across the floor and under the bed. He needed time to think before he could let anyone see him in his current condition. He was in the process of making a mental note to chew out the housekeeper for all the dust-bunnies under the bed when he heard Jeannie's voice inside the room. Much as he tried to stifle it, the bunnies got the best of him and he let out a violent soundless sneeze. Of course, Jeannie didn't hear it. That wasn't the giveaway. The force of his sneeze had caused Tie to rapidly uncurl, scraping the back of his celluloid legs on the bedsprings. His feet unfurled from under the bedskirt like a whale's tale from the sea.

Jeannie, facing the bathroom when it happened, caught the

movement in her peripheral vision. As she turned to investigate, she saw just the edge of something retreating under the bed. She pounced, felt around amongst the dust bunnies and latched on to something flat and slick. She pulled the object into the light and was aghast to find, in her delicate hand, one of those tawdry magazines dedicated to the display of giant female breasts. Meanwhile, Tie inched like a snail out the other side. Jeannie dropped the magazine like feces and bopped it back under the bed with the side of her hand. She rose and eyed the edge of the tailored bedskirt. She was sure she had seen something moving there. The hand that had held the magazine wiped itself off on the hip of her jeans, then ran through the short curls on the top of her head. She swiveled her body to survey the whole room, as if the lamps, the armchair, the dresser, the bed could offer a reasonable explanation. When none was forthcoming, she brought a finger up to her closed lips, tapped five times, turned and strode out through the sliding glass door.

Tie sighed soundlessly. The inchworm crawling from under the bed made him feel staticky—like when someone rubs a balloon on your head to stick to the wall. Except Tie's whole body felt that way, and dust was now clinging to him head to toe. He was still rattled from the effect of the magazine sliding beneath him—the aerodynamic ripple, the temporary loss of control of his movements. He seemed to be regaining his composure now, although the clinging dust was beginning to make him nauseated.

After a complete mental inventory of his body, Tie calmed himself. *Okay. Okay. I'm fine. No pain. Nothing broken.* Tie slowly, gently, raised his head. Again, his feet began to curl up, but Tie enforced a stringent control. He edged them up just enough to observe that his feet were covered by cowboy boots. Oddly, he found relief in the fact that the boots sported a bit of a heel. His lack of height had always been the bane of his existence. Tie allowed his eyes to wander up his legs, which were covered with fuzzy chaps. At almost the same moment that he realized he was dressed as a silent film cowboy, he also grasped that he was devoid of color. Whatever antique film stock his form was encased in was black and white—or, more precisely, brown and cream.

Shit! I can't go to the studio like this. We're shooting in color. Tie's lack of vocalization no longer surprised him. In fact, he felt rather unencumbered, being able to loudly and expressively vent without anyone hearing. *Well, so fucking what? I spend my whole fucking life doing whatever other people want me to do. Well, that's over now.*

Tie's rage at the studio flipped the switch of his denial about his current state back to "on." *Fuck the studio!* Reaping such giddy pleasure from the words, he repeated them even louder. *FUCK THE STUDIO!*

So immersed was he in his tirade, he didn't even notice that he was beginning to rock. *I work my fucking balls off for them and never make a peep. I'm out of makeup and wardrobe and on the set when those faggot-ass producers are just waking up.* As he became silently louder and louder, his form began to wobble faster and faster. *I do take after take after take and never say a word. They can just fucking shoot around me today. Fuck 'em!* It wasn't until Tie was halfway across the bedroom that he realized he was, once again, curled up and rolling and headed directly toward the open slider. *Oh, shit!*

"Whatya tell the driver?" Dorothy looked up from her crocheting as Jeannie drifted in through the kitchen door.

"Told him I thought Tie left already, but I don't know. Wouldn't we have heard him?" Jeannie's head was cocked slightly and her brows furrowed in thought. Her eyes landed on three tiny objects lying on the floor at the juncture of two cabinets. Squinting brought them into focus and Jeannie recognized them as the tightly wound dregs of a spider's dinner. The cleaning lady had been in only the day before. She had always been thorough—or so Jeannie thought. Had she somehow overlooked these tiny corpses? Or had the spider worked that efficiently, weaving a web, then wrapping and sucking the life out of the former insects in less than twenty-four hours?

"Oh, for cri-yi! Look at that!" Ted had noticed his daughter's silence and followed her eyes to the droppings. Squeezing himself out of the breakfast nook, he headed for the kitchen island and paper towels. "If your brother sees this, he'll have a fit." In moments he had gathered up the corpses and deposited them in the trash under the sink.

Jeannie found herself wishing he had left them. Everything needed to be so perfect for Tie. Her eyes fell upon her mother's face—a web of surgical procedures Dorothy would never have chosen for herself. What would she look like if she had stayed in Youngstown? Surely, her old friends didn't look like that. If she ever went back, would she still fit in? Everything revolved around Tie's career. Was it *that* fragile? Did it need to feed on *all* of their lives?

All at once, a sinking feeling settled into her heart, as if she had been speaking unkindly about the dead. She reminded herself that Tie was missing. She barely glanced at her parents as she started for the door. "I'm going to check his room again."

As Jeannie neared the kitchen slider, the cordless phone let out an electronic purr. "I've got it!" Jeannie leapt back, snatched the phone off the kitchen table, punched the "on" button and lifted it to her ear. "Hello? Oh, hello, Mr. Stein. Oh, of course. *Morty*."

Ted let his newspaper drop to the table and Dorothy looked up from her work.

"Yes. Yes, I did send the chauffeur back. Well, Tie isn't here. I assumed he'd called a cab or something. No, he's not." Jeannie wrapped her hand around the mouthpiece, gave a sidelong glance at her parents and continued in a whisper. "He's not fucking off. You know Tie better than that. What? What is *that* supposed to mean?" Jeannie now turned completely away from Dorothy and Ted and buried her mouth in the phone. "What do you mean, drugs? He wouldn't. He hardly drinks!" Her voice came out in an urgent raspy undertone. "Listen, Mr. Stein—*Morty*—if Tie needs too many retakes, it's only because he's being leaned on by that damned perfectionist director slug you hired. Lines?" Jeannie's voice rose now in spite of the eavesdroppers. "What? I'll have you know, my dear Mister Morty Stein, Tie comes home every night right after work and runs lines till he can't see straight."

"Tell him I help, hey."

Jeannie spun around and hurled a "Shush!" at her mother, then directed her attention back to the phone. "What? Fine. Come over. It'll be a wasted trip. I'm telling you he's not here. Pardon me? What? CREEP!"

The casing on the phone broke into four sharp pieces as it hit the table. Jeannie stood, eyes fixed on the pool beyond the door, clenching and unclenching her hands at her sides. Her parents, fearful of breaking the spell, sat gaping at their daughter, breathing through their mouths. The sounds of the children next door bursting from their house and diving into their pool broke the stillness. Jeannie, back in the here and now, spun on her heel and, in three giant strides, was out the kitchen door. "I've got to find Tie."

Tie cursed the expansiveness of his bedroom. A smaller room would have caused a slower, shorter roll, and the aluminum sill across the bottom of the slider would have halted his progress. As it was, he had gained too much momentum, and instead of stopping, he had glanced off the sill. Four more bounces landed him in the pool.

After an initial well-deserved panic, manifested by thrashing within his form while drifting slowly to the bottom of the pool, Tie discovered a valuable quality of his current celluloid state: He could breathe just fine under water and actually felt quite comfortable floating at the bottom of the pool. He seemed to be completely waterproof and never felt the least bit wet.

Tie dwelled for an inordinate amount of time on these qualities, testing and retesting, diving and surfacing. This was not out of any practical consideration, but rather to protect the multifissured candy-glass wall of his denial. That wall was about to be shattered as Tie floated face up on the light-dappled surface of his pool. Deep in thought about his hydrodynamics, he hadn't notice Jeannie cantering across the hot tiles of the pool surround.

Jeannie actually had one foot in the door of Tie's bedroom when, again, her peripheral vision alerted her to movement—this time in the water. Her body obeyed the automatic command of her mind to halt, turn around and walk to the edge of the pool. Standing with her toes hooked over the wet tiles of the apron, Jeannie saw her brother dressed in chaps, ten-gallon hat, vest, boots, holster and six-shooters, with a bandana tucked in a triangle under his chin. Although normal in height, he appeared to be two-dimensional and confined in a piece of film—sepia and ivory—with sprocket holes on the sides. Tie-sized, it seemed only large enough to contain his form with costume. Like the bystander at a gruesome beating, Jeannie's own denial system convinced her this was not happening. What she was seeing was a bit of prop, no longer useful, dragged home from the set by Tie as some sort of practical joke. Tie shattered her delusion and his own denial when he grinned sheepishly, shrugged his shoulders and wiggled his fingers at his sister. Her scream tore beyond Tie's property lines and alarmed the neighbor children bouncing about in their own pool. Tie's scream was silent, then he curled up and sank to the bottom of the pool.

When Morty Stein poked his head in Tie's bedroom slider, he saw Ted and Jeannie bent over the bed, asking it questions. Dorothy skittered like a tiny bird out of the bathroom, folding a wet facecloth into a neat rectangle. At his cheery greeting, Ted and Jeannie straightened and turned in unison.

"Mr. Stein, I'm *so* glad you're here." Jeannie traversed the room, hand extended. "There's something wrong with Tie. We don't know what to do." If not for the worry between her eyebrows, Jeannie could have passed for Hollywood's most gracious hostess.

It took Morty Stein a few beats to adjust to her change in attitude. He had expected more of the wrath Jeannie had fed him over the phone. He had been prepared to apologize and, oddly enough, to do so sincerely. Jeannie was one of the few Hollywood characters he took seriously. Perhaps it was because, although she wore the trappings of the typical casting-couch wannabe, she was not really in the system. He had often sought her out at Tie's parties, sensing a genuine solidity—a power hovering beneath the surface, a power she was probably unaware of. He had seen the same attributes in seasoned actresses as they sat politely listening while neophyte actors and directors analyzed a scene, attacking it from all angles, overthinking, worrying it to death. Then the cameras would roll and the actress would produce a character so seamless and powerful that the most jaded camera operator would forget to stop at the call of "Cut!" He wondered if Jeannie could act.

Morty Stein's pale eyes locked on to her deep amber ones while he covered her outstretched hand with both of his. His years of acting in doctor roles on the soaps had served him well. He could fake sincerity even while being sincere. "Jeannie, whatever it is, I'm sure we can fix it. Where is he?" He wondered if Jeannie would fuck him.

Jeannie led him to the bed, where Dorothy's hand hovered in the air, trying to decide the best application for the cold, wet facecloth. Morty Stein immediately saw her dilemma. Within his two-dimensional form, Tie's ten-gallon hat sat low on his brow, covering his entire forehead. Of course! Dorothy couldn't possibly place the compress anywhere effective.

When his mind allowed in exactly what it was he was seeing, Morty Stein's voice burst out in loud one-syllable laughs. "All right, who's behind this? Lucas?" He began to zigzag about the room, searching walls, drawers and cabinets for a projector or some other source of the image, all the while barking his rapid-fire laugh. He stopped at the sight of Tie's family, huddled now near the slider, and looked from face to sober face. "Dick Clark, right? It's one of those 'Bloopers and Practical Jokes' things, right?" Then he began shooting out his laugh again as he staggered back to Tie's bed. He ran the flat of his hand all over the air above Tie, checking for strings or a break in the image. Morty Stein pushed a facetious tear from his cheek while he pulled himself together. His eyes settled once again on Tie's flat shiny face, then turned once more toward the family. They hovered in a tight group, eyes glossy— puppies eager to please, but not understanding the command. As he realized they were looking to him for an explanation, he turned back to the Tie image on the bed. What he received from Tie was the same sheepish shrug and sappy grin Tie had given his sister. Morty Stein turned again to Jeannie, Ted and Dorothy.

Jeannie spoke first. "Mr. Stein—Morty—we were thinking of calling a doctor."

"Doctor. Right. Good idea." Morty Stein withdrew his cellular phone from his back pocket, flipped it open and dialed the studio physician—the *very discreet* studio physician.

Upon arriving, the doctor's reaction was roughly the same as Morty Stein's—up to the point when Stein had realized it wasn't a prank. The doctor stumbled out the poolside door, laughing, shaking his head and swearing to Morty Stein that he'd get him for this and just wait till the guys at the club heard about this one.

Again, Morty Stein stood facing the family. All wore the same somber questioning look. A slight breeze ruffled the tailored bedskirt and the room darkened slightly as a cloud passed before the sun. The children next door had abandoned the pool for the nearest arcade; the only sound was the petulant slapping of the water on the side of the pool.

Stein snapped back into action. Again, he flipped open his cellular phone and began poking the buttons. Dorothy and Ted and Jeannie looked at each other and nodded their approval. Mrs. Stein's eldest boy would fix everything. Morty Stein could be depended upon.

"Carole, I need you to contact Blanchard. Yeah. He should be on the set. Also, get me Matthesen, Granger and Goldman. Oh, and Tie Baker's agent—what's his name? Yeah. Howard. Get him on the horn. We need to change the shooting schedule. Yeah. Have them call me on the car phone. I'm on my way to the set." Morty Stein snapped the phone closed, stuffed it into his back pocket and, studiously avoiding the three pairs of staring eyes, ducked out the poolside slider. He wondered if he could save the film.

For the next several weeks, Jeannie passed most of her time on the phone, trying to cajole the doctor into returning and trying to contact Morty Stein, who seemed to be completely incommunicado despite the plethora of phones at his disposal. She spent some time with Tie, attempting to work out some system of communication. If she was unable to find out the whys and wherefores of his condition, she was determined to at least make sure he was comfortable and free of pain. He limited his communication to nods, noes and shrugs, first too impatient, then too depressed to try the Ouija board Jeannie placed before him. He emptied his days under the bed or at the bottom of the pool, anguishing over his condition. He hadn't quite figured out the whys and wherefores, but he had determined that his present physical form was a mirror of the superficial life he had been living. He was a star, not an actor. An image, not a person. He was as shallow as the film he inhabited and as grotesquely comic as the silent film cowboy he represented—and he had roped his family into the whole dismal scene.

As the days grew longer, the heat grew dryer. Tie became more staticky, more dusty, and his nitrocellulose surface became cloudy with tiny scratches until Jeannie could barely make out the one dour expression he had assumed. His parents made some effort to loosen Tie from his foggy mood. They tried reading out loud to him, but they were marginally schooled. Although Tie failed to react either nay or yea to their recitals, they grew impatient with their own skips and starts as they struggled to vocalize the printed words of *People* magazine. Receiving no encouragement from Tie, they eventually abandoned their visits to his room. Dorothy could no longer bear to see her son in his sad and filmy state, and Ted— well, Dorothy needed him with her.

Tie missed them. He was sorry that he hadn't reacted to their reading. He had been watching them grow back into themselves, and took comfort in the pounds Dorothy was gaining and the silver roots appearing at her hairline. Six weeks after Tie's metamorphosis, Ted and Dorothy announced they would be moving to a retirement village outside of Youngstown. Dorothy's sister lived there, and Ted still had the money from the sale of their house. He'd pay cash. They packed their clothes, Dorothy's afghans and Ted's La-Z-Boy recliner from the maid's room and trundled off to where Dorothy could grow old and fat and happy.

Jeannie had also changed. The orangy-yellow was gone from her hair. It was now its own chestnut brown, and her curls were clipped into a kind of Audrey Hepburn gamine look. How had he never noticed how beautiful she was in her own incarnation? How had he missed how capable she was? How intelligent? She had called in doctors, shrinks and scientists to try to get Tie puffed back up to his three-dimensional self. She even called in an expert from a film archives lab, who couldn't even venture a theory as to how it happened or how to fix it. He did, however, warn her that the film stock was prone to deterioration and was highly flammable.

She made at least a daily visit to Tie, but as his image faded on the film, her monologues to him became more like her thinking out loud, like a little girl bouncing ideas off her teddy bear. Tie missed her even when she was in the room. He made a few attempts to communicate, but by that time his image was too vague to even get her attention.

By now, Jeannie had muscled Morty Stein's secretary with

threats of publicity. She held a conference in Tie's bedroom with his agent, lawyer and publicist, the studio's people and Morty Stein. All but Jeannie avoided eye contact with Tie, propped up in a chair and so depressed that it took all of his attention to keep from curling up and rolling under the bed.

Jeannie proposed that she would report Tie as a "missing person" until they could return him to his natural state. She would take over the running of Tie's affairs and a press conference would be called, in which Jeannie would tearfully announce Tie's disappearance and appeal for information concerning his whereabouts.

At the press conference, Jeannie looked pale and fragile with just a touch of makeup. Morty Stein wore considerably more for his announcement that the film, already near completion, would be finished without Tie. He wondered if the press would buy it.

Three weeks after the press conference, on a day of spirit-squelching heat, a tree ignited in the valley, and Tie ignited on his bedroom carpet. He had taken to lying face-up under the bed, studying the bedsprings, abandoning himself to his limited life. Jeannie came to drag him out.

It was a mistake, the second significant mistake in Jeannie's life. She had been so preoccupied with telling Tie about the small speaking part Morty Stein had offered her in his new film (although she thought she would rather go into the production end) that she completely forgot about the fragility and highly flammable state of Tie's matrix. Reaching under the bed with both hands, grasping his brittle and cracking bottom edge, Jeannie hauled him out in a rapid whoosh and watched a spark leap from the carpet to her brother's silver nitrate form. He leapt from her hands, high into the air, and curled up in flames. In a blink, the blaze died and a puff of acrid black smoke drifted out the slider. A small, black, shiny ingot, threaded with silver, hung for a second in the air, then dropped with a thud on the expensive carpet.

Jeannie stood, listening to her own breath, gazing at the smoke, then at the lump that had been her brother. Although Tie had not spoken a word in over three months, his sudden absence blanketed the house in a new silence, almost palpable. Above the pool, the grains of black smoke attached themselves to moving air and drifted into the Hollywood Hills.

Beyond the trees that ringed the Baker estate, a motorcycle blasted its baritone song into the peace, and Jeannie stooped to pick up the ingot. She strolled over to Tie's night stand and picked up the cellular phone. While she turned the still warm coal over and over in her free hand, she dialed the number in Youngstown, and told her parents it was over.

Apéritif

Susan Raffo

She had her fingers around the thin stem of a martini glass when she asked me if I wanted to see her glass eye. I looked around the bar. Nobody was paying attention to us, but I wasn't sure what cool etiquette would apply here. I didn't know if I could pull off a gentle disdain as she popped out the piece of bright blue glass.

"Well?" she asked me, "Do you want to see it or not?"

Oh shit. I did want to see it, I mean I was pissing-my-pants curious, but I didn't want to see it here.

"Listen babe," I swaggered, "how's about you come home with me and take it out there." I hoped she was feeling awed by the way I stared meaningfully into her real eye, trying to look intent and in control at the same time.

She laughed. "Honey, I don't take it out in private. It's a public kind of thing for me. Like my spirituality or something. I don't do vulnerability behind closed doors."

I looked at her for a minute or two. A mutual friend of ours walked by and grabbed her by the arm, saying "hey" and then kissing her, hard, full on the lips. I picked up my glass and threw back a swallow while I watched them both flirt. Finally, the friend walked on by and into the restroom.

"So, you got ten seconds. If you don't say anything by then, I'm going to find someone else to expose myself to."

"Yeah, yeah . . . whip it out, babe. Let's see what you're good for. Lay it on the bar and don't let it get lost in the olives."

She smiled at me gently and let her head drop at the neck. She reached up with a hand and did some sort of tugging that was hidden by the long hair about her face, and then offered me her closed palm.

"Go on, take it."

I put my hand out and met the soft surface of her fist. She lay her hand in my open one and gently unlocked her fingers, the nails scraping against my palm as they spread. Something round and warm dropped against my skin.

"So," she said, "what do you think?"

"Yeah, just a minute. I haven't looked at it yet."

I pulled my hand close to my face and looked into her unblinking eye. The lights inside twinkled at me, laughter seeming to wander far away inside the glass globe, much farther away than was physically possible in such a tiny sphere. While I peered, I noticed that what had seemed just a blue eye was actually a mosaic of blue and black and dark, dark green. The colors ran into each other, blurring into some kind of hue that was unexpected.

"Well, it's pretty," I said.

"Of course it's pretty. I paid good money to make it more beautiful than any eye God could have given me. I've got to wear a contact on the other one to make them both match. I know it's pretty, but what else? What do you see?"

I looked again into the eye and watched the colors swirl.

"Rub it," she said. "Use the tip of your finger and rub against the surface."

I looked up at her. This was too weird and I wanted to shove it back in her hand and tell her to get a life. The thing of it was, the stupid little eye was so beautiful I wanted to touch it, to rub my skin along it and feel the way it must give, fluid like flesh. I wanted to know that it wasn't hard and made of glass.

"Go on," she said.

I held my finger just hovering over the top. I felt some kind of heat, but I guessed it was probably the smoke and noise of the bar. The music changed at the disco and a bass beat suddenly blared out of the speakers, making my bones vibrate and my teeth feel on edge. I pushed my finger down and rested it on top of the eye.

It was warm. Of course, I knew it had to be warm; it had just been resting in her body, picking up the heat of her skin and being moved by her muscles. I was a little creeped out, or maybe entranced, so it took a moment before I noticed her. She had gone slightly rigid. Her eyelids were closed and her face was turned to the ceiling. She was trembling and her mouth hung slack, her teeth just barely visible through her parted lips.

"Go on," she said, "don't stop. Just touch it."

The eye pulsed the smallest bit under my finger as I slid it along the curve, gently stroking one side of its surface. I could feel its heat rise, a slight sheen appearing along the blue. Across from me, she moaned a little and moved on the bar stool. I stroked my finger gently around the circumference, going around and around in regular circles, keeping with the beat that pounded across the room.

"Oh yeah," she whispered. "Oh god, you're good."

I rolled the eye over so that its underside faced the ceiling and, with two fingers, began a quicker, slicker motion, a friction up and then fast down and then up again. This was easy. I had done this lots before but never on something that I could hold so easily in the palm of my hand. By now her hands were gripping the bar stool and her head was tossing from side to side. Still her lids were closed—even clenched—shut. Her nostrils slightly flared, she was just on the edge of panting.

I looked at her while I kept on rubbing. I didn't want to end this yet, I wanted her to wait until I was ready. I slowed down the strokes and felt her frustration build.

"Oh please, please don't stop. Rub me, goddamn it, touch me faster."

I just laughed at her, a laugh deep down in my throat. And then I knew what I would do. It made perfect sense. Still rubbing gently, I raised my hand to my mouth and then suddenly popped her eye between my lips.

When the eye hit the hot wet of my tongue she shuddered and jumped, almost falling off the bar stool. Keeping my teeth away from the glass surface, I began to roll the eye against my tongue, stopping and sucking it, then rolling it again. It was like a fragile jawbreaker, a huge gumball, a shiny glass marble, and I sucked on it harder and harder until she screamed across from me and grabbed my arm, her hands tearing against my shirt.

Yeah, she was done.

I slowly wound down the suck, rolling the eye gently against my tongue as I watched her shudder still. Her face hung down again, the hair falling into her lap, and she leaned back, her spine resting spent against the bar.

I spat the eye back into my hand. It sat there, beautiful, blue and shiny. Raising it to my face, I blew against its surface and watched it slowly dry, the clouds of moisture evaporating into a silvery glow. She reached out to take the eye from me, but I held it away from her, waiting to see what she would do. "This babe is mine," I thought. "I know she's mine."

I could feel the shudders still carrying on inside her body, the aftershocks that made her waver a little on the stool. After a moment, she pulled her hand back and rested it, palm down and in her lap. I ordered another drink and looked at the mirror behind the bar. I watched as a group of dancers moved onto the floor, their bodies shifting to pick up the newest switch in beat.

After a minute she looked up. Her eyes were closed, but she was smiling. "I suppose you think I owe you something," she said, her fingers moving to toy with the bowl of olives on the bar next to her. "You must think that, or else you would have returned my eye to me by now." Although her eyes were closed, I could feel the intensity of her stare, the faint amusement that played around the lines of her face.

Looking down, I saw the same amusement reflected back from the depths of her eye. The blues and greens were laughing at me: There was something going on in there that made me stop and think. I liked this; it was weird, but I liked it. Not the usual Saturday night bar scene. I was about to look back up, thinking maybe I should return the eye now—I mean, it's gotta be a pain in the ass to sit there with that empty space hidden away behind your lid—when I saw some kind of movement.

I know it's impossible and no, I wasn't drunk, I was smooth, smooth like silk, so don't give me any crap about hallucinations, but I'm telling you what I saw and what I saw was the truth: That eye winked at me. No lids, no lashes, but damned if that eye didn't wink. Wink and then purse its little eye lips and blow me a kiss.

I looked up at her and she was just sitting there, her fingers playing with one of the olives in the bowl, slowly twirling the green sphere around and around. "You don't owe me nothing," I said, "but that doesn't mean I don't want something." She didn't say anything but just sat there, cooler than cool, still looking like she held the reins even though I was sitting there with her eye in my hand.

It almost pissed me off, but then I had an idea. I reached over and took the olive from her fingers and brought it to my lips. With a noise I knew she could hear, I put the green flesh to my mouth and then sucked as hard as I had sucked at her eye, a loud, wet noise with a lot of tongue. When I felt the red pimento slide against my teeth, I moaned real soft and then, even more loudly, I swallowed. She just sat there listening, her head cocked to one side and a faint grin on her lips.

Handing her the green shell minus the pimento and holding her glass eye in my other hand, I said, "Next time, I'll trade ya."

She took the green olive and put it in her pocket, then kissed me on the cheek. I felt the eye nestled in my hand shudder, a kind of clenching that then relaxed, something I never thought glass could do. Opening the eye that was still green and blue like the one in my hand, she whispered, "I hope I get to see you, baby, sooner rather than later."

And then she winked.

With her good eye.

And went out the door.

Author's note: This story was inspired by a friend who lost an eye in a car accident and thought a glass eye could never be sexy.

Feeding the Dark

Jean Stewart

Angrily scuffing her boots on the wooden floorboards, Emma followed her friend Toni across the barroom.

"I just can't believe they're lettin' Palmer live there," Emma griped. "A twice-paroled child molester movin' in right down the block from an elementary school!"

Toni half-turned, looking mildly exasperated. "Damn! You're like a broken record with this shit, Em. It's the old 'he paid his debt to society' crapola." She paused, waiting for Emma to come alongside her before she finished. "It's the law—Palmer can live wherever he likes until he's arrested for molesting somebody else. It sucks, but you can't do anything about it, so just get over it, will ya?"

Instead of dropping it, Emma shoved her hands in her jeans pockets and muttered to herself, "When did the law and justice become two different things?"

In the corner, beyond a pool table, a womanly form stepped out of the shadows. Dark eyes flashed at Emma.

Instinctively self-protective, Emma lowered her gaze.

Toni laughed. "Hey, girl, the law has always been the province of well-off white dudes." Leaning into Emma's shoulder, she gave a gentle shove and jested, "The likes of you and me are just equal opportunity window dressin'—don't you know that?"

Toni and Emma stopped before a gleaming wooden bar, where a youthful bartender sauntered over to wait on them.

"How ya doin'?" the bartender greeted. "I'm Angela. What'll it be?"

A tiny rhinestone on the right side of Angela's nose glittered in the light from the cash register lamp. Her mind still contemplating the modern paradox of law and justice, Emma simply eyed the nose stud and made no reply.

Mistaking Emma's steady regard, Angela preened and gave her a big grin.

Her face growing warm, Emma frowned and began pulling off her black leather motorcycle jacket. She was draping it over a bar stool when Angela seemed to speak to herself.

"Well, I think I just found my first candidate!"

Unwilling to be drawn into what seemed to be flirtatious banter, Emma replied, "A bottle of Sam Adams, please."

"Same, darlin'," Toni said, bestowing a warm smile on Angela.

As the young woman crossed to the hip-high refrigeration unit, Toni nudged Emma and whispered in her ear, "What's the matter with you, fool?"

Grasping the cold, long-necked bottle of beer that Angela handed to her, Toni asked, "And what's my friend Emma a candidate for?"

"A woman in leather came in here earlier," Angela answered. "She gave me a twenty to pass on names and introductions to the toughest dykes in town." Smiling, Angela handed Emma a beer, then finished. "So, of course, I'll be tellin' her about you two."

Tall, black and broad shouldered, Toni stood a little straighter. "Of course."

"We're cops, not thugs," Emma stated. Squinting against the

cloud of cigarette smoke being exhaled by a woman several yards away, Emma frowned harder. She felt like adding, *We're Philadelphia police officers, and that's a special breed. In this city of brotherly love, somebody's always busy gettin' in someone else's face.* Tired and suspicious, Emma sent an uneasy gaze around the bar. *If you're not tough, you die.*

From the disco downstairs, sultry dance music made its way up the narrow staircase at the side of the room. Though the melody had faded, a relentless, hypnotic rhythm reverberated through the smoky room like a monstrous heartbeat. Wandering easily between intermittent dark shadows and small islands of yellow light, women of all ages and shapes played pool and darts, and bellied up to the old mahogany bar that dominated one wall.

All around her, Emma saw women talking together, mildly flirting with one another. As ever, the sight of so many lesbians in one place made her feel shy and self-conscious. Yet she had to look, to feast her eyes on the creatures she would no longer let herself approach.

As Emma turned and scanned the far end of the room, a few bolder eyes near the jukebox began meeting hers. Then a Rubenesque blonde winked and blew her a kiss, while the woman next to her glowered.

Feeling ridiculous, Emma faced the bar again.

Beside her, Toni, who never missed anything, teased, "Girl, you've got half the women in this bar checking you out now."

Ignoring Toni, Emma began picking at the label on her beer bottle. "Angela, this woman asking for names . . . is she here, now?"

Clearly surprised by Emma's challenging tone, Angela asked, "Um . . . I don't think so. I don't see her. Why?"

"I thought you'd sworn off women, Emster," Toni remarked, her eyes lingering appreciatively on Angela.

In a patient voice, Emma elaborated, "Some woman is shelling out twenties looking for tough dykes. Does that tie in with a case you can think of?"

Toni sighed and took a swig from her beer bottle. Wiping her hand casually across the edge of her mouth, she commented, "Emma, I know you can't help this supercop shit, but god, you need to get a life. This is the first free Saturday night you've had in months. You've been in this bar for five minutes and what are you doing? Finding tie-ins to a case."

Intrigued, Angela demanded, "What case?"

Emma muttered, "Never mind."

"Oh come on," Angela whined. "Tell me."

Leaning forward, Toni quizzed, "You've heard about the mutilated male corpses that have been turning up all over the East Coast?"

Her eyes round with both horror and fascination, Angela responded, "Yeah. I heard about it on CNN. At first it was only in small southern towns, but now it's happening in Miami, Atlanta and D.C."

"Well, in each area," Toni elaborated, "there are reports—"

"Tone!" Emma hissed. "This is police business!"

Without pause, Toni kept right on talking. "—that someone was going around recruiting women for some kind of vigilante squad before the murders started goin' down."

Disgusted, Emma stated, "I can't believe you sometimes."

Toni gave her a smirk in reply.

Shaking her head, Emma picked up her beer bottle, grabbed her leather jacket and moved down the bar, away from Toni.

Though Toni was speaking quietly in her best bland, seen-it-all manner, Emma couldn't help listening as her friend proceeded to describe the torn-out throats and shredded phalluses of the victims. Overhearing her, most of the women near the bar gradually ceased their conversations. Several edged closer, horrified, yet intent.

Swallowing a wave of frustration, Emma found herself staring at her reflection in the large, rectangular mirror behind the bar. Beneath the old-fashioned painted letters of "Ballantine Ale," a tall, sandy-haired, thirty-year-old frowned back at her. Nothing remarkable. Just an All-American girl who had dearly wanted to contribute, to make a difference in the world. She had believed that a career in law enforcement would be the way to accomplish that dream.

Laughing grimly, she shook her head at herself.

Being a cop was like being a referee at a demolition derby, only instead of wrecked cars, what you ended up seeing was wrecked lives. The bad guys, for they almost always were men, raped and killed and dumped bodies, and the citizenry of Philadelphia had long ago become used to it. The majority of the cases Emma had worked in the past eight years were still unsolved. A few criminals had been indicted; fewer still had ever been convicted.

Emma no longer thought of herself as a servant of justice; she was concentrating too much on merely staying alive.

"So, is it true what they're sayin' on TV?" the bartender was asking Toni. "Those dead guys were all accused of rape or child molestation at one time or another?"

Coolly, Toni nodded. "Guess these attacks are someone's idea of justice."

"Death by castration," one eavesdropper pronounced. "Seems apropos for a sexual predator."

"God, no! They say it's like those guys were mauled by dogs," replied a woman farther away. "Murder is murder—no matter what they did. No one deserves to be torn apart. I mean—how medieval!"

Down the bar, another woman called out, "No more medieval than child-rape!"

While the voices around them rose, debating the point, Emma felt a strange sensation, as if a caressing hand had stroked her neck. She glanced over her shoulder, but no one was there.

Puzzled, Emma used the mirror before her to search the smoky barroom one more time. There in the glass, only one pair of eyes met hers.

Directly behind her, in the shadows, a woman was leaning against the wall, watching her. It was the woman she'd noticed when she and Toni had first entered the bar, the one beyond the pool table.

Seeing that she'd caught Emma's attention, the woman moved into the rosy light of the pinball machine. She was clad in a black leather miniskirt and a matching short-waisted jacket. Glossy, dark hair curled over her shoulders. Even in the half-dark, the woman's eyes seemed to shine as they slid over Emma, both teasing her and subtly taking her measure. Then, with a slight inclination of her head toward the staircase, the woman began to walk.

Emma turned and watched. Gracefully, the woman eased along the back of the crowd that had gathered around Toni's stool. At the top of the stairs, the stranger paused, meeting Emma's eyes again. In the dim light, Emma saw her dark brows rise in what was clearly a question.

The promise Emma had made to herself pushed past the pulsing beat of the music, past the promise of that lovely body lingering at the head of the stairs. *I don't want to be hurt anymore*, came the inner voice.

It was her mantra, recited at the sight of a pretty woman in a fervent hope to keep herself safe. It was her only protection against these ladies of the night. Long ago, Emma had learned the truth of these encounters. They never wanted her to stay in the morning. No one wanted to risk dealing with falling in love with a cop.

Emma had had enough of it. It was easier to be celibate than continually heartbroken.

With a chivalrous attempt at a smile, Emma shook her head, declining the invitation.

Staring steadily with dark, curiously burning eyes, the stranger in leather gave a languid smile. Slowly, she raised her hand and held it out, summoning Emma.

Emma felt an answering surge of sexual hunger, felt herself devouring the woman with her eyes.

"Come," the stranger mouthed, her gaze enticing.

Emma swallowed. For the first time in months her rosary was deserting her, leaving her powerless.

The woman descended the stairs in a smooth, quick glide,

leaving Emma peering at the shadows there.

Instinctively, Emma stood up to follow her, then hesitated, shooting a look at Toni.

"... so when the maimed male bodies start turning up," Toni was relating, "sexual assault cases plummet. Doesn't take an Einstein to figure there might be some lady perps taking the law into their own hands."

The little bartender blustered, "Hey, if there are sisters kickin' ass out there, I want in on it!"

"And I'll just bet you kick it good, too!" Toni laughed.

Tone is holding court here, Emma considered. *She won't even miss me.*

In Emma's mind, she saw the woman again, smiling as she invited, "Come." It had been a smile full of secrets. In the dim light of the bar, the woman's face had not been clear, but the odd glow in her eyes had been compelling.

She'll only hurt me, Emma thought cynically, *like all the others.* Bowing her head, Emma sank back onto her stool.

All at once disgusted with her own cowardice, Emma pushed uncertainty aside and stood up. "Jeez—so what?!" she muttered.

Without a backward glance she slung on her leather jacket and headed straight to the stairs. She rumbled down the steps in a noisy rush. Weaving through throngs of dancers, she crossed the crowded floor with her long stride. Her head was swinging from left to right, searching for that dark, mysterious woman, hoping against hope that she hadn't missed her chance.

A sweet-looking redhead caught her arm as she passed, laughing with the coquettish certainty of an accomplished vamp. "Dance with me!" the girl demanded.

"I'm ... uh ... looking for someone," Emma replied, sweeping her gaze back to the mass of writhing, sinuous bodies all around them.

And suddenly there she was, stepping close to the redhead and gently pushing her aside.

"You're looking for me," the woman stated.

Emma's eyes widened as she took in the seductive vision before her.

Frowning, the redhead protested, "Oh, I'm sure! I'm, like, talking to her first and then you come out of nowhere . . . "

The woman merely flicked a glance at her. "Go away."

Emma saw the redhead go slack-jawed. Wordless, the youngster spun about and disappeared into the crowd.

Emma blinked, struck by the suddenness of the abdication, aware that something had just happened, but not sure what. The redhead was slightly drunk and Emma had thought the girl was ready to make a scene. Emma knew it had little to do with herself and a great deal to do with Saturday night dance club drama. Yet, this unusually compelling stranger had quietly snuffed the outburst before it had even gotten properly underway.

How? Emma wondered. *In all my years of police work I don't think I've ever seen anything like that.*

Then the dark eyes flickered and the stranger was coming toward her. Though Emma stepped back, the woman caught her by the elbows and checked Emma's retreat. She managed to brush her body along Emma's side as she moved into Emma's arms.

"Shall we be partners, then?" she murmured. "To see how we fit?"

Astonished by the sensations roaring through her, Emma could only gasp, "I—I—don't dance." Wherever the woman touched her, her body was responding with a reflexive neediness that was a little frightening.

The woman slowly leaned into her. "It's alright. I know you're afraid . . . but you're afraid of the wrong things."

"What?" Emma asked. Her head was swimming, her heart was pounding loudly in her ears, matching the driving beat of the music that enveloped them in a primordial embrace of its own.

She was more than afraid. She was terrified.

This is a fast dance, Emma thought inanely, as the woman in her arms embarked upon a slow grind.

For a moment, Emma thought she might faint.

Shit! This feels great, her mind crowed. Aroused and reckless, her body was screaming for whatever relief this woman might provide, even as her mind warned her that this, too, would be a one night stand. *I don't care,* Emma swore. *I don't care. Just let me hold her, love her, do whatever she wants. I need it. Oh god, I need it!*

Gradually, Emma's rigid posture relaxed. With enticingly tender hands the stranger was pulling her hips closer, melding Emma's shape to her own. There were warm lips on her throat, and the dance was becoming barely restrained foreplay.

Then the woman leaned back and stared into Emma's eyes. "Come with me," she urged.

"Yes," Emma breathed.

The woman gripped her hand and then they were moving briskly across the dance floor. With a surprising firmness the stranger was pushing past bodies, clearing a determined path to the door.

At the club exit, the burly bouncer rose from her stool, about to engage the dark woman in conversation, but the stranger did not slow. Instead, she threw a placating grin at the bouncer and announced, "Found who I wanted, thanks."

Mutually perplexed, the bouncer and Emma traded a look before the stranger hauled Emma past the woman, through the threshold and into the night.

Once outside, the stranger gripped Emma's hand fast in her own and turned right. She was moving steadily, dragging Emma along with her. They hurried down the alley, Emma's boots and the woman's flats echoing on the grimy brick pavement. A cold, drizzling October rain gathered quickly on their hair and shoulders, and their breath formed in small pale clouds before their faces.

As they left the small, overhead light of the bar doorway behind, they plunged into total blackness.

Eyeing the faint outline of the smaller woman beside her, Emma wondered, *What am I doing?* The bar was in a high crime area, and her .38 was in her car around the corner, hidden beneath the driver's seat. Feeling nervous, Emma began moving her eyes over the velvet black shapes of the warehouses they were passing. *Where's she taking me?*

The woman made another sharp right, pulling her into an alley Emma would have missed in the darkness. Slowing, the woman whispered, "Over here," then guided Emma deeper into the ebony cocoon before her.

"Jeez . . . I can't see anything," Emma whispered. "You know, this isn't very safe."

There was a short, breathless chuckle that ended in a growl, and the hair on Emma's neck stood on end.

Caressing hands slid up the sleeves of her leather jacket, to her broad shoulders, turning her, pushing her. A hard wall thumped against Emma's back.

And then the woman was pressing into her, her voice deeper and menacing as she repeated, "Safe?"

Emma heard her own breathing speed up in response. She made a subtle effort to slide to the side and the stranger placed a firm, restraining hand on her shoulder. Emma found herself pinned, trapped against the cold bricks by the surprising strength of the other woman's body.

A whisper began caressing Emma's ear. "You are so strong," she rasped, "so good. I can see it in you, in the colors that surround you. But you have been alone for a long time, in spirit and in flesh. The loneliness has made you weary."

A soft, warm mouth began nibbling the length of her neck and Emma groaned.

"You have a need," the woman whispered.

Hands slipped inside Emma's open motorcycle jacket, coasting boldly over her ribs, her stomach, then up and over her breasts. The fingers lingered there, gently strumming the hardening nipples that rose through Emma's T-shirt.

Stunned by the erotic force being unleashed in her, Emma could only tremble and react, as mind and body yielded to the play of the stranger's hands.

"I can give you so much . . . if you allow it . . . "

In the distance, Emma thought she heard dogs barking. The cop part of her went on alert, and she turned her head toward the noise.

Then the woman's teeth nipped down her neck, to the place where her T-shirt collar rested.

"Shall I restore your strength, mighty warrior?"

What the hell is she . . . ? Abruptly, she lost the thought, as a hand dove between her legs, insistently rubbing, then just as quickly leaving.

Gasping, Emma clung to the woman.

The hands on her breasts became sweetly rough. The mouth on her neck was making her crazy.

"Kiss me," Emma begged. Her every breath was a soft, helpless moan. She was covered with goosebumps, defenseless against the hunger that was overtaking her. "Kiss me!"

"Let me into your heart . . . Let me change you," the woman crooned, reaching lower, massaging the crotch of Emma's jeans.

Shivering, Emma felt her hips moving of their own volition. She couldn't believe she was doing this. Shrouded in cold rain and night, she was about to let this woman fuck her in an alley. Her proud, aloof self-image had been shed like a burdensome cloak, thrown down before this relentless force in her arms.

A knee was nudging her leg, moving it aside.

"You must ask for what you want," the woman coaxed.

"Oh goddess, please . . . " Emma gasped.

Somewhere, several dogs sent up a chorus of full-throated howls. Distractedly, Emma thought they sounded closer than they had earlier.

"Finish the sentence," the woman demanded, rubbing soft, worn denim with a firm, rhythmic stroke. "What do you want?"

Emma writhed and pleaded, "Take me."

In a quiet, imperative voice, the woman proclaimed, "Pledge yourself."

"What?"

"Pledge yourself to me," the woman urged, her hands moving to the buttons of Emma's jeans. "Say that this is only the beginning."

Impatiently, Emma repeated the words, "This is only the beginning."

Teeth brushed against her neck. "Say you are mine."

Desire engulfed her. Emma choked out the promise.

The woman was undoing her jeans, slipping a hand into her underwear, forcing the fabric down.

Emma arched. With a mere fondle of the woman's fingers, she was flooding. She forgot about dogs or danger or anything else except what this woman was doing to her.

Stroking slowly, building a delicious anticipation, the woman completed her capture. Emma's legs shifted farther apart as her body opened. She was liquid, she was quaking, she was swaying in supple response to each slide of those fingers into her cunt.

Never had she felt anything like this.

Aware of everything—the chill mist on her face, the spicy, wildflower scent of the woman's hair, the taste of the tongue at last teasing her mouth, the sound of her own stifled cries—Emma leaned back against the rough brick and allowed invasion. Trembling, awash in need, she hovered on the edge of sensual bloom.

"Give yourself to me," the stranger growled.

Rapture shot through her. If the woman had not been holding her up with one arm, she would have collapsed, for her legs were gone. Charged with lightning, transformed into driving, ethereal energy, she spasmed helplessly on the ends of the stranger's fingers.

"Yes, that's it," the woman cajoled, her hand relentless. "All deathless spells start here, at the source of power."

Like hounds on a hunt, dogs were baying, yipping excitedly, and the noise was echoing off the walls of the alley just outside the one where they stood.

Emma heard them, but the woman clutched her closer and with another play of her enchanting hand sent Emma into a near swoon. All awareness of the outside world left her. She only knew that something hot and dark was suffusing her, flowing into her from the entire length of body that pressed her against the wall.

It was as if the black night had taken shape and was consuming her.

She could no longer see, no longer hear; she could only feel the blazing, exotic other that sank into her flesh and sinew with fiery abandon.

"Ahhh yes . . . " the stranger breathed in quiet triumph, and Emma felt herself saying it with her.

Savage and merciless, the being within her flexed Her authority, causing Emma to come again. Delirious with pleasure, she felt herself falling. She realized dimly that she was in the grip of something she had not known existed, and even in the midst of orgasm, terror rose.

With all her will, Emma began to fight for her wits.

"Shhh, now," a voice in her mind soothed. "I am Hekate, the Dark Goddess. And you are mine."

Wooly-headed, Emma found herself on her hands and knees. A heady mix of wet dog, street grit and wildflowers filled her nostrils. From above, a gentle, icy rain was falling, and visibility in the dark alley was suddenly greatly improved. In the murky dimness, Emma could see the outline of bricks in the wall opposite, the empty beer bottles lying on the pavement near a crushed corrugated box.

And at the entrance to the alley, she saw a milling cluster of big, black dogs. Their eyes were gleaming knowingly, and they panted as they watched her.

The strange seductress was nowhere to be seen.

Emma struggled to stand.

And discovered she could not.

Where her hands had been, there were paws.

Astounded, she froze.

One of the dogs walked slowly toward her. *Don't panic*, came the amused, womanly voice in Emma's mind. *You're not insane.*

The change will not last. It's only good for the night, and only happens when Hekate calls you. You'll always shapechange back to human form about an hour before dawn.

Emma blinked at the sleek, young Rottweiler before her, not quite believing that this was happening.

Her tone careful and kind, the Rott informed her, *Tonight, it all seems so bizarre and frightening, I know. But you will learn to love this gift.*

A rapidly compounding hysteria crept up on Emma. She wanted to flee, to run. She actually burst into bounding flight, then screeched to a four-legged stop, shocked by the joyful familiarity of the motion. She looked her dog-body over, then gazed up at the Rottweiler before her, completely at a loss.

Yes, you know that body, the voice assured her. *You've belonged to Hekate many times before this life. Some of us wear many shapes in our visits here.*

Making a deliberate effort to control the terror, Emma sniffed the air. *Do I know you?*

Large, intelligent brown eyes stared directly into her own. *You will. As people, we haven't met, yet.*

Breathing hard, confounded, Emma could only stare at her.

The other dog came closer. *You can leave the pack whenever you choose. You'll awaken in this alley with no memory of how you got here, and go back to what you were before you answered the call.* A cold nose nuzzled Emma's ear and Emma took a surprised step back. *But most of us choose not to do that.*

Emma swallowed. *Why not?*

Because we're Hekate's magic: justice in an unjust world. With an encouraging twitch of lip, almost a smile, the dog finished, *Run with us. You'll see.*

The dogs near the entrance of the alley were barking excitedly, but in her mind, Emma heard what they were truly saying.

You'll be invincible! one called.

Come on! another demanded. *We're needed!*

And then the disembodied voice of the stranger came to her.

You fed on the dark, my sweet one. You gave yourself to me of your own free will. Out in the night, there are men doing wrong.

Emma glanced around, but even as she did she knew somehow that she would never see the Goddess in human form again. Her recruitment had been deftly accomplished, and now, it seemed, service was required.

A man named Palmer, the menacing voice of the Dark Goddess hissed. *He who ravishes little children. It's time he met my hounds, I think.*

Emma stiffened with shock.

Beside her, the Rottweiler waited, eyes glimmering with anxious hope.

Gripped by consternation, Emma tried to think. *I'll be breaking the law if I do this.*

Hekate's voice came again. *There is law and there is justice.*

Uncertain, Emma hesitated. *Who am I to mete out justice—to take a man's life?*

Who are you not to? the Goddess asked. *Will you stand aside and let monsters devour the innocent? Who better to stop them than you?*

In an agony of doubt, Emma shook her head. *I can't. It's not right . . .*

Quietly, the Rott spoke in Emma's mind. *Palmer's already picked out his next victim.*

Her breath coming fast and sharp, Emma bowed her head. *No, no, no . . .*

Feeling helpless against her fate, she charged forward.

The Rottweiler raced alongside her.

At the entrance of the alley, the pack waited for Emma and the Rott to pass, before whirling and following in a collective burst of speed.

Without allowing herself to examine exactly what she was doing, Emma instinctively understood that she was leading the black beasts that streaked through the night behind her. Still feeling oddly dazed, she looked back several times as she ran, trying to count how many were in the pack. She had surmised eight before she realized her distracted glances had set them to baying again. Two of the burlier dogs began showing off, capering up close to her heels to attempt a playful nip. Then suddenly, the young Rott who continued to position herself next to Emma lunged at them with a feral snarl. Cowed, the two fell away. Startled and confused, Emma's attention snapped back to the street before her.

There was some sort of canine etiquette at work here, but for the life of her, Emma could not begin to fathom it. She was having enough difficulty just trying to keep the panicky despair under control. Her mind kept insisting that none of this could be real, while over and over her own shaggy black paws rose and fell on the grimy, wet pavement before her. Sensuously powerful, her four legs were stretching and gathering under her in a rhythmic flow. Stunned, she discerned her dog-body was propelling her along the dark, wet streets at a speed that did not seem possible.

In the periphery of her vision, a surreal gleam of colors moved like an eddying stream. Ahead of her, a silver-gray fog hovered. And then, all at once, the fog enclosed her, removing everything from her sight, even the street beneath her. Though the ground below seemed solid enough as she continued to race along, Emma had the distinct impression that it was no longer there. She was running so fast that she left even fear behind. Glancing quickly around, she could no longer see the pack behind her, or even the Rott who'd stayed on her right.

A low voice was crooning in her, *This night is yours.*

She knew it was Hekate. Once more, she felt the erotic rush of magic surging through her. Even now, shapechanged as she was into this bizarre, frightening thing she had become, Emma felt her body responding with an intense, corporeal yearning.

The first Blooding is the worst, the tender voice went on, filling her head. *Just know that there will be death with the morn, regardless of what you do or cannot do in the hours before dawn . . .* The chill finality of the words sank through Emma. Quivering helplessly with the carnal anticipation this voice caused, Emma was also terrified.

She staggered, but managed to keep running, as the fog beneath her feet thinned and cleared. Far below, there were small, glowing, milk-white pools—street lights—and then shrouded in rainy darkness, she glimpsed the roofs of hundreds of row houses.

Shocked at how high she was, a small cry escaped her.

As she flailed helplessly, her paws struck air and she soared lower. From the corner of her eye, she again noted those odd swirling streamers, like rainbows of some altered reality. Then the Rott burst through the thick clouds above and with a casual lean of her shoulder slipped down to Emma's side. Effortlessly, the dog with the soulful eyes matched Emma's slowing pace. Hearing a series of excited barks, Emma glanced back and found the rest of the pack racing across sheer night air and rain, straining to stay close.

In Emma's mind, the Goddess whispered, *It is your choice. The prolonged rape and strangulation of an eight-year-old . . . or the swift gutting of a ravening animal.*

All at once, something in Emma knew which house she wanted. She was sweeping lower, coming in fast. The dark, wet street rose up at her. Her paws were scrambling, then skidding across slick macadam, and she ended up tumbling head over tail in a hard, awkward landing. She rolled to her feet, bruised and stiff-legged, and trembling with nerves.

Before her, in the surface of a large puddle, she was suddenly confronted with her own image.

Arrested, Emma stared. A long, dark snout, stiffly erect ears, glittering ebony eyes, a shaggy, charcoal-colored coat. *Shit!* she thought, while the German Shepherd gave a low growl.

With all the grace of practiced flyers, the others began smoothly descending around her.

The pack looked over the houses before them, panting, some shaking the rain from their shining dark coats, some whining and anxiously pacing.

Padding forward, Emma surveyed the row of brick houses. She lowered her head and her nose twitched the man's distinctive scent from the moist strip of grass by the curb.

She followed the trail to the gate in the picket fence, then stood there, eyeing the house through the misting rain.

Even without the trail he had left, she would have known Palmer's house. Friday morning she had sat across the street from this place in her cruiser. Grimly, she had watched as a man already paroled on an earlier rape and murder stood framed in the curtains of his wide picture window. He had smiled at her, and waved, while on the sidewalk before the house, the neighborhood children had paraded between them. In her mind's eye, Emma could still see the straggling line of girls and boys making their way to school.

The pack gathered behind Emma on the sidewalk. Though eerily quiet, they milled restlessly in and around each other, their eyes fixed on the house. The sleek, young Rott eased forward and stood beside Emma once more, her calm, dark eyes shifting to Emma's own.

Feeling suddenly raw and exposed, Emma challenged, *If the choice is between this . . . awful man and any child . . . then there is no choice, really. Is there?*

The Rott replied, *There is always a choice.* Turning to gaze up at the black, rain-streaked windows of the house, she finished, *It's simply that some will not make it. And those like Palmer have learned to count on that.*

Still, Emma hesitated, her thoughts spiraling inward. *It's murder! I can't go against everything I've ever believed in!*

And then, all at once, she was seeing herself here in daylight, walking past the yellow police tape, sickened and trembling and pierced through the heart with the knowledge that a child lay dead in the basement.

Roaring with fury, she sprang over the gate before she even knew she was moving. The house seemed to come rushing at her, and then she was crashing through the huge picture window. Shards of glass showered over her dog-body, slicing her legs, gouging her shoulder. In a distant part of her mind, she felt the knifelike pain, felt more wounds as the razor-sharp glass crunched beneath her paws on the carpet. Then she was taking the stairs in a series of leaps. By the time she confronted him in the bedroom, deep, rumbling growls were escaping with each breath.

Palmer sat up in bed. "What the fuck . . . ?!"

Momentarily frozen in the bedroom doorway, Emma's eyes swept over the array of photos adorning the bedroom walls. There in all her eight-year-old radiance was the next victim, captured already, if only on film. In one photo she was kicking through piles of leaves, in another she was smiling as she played with her friends. In yet another, she was walking before Palmer's house, running a muddy stick along the white picket fence. And in all of the photos, it was apparent that the child was completely unaware of the stalker readying to take her.

A new psychic flash engulfed Emma. The dank, musty smell of a basement, the huge shape of a man wrestling down an impossibly small girl, who gave one terrified shriek before a massive hand closed on her throat.

Inhaling sharply, Emma closed her eyes and staggered back a few steps.

Before her, Palmer was fumbling with the night stand.

The Rott was suddenly beside Emma, barking furiously at the man.

Still twisted around toward the night stand, Palmer was reaching into the top drawer, shouting venomous curses at them. Then, Emma saw the dull-black Glock automatic in the hand he was drawing clear of the drawer. Swinging around, Palmer aimed at the Rott and fired.

Even as Emma launched herself at him, the gun fired four more times in quick, explosive succession. She heard the buzz, felt the rush of air as the bullets sliced past her, then her front paws were smashing into his chest, knocking Palmer and the automatic in two different directions.

She was on him and over him and he was screaming now, pleading for a mercy he had never given. Her ears rang with the savagery of her reply.

In an instant, it was over. Silence echoed in her ears and the body sagged, the dead weight of it a steady pressure against her jaws. Slowly, she came back to herself.

She realized her mouth was full of hot blood. With a cry, she let him go.

Gagging helplessly, Emma clambered away.

With a soft whine, the young Rott snuffled Emma's left ear.

Dazed, Emma looked her friend over before commenting, *You're not hit?* She was shocked to realize it, for the shots had been aimed with deadly intent from a distance of less than ten feet.

There's still a lot to explain, the Rott softly replied.

The rest of the pack flowed into the room like big, black shadows. With an expeditious violence, they fell on Palmer. In seconds, the room was filled with a chorus of spine-tingling snarls, with the sounds of tearing flesh and splintering bone.

Aghast, Emma's only thought was fleeing.

Breathing hard, she shot down the stairs, crossed the glass-strewn living room and bounded through the open window. She dashed over grass, then hopped the neat picket fence and unleashed herself. She was racing down the street, heedless of the blood streaming from numerous superficial cuts she carried, oblivious to the deep wound in her right shoulder.

She ran, desperately hoping that if she ran fast enough she could escape what had happened back there in Palmer's house. The rain fell harder; the cold wind rose to a frenzy and lashed through the trees. And dimly, Emma heard her own voice rising in terror, raving in the language of dogs as the night's madness fully consumed her.

Quite unexpectedly, she was limping, then the gleaming, wet pavement rose up and crashed against her face. She struggled twice to her feet, only to collapse again. She, who had become expert at protecting herself, at distancing herself from others, had no protection for or distance from what this night had brought her.

Pain. So much pain.

Her eyes closed. She groaned, feeling her body surrendering to the icy darkness creeping over her.

And in the distance, like something out of a horror film, she heard the pack howling.

Oh, Hekate, she breathed. *Help me.*

As if in answer, the black night enfolded her.

She was down deep, struggling through layers and layers of something dense and warm, fighting to get free.

She opened her eyes, then simply lay there, blinking wearily, unable to comprehend anything else. Without knowing how, Emma knew that she had been trying to awaken for a long time.

Like an avalanche, hushed and devastating, memory slammed into her. Adrenaline flared, then blasted aside the last vestiges of heavy sleep as the entire evening swept through her mind with harrowing clarity.

The cunning, voluptuous grace of the woman in the bar, the overpowering desire to follow her, the breathtaking command of the hands moving over her in the darkness of that alley. Then, the unbelievably exquisite feel of running and leaping as a big, powerful, exuberant dog! And the coppery taste of Palmer's blood gushing into her mouth!

God! Gasping, Emma sat up, her hands on her face, then her arms, then her legs. *I'm human!* She was nude, but she was unhurt, and she was certainly not fur covered or shaped like a seventy-pound Shepherd.

Utterly relieved, her knees rose up, and clenching them, she curled into a self-protective ball. A barely restrained sob choked free.

Long minutes passed. Then gradually, as her heart slowed and she relaxed enough to control her breathing, the first threads of rational thought pressed forward.

That can't have really happened....

Frowning, she turned her head and surveyed the dark room. With a sigh of relief, she noted the presence of her clock radio, the glowing red digits stating that it was 5:22 A.M. In the faint illumination from the night light in the bathroom, she could make out the murky features of her spartan bedroom. The long bookshelf by the window, her well-loved novels side by side with volumes on police theory and criminal psychology. The stocky bulk of the dresser. In the corners, she recognized the huge speakers of her archaic stereo system; each of the units served as platforms for her cherished jade plants.

There, on the floor by the spindle-backed chair, was a pile that appeared to be her cast-off clothes. Nearby she spotted the contour of her boots.

Where's my weapon? she wondered.

Driven to find out, she slapped back the covers and sprang out of bed. With a sharp breath, she halted, grimacing.

She was stiff all over, and her right shoulder ached with a dull throb. The pressure of merely standing was causing the soles of her feet to burn!

As if... Stubbornly, she shook her head, clearing the dizzying wave of uncertainty clouding her mind. *It was only a dream!*

All the same, she winced as she made herself walk the few steps to the pile of clothing. She nudged aside the jeans, socks and T-shirt, found the heavy leather of the motorcycle jacket and then rummaged beneath it.

No gun.

Damn! She sat back on her haunches, impatiently scrubbing her face with her hand. *Did I leave it in the car?*

Feeling tired and clumsy, she moved to the window. She used a finger to separate the blinds and peered outside. Her car was not parked in the designated space in front of her apartment building. Swallowing nervously, she angled her face closer to the windowpane and searched the street. Her car was nowhere to be seen.

Uneasily, Emma probed her memory. *How did I get home?*

The last events of the evening came abruptly to mind: collapsing, wounded and frightened in the rain, praying to Hekate to help her.

Angrily, Emma rubbed her sore shoulder. *Oh, right! When I was a dog!* She rolled her eyes to the ceiling.

Once more she turned toward her clothes. It was so completely uncharacteristic of her to throw them on the floor like that, rather than hang her jacket and place the soiled clothing in the laundry basket. She had to have been drunk.

Go find your car, Shit-for-Brains! she railed at herself. *Maybe you'll be lucky and the .38 will still be under the goddamned seat!*

Disgusted with herself, she stomped toward the shower, then had to slow and move more carefully as the aches flared.

What the hell happened to me? she worried. *How the hell did one bottle of beer fuck me up like this?*

An hour later, Emma parked her old Subaru in front of her favorite diner. As she unfolded her tall form and climbed out of the vehicle, she held her breath. The aches she had woken with were getting worse.

She was thankful now for three things. It had taken the expense of hiring a taxi, but she had found her car exactly where she had parked it last night before entering the bar. Her police revolver and holster were under the driver's seat, undisturbed, right where she had wedged them. And the last piece of luck was the best: Bless the Goddess, today was her day off work.

Emma limped stiffly past the diner's chrome-framed windows, opened the front door and headed toward her usual booth. Gail, the proprietress, called good morning, then turned to the coffee urn to fetch the cup of black coffee she knew was wanted.

Emma slid into her booth, an involuntary groan escaping. A moment later, Gail placed the coffee before her and inquired, "Scrambled eggs and ketchup, kid?"

It'll look like . . . For a brief instant, her ears were filled with the crack of bones; her nostrils were assaulted with the aroma of blood-drenched flesh.

Swallowing an unexpected surge of bile, Emma hunched over, gripping the chipped formica table top.

"Hey, you alright?" Gail asked. "You don't look so good."

Nodding quickly, Emma muttered, "Yeah, I'm okay." She passed a hand over her eyes, trying to reassert control. "Nothing for now, I guess. Just want to sit here for a while, okay, Gail?"

"Sure, honey. You know to holler if you change your mind."

As Emma nodded, Gail patted her shoulder. Several other customers came in and Gail went off to take their orders.

Emma wrapped her left hand around the white, porcelain mug, frowning at the steaming, dark liquid. Unconsciously, she flexed her shoulder, trying to ease the cramp that sat just beside her right scapula.

Despite her best efforts, she was finding that she was completely unable to reconcile that dream. There was something . . . intensely visceral . . . about the images, the sounds, the smells, the sensations.

Sighing, Emma closed her eyes. *What the hell happened to me?*

She felt the table jar beneath her elbows, and Emma opened her eyes to see a young woman easing into the seat across from her.

"Hey," the woman greeted softly, then took a nervous sip from the coffee mug she carried. "Hope you don't mind. The counter was getting way too crowded for me . . ."

Emma glanced over at the row of chrome stools and noted the husky male shapes that were sprawling knee to knee. The one empty spot was already engulfed by the two offensive-lineman types on either side of it.

"S'okay," Emma replied, automatically sitting up a little straighter. *Damn, she's cute . . .* Then the warning bells went off. *Like I haven't learned this lesson yet. Like whatever happened last night didn't have something to do with letting a strange woman pull me into an alley . . .* Immediately, self-doubt crept in on the heels of that thought. *Didn't it?*

Unable to help herself, Emma stole covert glances at her companion. The young woman looked tired. The shoulders beneath her oversized oatmeal-colored sweater were slightly hunched, and even though her eyes were directed downward, Emma could see they were at half-mast. She was well dressed, in a relaxed, Sunday-morning sort of way. Her skin was a rich, dark, earth shade, with a rosy hue about her cheeks that made Emma wonder if the girl was blushing. Silky-looking, curly black hair was swept back from her face and held in a short, efficient braid that complimented her square-jawed face. There was strength in that jaw and, Emma suspected, stubbornness.

In the midst of Emma's contemplation, the woman raised her eyes and met Emma's stare. For a heartbeat, Emma felt shy, and embarrassed to be caught looking. Then, just as Emma's gaze began to drop, recognition hit her like a sucker punch.

She knew those eyes. Those wise, calm, brown eyes.

The Rott!

Startled, Emma moved back so forcefully she jolted the entire bench unit. The young woman quickly reached out and touched the hand Emma had locked in a viselike grip around her coffee mug.

"Don't go," the young woman said, her voice so quiet that only Emma's eyes on her ruby lips confirmed the message. Fingers brushed lightly over Emma's hand, then smoothed the tender skin on the inside of Emma's wrist.

For a moment, Emma couldn't breathe. Riveted, she stared at the stranger across from her, while her flesh erupted in erotic presentiment.

This is just like . . . Involuntarily, Emma allowed the stranger to peel her fingers from the porcelain cup. *Feels so good . . . electric . . . like . . .* Deliciously tormenting fingers were caressing Emma's palm. *This can't be. . . .*

"We should have coached you a little more," the young woman was saying.

Vaguely disturbed by her abrupt lack of will, Emma could only watch as the woman took Emma's hand in both of her own. A warm, tingling rush passed from the young woman's hands into Emma's. It was irresistible, and all-encompassing. Emma found she had to concentrate to make sense of what the woman was saying.

"When you went airborne so easily, I guess we all thought you were some kind of natural," the woman went on, her voice low. "Once we were in front of the house, well, we all get kind of freaked, no matter how many times we've been on a hunt. . . . "

Emma whispered, "Oh god, no. It was real?"

The woman bobbed her head once. "I guess we expected you to remember that the form is adaptable to what circumstances demand . . . ghost-shape in order to fly or pass through walls, only going solid long enough to make the kill. . . . "

Dazed, Emma uttered, "It was real."

"And necessary," the woman stated. "You changed more than one person's future, you know. This morning, a little girl will pass by that house and live to go home again. . . . "

Emma could think of nothing to say.

The young woman stroked her hand. "No more children will die hellish deaths at the hands of that man." Then, the quiet voice finished, "If that's a crime, then we should all be criminals."

Unwanted tears sprang into Emma's eyes.

"And I'm sorry to tell you this," the woman said gently, "but you'll carry the guilt of what you've done for years." The woman went on, "That's why you were chosen. You're strong enough to bear it."

Emma bent her head. Her cheeks were quickly wet. Fat, useless drops fell on the table top, and bitter, barely suppressed sobs choked free. In a rush of despair, she tore her hand from the woman's grasp, slid out of the booth and headed for the door.

A voice in her mind was nagging her about stiffing Gail on the coffee; another was shrieking "Murderer!" Above them both, one unquenchable voice was insisting that she should *not* walk away from the young woman she was leaving in the booth.

Somehow managing to ignore that last voice, she kept walking, pushing open the diner door and striding out onto the sidewalk. Agitated, she stopped there, using the sleeve of her leather jacket to impatiently wipe her eyes and face. She glanced once at her car, then turned away and trudged through the pre-dawn light.

Head down, hands in her pockets, she thought as she walked.

Nearly an hour, several miles and many tears later, she was no closer to coming to terms with what had happened.

Maybe I'll never understand any of it, she finally reflected. *Maybe the only response is this sickening feeling that I've desecrated something . . . my humanity . . . my honor . . .*

She stopped walking and studied the collage of yellow maple leaves plastered to the sidewalk by last night's storm. *In trying to stop darkness, I became darkness. . . .* Frowning, she knew that wasn't all. *Law and justice. Law is just words, a pact civilized people make among themselves. Justice is the Goddess's realm—a terrifying place. One I don't think I ever want to visit again.*

Someone touched her shoulder, and Emma gazed into warm brown eyes. "You followed me," Emma stated, surprised. Feeling incredibly vulnerable, she tried to get her inscrutable cop-mask back in place.

"Wasn't hard," the woman replied, passing Emma a handful of diner napkins. "You were walking pretty slow near the end."

After briskly wiping off her cheeks and blowing her nose, Emma sighed once, then stuffed the wad of used tissue in her jacket pocket. She looked over to find the woman watching her.

Warmed by the woman's concern, Emma gave up the effort to hide herself. "I don't even know your name," she said wonderingly.

"Lesley," the young woman replied, then held out her hand.

"Emma," she returned, slipping her palm into place.

They stood looking at their united hands, one freckled, one peat-colored. After they'd drawn out the greeting longer than really necessary, they both let go.

Emma began shifting her weight from one leg to the other.

"Why do I feel like . . . ?" she paused, unwilling to put words to so ridiculous a notion.

" . . . we're involved?" Lesley finished.

Emma gave a nervous laugh, then glanced away, overcome. At last she confessed, "Every time we touch, I feel . . . Her."

"Hekate," Lesley supplied with a knowing smile.

Giving a quick nod, Emma once more fell to examining the bright gold leaves underfoot.

"Well, She's in us, you know," Lesley explained.

Alarmed, Emma's head jerked up.

"Just a little sliver," Lesley added, a little too quickly for Emma's comfort. "Nothing to worry about, Officer."

Emma watched her carefully. "How do you know I'm a cop?"

"As they say, takes one to know one."

"Oh." Bemused by this piece of information, Emma found herself examining Lesley's slight but definitely wiry build.

"Besides, in case you haven't figured it out yet," Lesley went on, "we're fated."

Frowning, unsure if she was being teased or not, Emma watched the slow smile spread across Lesley's lovely face. "We are, huh?" Emma said softly.

In reply, Lesley leaned slowly closer, went up on tiptoes and then nuzzled Emma's ear. A small tremor of desire raced through Emma, and she knew Lesley felt it.

Close to Emma's ear, Lesley whispered, "After all . . . there are some blessings to being called to the pack."

She wound her arm around Emma's, then tugged her into an ambling stroll beside her. Arm in arm, in the Sunday morning sunshine, they began walking back the way they had come.

Curious, but dreading what she might hear, Emma finally asked, "So is this an every-full-moon kind of thing?"

Lesley gave Emma's arm a reassuring squeeze. "You're not a werewolf. You're one of Hekate's dogs—a far more ancient and lethal breed." In a half-serious, half-jesting display, Lesley made a soft growl that caused the small hairs on Emma's neck to rise in answer. "She doesn't call often. Only when the worst kind of animal needs hunting . . . " With a small sigh, Lesley ended, "And each time, you can decide to go, or not."

Emma nodded, considering. *I don't think I can ever do that again. . . .*

Beside her, Lesley suddenly broke into laughter. "Meanwhile, the rest of the gang can't wait to see what you look like as a woman," Lesley remarked, grinning wickedly. "You're a very handsome dog, you know."

Far, far above them, on the currents of a southeast wind, a Goddess laughed.

The Acolyte

Toni Brown

The families filed into the church, each member carrying a parcel wrapped in white butcher paper. The bundles, marked with the individual's name, contained a set of clothes. Each man, woman and child carried his or her own, as was the custom, and left it stacked with the others in the coat room. As the last family settled into their pew, the huge oak doors were closed and locked by the acolyte. The key was pushed outside through a narrow slit in the wood. This was a monthly sunset service at St. Luke's Episcopal Church.

The acolyte, wearing robes of black and red and purple, stepped out of the shadows and walked slowly down the aisle to the pulpit. As he passed the families seated in the pews, he held his head up, proud to be part of this enduring lineage, proud to be the appointed keeper of the key. The acolyte tried to push away the gnawing in his heart, the monthly reminder that this was as close as he would ever be to this Congregation.

A birth defect, a genetic mutation that affected one in every generation, had left him to be the keeper of the key. The birth defect that made him the only one to be trusted with this great task also separated him from his family members sitting in the pews around him. He felt their eyes on him as he tried to ignore the spidery fingers of fear closing around his testicles. Once a month he felt this fear. Once a month he felt the loss.

The acolyte carried a large leather-bound book, which he placed on the ornate rostrum. Then he stepped back into the shadows.

The body of the church stood with heads down as their leader entered from a side door and made her way to the pulpit.

"Please be seated," she intoned. The Congregation, never looking up, sat with a soft, rustling sound.

"We gather here each month for fellowship and the protection of these walls that we might experience the essence of what we are in safety and joy. I will read from the book of *Our Beginnings* to carry us to our moment of transformation."

She opened the book to a page marked with a red ribbon and began to read.

"And it is written that sevens of hundreds of years ago, there was a lone one who had fled the staring eyes and sharp teeth of his kind and set out long distances to establish a family of his own. This one called Grey-Back was crossing an area thick with trees when he smelled an animal but could not tell what it was. It had been many days since he had eaten, and so he altered his course to find what it was he had smelled. As he came closer, he found a furless female covered in the skin of the sheep, thus his confusion over the smell."

Some of the Congregation snorted knowingly.

"Grey-Back licked his tongue over his teeth trying to decide whether to eat the flesh first and the sheep skin next, or everything all at once, when the female spoke to him. He was surprised that the hairless creature could speak. Used to being last of the pack, he did not express his wonder at this but asked instead where she was going.

"And Grey-Back was reported to say—*speak the words with me*—'What are you doing in the woods so late and all alone?'" The Congregation repeated the words as was the custom, then quieted.

"And she was surprised that a wolf such as Grey-Back could walk on two legs, but she said, 'I'm not alone, my family lives just over there.' She pointed into the darkness behind her. 'And my granny lives over there.' She pointed into the darkness in front of her.

"It is believed that Grey-Back was mystified by this female, but also interested in filling his belly, so he ran in the direction the female had indicated and soon could smell the old one inside the wooden structure. He pushed the door open and found her in her bed. Grey-Back leapt upon her and satisfied his hunger. He buried the rest as is our custom. But he was still hungry, and decided to wait for the female to come, that he might be filled. He waited in the bed of the old one, and soon the female did come.

"There was a fire in the hearth, which made the room glow with red shadows. The floor was sticky and pulled at the female's feet as she made her way to the bed in the corner. She could not see well in the shadows but thought she could make out the old one's shape sitting up in bed. She must have heard Grey-Back growling softly in his throat and wondered why the old one should make such a sound. As the female got closer to the bed and her eyes grew accustomed to the darkness, she noticed how big and yellow the old one's eyes were, how black and wet her nose looked and how big and sharp the old one's teeth were. As if reading her mind, Grey-Back leapt up and pushed her against the wall, pinning her with his sharply clawed paws. He was drooling with anticipation. The female stiffened her body and pretended not to be afraid. 'You'd better make it quick because my family is just on the other side of these woods. My father is coming and he will take his gun and blow your head off!'"

The Congregation bristled at this passage. Some youngsters

whimpered and were comforted.

"Grey-Back's stomach growled; his breath was like a hot blanket of rot. He stepped away from the female, breaking his grip on her arms. The female closed her eyes. She felt a warm breeze on her face. It is said that when she opened her eyes, he was gone.

"We believe that Grey-Back was again fascinated by this female who could speak his language and was brave enough to be walking the woods alone at night, and so he hesitated to devour her. It is written that the female stayed in the old one's den for the night. She did not go back into the woods nor did she look under the bed where what was left of the old one lay buried. She took off the sheep skins, climbed into the bed and covered her head with the thick quilt. We believe she comforted herself by thinking that Grey-Back had been frightened away.

"It is written that Grey-Back was still very hungry after despoiling the old one, and hearing that there were more hairless ones on the other side of the wood, he ran through the darkness until he came to the clearing. By the time the moon had climbed to the other side of the sky, there was no one left alive in the den except a full and satisfied Grey-Back.

"As we now know, our father Grey-Back returned to the den of the hairless female and looked upon her as she lay beneath the thick covers. Grey-Back was no longer hungry, and with this need satisfied, the original desire to found a new pack was reawakened. The female awoke to find something large, wet and hairy climbing into bed with her. By the vile stench of Grey-Back's fur she knew just who it was.

"And Grey-Back did couple with her, founding the beginnings of the great pack that exists today.

"And we are grateful to the hairless female, whom we now call Mother."

The Congregation intoned "Mother" in gruff whispers.

" . . . and we are grateful to Grey-Back, whom we now call Father. ('Father.') And each full moon we cry out in their honor. Join together in their names."

The Congregation harmonized in a howl that lasted several minutes.

"This concludes the reading of *Our Beginnings* in the *Book of the Free*. As the moon climbs in the sky, I can feel the blood of our Father and Mother coming to claim us. Try to remember that we are safe here until morning."

The Acolyte backed off of the pulpit and out of the side door, which he locked behind him. He hurried through a narrow hall where choir robes hung, and quickly stripped off his own robe. He continued to the minister's quarters. The howling seemed to grow louder, and he hurried to a heavy door that he closed behind him and locked. He was out in the courtyard, his breath coming in quick shallow blasts. His heart felt like it would burst from his chest. He wanted to run far away from this place, this task. As he stood in the night's chill he began to shiver, but there was one more thing he had to do.

He could hear the sounds of their transformation but he had no desire to look in the window and witness it. He made his way to the front of the building and found the key where it lay on the stone steps. He could hear guttural cries and the ripping of cloth. Snatching up the key he hurried over the grounds and through the iron gates.

Once on the streets where the ordinary—unknowing—innocently walked, he slowed his pace and pulled a handkerchief from his pants pocket. He wiped the sweat from his face and hands. Replacing the cloth, he fingered the key. The street lights blocked the cold moon from his view. He joined the others walking toward home in the crisp autumn air. His fear soon left him with a lonesome, empty feeling that he carried to his darkened house. It would be a long night without his family.

In the morning he would return once again to the church on the dead-end street and let them out.

Pierced

Linda K. Wright

A woman your age! Getting your eyebrow pierced!" Terry's mother demanded an explanation over the telephone. "I couldn't believe it when Gerald told me."

"A lot of women older than me have it done," Terry had answered quietly, trying to be patient. "I'm not going off the deep end."

Her mother interrupted. "You've changed. You're turning into someone I don't know."

Well, Terry thought, she *was* changing; her mother's reaction just confirmed her own gut feeling. She couldn't share her new life with anyone, except Mr. Sims. No one else understood. She'd had to do something after Malcolm was killed.

"Mom, don't worry so much, okay?" Terry said patiently. "I'll talk to you later."

Terry hung up the bedroom phone and looked at the clock on her night table. Seven-fifteen. She raised her dark brown hands to shoulder level and held them there a few seconds. They didn't shake. Today the grand jury hearing would start. She was ready.

Terry had run out of the shower to answer her mother's call. Ordinarily, she would have let the answering machine take the message. But she knew she needed to prove to herself that she was ready to face what came today. Besides, the call could have been her lawyer or someone from the media, people who were going to help her get justice for Malcolm.

Considering she'd been a divorced mother for most of her three children's lives, she thought she'd raised them pretty well. Ronnie had served in the army and was now working in a bank. Gerald followed him into the service and, after he'd returned home, found a job with a trucking firm. Terry smiled proudly. Her boys had made a place for themselves. They'd fought overseas, then come home to fight the subtler battles, pervasive in a country that congratulated itself on having resolved most of its racial conflicts. Her sons had done her proud. They'd survived.

And so had she.

Still wrapped in a towel, Terry opened the dresser drawer where she kept her underwear. She wore only cotton lingerie now, as Mr. Sims had advised. It cut down on the risk of infection, although she thought the coolness of silk or polyester would have felt better. She'd also had to buy larger bras—a much less painful fit.

As Terry stood looking at herself in the mirror, she carefully touched her stomach, just below the navel. She knew she was getting heavy. Pounds that had never shown themselves before had suddenly appeared in force. That's what happened when people turned forty. She pulled her half-slip carefully over her navel, remembering the pain she'd felt when she'd rushed dressing once before and her slip had gotten caught on the small ring that she wore there. It wouldn't happen again.

Terry looked in the mirror, noting that her physical appearance showed little of the pain she'd experienced. She'd gotten a little heavier, but people still thought her attractive. They were always complimenting her on her striking looks. Her ex-husband—

now remarried and a church deacon railing against the sins of youth—always said, "You are one fine black woman."

While the army had given his brothers respite from the temptations of the street, Malcolm refused to follow in their footsteps. Physically he was a lot bigger than they were, but he was of a gentler disposition. He'd never seemed tough enough. Terry had done a lot of praying for him.

When Malcolm graduated from high school, he decided to work at a homeless shelter. Once there, he couldn't see himself working anywhere else. At nineteen, he still lived at home and over dinner would tell Terry stories about the men he met and their feelings of hopelessness.

He would have made a great minister. God, he had been a lot like his father, but he had differed in one important way: his innocence—that's what had killed him—his belief in treating others as he expected to be treated. Terry thought she'd taught her boys that not everyone played by the rules. She thought she'd hammered this idea into her idealistic Malcolm.

"You trust other people to be fair with you," she had told her youngest child. "That's a mistake. You hope they will be, but you can't count on it. Counting on it will get you hurt."

Why hadn't Malcolm listened?

Terry had learned quickly about not being able to trust. She'd married young and gone straight from her mother's house to her husband's. She had stayed with him long enough to have three sons in quick succession.

It had taken longer to make the transition from self-doubting single mother with a high-school education to capable manager of a retail store. She'd gotten her college degree one course per semester. Except for a few short-lived relationships, she hadn't gotten involved with anyone. Raising her three boys had been much more important.

Terry sneezed. *Damn, am I getting a cold?* She reached over to the tissue box on her dresser and wiped her nose carefully. I'll take some decongestant, she thought. Having the small bead in her nose made her feel uncertain about how to handle head colds. She reassured herself that she'd learn—like she'd learned how to deal with everything else.

After Malcolm's death, Terry had taken a leave of absence from her job. It had been tough getting out of bed. Late mornings, she dragged herself to the cushions of the living room sofa and stared into space. It had taken so much effort to get even that far. Why then didn't it change anything? Why did everything still seem unbearable?

Terry still remembered the last view she'd had of her son in the morgue. Permanently fixed on his face had been an expression of surprise and—what else?—shock. As if his last thought had been, "I was trying to help. What did I do wrong?" His clothes displayed bloody, ragged holes caused by the six gunshots that killed him.

Malcolm was leaving the shelter after a long day. The police were in the area answering a call about some drug dealers. Malcolm was big, intimidating in the dark. A tall, imposing nineteen-year-old black man. He must have told them he was just reaching for his ID. In the noise of the sirens, the crowd, the confusion—did the police hear his words? They said they thought he was reaching for something else.

Malcolm had made a mistake. He'd trusted the police would know what he was doing, would know he was no drug dealer, carried no weapon. The police made a mistake and blew him away. Two mistakes, neither of which could be remedied.

Terry picked up the skirt of the outfit she'd laid out on the bed: a black, two-piece suit with a dark blue blouse. For some reason, people seemed to think ten months was more than enough time for her to get over her son's death. She was still in mourning.

She put on the blouse and stepped into the long skirt, lifting it carefully over her hips, making sure the slip lay between her skin and the skirt waistband at the navel. She reached back gingerly to zip the skirt.

How difficult it had been, Terry remembered, after they'd buried Malcolm, to leave the relative safety of her row house. The first day she'd tried to go out, she'd gotten as far as the front porch. She'd stood there, unable to make herself move any farther. Her body wouldn't stop shaking. Finally, one of the elderly neighbors coming out to walk his dog had seen her.

"Mrs. Wilson," Mr. Carter had said soothingly as he escorted her back into her house, "you just come inside with me. No one's going to hurt you."

She'd kept trying to go out by herself. She knew she had to get better. It was the only way she could avenge her son's death. She had to be strong enough to face his killers. A grand jury was being convened to look at the case. She needed to be in court. If she were there, it would remind the people who had killed Malcolm what they had destroyed. Terry's son had inherited her strong facial features; when they looked at her, they'd see him.

When Terry had finally been able to walk past her front porch, she headed toward the Avenue. The bright murals and colorful sidewalk stands assaulted her. People were calling to each other, laughing. A few sidewalk vendors hawked their wares.

Terry was furious. Life hadn't stopped in deference to Malcolm's death. Tears blurred her vision; the writing on store signs kept running together. She couldn't decipher the names or understand what the words said. One storefront stood out for its quiet simplicity. On the left side was a picture of a proud, beautiful black woman, sporting large, silver earrings.

On the right side, in large, dark lettering contrasting with the omnipresent barrage of color everywhere else, were the words "Body Piercing."

The woman on the sign looked untouchable, yet she seemed to understand. Terry felt drawn to her. She'd thought about getting her ears pierced for years. Why not now? She was middle-aged and divorced. Who did she have to answer to? Most women her age had pierced ears, after all.

Mr. Sims, the thin and graying shop owner, had been so kind. With a light touch, he examined her ears almost before she'd realized it. There was no one else in the store and she told him her story.

"The pain," she'd whispered, sobbing, "it won't go away."

"Piercing cleanses," he'd said gently. He brought her a cup of tea from his hot plate in the back of the store.

"The needle excises the pain," Mr. Sims said. "It helps strengthen you for the bad times life brings to us all." He showed her his special needles. They weren't the disposable ones he used for the routine piercing of a teenager's ears. He kept his special needles in a carved wooden box, his long fingers slowly caressing each one as he showed them to her.

"You can overcome the pain. Just allow the needle to cleanse the hurt."

That first piercing—it had only been her ears—had given her the courage to leave the house more regularly. The pain of leaving the house had been replaced by the slight pain in her earlobes. The sites became infected, and Mr. Sims soothed them with unguents and healing words. He told her the infection showed how poisoned her system had become. He gently suggested that more cleansing was necessary.

Even after the first infection had cleared up, she was unable to stop going to the shop. Warm and fragrant and filled with old instruments Mr. Sims said he'd found on his travels abroad, the shop itself comforted her. Mr. Sims told Terry stories of places he'd traveled where the wisdom of healing was still alive. He helped her to understand that healing was a process that she had to follow to completion. He was patient with her fears. He didn't try to rush her through her grief.

Terry allowed him to help her heal the hurts and fears: the betrayal in her short, destructive marriage; the long years of wondering how she'd stretch the little money the boys' father gave her; the daily worry of what could happen to her boy children as they walked the menacing urban streets.

For each hurt, for each fear, Terry accepted another site on her body for healing.

She went back to work. She was even able to smile when she thought of Malcolm.

An ache remained, a pain so wounding that no matter how hard she tried, she couldn't erase it. She felt it when she set one place at the table for dinner. She felt it when she did the laundry and the clothes didn't make a full load. She felt it on Mother's Day when Ronnie's and Gerald's were the only two cards on the mantelpiece.

Malcolm's father waited in anticipation for a trial. He punched his fist against his open palm. "I'll make sure the grand jury gets those bastards for what they did to my son. An eye for an eye."

Terry looked at him. She'd always felt he was wiser than she about the way the world worked. Now she stared at him, amazed. His anger was apparent, but what had he done with his pain?

Did she not have repeated dreams of Malcolm's death? Did she not repeatedly hear those six shots? Did she not constantly jerk awake, tears and sweat all over her body? The tears and sweat of the fear Malcolm must have felt as he lay dying on that dark street?

She needed a final treatment.

She told Mr. Sims of the omnipresent pain that would not yield.

"You suffer deep inside where only a mother can feel," he'd said softly, sympathetically. "Your son was shot six times."

"And," Terry said slowly, "I have only had five treatments." She looked at him and understood. Mr. Sims had always instructed her that one must complete the process.

He looked back at her. "You must pierce the area. In the healing will be wholeness."

She wasn't sure she wanted to heal.

"You have trained for this," Mr. Sims said, with an insistent gentleness. "Your entire life has prepared you for this healing."

That piercing, deep inside . . . she didn't remember it now. Like the pain of childbirth, it had disappeared from her memory.

She told no one. They would not understand. She needed to do this alone. She knew—when she looked at the evidence of her cleansing, her healing, she knew—she would survive.

It had taken Terry a while to recover. The area had become greatly infected. Mr. Sims had explained that it was because she held so much of her pain there. It needed to be cleansed more than once. He had been very thorough. She would have no more children anyway. There could be no one to replace Malcolm.

Today was the first day of the grand jury hearing. Terry looked in the mirror.

Malcolm looked back. She no longer felt the pain. She was whole.

Silkie

Barbara Wilson

I went down to the sea again this morning, early this morning.

I did not see you.

Kelp only, bullwhips of it, and tangled lace, thick upon the shore. Once the people here would have gathered the seaweed into woven baskets, brought it home for drying. Made delicate soup that smelled of the ocean.

Now they eat oatmeal or eggs and bacon with brown bread. There had been a breakfast like that waiting for me. Mrs. Corley had made it for me, as she'd made it every morning for the last six weeks.

She didn't ask me where I'd been when I came in, windblown and smelling of the sea.

She no longer asked me what I'd be doing that day or when I'd be leaving.

I was the last guest to stay on at her bed and breakfast. When I first arrived, in late August, she mentioned that she always closed down October first and went to stay with her married daughter in Galway.

It was in autumn that the storms would rush in, nothing between the sea and the hills to stop them, Mrs. Corley told me. The storms knocked out power, the dark came early, the roads were unsafe and the neighbors far between.

"When my husband was alive, I stayed all year then. The farm was going strong then, well, not strong, but going. And it was a pleasure to be in of a winter's night, snug as we were, and to hear the rain against the roof. I didn't mind it. Neighbors would come by, we had our work to do, and the radio and books. And we told stories then, to pass the time."

I had no stories to tell, but I was always a great reader. I had brought many books with me, as if anticipating a long stay, and when I finished those I took a bus to Galway and carried back another bagful.

"Always reading," said Mrs. Corley. "And what is it you're reading?"

Children's books, I told her. Folktales, too. But mostly books for children.

This morning when I went to the sea it was not raining, but there was a heavy mist. I walked the path from Mrs. Corley's white-washed farmhouse to a dirt road edged with dry stone walls. There were no other inhabited houses along the road; only a farmhouse here and there with its roof collapsed, its red door splintered off its hinges or faded to pink, or a cottage that was rented out to tourists in the summer and now sat secretive and empty.

About midway between the sea and the farmhouse there was an old school bus pushed off the road, the tires removed but otherwise unvandalized. It was still bright yellow and on the sides was lettered SCOILE, Irish for school. In late summer, when I first began to walk this road, the old bus had charmed me. Golden flowering weeds and tall red-hot poker flowers had grown up around it; the windows reflected the sun.

As fall had deepened, the bus had come to have a desolate

air, mist all around it like a chill shawl, the weeds tall and gray, scratching at the paint. It always made me remember that this was the first autumn since I'd begun kindergarten that I hadn't gone back to school.

Mrs. Corley never asked me much about myself. Never asked me why I chose to stay on and on in a bed and breakfast in a western corner of the stony Irish coast. From time to time, when there were other guests, I'd said a few things that she must have overheard in the breakfast room, about having been to Europe once some years ago, when I was a college student. Now I was a school librarian, had the summers off.

I lied.

Dublin had been the last stop on a pilgrimage to many of the places I'd gone to years ago, cities where I had hoped and failed to find some remnant of my younger self. I was there a few days, then one morning I'd simply stepped onto a train going west and then a bus, and then I walked until I came to a sign that pointed to a white house with a red door. With a hand-painted wooden sign saying SEAL POINT FARMHOUSE.

Almost everyone else who came to Mrs. Corley's had come by car and because her bed and breakfast was listed in some guidebooks. They stayed overnight, rarely more than three days. They were on two-week holidays and had to see as much as possible.

They came and went and sometimes we exchanged a few words. One morning at breakfast, an older woman, stout, gray-haired and British, rather sharp and inquisitive, grilled me about my work.

"A children's librarian," I told her, aware of how little that conveyed. How could I tell her about the old elementary school on a hill, brick with worn wood floors that echoed late in the day, or about the long room that ran the length of the west side on the second floor, with its many-paned windows and its view of the mountains in the distance? How could I tell her about the books I loved to shelve—*Curious George, Caddie Woodlawn, Matilda*—or about my seasonal displays, autumn leaves, snowflakes, crocuses, resurrected yearly from a cardboard box?

"I'm a children's *author*," she said and told me her name. I recognized it of course, but pretended I didn't. "I'm here in Ireland to do research," she went on. "I went to Scotland and now here. I've been collecting stories about seals. I thought the people here would be eager to tell stories; that's what I've always heard about the Irish. That hasn't been the case. And I haven't found any actual seals either."

"Maybe it's not the season," I said.

"Perhaps." She told me about her husband and her grandchildren. I realized she was lonely, and unbent a little. Then she asked if I had children.

I hesitated, then said, "Yes. One."

She looked at my finger and did not see a ring.

"Divorced?"

"Yes."

"Then your child must be almost grown-up for you to travel like this." Her eyes, which a minute ago I had seen as lonely and in need of a listener, now struck me as cold and judgmental. I remembered that I had never liked *Badger's Holiday in the Cotswolds* and had thought, *I could do as well myself.*

"No," I said. "She's only eight."

And then I left the room.

This morning when I came to the sea the tide was out. The rocky promontory called Seal Point was almost totally exposed. Once there had been a large colony of gray Atlantic seals who lived on those rocks, but now they were few, hunted almost to extinction, Mrs. Corley had told me.

Only stories about them were left.

I picked my way to the very edge of the sea, over rocks covered with the leathery soft skin of the kelp. The sea was gray-green with a white mist where the waves lapped through the stones.

I stood there for a long time, calling your name. One of the names I had for you.

Silkie.

It already sounded like something lost and long ago. A story I told myself to help myself. A children's story.

I had to repeat it to myself, as I stood there on the empty shore: *No, you were real.*

Bad news comes by threes, I've always heard. This year I learned that for a fact. In my first misfortune I was not alone: All the elementary school librarians in my district lost their jobs at once. The taxpayers spoke and the budgetary ax came down. Children's librarians were a luxury and must go. The mountains in the distance would remain, but I would not be there to see them. Teachers, my friends already so underpaid and overworked, would help the children choose books and check them in and out. My autumn leaves and snowflakes would stay in their box. No longer would I try to teach the Dewey Decimal system or read a book aloud to a lively group of second graders.

I got the news on a spring day and came home in a rage. An hour later I could barely remember that rage, so quickly was it blanketed by something larger—as if a fire truck had arrived to deal with a sudden hot blaze in one room of the house, and had then hosed water and flame retardant over everything. Destroying it all.

"I know there will never be a good time to tell you," blurted Diana. "But I have to go."

Maybe she thought that, thrown off course by news of my dismissal, I wouldn't have the courage or the anger to fight back.

She was right.

My eyes blinked back shocked tears. I whispered, "Tracy?"

"I'll take her with me, of course," Diana said harshly, for she couldn't afford to be tender. "After all, I'm her mother."

Three pieces of news, all unexpected, and all bad.

Instead of anger, hopeless bitterness in a gray cloud fell over me like ashes.

You came to comfort me, though I didn't know it at first. I felt only what I thought was lust, the desire to be touched again and to touch.

It was about 7 A.M. when I found you sleeping on the shore. No one else was about. I'd woken at four, full of unhappiness. Dreaming of Diana. In that pathetic way of dreams, I'd found myself on my knees, begging her to return, sobbing that there must be something left: We had been together six years. I had helped her raise her daughter, given money, given time, given all the love I'd known how to give.

Waking, my mouth was dry and salty, as if I'd fallen asleep chewing a cracker. I felt self-revulsion to my fingertips. I had never begged, thank God. I had stood aside, in deadened condemnation, while she made moves to leave. In the end, because I couldn't bear to see Tracy uprooted, I'd left the house we'd bought together three years before and moved in with a friend. A few weeks later, when school ended, I'd emptied my bank account and set off for Europe.

As soon as it was light I came to the stony beach, to burn away the humiliation of feeling anything for Diana still. I came to scour out the longing for the daughter I had once believed, had been told, was equally mine. Underneath my sweater and jeans, I had on my swimsuit, for I meant to swim, as I had been swimming the last week, before breakfast, in water so cold it took my breath away and stopped me from thinking.

I assumed you were French when I saw you lying there, naked, without even a towel beneath you. Mrs. Corley had mentioned that a group of French tourists had rented a house along the coastal road. Your short hair was dark and your pubic triangle black as wet kelp. You were darkly tanned, without any sun lines, and lightly oiled, so that your skin had almost a sheen of water. Your breasts were high and small, your hips wide. Your feet were thin and very long, your hands the same.

The tide was out, and you lay lightly, as if tossed ashore on the smooth gray stones of the little beach between the rocks. To the side was your knapsack, made of a curious material, gray-black oilcloth perhaps, with a clasp that seemed to be of bone or polished white coral.

I couldn't help myself; I sat on your knapsack, stared at you in longing, willed you to wake up, and yet feared it. For I knew that once you did, you would look at me in horror, would feel, quite rightly, that you had been violated by my gaze. I wouldn't be able to explain in time that I was only lonely, that my lover had turned away from me and left me doubting myself and loathing her. I wouldn't have time to explain, for you would jump up and shout at me in French, something vile about *perversité*.

You didn't wake up. You kept on sleeping. Gently, like a baby. And gradually I quieted in myself, watching you. As if I were watching Tracy sleep, as I had watched her since she'd been a toddler.

"Could I have asked for anything more?" Diana had once said, a year into our relationship, lying in my arms at night. "A woman who loves my daughter as much as I do."

"Our daughter," I dared to say for the first time, and Diana drew in her breath and her beautiful dark eyes looked deeply into mine and she repeated quietly, "Our daughter."

It was two or three years later that Diana began to draw away from me, by imperceptible degrees. Did she draw away, or did something opaque and heavy begin to form, like condensation on a glass, each drop composed of some invisible wrong step I took? I never knew, and she would never tell me. "You're not doing anything," she would say, impatient. "I'm restless in myself, I don't know why."

All this I thought about and remembered as I looked at you and then at the ocean's horizon. Thousands of miles away Tracy was starting school and Diana was probably with someone else, someone Diana could feel passionate about for a year or two, someone who might also begin to believe that Tracy was her daughter.

When you finally spoke, your voice was strange, with a rough, fogged sound, as if you were getting over a cold. It could have been French or some other older language, like Basque perhaps, or Gaelic.

"Hello," you said. You didn't seem alarmed to find me there, but your large brown eyes were fixed on the knapsack.

"I'm so sorry, I'm sitting on your things," I said, jumping up.

But you never engaged in social chat. With you there were no introductions, apologies or how-are-you exchanges.

"Take off your clothes," you whispered.

And I did.

If I were writing a lesbian erotic novel, of the sort that had increasingly piled up by Diana's side of the bed, what happened next would be easy to explain. I met a strange foreign woman on the beach. Her nipples were hard, her cunt was wet, our passion flowered and burst before we had time to say our names.

It wasn't like that.

"Lie down beside me," you whispered.

And I did.

Your skin was soft and slippery and warm.

"Don't be afraid."

I wasn't. My eyes closed almost automatically, as if I had been very tired, so very tired, and needed to rest. All the same, my body was awake, and all my senses. I felt the stones beneath me. I felt your skin down the length of my body. I smelled the sharp dank smell of the sea, and I heard the waves rising up along the shore, heard them crash and pull at the stones as the water sucked back.

Heard the tide come in. It touched my toes, very cold, and then my ankles. Moved up.

"Don't be afraid," you whispered again.

And I wasn't. I remembered sleepily how my mother used to dip me toe by toe into the backyard wading pool, and how I taught myself to enter the ocean as a child: Foot, calf, knee and thigh, and all at once, I was in.

Like now, with you.

"Hold on," you said, and I held on, for your arms were moving in the water, powerful arms, and your legs were melded together all of a piece, able to propel us fast and fanlike.

Now you spoke to me no longer. I remember thinking clearly: I must not open my mouth.

I knew it was water we were in, deep water, and that it was dangerous to me, but safe to you.

As long as I held you, I would be all right.

I don't remember much else. No kingdoms of the deep, no sunken palaces or mermaids and sea horses. Only veils of green and dark blue flying past, thin as wet tissue paper, and streamers of golden light flickering from a light source high above.

No sense of cold or of strangeness. More the sense of being enveloped, held close up to you but also in my own skin.

Rocked.

Then we were on the shore again.

Had we made love?

I didn't know. You were breathing hard and glistening all over with a beaded sweat. My body was euphoric, dazzled in the sudden sunlight, wet.

I fell into a deep, calm sleep and when I woke was rested as I had not been in months. My watch said ten; my clothes were neatly piled next to me on the rock where I lay.

Your knapsack was gone and so were you. In the distance, on the rocky promontory, I thought I saw a rounded shape.

From far away you called to me in a long and sweet lament.

I had run out of all my traveler's checks by the time I'd arrived in Dublin, and I'd taken out a cash advance on my Visa card. It was a large enough sum to let me travel in Ireland for two weeks and to get me back to London for my flight home in September; large enough too that I wondered how I would pay it off.

I wrote Diana to tell her I was not returning in September or anytime soon and to ask her to forward my mail to Mrs. Corley's at Seal Point. I enclosed a note to Tracy to say I thought of her often and would have a lot to tell her about my travels when I saw her.

A week later I came in one day to find a manila envelope with my old house as the return address. Inside was the dreaded Visa bill with a Post-it note from Diana: "Call me when you get a chance. Glad traveling suits you."

And a letter with drawings from Tracy that told me all about school and her friends and ended, "I miss you so *much*. Please write soon!"

Mrs. Corley found me crying in the small parlor.

"There, there, dear," she said. "I've got the kettle on. I'll bring you a cup of tea. Not bad news, I hope."

"No, no," I said (though the Visa bill was definitely a problem). "It's from a little girl I know."

"Your daughter?" she asked, and it was the most personal question she'd ever ventured. It shot past her usual reserve.

"Yes. I mean. She was . . . it's hard to explain."

"But you miss her."

"Yes."

Just to say it aloud was a relief. Mrs. Corley came back with a pot and two cups. She didn't ask more questions, but began to talk on quite another subject.

"Have you heard the seal out on the rocks? I heard it last week a time or two and then again today. It's just the one seal. There used to be so many. Hunted off a long while ago. Just the one now and making quite a noise sometimes. There's some say that a seal sounds like a baby crying or a woman. They've a kind of human sound to them. Asking for something."

"For what?" I drank my tea and didn't meet her eyes.

"To be a relation to us maybe. You know a seal is an animal that can't be at ease, either on land or sea. When she's ashore she looks at the ocean, and when she's swimming she puts her head up and looks at you—have you seen it?—as if she wants to come up on land again."

"I know someone . . . a woman back home . . . just like that."

"They're some who are like that, they can't help it, poor souls," Mrs. Corley nodded. "But have you ever heard the story of the Selkie Wife?"

I shook my head.

"Selkie, that's an old Gaelic word for the seal. Selchie. Silkie. All those words are the same one. So, then, there's a story that a man found a beautiful woman sleeping on the shore, without her clothes if you can believe it. He watched her that day and others, and saw how she slipped in and out of the sealskin she had nearby to her. And he determined to steal that skin so she could never more swim away. He wanted to have her for his wife, do you see? And he did take the skin and hid it away, and she did become his wife.

"He brought her home and she gave him one child and then two more, and was always a good wife to him. But never was she completely happy, never was she at ease. Always walking by the shore, she was, and staring out. And from time to time she tore the house apart looking for that skin of hers.

"And her children knew that she was looking for something, and one day her little boy found it hidden away where his father had put it, and he gave it to her.

"And she was off. From one day to the next, gone."

I thought of you when I heard this story; but mostly I thought of Diana. Diana who had married young and had had a child so soon, only to decide, when Tracy was just six months old, that she had to leave her husband and find herself, her lesbian self.

Diana was ten years younger than me. She'd never had a job she really liked, had never held one for more than a year. She wasn't yet thirty, and yet she was convinced that life had passed her by. All the time I'd known her she had worried and complained about this, but in the last years it had come up again and again.

"I never had a chance to really live, to experiment, to be young, to be a young *dyke*," she said. "I dropped out of college to have Tracy and ever since then I've been somehow gasping for air. My head is just above water, my eyes never seem to clear enough to let me see what I really want."

I thought that I could make everything right for her. For both of them.

"You're so stable," Diana would say to me the first year. "What can you possibly see in me?"

A woman that I loved right from the start. With a daughter I could delight in and raise as my own.

"It's not fair," Diana used to joke. "How can I compare you with anyone? *You've* had half a dozen girlfriends before me. I've never had anyone but you."

"Sex is always the same, in the end," I told her, lying. "But love hardly ever comes along."

But in the end she wept. "I feel so trapped by life, by Tracy, by you. You know what you want. I've never known."

I never wanted to possess you, Silkie. I could have taken your knapsack, could have brought you back to Mrs. Corley's and made you my wife. Or just my new roommate.

Mrs. Corley wouldn't have minded. "Seals used to be human," she had ended her story. "Or maybe it was the other way around. Then we were separated, and one of us began to kill the other."

I could have tried to hold on to you, after you pressed me to your warm, damp body and took me where you took me, to some lush wet dark kingdom bannered and splintered with light. But you always left me on the shore, not satiated but complete, and I let go of you and slept and woke refreshed and quiet.

Even when it rained, even when the weather turned wilder

and rainier in late September, I went looking for you. I stood on the shore and called your name.

You answered and you came. You took me in your arms and enveloped me, so that the salt water was no longer bitter on my lips or stung my eyes. Until I had no more longing for what had been or might have been, but was content and was complete.

I called Diana a few days ago. Since then I have been looking for you every morning and haven't found you. This morning I went earlier, hoped to find you sleeping with your knapsack a few feet away. Imagined sitting on your sealskin and capturing you.

I can understand why you would stay away.

Two weeks ago I wrote to Tracy, a long letter all about the travels that brought me to the Irish coast. Back came another letter from her, large-lettered and urgent. "When are you coming back?" she wrote, and then, "We MISS you."

I called Diana. She was hesitant. Things were pretty good, she said. They had roommates in the house to make the mortgage. "A couple," she said. "I watch them and I'm both envious and not. My life's so busy now, I don't want to be involved. I've gone back to community college. I'm going to finish my degree. I will! So I'm in school every evening."

"Diana, that's great!" I said, without another thought. "But . . . Tracy?"

"Baby-sitters, or Helen and Tina keep an eye out for her. It's not the best, but . . . "

I wanted to say, "Let me come back. I'll take care of her every night." My heart broke to think of my Tracy all alone.

"She misses you something terrible," Diana said. "I'm just not the same, even when I am home. It was a world you shared, books, games, magic things I didn't even know about. I always thought it was because you worked in the schools, were a librarian, that you had some special way with kids. You know," she paused and sighed, "I was always a little jealous of you. The fun you could have with

Tracy while I sat and stewed about all the things in life I was losing out on."

A pause. Then, low, she asked, "When will you . . . will you . . . ?"

I won't deny that it was tempting. To say, "I'm coming home. Let me back in your life again."

"There's someone else," I said instead.

"I thought so." She was strong. "It's why you didn't come back in September, isn't it?"

"Yes."

"Tracy will be so disappointed."

"Tell her that I'm happy. And I'll write to her every week and tell her stories like I used to. And I won't be gone forever. Only for a while. Till this is over."

"It's ironic," said Diana. "I thought I was leaving you, for a brave new life. And you're the one who found a new lover."

"You do have a brave new life. And I'm proud of you."

When I hung up the phone, Mrs. Corley was nearby, offering tea. "Was that your daughter you were speaking to, then?"

"My daughter's mother," I said, as plainly as I could.

I think she understood me. She said, "Well then, that's all right then."

I went down to the sea again this morning. Called your name. There was no answer from the rocks. The waves dashed cold at my feet. I could not imagine going in the water by myself to look for you. For I would surely drown. Perhaps you'd said good-bye the last time and I hadn't heard you. Perhaps you knew that I had it in my heart to leave you eventually and return home, and wanted it to be now, rather than later.

I came in windblown and Mrs. Corley didn't ask me where I'd been. I ate my breakfast, went to the parlor and began to write a long letter to Tracy. It was about Ireland and the seals.

I told her the story of the Selkie Wife.

Late this afternoon, I read it to Mrs. Corley, asked her if I had the details right.

"Now I see why you are always reading those children's books," she said. "You're going to write one of your own, and here's your first."

"No, it's a letter to my daughter, to Tracy," I said. "I just wrote down the story that you told me."

"But I never told you about the water being veils and how the rocks felt when the seal came up on land. You wrote that all yourself."

I was taken aback. I had.

"And you never wanted to be a writer?" she asked.

"Well, yes. Once. But I never thought I could. So I went to library school, and got a good job and was happy there."

The past tense had slipped out. I added, determined to be truthful, "I lost my job last spring."

"Then you're lucky," she said. "For now you've found a new one, and it suits you."

I took a nap soon after that and slept as sound as I ever had and dreamed of you. You were in your sealskin, but with your human eyes, and we were in the water together. For the first time you did not hold me and I did not hold on to you. We swam alongside each other, me with my arms and legs and you with your fins. We swam a long time in the shallow water and then the deep, and then you led me back to shore. We raised our heads above the water and stared full into each other's eyes. We made a cry that could have been a long lament; it could have been a peal of joy.

For everything that we had lost.

For all that we'd been given.

Mud

Judith M. Redding

Philadelphia Police Department Computer System
Log-on ID: Dash 5477 Password: XXXXXXXX
Case # 6745 Robert Frazier, age 57, Caucasian
Officer: J. Teresa Dash, 6th Detectives
Badge No.: 5477

Date: October 23
5136 Morris Street, Germantown, 14th district

Homicide occurred during break-in and attempted robbery. Glass in French doors leading from walled back garden was broken with a brick. Indistinct muddy footprints were found trailing throughout the house, and muddy palmprints were found on walls and doorways. Samples of the mud have been sent to forensics for analysis; prints could not be lifted from walls.

The victim was suffocated by having mud forced down his throat; medical examiner Dr. Deepak Mehta states that it is likely that Frazier was conscious during this and was aware he was suffocating. Mud has been found under his fingernails.

Frazier lived alone. He ran a small but profitable mortgage brokerage, which offered home-equity refinancing to high-risk borrowers. His body was found at 8:45 A.M. by his assistant manager, Maria Lopez, who came to his house for breakfast, apparently a Monday morning ritual. Medical examiner estimates time of death to be between 8:30 P.M. Sunday and 12:30 A.M. Monday.

Miss Lopez provided a print-out from Frazier's laptop computer listing the tenants of Frazier's rental properties. She said she knew of no specific enemies, but knew that many potential customers became irate after being telephoned by Frazier's autodialer machine. Miss Lopez also provided a list of past and current employees.

Carl Green, Frazier's next-door neighbor, noted that Frazier had purchased the house three years previously and done extensive renovations, including adding the French doors. Before that, Frazier had lived in the 4900 block of Morris Street; that house was converted into the mortgage brokerage offices.

Miss Lopez was unable to ascertain whether anything was missing from the house, noting that Frazier did not own many possessions, and those he did own could be classified as either furniture or books. She did note that Frazier's three-year-old pitbull terrier, Shorty, was not in the house or garden when she arrived. Fraizer's datebook was found in his briefcase: He had an appointment to play chess with a former employee at 5 P.M. Sunday.

Question: Who disliked him enough to murder him?
Question: Why was Frazier choked with mud?
Question: Who stands to profit from his death?

October 24

Frazier's chess appointment was with one of his former loan officers, Newman Hayes, who lived three blocks away on Erringer Place. Hayes now works in the underwriting division of a center city mortgage firm. Hayes stated that he quit his job with Frazier because it was a commission-only job, and he wanted a guaranteed income. Hayes also noted that Frazier's firm brokers a large volume of loans for his present employer. Hayes went to Frazier's house to play chess; they played and drank beer from 5 P.M. to roughly 8 P.M., when Hayes went home. There were no disturbances on the street while Hayes was present. [Note: This has been confirmed by 911 phone logs.] Hayes said that, in all likelihood, Frazier would have read "serious fiction" until 9 or 10 P.M. and then gone to bed. Hayes also noted that Frazier's chessmen were hand carved and worth about $2,000.

October 25

Review of the crime scene: Frazier's chess set, although scattered about on the dining room floor and covered with mud, is intact. A collection of fine wines housed in the basement is untouched. No mud has contaminated the bookshelves in Frazier's second-floor library; apparently his assailant knew to find him in his upstairs study. The bathroom is likewise untouched, although the bedroom and study have clearly been rifled through, with muddy markings on walls and furniture.

The "serious fiction" which Frazier was reading immediately before the break-in was a collection of stories by Argentine writer Jorge Luis Borges; specifically, the short story "Death and the Compass." The book is open and the pages are caked with mud.

Report back from forensics: The mud found in Frazier's house does not match the soil taken from Frazier's walled garden. The mud found in the house is river mud, containing a high percentage of silt. The laboratory's best guess is that the mud came from along the nearby Wissahickon Creek.

Call from Erie Avenue SPCA: Shorty was picked up as a stray in Laurel Hill Cemetery, and was identified by registered tattoo. Veterinary technician Hakim Aziz noted that the dog was brought in covered with mud which, even considering the wet weather and the dog's stray status, was unusual for a short-haired dog. Other than cuts on her feet, Shorty is uninjured. Miss Lopez has applied to adopt the dog.

Have reserved a copy of Borges's *Ficciones* at the Philadelphia

Free Library. Tonight I read "serious fiction."

October 26

Frazier's house was broken into again last night; the intruder pulled off the plywood that was nailed over the French doors. Found on Frazier's desk were a scattering of playing cards from the children's math game "24" and a torn piece of notepaper with Hebrew characters written on it. Otherwise, the crime scene is unmolested.

Detective Lenhart's background check turned up an ex-wife, Catherine Frazier, now living in Lancaster. According to Catherine, Frazier was the son of Protestant missionaries to Nigeria. He has a younger brother Andrew, but she is unsure as to how to locate him, and suggested that Andrew might be listed as the beneficiary to Frazier's life insurance policy. Frazier moved to his previous house on Morris Street when they separated; she was unaware that he had purchased a second house.

The Borges story "Death and the Compass," which I presume Frazier was reading, is a detective story heavily laden with cabbalistic allusions. The points of the compass, the colors of a rhomboid, the letters of the name of God all provide the clues to a series of murders, culminating in the murder of the detective himself: *The first letter of the Name has been spoken.*

Our contact at the Annenberg Center for Near Eastern Studies explained that the words *malache habbala* written on the scrap of paper describe a class of angels, the dark angels of destruction who wander the world by night.

Detective Lenhart has located Andrew Frazier, who after being sent to Africa by the Peace Corps, decided to stay in Sudan when his term of service was finished. A transatlantic phone call revealed that Andrew had not spoken to his brother in over seven years.

Mutual of Omaha Life Insurance has confirmed that Frazier listed the sole beneficiary of his $500,000 policy as Jonathan

Lozano, his son. Mutual of Omaha had no further details as to Lozano's age or address. Catherine Frazier says she knows nothing about Frazier having any children, and that the name Lozano means nothing to her.

October 27

Interviewed Maria Lopez. She knows nothing about Jonathan Lozano. She said Frazier rarely spoke about his personal life, other than to relate stories about his childhood in Nigeria.

She was not aware that he had an ex-wife. Miss Lopez referred to making money, chess, and books as Frazier's "three passions in life." He did not smoke and rarely drank; he was extremely frugal. Purchasing Shorty as a puppy for $400 is the only instance she can think of where Frazier showed any impulsiveness in spending. Miss Lopez did point out that Frazier was generous with his employees, giving them cash advances against commissions, handing out Christmas bonuses and giving the two long-term employees—herself and Darrell Sampson—a stake in the business.

The contents of Frazier's bank safe deposit box: $10,000 in $50 and $20 bills; an expired passport with visas for Argentina; a photocopy of a birth certificate for Jonathan Malachi Lozano Frazier, listing Frazier as the father; correspondence from Mercedes Ruiz Lozano with return addresses in New York City and Buenos Aires.

The medical examiner's preliminary findings: Frazier suffocated on mud. Dr. Mehta is unsure exactly how the mud was forced down Frazier's throat: There is no evidence of an instrument. Although there were lacerations and abrasions inside Frazier's throat, they appear to have been made from hardened mud. A clay funnel?

October 28

Checked with Immigration at Philadelphia International Airport: Jonathan Malachi Lozano entered the country on September 1, listing the Adam's Mark Hotel on City Avenue as his address. Lozano played in a ranked chess tournament held at the Adam's Mark on September 4 and 5, coming in third out of forty-five professional contenders. The Adam's Mark confirmed that Lozano stayed two additional nights before checking out on September 8. His expenses were paid as part of the tournament appearance; he paid cash for the two additional nights. Martin du Plessis, the tournament director, confirmed that Lozano had an open return plane ticket to Buenos Aires. Lenhart, Goshow and Strepansky are canvassing hotels.

8:30 P.M.: Met with Dennis Richards of the Philadelphia Chess League. Lozano is a top-ranked Argentine chess master, having achieved the title of international master at the age of fifteen. Now twenty-five, Lozano limits his tournament appearances; the bulk of his income comes from endorsing a line of chess computers and from tuition paid by his private students in Buenos Aires. Richards also noted that Lozano is an Orthodox Jew and is very popular in Israeli chess circles.

The second letter of the Name has been spoken.

October 29

Attempts to locate Lozano have failed.

A woman walking her dogs along the Wissahickon Creek found what she described as "an empty grave" about fifteen feet from the creek bank. Patrol officers from the 14th District checked with the Wissahickon Nature Center; volunteers there knew nothing about the hole. When Goshow and I examined it late this morning, we were startled to find a six-foot-deep rectangular hole, but *no displaced dirt.* Fallen leaves covered the grave's floor, but Goshow discovered several burnt pieces of paper and a charred card from the game "24."

Soil from the grave has been sent to forensics for analysis.

October 30

Soil from the grave by the Wissahickon matches *exactly* the soil found in Frazier's house.

October 31

Frazier's house was broken into again last night; the police apprehended Jonathan Lozano at the scene. Lozano was sitting at the kitchen table, drinking coffee, when officers arrived. He was spattered with mud. Officers found a life-sized mud sculpture of a one-armed man lying flat on its back on the dining room floor. Hebrew letters were inscribed on the sculpture's forehead. Lozano refused to give any statement other than he had the legal right to be in his father's house.

Before interviewing Lozano, I took a Polaroid of the sculpture's head—where the Hebrew letters were written—over to Dr. Ethan Hirsch at the Annenberg Center for Near Eastern Studies. Hirsch noted that the word written on the statue's forehead, *meth*, means death. Hirsch believes that the sculpture was an attempt to create a golem—a Hebrew zombie made of mud or clay. One writes the word *emeth*, meaning either life or truth, on the creature's forehead to bring it to life; by erasing the *e* and changing the word to *meth*, meaning dead, the creator returns the golem to its inanimate state.

Hirsch noted what he believes are two pertinent points: First, a golem can never be completely controlled, and inevitably runs amok. Second, creating a golem is beyond the purview of an ordinary Jew—only a cabbalistic scholar who knows the "alphabets of the 221 gates," which must be recited over the golem's various organs, can actually create one. Hirsch also said that only the creator of a golem can kill it.

Interviewed Lozano. He is still boyish, pale, with intense eyes and a distracted manner. He declines to give details: where he has been living, whether he knew his father well, whether he knew his father was dead, where the clay sculpture in the dining room came from. As he sits in the interview room, he plays with "24" game cards, flipping rapidly through them.

"Twenty-four letters in the Greek alphabet. Twenty-four ribs in the human body. Twenty-four books in the Old Testament. Twenty-four seasons in the Chinese year. The ancient Egyptians divided the day into twenty-four hours. Baseball player Willie Mays wore the number twenty-four." Having recited this litany, he looked up, gazed at me intently.

I said, "And yet there are 221 gates with 221 alphabets." No response, so I pushed the Polaroids of the clay man across the table to him.

"This was found, with you, in your father's house. Am I correct in thinking it is the golem you made to kill your father?"

He glanced at the photos. "Did you know that in Hebrew the word *golem* means 'nothing'? Literally, a being without spirit or life. Until one writes the word *life* on its forehead, in which case it becomes alive but is still referred to as 'nothing.'

"Tibetan monks who concentrated hard enough and for a long enough period of time could create a *tulpa*, a golem made out of sheer concentration that takes on corporeal form. A holographic golem, if you will.

"The *Westcar Papyrus* tells the story of an Egyptian magician who made a crocodile out of wax, fed his unfaithful wife to it and then sent it into the Nile. A Jew, of course, could not perform the same trick, as the Hebrew world is composed of three elements—*Aleph,* or air, *Mem,* or water, and *Shin,* or fire. Wax, obviously, is not one of these three elements. Numbers might be considered a fourth element. It's a concept that goes back to the beginning of time—gods are represented by letters, letters make up words, words represent ideas, ideas can be converted to numbers, therefore making numbers perfect signs, which are elements. The great Hebrew sorcerers taught the Egyptians everything while Israel was in captivity—Aaron and Moses and the parting of the Red Sea—

they just never told them God's true name."

"What about," I continued, "earth? Isn't earth the fourth element? How could one make a golem out of clay without earth?"

"Earth is corrupt, and therefore not an element. *Mem* represents earth, *Shin* represents heaven, and *Aleph* mediates between the two."

"What about the *malache habbala?*" I asked.

"Angels of destruction. A conundrum, really, in cabbalistic thought, because angels are supposed to be perfect creatures. Angels of destruction would then be demons and not angels. But then Lucifer is an angel who behaves like a demon in order to do God's bidding."

He leaned back in his chair. "I'd really like a cigarette," he said.

Goshow fished a crumpled pack of Camels and a lighter out of his jacket pocket and handed them to Lozano.

"Do you know what I think?" I said, watching as he lit a cigarette. "I think you made a golem out of Wissahickon mud and sent it after your father. I think your golem killed him by forcing its arm down your father's throat and leaving it there. And then you went back to the house, later, looking for something, found the golem, and erased the word *life* from its forehead."

His blue eyes regarded me through the scrim of cigarette smoke that hung in the air between us.

"Some history, Detective: The first golem was created by the rabbi Judah Loew ben Bezalel of Prague in the early sixteenth century to defend the Jewish community there. The golem has always been a protector. Why would I need protection from my father?"

"I think what you wanted were the proceeds of his life insurance policy. You wanted the $500,000. You wanted his money, but you wouldn't even use his name."

"For a black American detective, you seem to know a lot about golems. But you don't know much about Judaism. Like, for instance, that Jewish blood is carried through the mother's line. That in Argentina, one is given two surnames: one's mother's, and then one's father's. My mother comes from a long line of Marano Jews, Jews who left Spain and settled in Buenos Aires. When I was two, my mother brought me here, to show my so-called father. He wouldn't see her. When she was pregnant, he refused to marry her. Because he was in the United States and we were in Argentina, he didn't have to pay child support. I have supported my mother and my grandmother since I was ten by playing chess."

He paused, and ground out his cigarette.

"My mother died last year. I went to my father's house to get the letters she had written him. Once I had burned her letters, she could be at peace. And I would never have to have anything to do with him again."

At that point, Lozano's attorney entered, and the interview was terminated.

The last letters of the Name have been spoken.

December 4

Frazier's body was unclaimed and buried yesterday in a potter's field.

Lozano was released from custody on November 2 and returned to Argentina on November 4. He has not claimed the $500,000 pay-out on Frazier's life insurance policy.

The Frazier case remains open.

Keys

Ruthann Robson

Summer is driving down Utopia Parkway with the key. A ring of keys, actually, because more than one key has become necessary to achieve almost anything. And Summer wants to achieve something. Something grand and treacherous. Something stupendous. Yet simple.

Simple if Summer could figure out which key was appropriate where. If Fox were here, Fox could help. And Fox should be here, Summer pouts. Fox, her friend—or perhaps former friend—who used to be so radical about animal rights. Radical enough to rename herself and write a dissertation about the arctic fox. But now, when something can be done that isn't just writing a letter to a congressperson or buying an endangered species calendar or doing yet another study with a volcano of footnotes, Fox has gotten timid. Summer had sought assistance from Fox, but Fox had replied with platitudes about limits and risks, about her future as an academic.

But, Summer had noticed, Fox had mostly talked about her

new girlfriend, the Chief Veterinarian. How Fox could not betray her. How Fox could not disappoint her. How Fox thought she loved her, thought she really loved her. And Summer had thought, but had not said, how can you love a woman, really or otherwise, who is the chief veterinarian for an animal shelter? Don't you know what that means? She's the supervisor of extermination. She's a murderer. No, Summer had not said that to Fox. Because she didn't need to. She knew that Fox was already thinking that. She could feel Fox feeling it. Feeling the deaths.

It had been something Fox had had to overcome before she even went to the movies with the Chief Veterinarian. They had seen a popular disaster movie, and Summer had heard about the exact moment the Chief Veterinarian had put her hand so casually on Fox's knee. By the time—several movies and progressively more lingering touches later—they had fallen into bed at Fox's apartment, Fox seemed completely resolved to the Chief Veterinarian's role at the Animal Shelter.

Although maybe Fox hadn't gotten over it, not completely. Because Fox had given Summer the ring of keys. The ring of keys that the Chief Veterinarian had lost. The ring of keys that Fox had found burrowed among the dust bunnies under her bed, weeks after the Chief Veterinarian had given up hope and had replaced them. The ring of keys that Fox had simply placed on the counter between herself and Summer, not handing them to Summer, but not stopping her from picking them up. The ring of keys that Summer is taking from her van, closing her hands around them right now. Now, outside the Animal Shelter, after it has closed, while the sun still flares.

The last commuters, with their desperate strides, have long since passed by the back of the Animal Shelter, taking a shortcut from the train station to their homes, through the alley where Summer's van is now parked. No one lingers on the short street, the dead-end street, the barely paved lane in front of the Animal Shelter. The many who dropped off unwanted animals today and the few who came to "adopt" are dispersed throughout the suburbs.

The workers, too, have gone home to their suppers of cold chicken and coleslaw, including the receptionist who Summer had screamed at the last time she had been here.

There seems to be no one to spy on Summer, a woman who, if anyone had been spying, might have been judged as slightly dangerous, or at the very least someone who did not belong on Long Island. Most alarming was Summer's head of tangled feathers and tiny braids woven with pieces of fur, her patch of shaved skull as if from some surgical procedure. Her dress was not any more reassuring: It was the dress of an old woman or an overgrown doll. Gingham: the key lime green checks offset by squares of dirty white meringue. The hem had been made with pinking shears.

The smallest key on the ring confirms Summer's belief that there will be an alarm. After she gets inside, through the thick metal door, all she has to do is locate the alarm and figure out how to shut it off. And if she doesn't? Only a few minutes to escape. Her fingers caress the smallest key. Yes, the small key means it is not a combination, some secret series of numbers that she would never be able to guess in a million years. Nevertheless, she is sweating in the cool evening. A trickle runs down her back, blotted by the green and white gingham.

She thinks for a moment that she could simply walk through the concrete wall. Forget the ring of keys. Forget the steel door and the locks and the alarm. But that is not the way things are done. She listens for something that might tell her otherwise. There is only silence until she hears a train.

Once inside, she cannot hear the train. And she can no longer hear the silence. All she can hear is the screaming.

Terrible screaming. Not out-loud screaming, but screaming that comes from the inside. Inside her own flesh. From inside the marrow of her bones, that delicious part of her that could be sucked out if she were a meal. Screaming so intense that she almost forgets about the alarm, until the smallest key presses itself into her palm, and then seduces the little red box. The alarm so innocent, so brilliantly obvious, so metallically quiet in the midst of the din.

She is in hell. Hell will be loud, Summer knows.

And hell will not be filled with fire, but with wire. There are wires everywhere. Cages behind cages. Neat in rows on the other side of a wall of wire. There is a wire door in the wire wall. It has a lock, but the lock is not wire. The keys, though, feel sharp as wires in Summer's hand. She tries one and then another until she finds the one that slips into the lock as precisely as Fox's tongue must have slipped into the Chief Veterinarian on the afternoon she lost her keys.

Don't think about that, a voice says. Not Summer's voice, but inside Summer. Somewhere different from the place where the screaming originates. But close, close to that soft marrow.

Summer presses her back teeth together and begins to move among the cages.

She had expected the dogs. And the cats. But there are more raccoons than she thought there would be. And a few skunks; she hadn't really considered skunks. And a rabbit as large as an armadillo. Summer loves armadillos. The range of their voices. She doesn't hear any armadillos in this shelter.

She is searching for a large cage, the goal of her breaking and entering. She is looking for the wolf. The wolf with the one blue eye. The wolf-dog, a hybrid of some sort. Taken from Queens, driven on Utopia Parkway to this shelter on Long Island because the City shelters preferred not to accommodate "wild animals." Taken from the man who had kept the wolf chained in the small yard. The man is being charged with animal cruelty. The wolf-dog is being scheduled for destruction.

Summer is here to rescue the wolf, the wolf-dog, before it is killed.

Before it is put down, as the Chief Veterinarian might say. If she were saying anything at all. Even when Summer telephoned, pretending to be from a newspaper, the receptionist had replied with an officious, "We are not at liberty to release any information." But Summer knew. Summer knew.

And Kia, Summer's lover, had confirmed it. It had not taken Kia the lawyer very long to find the New York statute that provided that any part wolf/part dog animal was to be considered a wolf. And treated as such. A wolf and therefore a wild animal and therefore not able to be possessed by any ordinary person. A person would need a special permit and the Department of Wildlife was not granting those permits to "ordinary citizens." "What does that mean?" Summer had asked. "You have to be a dealer in exotic animals," Kia replied. Summer had predictably exploded into a tirade about commerce and exploitation and profit while Kia almost listened.

It had not taken Kia that much longer to locate the regulations and policies of animal shelters dealing with unadoptable wild animals. There was even a new regulation prohibiting the sale of the wild animal to laboratories as not being humane. *Humane!* Summer had squealed when she had heard that word.

Unlike Kia, Summer's research was not done with books, or even on computers. Summer got into her van and drove around Queens, crossing Utopia Parkway now and then, thinking about directions and maps, about places she had been and people she had heard about. Then she came back home and settled into a beige chair with pink roses, rescued from some refuse pile on bulk collection day. She started to dial the phone and to put numbers and names on one of Kia's yellow legal pads until she was satisfied.

"Havre de Loup," Summer announced to Kia.

Kia's language skills, mostly derived from the high-school Latin so beneficial during law school, were sufficiently competent to piece together the idea of a wolf sanctuary.

"Where is it?"

"Quebec."

"So that explains the French," Kia said, "but how will they get the wolf-dog? Is there some sort of program or something?"

"We are the program." Summer said. She looked at Kia for a long time and Kia looked back, neither one of them twitching.

Their love stretched between them, flat and heavy and taut. Kia finally closed her eyes.

"Let me decide on my own, Summer," Kia said.

"I will," Summer smiled. For she knew then that Kia would, that Kia was only making sure that she wasn't being overpowered by Summer's desires, that Kia was only testing the voice inside her head to make sure it was her own.

Kia turned away from Summer and suggested they go to dinner. To Lorenzo's, their usual restaurant. It wasn't until the door to Lorenzo's was closing behind them and Summer was driving them home in the van that Kia had said, "Okay. But it will have to be the weekend. I'll get Monday off or something. And remember I have to work a little late on Friday. I need to monitor a visit at the park between one of my clients, Joy, and her mother." Kia's clients are always children. Abused children.

Summer hurries now thinking of Kia, who will be waiting at the park when Summer casually pulls up, the girl in the park having visited with the mother who had abused her, the wolf safely in the carrier in the back of the van. Oh damn, the carrier! She left it in the van. Well, she'll simply walk the wolf back to the alley on a leash—a rope or something—like an ordinary dog. If she can even find the damn animal. Too many cages. All this wire is giving her a headache. Which makes it difficult to hear. To hear the wolf's voice among all the other screams.

Summer walks back toward the door, toward the alarm. From this far wall, she retrieves the largest size collar and leash on the display. Rips the small tag from the imitation leather. Overpriced, Summer notes. A small exploitation of the people who come to adopt the animals that would otherwise be exterminated. "You'll need a collar and a leash," Summer can almost hear the receptionist, her voice liltingly sweet. "Oh yes," the new owner will reply. And shell out some money.

Then she scans the concrete hell. Listening. Listening.

Suddenly startled by an absence more ugly than the incessant screaming. She walks toward the pool of silence. Past and through the labyrinth of metal mesh. Finally sees the mute animal in the cage and certainly it has one blue, unblinking eye. But it doesn't look like a noble wolf. Or even a mangy coyote. It looks excessively average, like a dog. Pitiful. But then what doesn't look pitiful dissected by wires?

Summer bends her head close. Listening. Hoping to hear . . . what? Not the horrible screaming that is coming from inside the other animals, but something else. Some majestic sound that will convince her that her risk is a worthwhile one. Some voice. Sensate and sensible.

The wolf-dog maintains its silence.

Summer shifts from foot to foot, waiting for some sign, smelling the harsh metal. That same metal smell when the man who was her father came to her fourteen-year-old body. He must have always shaved first, some flecks of his steel razor remaining on the face he pressed into her. Or maybe the metal was from the huge candy machines he kissed in order to make his fortune. His breathing was noisy, noisier than any factory, roaring in her ears. This was when she learned to hear voices, to hear screams. To be so still and silent that what was deep inside could wrap itself around language and vibrate into voices.

This was when she tried to bend back the cage of his body with her fingers until they bled. Too many nights they bled. And she tried to tell her mother about the blood running down her hands, but her mother probably couldn't hear her over the screaming. Or perhaps it was too noisy to hear anything, even your daughter, when you were cleaning toilets in the home of the man. In the home of the man's wife. They were always having a party. The man and his wife. And sometimes Summer's mother, one of the maids, brought leftovers back to the little cottage.

The metal tells her to relax. To forget. It sings the lullaby of denial. The suck of giving up. How easy to slip through the thin silvery wires. To curl next to the wolf-dog. To wait until it is the correct time to die.

The wolf-dog's fur is softer than Summer thought it would be.

Too much dog and not enough wolf. A wolf would have wire for hair. A wolf would not have been caught like this. A real wolf would be ferocious and have two yellow eyes that could burn a hole through the hell of the wires. A real girl would not let her father rape her.

Summer puts her nose next to the wolf-dog's nose. Summer inhales the animal's exhale. Summer sniffs the dampness from its nostrils. Summer puts one hand on each of the animal's ears, as if she is going to pull it even closer and kiss it deeply. But she doesn't. Doesn't pull it closer and doesn't kiss it. Doesn't have to. There is no need. There is nothing more.

She is in the cage with the wolf-dog because this is all she deserves. Or she deserves worse, really. Yes, much worse.

The man who was her father—although she didn't know he was her father then, didn't know until much later, when her mother told her—had kissed her neck, once. A little farewell peck. Nothing vampirish about it. Nothing wet or selfish. Just a simple kiss. On the neck.

And it was nice.

So nice that Summer had started to sob. She had not cried before, not while he was still there, anyway. She had not cried when she bled from trying to bend back the steel smell from his body. She had not cried when he had put his knee between her legs, or when his heaviness collapsed on her chest, so that she felt as if she would suffocate although she was still breathing. No, she hadn't cried. Until now.

And he hugged her then.

And she hugged him back.

She hugged him back.

She could hug the wolf-dog now. She was so close she could twine herself with the unexpected softness, kiss the wolf's moist black nose, cry in the wolf's muscular neck. She belongs with the animal. Belongs in the cage, waiting to be exterminated. Waiting for the receptionist, the Chief Veterinarian, the assistant who will administer the lethal injection.

Don't be a dry stream.

The voice is in her head.

The voice must belong to the wolf-dog. Yes, it is so rough and impatient. So wolf. It is a few octaves lower than the screams, but still a few octaves higher than she would have imagined. If she had imagined. Which she hadn't, not really. Not clearly enough.

Hadn't imagined being here. What would come next. Hadn't thought it through. "We need to think things through," her lawyer had said. A feminist lawyer, a good woman, a woman who took time with her, acting almost as a therapist instead of as a lawyer. The feminist lawyer who had taken her case. Had sued the man who was her father, the man who sexually abused her, the man with a lot of money who should give her some. And he did. He did. The feminist lawyer settled the case for a comfortable sum. A sum that made everyone feel comfortable. A sum that was supposed to help Summer feel as if she wasn't still in the cage of him.

She was supposed to be the alpha wolf. Yes, that's what she had imagined. Was supposed to be a leader. In control. Inspire confidence. Be someone to follow. And then lead them both out of here.

She wasn't supposed to be in a cage.

Not anymore.

Never.

Summer feels the keys in her hand. Sharp keys. Heavy keys. But none of them call out to her to fit the lock of the cage. Because there is no lock. Just a latch. A simple latch.

Summer snorts.

The wolf-dog remains sullen, biting at a paw that does not have fingers, a paw that can tear and scratch but not unlatch.

Summer opens the door of the cage.

The wolf-dog does not lunge. Summer flattens her palm toward the wolf-dog. Commands "come." The wolf-dog doesn't move.

They repeat their dance.

Flat palm.

"Come."

Motionlessness.

Summer reaches into the cage. Bares her own teeth. Pulls the wolf-dog by the scruff of the neck. Slips the collar over its head. Tugs on the attached leash.

No.

The wolf-dog's voice is less impatient than before, more determined.

"Listen," Summer says in her best alpha-wolf voice, "we are leaving this place before you get killed. You don't want to have a short life spent in a goddamn cage, do you?"

Others.

"Oh, this is a fine fucking time for charity. We can't perform the rescue of the century."

Though now, once she has heard the voice over the screams, has the idea in the spaces between the screams, she knows she cannot free only the wolf-dog.

And besides, this will be more sensible. It won't point so directly toward a search for the wolf-dog. It will seem more accidental. Inexplicable. All the animals escaped. Found a set of keys under the bed and the raccoons opened all the locks. Or maybe a fire? Can one set hell on fire? All this steel and concrete? Even if . . . no, too dangerous.

But it is not the wolf-dog's voice inside Summer's head giving reasons and rationalizations. Giving a concrete shape to the plan: The rabbit first or last? The skunks and raccoons? Cats, then dogs? It is Summer's voice. Only Summer.

Only Summer, admiring the lope of the wolf-dog as she guides it out the door, down the lane, back to the alley, into the van. What once were screams inside Summer are now howls and yelps, outside the world of the wires. Summer is surrounded by the sounds of trapped animals enjoying their escape, even if it proves temporary.

Maybe all escapes are temporary.

Maybe not.

Summer asks the wolf-dog what it thinks as she navigates the van on the crowded highway, toward the waiting Kia and the girl Joy.

It doesn't answer.

"Don't be a dry stream," Summer says, smiling.

She wonders how a wolf-dog smiles. If she could twist around and see inside the carrier, could she tell if the animal was smiling? Or is the carrier too much like a cage for the wolf-dog to smile? How can she tell it about the plan to transport it to Quebec? To a place where it can run free, among wolves and hybrids. How can she convince it she means no harm?

Keys.

Summer hears the command, the question, the slightly less sullen voice inside herself and wants to laugh. Thinking of the Chief Veterinarian, and the man who was her father, Summer realizes that she—maybe more than the killer or the rapist—is the criminal, with an animal for an accomplice and a possible plea of insanity and a piece of evidence. She wipes the keys off on her gingham dress and throws them out the window, into the summer twilight, contributing to the garbage that lines the Utopia Parkway.

Vengeance of Epona

Susanna Sturgis

"Which one's the horse?"

Ha. Ha. Ha.

This time it's Dwayne, straggly haired Dwayne, third-string center on the high-school basketball team. Most guys only act like assholes when they're in groups—why keep up appearances when there's no one else around? But dorks do it when they're alone, because they want so badly to belong to the asshole club that they practice, practice, practice every chance they get. Dwayne's a dork of the first magnitude. I figure his parents saw what was coming and named him Dwayne to let fat kids know what they're dealing with.

If only he knew.

I glare down at him like the Witch Queen of Chilmark, my lazy-daisy hometown. If I weren't riding incognito today, I'd lop his pitiful head off with one stroke of my invisible sword. Dwayne adjusts his backwards baseball cap with both hands, then hitches up his baggy shorts. He looks over his shoulder at the well-worn path that leads to his parents' house, doubtless assessing his chances of escaping if I decide to ride him down. *Don't flatter yourself, asshole*, I think at him. He cups one hand behind his ear and makes a retching noise in his throat. "Step on a crack, break your horse's back," he sings.

Then he turns and sprints down the path, arms pumping as hard as his skinny white legs. His shorts slip rapidly south, exposing most of the crack in his butt. "Get a belt!" I yell after him.

Gal whuffles, rattles her curb chain and ducks her head to rub a mosquito off her pastern. The reins slide smoothly through my fingers. When she's done scratching, I gather them back, move my left seat bone forward and squeeze my right leg behind the girth. We ride on. I almost manage to forget the scrawny prick.

Asshole.

Gal settles into a steady trot. I simmer down enough to notice the golden oak and birch leaves overhead, the deep russet red of huckleberry bushes below. This trail meets the dirt road far enough down so you don't run into much traffic this late in October. They unlock the gate in mid-September, when the summer people leave, and after that it's mostly locals, coming down to fish or walk or watch the birds.

Gal starts dancing in place as I look both ways and see nothing coming. We canter around the bend to the right and the sharp swerve to the left, through the open gate, all the way to the sandy parking area. Brisk air streams along my cheeks. All the way up into my belly I feel Gal's hooves beating the dirt, da-da-DUM, da-da-DUM. Scrub oak gives way to stunted brush and bramble, which thins out till the only vegetation is beach grass, dusty miller and poison ivy. Behind the dunes the Atlantic crashes again and again, like applause in a giant stadium.

As usual, I ride up to the footbridge over Crab Creek. Its weathered planks are solid enough, maybe two feet wide, but there's no railing on the right side. I hallucinate Gal shying to the right and falling into the creek. Can't do it. So we ride left a ways to the best ford. Both the creek and the adjoining pond are high with rain run-off; the water touches the bottom of my stirrups.

South Beach stretches sandy and pristine as far as the eye can see. It's everything a beach should be. Right about now you're thinking how lucky I am to live on Martha's Vineyard, yes? Not quite. Even when the gate's wide open, there's a big, blaring, invisible KEEP OUT sign for people like me. Any fat female who goes swimming at a populated beach is a world-class masochist. "We're trying to beautify the beach," they say, "would you mind covering yourself with this muumuu?" Those are the polite ones, the ones who aren't wondering out loud what the horse is doing in a bathing suit. People who screech to a halt for every pedestrian in a crosswalk—for a fat woman they're more likely to gun the accelerator and steer straight for her.

Ha, ha, ha.

Ha, ha yourself. I know what you're thinking: You're thinking those people are boorish as hell but haven't they got a point? Pudge is unhealthy, and worse, it's *unsightly,* and surely I could lose fifty pounds if I joined a health club and stuck to a diet.

I got news for you. I muck out six stalls a day in the off-season, eleven in summer, and I bet I could work you into the ground any day in the hay fields.

On the other hand, I wouldn't give up coffee-toffee crunch for a million bucks. A million bucks *a year?* Make me an offer and I'll think about it.

Once the water gets too cold to swim in, the beach is safe enough. Way up ahead two guys in waders are casting flies into the surf. Gal snorts at an artist who's set up her easel just above high water and is studying incoming waves through Polaroid lenses.

"Beautiful horse," says the woman, peering over her glasses. "Morgan?" The braids hanging over her flannel shirt and down vest are one-third dark brown, two-thirds silver gray.

"Yeah," I say, pleased. "Thanks." The suspense is killing me: Is she going to purse her lips and wonder—politely, of course, which is to say, in silence—*Which one's the horse?*

She isn't. She studies Gal's cresty neck, broad forehead and twitchy little ears. "Ben Don breeding," she says, "unless my eyes are failing."

I consider asking this woman to adopt me, never mind that I'm twenty-one and self-supporting, thank you very much. Someone who not only knows a Morgan when she sees one, but who can actually talk bloodlines?! "Great-granddaddy on both sides," I tell her. "Mind if I look at your painting?"

"Be my guest," she says, standing aside.

It's South Beach all right, at least in the foreground, where sanderlings cast tiny shadows as they skitter up the sand. But the glowering sky looks about to spit lightning, and the cavalry is riding in over the water. The horses look like Arabs, their coats the colors of smoke and dappled sea foam. The lead rider, red pennant flying, skin glowing warm as brandy, is definitely female. I'm impressed. "Wow," I say.

"For now I'm calling it 'Vengeance of Epona,'" she says.

"Epona?" I wonder out loud. Shit. Now she's going to think I'm a world-class ignoramus.

"An ancient European mare-goddess. Not terribly well known these days, but at least one source says she's an aspect of Demeter."

"Demeter, as in 'Persephone and . . .'?" I never paid much attention to those Greek goddess types. As role models they pretty much suck. Their husbands treated them like shit, for one thing, and for another, they were drop-dead gorgeous, every single one of them. With my luck, I'd pray for love, wealth and a stable of my own horses, and one of them would appear in a sparkly cloud and give me a prescription for diet pills.

"The very same," the artist answers. "I don't exactly see her as someone who wanders the world tearing her hair in grief, however."

I'll say. All the riders in the painting are women—dark women, pale women, determined and fierce women; I bet the horses are all mares. My opinion of Demeter heads for the stratosphere. I'd love to gallop right into the painting and ride with them. Da-da-DUM, da-da-DUM all the way to Dwayne's house, then we'd circle the house, round and round, and Epona would issue an ultimatum: *Mend your ways, Dwayne Stringbean, or suffer the consequences.*

The woman looks at me. Am I blushing or what? "What's the vengeance about?" I ask.

"Well," she says, studying the painting for a moment, "there's a story that Demeter was pursued by Poseidon, the sea god, but she wanted nothing to do with him. She disguised herself as a mare and tried to hide in a horse herd, but Poseidon changed into a stallion and raped her."

Stupid, stupid, stupid. A nasty memory of my own threatens to well up from my gut. I stomp on it, hard. *If she'd been smart, she would have turned herself into a stallion.* "Take back the sea," I say. The woman beams at me so broadly her cheeks rise, and the skin crinkles around her eyes. I feel like I've aced an exam in quantum physics or something.

"Their horses are their power," she says thoughtfully, as if she hadn't considered it quite that way before.

This gives me the shivers. How much does she know, this artist? *Does she recognize me? Maybe this Epona was my great-great-hundred-times-great granny.* When I was about eight years old, I started crossing my fingers that someone would gallop up to my front door and tell me I'm the long-lost daughter of my father's secret marriage to a—well, what? Someone a lot more cool than my mother, the nag. I thought I'd resigned myself to reality. Maybe not.

The artist's name is Kate McKee. She invites me to drop by her studio, which is back in the woods off the South Road, within sight of the King's Highway, she says. The King's Highway is just an old dirt road traveled by walkers, runners and more prepubescent dirtbikers than have any right to exist. I'm up there all the time, one way or another.

Kate McKee watches a swell move in to shore. At the last minute it arches into a little wave and breaks. Her brush moves quickly in the fair-weather foreground of the canvas. The water withdraws, leaving a long, looping garland of froth that breaks up and blows away in the quickening breeze.

"Wind's shifting," I observe. "Southeasterly."

"Storm wind," notes Kate. She throws her head back, closes her eyes and bares her teeth to the sky. I think she's grinning.

Way out to sea the clouds are gathering. If I squint, I can almost see the mare-riders coming, banners, braids and horse tails flying.

"Most people," Kate says, "think the shoreline is just the end of the land." She glances at me, obviously expecting something. What am I supposed to say? "It's the end of the sea as well, and it never stops changing."

Everything I think of saying is monumentally banal, so I don't say anything. She studies me like the shrink my mother made me go to freshman year of high school, after I gained forty-five pounds in one year. I didn't need any fucking shrink; I just wanted someone to help me survive adolescence. No such luck. My insides dissolve and start rolling back and forth like a caged ocean. Gal senses my panic and edges sideways, shaking her head.

"She wants to get going," I say.

"Can't say as I blame her," Kate replies. She looks like a hawk who's landed and drawn in her outstretched wings. Not physically, of course; as far as my eyes can tell, she hasn't changed a bit. I wish I could read auras. I bet Kate McKee's could tell a few tales.

"Stop by sometime," she tells me again, repeating the directions. "I mean it."

"I will," I say. It comes out like a promise.

Gal and I find the stretch at the water's edge where the wet sand is packed hard enough to trot on. The two fishermen up ahead go up-down, up-down as I post, getting closer all the time. I imagine naked sunbathers stretched out on the sand, not a beach towel in sight, their heads to the dunes, tails to the sky, toes pointing toward the sea. Males and females both, they are bronzed, long and lean. I hope they get skin cancer before they turn forty.

Gal breaks into her best show-ring canter: a steady, slow

cadence, no stride longer or shorter than the one before it. The two fly-casters ignore us as we pass.

Most people stick to the paved roads, you notice that? They cruise along on total autopilot. If Will Shakespeare himself stuck out his thumb on the side of the road, they'd figure he was just another psychotic ax-murderer. When was the last time you picked up a hitchhiker?

There's more to me than meets the eye. That's a joke. I'm not a psychotic ax-murderer. Yet.

Horses see differently. With eyes on the sides of their head, they don't see so well straight in front, or straight behind, for that matter. Right and left they're fine, though their depth perception isn't great. You ride a lot and eventually you start seeing like a horse. You understand why a rabbit that breaks cover and bounds across the trail is scarier than an old Ford truck rattling down a dirt road with shovels, rakes and god-knows-what-else in the bed.

There's plenty going on off the paved roads of this island, let me tell you. Kids go back in the woods to drink, smoke and make out, just like they did when I was in high school. Not that I ever did, of course. Fat girls don't qualify unless they have hidden assets, like access to free booze or a willingness to go all the way. I'd go as my alter-ego, so to speak, just to see what I was missing. Grunting and pawing and guys barfing in the bushes: big thrills, in other words. Home Ick class was riveting in comparison.

Stallions and guys aren't all that different, except your average stallion doesn't give a damn what you look like, as long as you're in heat. Once upon a time, I figured that had to be an improvement, but having twelve hundred pounds of horse bearing down on me like a runaway locomotive changed my mind real quick. If I'd been Demeter, Poseidon would have been charred dog food *tout de suite.*

I'd half-decided Kate McKee was a figment of my imagination that had given me directions to never-never land. But her studio was right where she said it was, shining through the trees within hailing distance of the King's Highway. It's a cedar-shingled cottage set toward the back of a clearing that slopes down from the highway. It's got plenty of windows: three skylights, a slider opening on the west-side deck, and plate glass on the south, not to mention the three six-over-sixes in the kitchen.

The oblong windows on the north side, the King's Highway side, were placed high in the walls and sheltered by the eaves. I stood there and peered in. A big woodstove on a semicircular brick hearth dominated the main room. Kate had pulled her easy chair up within an arm's length of it, and there she sat, one ankle resting on the other knee, reading. She turned one page, then another. She chewed idly on the end of one braid and gazed at the fire, visible as pulsing yellow-orange through the stove door's thick glass window. She reached toward it and drew back a ceramic mug of something steamy. She sipped, still watching the fire, and settled the mug into her lap. I was entranced.

A few feet off to her left stood one easel; a few feet off to her right stood another. Apart from the chair, a square end table and what seemed to be the foot of a folded-out sleep sofa, the furnishings were strictly studio: utility shelf, file cabinet, another metal cabinet with a dozen drawers wide and shallow enough for oversized papers.

Preoccupied as I was, I didn't notice the black Lab till she'd risen from the hooked hearth rug and come growling toward the north wall. Her eyes shone green as sun through spring leaves. Kate sat up straight, alert but definitely not worried. Carefully she closed the book in her lap and set it on the little table beside her coffee mug. Rising, listening intently, she followed the dog's gaze. "Want to go out, Callie?" she asked.

I panicked. Around the house I raced, remembering at least to stay outside the perimeter of light that spilled through the half-open curtains and over the deck. Abruptly the floodlights came on; I swerved just in time to miss crashing into the left fender of a silver Subaru wagon. *There was no fucking way out of the damned clearing!* Just dense underbrush and oaks growing so tight that even skinny Dwayne couldn't squeeze through.

Had the door opened, was the dog coming? I was making such a racket that I couldn't tell.

Sides heaving, I paused long enough to realize that the white sand dusting the driveway, touched by the radiance from Kate McKee's cottage, was showing me the way out. A voice called out behind me. I didn't understand the words; I couldn't stop to inquire. I followed the white glowing sand through the trees to the South Road and, eventually, home.

I'm still kicking myself: *dumb, dumb, dumb!* Kate McKee knows; I know she knows. *You're paranoid*, I tell myself. *I've fucked up before and left no one the wiser.* But most people don't see what's doing handsprings right in front of their noses. Kate McKee sees horses galloping on the ocean. I decide to avoid South Beach, and the King's Highway too, anywhere I might run into Kate McKee. Surely she'll be leaving the island before the weather gets much colder, won't she?

Tell you a secret? You can't tell, you *really* can't tell. Cross your heart and hope to die: not a single soul.

Come to think of it, go ahead and tell. After they put you in the loony bin for having paranoid delusions, I'll smuggle you all the rum and Hershey bars a girl could wish for.

I can turn into a horse.

No, I'm not going to prove it. You think I'm crazy? If anyone else knew *for sure*, I'd be locked up in a research institution and vivisected, or worse. That wretched teenage fat camp my mother packed me off to one summer would start looking like the good old days.

I hardly realized it at first. I mean, I was one of those kids who never runs, she canters—da-da-DUM, da-da-DUM. Through the woods I galloped, flying over running brooks and fallen logs. I showed up for riding lessons earlier and earlier, so they put me to work: sweeping, mucking out, cleaning tack. Horses in pasture that hated being caught would let me lead them in with just a hand in their manes. Rather than go home to the family feud, I'd sit unnoticed in one of the stalls and hand-feed hay to whatever horse wanted to talk.

At first I thought it was just dreams: Thundering down the beach under a full moon, only I wasn't riding, it was *my hooves* the water was lapping at. But outside the house there were hoofmarks in the soft earth where hoofmarks shouldn't be, and I started to remember . . .

I'm a mess. In my dreams some nights the mare-riders thunder ashore and gallop double-file down the Quansoo Road, but then I wake up. *What happens next? Where do they go?* I'm dying to see "Vengeance of Epona" so bad that I find myself halfway to Kate's studio without knowing how I got there. Other nights Kate McKee points her braid at me with a knowing glint, and I gallop away pursued by a pack of green-eyed Labrador retrievers. They draw closer and closer to my hind heels, and I wake up sweating with my sheets wrapped around my legs.

At the stable where I work, I go around tripping over buckets, knocking pitchforks off hooks and growling at everyone who looks at me cross-eyed. "What's your problem?" asks Erica, the riding teacher. "You can't have been on the rag for three consecutive weeks." Startled, I realize I haven't nursed my Erica crush since this Epona thing started. It comes back in a rush, like being in heat.

Erica's built like a Saddlebred, high-headed and leggy. She has long, thick, near-black hair that she wears in a French braid because I showed her how to do it. Go watch her ride someday. It's like her fingers, her seat and her legs are connected directly to the horse's brain. She looks so good on a horse that sometimes I can't stand to watch. The rest of us might as well give up, you know what I mean?

Erica gives me free dressage lessons because I'm the only one she trusts to exercise Justice when she's unable. Justice is her Anglo-Arab mare, a gorgeous dark bay, a shade over sixteen hands. She can't abide heavy-handed riders who flop around in the saddle; for me she goes like a dream. Erica's off-island a lot, giving clinics and judging shows.

She also, believe it or not, has the world's most disastrous love life. Whenever she gets jilted, or falls for another married Grand Prix dressage rider, she mopes around the farm till I sit her down in the tackroom with rum, Coke and ice in two tall glasses and make her tell me all about it.

When we hit the maudlin stage, after I've pointed out how she's either repeating an old pattern or starting a new one that's equally unpromising, she usually says something like "You're so smart, why aren't you married?"

"Same reason you aren't," I say, knowing she's too drunk to get it, and if she gets it once she sobers up she'll think she heard me wrong. People hear what they want to hear.

Once I sober up, I get pissed. Why can't I ever say something incisive like "Hey, when's the last time you were attracted to a zaftig, statuesque or another polite-euphemism-for-fat female person? Like me, for instance? Supply and demand, honey; it's all about supply and demand."

One of these days she'll ask, "Why aren't you married?" and I'll say, "So ask me to marry you, why don't you." Then an atomic bomb will obliterate Martha's Vineyard and the world as we know it will come to an end.

Last July Erica came back from an art opening of a friend of hers and started gushing about the new gallery owner. A few days later I was sitting out front on the mounting block, taking a bridle apart so I could clean it. Brand new white Saab drives up in a cloud of dust, stops dead center in the stable yard. Woman gets out with great difficulty because her skirt is almost skintight around the knees, and matters don't improve much then because her sandals have three-inch spike heels that sink into the dirt.

"I'm looking for Erica Anthony," says a Lauren-Bacallish voice that could not possibly be coming from this wispy blonde. I glance around for the ventriloquist. "You're not planning to ride in that get-up, are you?" I ask.

"I don't ride," she replies. I stare at her. She raises her voice. I almost tell her that my ears aren't the problem. "We have a date," she says. "She told me to meet her here."

I catch on. I imagine White Saab Lady and Erica smooching on her couch, tipsily climbing the stairs to Erica's bedroom. My finger muscles turn to Jell-O and the pelham bit I'm holding drops into a too-full bucket of dirty soapy water. My right arm, side and thigh get splashed.

Right on cue, Erica appears leading Justice in from the lower pasture. White Saab Lady apologizes for being a little early. She doesn't comment on Justy's broad forehead, deep chest and unblemished legs.

Flustered, Erica rubs her free hand on her exercise jodhpurs. Her gaze darts from the blonde to me, back to the blonde, back to me. "Would you mind putting Justy away?" she asks.

"I'll take care of it," I tell her, meaning every word.

In the morning the Saab's passenger-side door is stove in but good, and there are some pockmarks on the right-rear fender and trunk that neither of them notices. White Saab Lady doesn't come back. I wonder if I've gone too far. For a couple of days Erica bitches about our neighbors up the road, whose horses are always getting out because they don't keep their fences fixed, but she's not all that upset. "Serves me right to try to get a romance going in summer," she sighs. "There'll be more time in the fall."

November closes in, two good blows knock the last leaves off the trees and the sun's grown so feeble it only warms your face between noon and 1 P.M. Ordinarily I would take heart from the fact that no human types have been hanging around Erica lately, but I haven't been sleeping well. I'm one hundred percent certain that Kate McKee is lying in wait for me somewhere. First I take rides in directions too boring to attract any self-respecting artist. Then, more and more, I stick to the ring. Erica arches both perfect eyebrows at this. "You'll be teaching the beginners class next," she says.

"In your dreams," I reply.

It's late morning the week before Thanksgiving; the sun is out, the sky is blue and I'm sick to death of sticking close to home. Gal and I head for Waskosim's Rock. Up there the trails wind up and down through the woods and across a rugged meadow. We make a beeline for the Top of the World, where you're ringed all around by the Chilmark hills and there's hardly a house in sight. Gal's powerful haunches propel us up the short, steep path to the clearing.

Big mis-fucking-stake. Kate McKee's sitting at her easel, not fifty feet away. Why, you may ask, didn't I come in from the other direction, so I could have seen her well in time to sneak away? 'Cause I like galloping up hills pretending like I'm charging San Juan Hill, that's why, and if you tell anyone, I'll deny it.

Briefly I contemplate wheeling around and disappearing back down the hill. Nope. Now that we're almost face to face, my terror seems even more paranoid than usual. Beaming like a long-lost relative, I ride sedately toward Ms. McKee.

The black Lab rouses herself from under the easel. Kate puts me on hold with a smile that says *wait a minute till I finish this little bit*. The dog takes a few steps in my direction, glaring with those bizarro green eyes. She growls. "Shhh," says Kate. The dog keeps coming, barking all the way. Her whole body vibrates.

"Callie! Enough!"

Callie sinks into a sphinxlike crouch. I am not convinced. Neither is Gal. She blows hard through her nose.

"She won't bother you," Kate says.

Right. I coax Gal forward with my hipbones and then with my calves.

Kate waves a brush at her canvas. "I just started today. What do you think?" she asks.

I think she doesn't go in for the picturesque land- and seascapes that keep the likes of White Saab Lady in business. On her canvas the sky is broody gray, not blue. Shapes are pushing through from the other side. Some are long and slender like pawing hooves. The trees are barely sketched; their skeletons lean into the west.

As I watch, Kate's brush conjures the lead rider, bare-breasted and dressed in black buckskin breeches and black leather boots. She has Erica's face.

I yank Gal around and take off down the steep path. Fuck what anyone thinks.

That night, and every night for a week, a dapple-gray Arab mare thunders through my dreams, with a green-eyed black Lab at her heels.

I'm in big trouble. Why did I have to blow it like that? If I'd taken a second look, it wouldn't have been Erica at all. I know this. How could it be? Now I'm so desperate to see "Vengeance of Epona" again that I get how drunks need their next drink, and smokers their next smoke. I sort of know why, but I sort of don't. You know what I mean? That painting turns me inside out. If I study it long enough, maybe I can figure out how.

The logical plan is to hang out in the woods till Kate McKee drives away, with that damn dog of course, then sneak into her studio. Piece of cake: No one ever locks their doors around here. Except Kate would know I'd been there. I'm sure of it. Even if she never said anything, I'd know that she knew. And no matter how hard I tried to avoid it, I'd run into her somewhere, like the post office or the supermarket parking lot.

So one dark, frigid December evening I park the farm's ancient station wagon in a vacant driveway two houses down from Kate's and walk up the dirt road. If I chicken out, I don't want her to suspect anything, right? Kate's lights shine almost to the edge of the clearing. The Subaru is pulled up close to the deck. It's so branch-cracking cold that I'm actually glad she's home.

Callie saunters over to greet me, stretching one hind leg and then the other. She sniffs at my knees, fixes her green eyes on me and returns to the woodstove, where she circles round and round before flopping down like a rag dog. Kate welcomes me warmly. "Of all nights!" she says. Before I can mumble a reply she offers me a hot toddy, heavy on the rum. I accept.

Her hair cascades loose over a spectacular sweater, knitted in intricate whorls and spirals the colors of sunset. Her navy cords fit like a second skin. Her gray wool socks look just like mine.

Once she disappears into the kitchen, I scan the room. "Vengeance of Epona" hangs, unframed, on the north wall, but my attention is distracted by its neighbor, on an easel close by. It's the canvas she'd barely started at Waskosim's Rock. Now the mare-riders swirl down from the sky like a cyclone; the lead horse's hooves have just touched a bleak and rocky hilltop. The lead rider's hair is blacker than Erica's, her face a little broader.

I imagine riding with them, plunging down with the clouds and streaming along hidden trails. We'd circle Dwayne's house until his parents pushed him, clutching his belt loops, out the door. *You decide his fate;* the lead rider's thought would appear in my mind without words. Possible punishments fan through my mind like so many playing cards, each more grisly than the last. I point at his stringy self, mildly surprised that my finger isn't shooting sparks. "Let him spend a year as a fat kid," I say. The women laugh and cheer, all without sound.

Two hands close mine, pointing finger and all, around a warm dark-blue mug. The rising steam smells of rum and orange and a hint of nutmeg. "So what do you think?" asks Kate McKee.

No—what do you *think, me pointing and chortling to myself with no one else in the room?* Kate McKee's breath is warm on my neck. She smells like wood smoke. "Could you put me in the painting?" I blurt out.

What the fuck did she put in this toddy? Something's pulling secrets out of my brain and broadcasting them in my own voice. I consider bolting away, diving headfirst off the deck if I have to. Too late: Callie has stretched herself on the floor between me and the sliding door. She raises her head, smirks and goes back to dozing.

During the next excruciating minute I begin to hope that Kate didn't hear the question. She isn't laughing out loud, for one thing. She isn't saying, or even thinking, *Come on now! Do you see any fat women in that picture? What do you think this is, a sitcom?* I sneak a look. She's frowning at the painting with lips pursed tight and eyebrows nearly touching.

"Look at them," she says at last. "I wanted all kinds of riders in that painting. They're young; they're old; they're short; they're tall; they're black and tawny, brown and pale. And skinny as rails, every single one. You'd think no one above a size six ever had reason for vengeance, wouldn't you?"

I think of Dwayne Stringbean, and White Saab Lady, and my mother's unceasing efforts to make me shrink. Memories coalesce in my belly, swirling and churning like nausea, only worse. My vision blurs, my center of gravity shifts upward . . .

Shit, I'm starting to change, right in the middle of Kate McKee's studio!

If I'm a horse, I can't talk, right? If I keep talking, maybe I'll stay in my human form. I talk. I babble. Whatever words come into my head shoot out of my mouth like machine-gun bullets and ricochet around the room. I yammer on about my mother and her diets, my father's obliviousness, all the Dwayne Stringbeans who ever asked "which one's the horse?," being voted class clown year after year, and finally Erica always sobbing on my shoulder, why couldn't she see that I . . .

The torrent skids to a halt just this side of a humongous stone jetty. My vision clears, the nausea is gone; my feet are still feet, encased in battered brown Wellingtons. My face is slick, my tongue bone-dry, my lungs burning for lack of air. I take a long, long sip of my toddy.

Kate McKee is nowhere to be found. The dog, however, stands whining and scratching at the sliding door. I search in the kitchen, behind drapes, even under the chair. I call Callie to the front door but she doesn't come. "Silly dog," I tell her. "You planning to jump eight feet off the deck?"

I pull the door open twelve inches or so. Callie slips between my leg and the metal jamb. I step through the curtains and let them swing closed behind me. My eyes adjust to the starlight.

In the clearing a dapple-gray Arab mare stands, her forelegs dancing back and forth. As I watch, she trots to where the woods begin, balks, whirls and gallops back, tail flying high. For a second she stands stock still. Callie squeezes between the deck rails on the uphill side, where the drop is only four feet or so, and jumps. In a moment she is racing circles around the horse. The horse is looking at me. She breaks toward the driveway and pauses, executing an impatient piaffe in place. Then stones fly as she canters down the sandy track, Callie loping at her heels.

I race through the studio, feel the brief heat of the woodstove, bang my thigh on the kitchen table and throw open the front door. I hear its latch catch behind me. Then propelled by my hindquarters I leap, stumble slightly and follow after.

Soon, very late on a full-moon night, Erica will wake to the drumming of horse hooves outside her house. First she will think she is dreaming, then she will know she is not. Swinging her long legs out of bed, she will smooth her flannel nightgown down her thighs, tuck a stray lock of hair behind one ear and go to the window. There she will see Justice—*her* Justice—rearing up, pawing the air by way of invitation.

Oh God, oh God! she will think. *I must not have shoved the bolt all the way home!* Wide awake, she will pull on her jodhpurs, tuck her nightgown into the waistband, find socks and boots and put them on too. Her hair she will tie back with a barrette, or a rubber band, or maybe an ascot scarf. Hurrying down the stairs she will grab her parka from the back of a dining-room chair and shrug into it as she goes out the door.

In the silver moonlight she will be reassured to see Justice nibbling at the paltry half-frozen grass. How will she account for the mare's bridle, a gossamer thing that never hung in our tackroom? It's there; she will accept that without thinking much, and even be grateful that she doesn't have to rummage through her messy old Volvo wagon for a halter, a leadline or a length of rope.

Justice will rub up against her, feeling unbound breast even through down and rip-stop nylon. *Why walk?* Erica will think, *Why not ride?*

Why not! She will consider leaping aboard, as she did as a kid and occasionally does now, when she thinks no one is watching. *No, it's too late; I'm still half-asleep.*

Instead she will lead me up to the Volvo's right fender, step up on the bumper, and launch herself gracefully onto my back. I will shiver at the pressure of her thighs against my flesh, sense the touch of her hands. With her right hand she will stroke my neck and scratch my withers lightly, ever so lightly, while I dance coyly a few steps to one side.

As we draw near the barn, with the single carriage lamp glowing to one side of the door, she will think, *Why go back to bed now? Why have I never, ever gone riding in the middle of the night?*

Taking my cues from her hips I will veer away from the barn, following first the dirt driveway and then the path that bears off at an angle and comes out across from the Quansoo Road. My hooves will rap an impatient tattoo on the pavement till they find dirt again. Experimentally, cautiously, because no one will know, Erica will lean forward and squeeze my sides with her upper thighs.

For joy I will run, pausing only to scream a challenge near Dwayne Stringbean's house, then race on toward the ocean.

At Crab Creek I will clatter across the footbridge and up over the dunes, just as Epona's mare-riders gallop in from the sea. This time it will be Erica who cries out to greet them while my hooves mark impatient time on the sand. *Ride with us!* the lead rider will cry, and we will fall in with the charge, long hair and mane whipping back in the wind of our passing.

Breech Birth

Meredith S. Baird

I was born April Fools' Day. One minute after midnight. That was some joke on my Mama, they said. They said she took one look at me and started to scream. Didn't stop until the doctor stuck a needle into her and made her go to sleep. But that's not true. Mama was so tired, she went to sleep long before I found my way out of her.

I was inside Mama for as long as I could remember. Hot. Wet. Dark. Safe. Safe until that day, that April Fools' Day when, without warning, the rubbery walls around me quivered, shuddered, caved in on me. The warm fluid I'd floated in for so long flooded past me, left me behind—crushed deep inside her. I couldn't breathe. After a while—not too long—I didn't want to breathe. I just wanted to stay with Mama. To go to sleep like she did. I linked my mind with hers and welcomed the darkness.

But they wouldn't leave me alone. Not then. They didn't want to leave me alone until after it was too late.

Pain exploded through my body, ripped me from my peaceful

retreat. Barbed fingers gripped both sides of my head, clamped into the soft, defenseless tissue. My skin and bones dented, then tore. Hooked like a fish, I fought to get away, but the claws dug deeper into my flesh, paralyzed me with pain. Helpless with shock and fear, consumed by exhaustion, I gave up.

They dragged me through my mother, tore me from her body, swung me by my legs through the cold air.

Silence.

Then it started. One nurse screamed. Another. And another. The shrill chorus of voices splintered inside my head. My body jackknifed, tried to get back to Mama.

But Mama was asleep. She slept on and on. That's how I know all those stories about her carrying on weren't true.

They couldn't be.

My mama didn't scream until the next morning when she woke up and they brought me in to her.

The holes from the forceps were all covered up in a pink knit hat pulled down to the tip of my nose, but it didn't hinder me none. I recognized Mama right off. The warm, sweet-powder scent of her welcomed me into the room. Mama took me from the nurse and scolded her for covering my face. Then she fitted me close against her body and pushed my cap up.

That's when Mama screamed.

I never found out what scared her so. She didn't know about my tongue yet—how it was so little they could barely see it twitch and wag at the back of my mouth. My arms—what Mama always called my arms—were hidden under the blanket the nurses wrapped around me. I felt the little flaps strain toward her. Sort of how a flower turns to the sun. Sometimes I think it was the way my skin grew smooth and tight over where my eyes should be.

But there was no time to wonder about such things right then.

The door banged open. Footsteps pounded into the room. An angry voice, a man, demanded to know what was going on. It was the doctor. I remembered his voice from the delivery room, the sharp, nasty smell that covered his hands. He cussed at the nurse for taking me out of where he'd hidden me. For bringing me in here. For letting Mama see me. The nurse started to cry. She sounded so sad. Like her heart was broken. Then she said something soft and quiet about Mama having the right to know. The doctor cussed at her again and told her to get out and not let anyone in the room.

The nurse was still crying as she obeyed the doctor. I heard her stumble and then felt the bed shake. She must have grabbed hold of it to steady herself. "I'm so sorry," she said to my mother. She started to say something more, but the doctor shouted at her to get out. I listened as her soft footsteps faded away from the bed. The door slammed shut. It was quiet now. Mama had stopped screaming when the doctor came in. She lay very still in the bed, barely breathing. Her arms pressed me into her covered breast.

"What happened to my baby, Tom?" she asked the doctor. Her voice was flat. Matter-of-fact. She could have been asking about the weather. Only her heart, a battering ram against my cheek, gave her true feelings away.

"I . . . I don't know, Evvie," he said. He started to say something else, but Mama cut him off.

"What went wrong?" she said. Her voice had changed. It was harder. Direct. The heat of her body radiated through the thin blanket wrapped around me. I stiffened slightly, sensed danger in the room. "You know, don't you?"

"There's no way of knowing, Evvie," he said. His voice trembled slightly. A sour smell reached off his body. Fear.

"I told you how dangerous it was for you to have a baby—much less your first—at your age. Forty-eight is just too old. Too risky."

"You made me believe *I* was the one in danger, Tom. Not my baby." Mama held me tighter. My heartbeats equaled hers now. I matched her breath for breath. I'd shared all her emotions for the last nine months. Her life was my life. She was all I knew.

"You're wrong, Evvie," he insisted. "I told you. You just wouldn't listen because of Carl."

"That's right, Tom," she said. "We all knew how bad Carl's cancer was. This child's daddy is dead and she's all I have left of him. Carl couldn't even hold on long enough to see her." A terrible sorrow weighed down the anger in her voice. I'd shared this sadness in her for as long as I could remember.

The doctor must have sensed she was weakening. That this was his one chance to get through to her.

"Listen to me, Evvie," he said. His voice was soft and gentle. Every sense I owned screamed *danger*. For the first time, I wasn't in sync with my mother. She'd turned inside herself. Given over to the grief. He continued, lulled her with his sympathy.

"Evvie, I want you to think of Carl now. How he would have protected you and done the right thing by this poor baby." Mama picked up her head. The doctor continued. His voice took on a positive, persuasive tone. "Let me take the baby away, Evvie. You can't hope to make her any kind of a life. You don't know the half of what went haywire here."

Mama shifted me in her arms, brought me up closer to her face. Her breath, faintly scented with orange from her morning juice, warmed my cheek. Despite the comfort I felt in her closeness, it was the veiled menace in the doctor's voice that dominated the room.

"You know I'm right, Evvie," he continued. "Carl, who's up in heaven crying for you to send his baby to him, knows I'm right."

Mama turned away from him, shielded me between her shoulder and the crook of her arm. Her hot tears splashed on to my face.

"This is my child, Tom. My only child," she replied in a desperate voice. "There must be some kind of operation you can do. Some medicine she can take."

"There's nothing, Evvie," he replied impatiently. "Just give me the baby. You know how the people are in this town. What they'd say. What they might do. I'll take care of that fool nurse.

No one will ever have to know."

"*I'll know*, Tom," Mama shouted at him. She sat bolt upright, pressed me deeper into her shoulder. Fury forced her voice into hard, sharp points. "I'll know for the rest of my life."

"Evvie," he started, but Mama wasn't finished.

"Are you talking about murdering my child, Tom," she said, "or are you just planning on some fancy experiments?" Deadly silence hung in the air.

"You shouldn't have said that, Evvie."

Heavy footsteps charged toward the bed. Mama clutched me against her but his hands, like the forceps, were too strong for her. His fingers dug into my body, tore me from my mother's grasp. She cried out for me. I replied—a strangled whimper all I could force from my malformed throat. The doctor turned me in his hands, stripped the blanket from my naked body and thrust me toward Mama's face.

"You think an operation or a few pills can fix this abomination?" he shouted at her.

Her breathing faltered, stopped. "Oh, my God," she whispered.

The cold air assaulted my dangling body. I didn't understand what was going on—only that I had to return to the safe place he'd ripped me from. I whimpered, reached for the sound of Mama's voice.

"Give her back, Tom," she said.

"You have to listen to reason, Evvie."

"Hand over my daughter." Her voice was final.

The doctor sighed and passed me to Mama. Her reassuring scent surrounded me as she snugged the blanket around my body.

"You're safe with me, little one." She cupped her hand around my chin and pressed her lips to my cheek

A shock racketed through me, shattered inside my head. Mama cried out and reared back against her pillow. I opened my mouth, tried to get some air, but Mama's hand slipped up and clamped firm across my lips.

That's when it happened.

Something took hold of me, slammed me into a new place. The horror of being torn from my Mama again was almost unbearable. My senses dimmed out as I struggled against this new outrage. I knew Mama was somewhere nearby. I could hear her cry, her voice thin and distant—more like something in a dream. I couldn't feel her against me. An intolerable heaviness overwhelmed me, engulfed me from all sides. I struck out against the intense pressure, tried to make room. My boundaries shifted slightly, then clamped back down.

Terrible as the defeat was, I had to try again. The brief instant my prison had relaxed, I'd been close to Mama. I could smell her, hear her. She was on the other side.

I rested for a moment, gathered strength. I knew what I had to do. I pushed harder. The barrier resisted, then relaxed a bit. I slipped into the tiny space, expanded.

"My head. Make it stop, Tom."

It was Mama. I could hear her plain as can be.

Mama, I cried out. I rammed the barricade, determined to get to her. A tremor shuddered around me, threatened to crush me.

"The pain," Mama moaned. "The pain. The voice. What's happening to me?"

That's when I knew.

It's me, Mama. Your daughter. Carly Hope.

Silence.

Mama?

No one knew that name. Carl and I picked it out right before he died. I didn't tell anyone.

I heard you, Mama. I heard everything.

It's not possible. I must be having a spell from the shock.

You've been talking to me for as long as I can remember, Mama. Papa, too. I talked back. You just couldn't hear me.

How can I hear you now? How can you speak? How can you hear me?

I don't rightly know, Mama. They took me away from you. I had to get back.

"Open your eyes, Evvie. Look at me."

I shifted slightly at the sound of the doctor's voice, melted into my surroundings.

Mama lifted her eyelids real slow, like she was trying them for the first time.

"Are you alright, Evvie?" The doctor crouched down, blue eyes all squinted up. He stared at Mama. At us. His face was long and thin, like his body. Brown hair curled over his forehead and joined the heavy beard that bristled across his cheeks, leaped off his chin.

I can see him, Mama. I can see him through you.

The colors pulled me. Bands of colors—deep blues, greens, purples—twisted and shivered around his face. The colors told me all about him. He cared about Mama. He never meant me any harm. He only wanted to protect Mama from being hurt.

It's okay, Mama. He wants to help us. Look at his colors.

I believe you, Carly Hope. I don't know yet if you're real or something I've dreamed, but I'm thankful for this gift.

"I'm fine, Tom. Just fine." She—we—looked down at the limp body of the baby she held, the shallow rise and fall of the stomach the only movement. No colors bounced around the baby. Nothing was in it. I could feel Mama's mouth turn up in a smile. "My head went swimmy for a minute is all."

I was back with Mama, alright. I was in Mama.

Years later, Mama told me about the first time I came into her. How hard she had to fight to stay in her own body, not swap into mine. She figured she won because I was just a baby. Over time, she'd learned how to make room for me, to resist the strong pull down into my body. How to help me find my way back into my own body. After that first time, she never let another person touch my face.

Folks around here, mostly farmers, were afraid of me when Mama first brought me home—just like Dr. Tom said they'd be. Some of them whispered rumors that God had punished Mama for something she did. Others told crude jokes. Dr. Tom said it was the only way these people knew how to deal with their fear and ignorance.

One morning, when I'd only been home a week or so, Mama found a dead chicken on the front porch. Bloody words and strange pictures were smeared all over the door. I know she was fearful and angry, but she never let on. Just propped me up in a sling on the sunny side of the porch and began to scrub that door clean with lye soap. The soap smelled like Mama's anger. Fierce and strong. It stung the insides of my nose, but I didn't cry. I was listening too hard. I could hear something around the house now. It sounded like the woods were creeping closer. Twigs snapped, bushes rustled.

I puffed the lye fumes from my nose, picked up a new smell. Sweat. Dirt. Muck. I recognized the stink from the crowd we'd pushed through when we left the hospital. Farmers. Mama must have heard them, too. I heard her rag splash into her bucket. She stepped in front of me, blocking the warm sun from my body, and reached down to pick me up. She grunted softly from the pain of bending down so soon after having me, but I don't think they heard her. Not until she'd gotten me and straightened back up. She touched my cheek.

I could see them now.

They looked like pieces of the woods. Weathered faces, bodies covered with stained, shapeless clothing. Their colors—dark green, almost black—snaked around their bodies like kudzu vines.

"I want to thank you kindly for this chicken," Mama said in a strong, clear voice. "I'll be making a fine stew with it. We, Carly Hope and me, hope you'll come by to visit again real soon."

They never said a word. Just backed away into the trees until you couldn't hear nothing but the wind whisper through the few leaves that had escaped the choking grasp of the kudzu. They didn't come back that day, but after a while, after things started to happen, they came all the time.

They bring chickens now, other things too, but it's as a gift to Mama and me. She takes their gifts and we tell them what we see—what their colors tell us. Sometimes it's not what they want to know, but folks around here have a way of dealing with things that maybe other people might not understand or agree with. Mama says that's part of how they get along, how they fix things that don't seem right. I guess that's how they come to accept me.

After all, they'd say, Carl was one of the finest men ever to walk the earth. And Evvie. She was the prettiest thing anyone in this town ever laid eyes on. All that curly black hair, dark eyes and sweet curves. But Evvie was never stuck up or prideful of her looks. No sir. God filled Evvie with a soul as pure as any woman could ever hope to have. Why, when she was just a young slip of a girl, she'd sneak into the church and watch old Rosemarie Havers playing the piano—you know, practice for Sunday meeting. Now, years later, Evvie sits up front every Sunday morning—with Carly Hope right next to her—plays hymns and leads us all in prayerful songs. And she never took one lesson. Not a one. God reached right down and touched her—gave her the gift of music. But that ain't all. Evvie was always the first one showing up at your door with a stewed chicken or some calvesfoot jelly when you were sick or maybe lost a loved one. Sometimes she'd come calling before anyone could possibly know you were ailing. Like she knew things ahead of time. It spooked folks at first, but then they got to like it. Now people, especially the women, are always going to her for advice. They believe she has "the sight." And it got stronger after Carly Hope come. It's like Evvie can look at you and tell you what's going on in your mind.

And what about Carly Hope? Well, sure, the baby took some getting used to, but Evvie stuck by the baby and Dr. Tom stuck by Evvie and pretty soon everyone come to accept her. She ain't so awful, once you get used to her. Evvie keeps her arm-things covered up with pretty sack dresses. Carly Hope's legs ain't worth much. Sort of floppy, but Evvie just pulls the dresses over them. All that curly hair—black like her mother's—just covers over her shoulders and part of her face. She smiles all the time, so I guess she's happy. Evvie keeps her by her side, always touching her face. No sir, God would have no call to punish Evvie with a freak baby. Carly Hope was a miracle. A sign.

It's my birthday again. This day has come and gone eighteen times since I was born. Eighteen years of living my life and seeing the world through Mama. Eighteen years of watching people's faces when they looked at me. Eighteen years of knowing their thoughts before they did. Eighteen years of superstitions, hate and fear.

Mama is laying next to me here on the bed, propped up with four pillows to help ease the pain of the sickness that's eating her alive. The bedroom window is open, welcoming a lazy breeze rich with the scents of wet earth and new green plants. A tiny set of wind chimes sways gently over our heads, tapping sweet, random notes that echo the mountain birds. I can feel the warm sun slant across the bed—across Mama and me. Mama always said that spring, like all nice surprises, is always here on April Fools' Day.

I feel Mama shift slightly, trying, I think, to find a more comfortable position. A resigned moan escapes Mama, the quiet sound telling me she's found no relief. I snuggle into her, letting her know I'm nearby. I haven't gone inside her much these last few weeks. Not since she got so sick. It uses up too much of her strength to share with me. So I just sit here, in my dark world, wondering what will happen after Mama dies.

Cousin Jessie and Billie Sue, his young new wife, have been here helping out this last week, ever since Mama took so bad. Billie Sue has pale, almost-white hair that curls over her shoulders and down toward her slender waist. The women say she's too skinny, but I notice the men watching her every chance they get.

They can't see the colors snaking around her. Mostly muddy blacks and grays with strange crackles of red light. I've never seen colors like that before, but they scare me.

Billie Sue and Cousin Jessie are all the kin I'll have left in this world when Mama dies. Cousin Jessie promised Mama a time ago, right before he moved away and got married, he'd take care of me if anything ever happened to her. He's here now, so I guess he remembered. He's almost old enough to be my daddy, but I never think of him like that. I think he's wonderful and I love him with all my heart.

I can hear them in the next room, packing up Mama's things. The wind chimes Mama hung for me in each window of the house clash and chatter as they're torn from their airy shelters and thrust into paper shrouds. Dishes, pots, rag rugs, embroidered samplers—all hidden away, like they're shameful.

"Not much worth saving," Billie Sue complained to Jessie. Her whiny voice carried easily through the thin walls. "Certainly not enough to pay for taking care of . . . " Jessie shushed her before she could finish.

Mama stiffened. Even that slight movement caused a gasp of pain that she quickly stifled. Cousin Jessie and Billie Sue must not have heard her. I could still hear them in the next room, but I couldn't make out what they said. It sounded like an argument. Then I felt Mama try to turn toward me. She lifted her right arm, tried to put her hand on my face to make the connection.

Nothing much worth saving at all, I thought. I leaned closer to link with Mama. Only my whole world, fitted into a few boxes.

"Carly," Mama whispered, her hand groping for me. "Carly, I need to tell you something. Before I die. Before it's too late." And then she reached me. Her bony fingers, sharp slivers of chilled flesh, barely touched my forehead, but it was enough to make the connection. I flashed through the link and, probably for the last time, entered into my mother's mind.

The soft knock on the bedroom door startled me. I'd felt so familiar and safe during my link with Mama, I'd almost been able to forget about my kinfolk in the next room. Kin who would have complete control over my future. The fear came back. Fear for Mama, for myself, for what my life would become after she died. And she was going to die. Soon. She told me so.

The door opened slowly, creaked on old rusted hinges. Cousin Jessie and Billie Sue walked in, the now-familiar sound of their shoes racketing on the wood floor. They stopped near Mama's side of the bed. The mattress sagged deep at the end and a wave of sick-sweet perfume washed over me. Billie Sue must have sat herself down.

"We've packed up all the small stuff, just like you wanted, Aunt Evvie," said Cousin Jessie in a forced, cheerful voice. "What do you want me to do now? Can I get anything for you?"

"You can tell that fool girl to stop jiggling this bed," Mama snapped. Her voice was stronger than it had been for weeks.

The bed shook again. Sudden-like. I could hear Billie Sue's shoes hit the floor with a sharp smack.

"Who's that old woman callin' a fool?" Billie Sue screeched. "I've worked and slaved here all week, taking care of her and that . . . "

"Shut your mouth," Cousin Jessie commanded. "You just shut up and start apologizing right now."

"Me?" Outrage notched her voice up higher than usual. "You're telling me, your wife, to shut up? To apologize? You're supposed to defend me. Not dishonor me to some backwoods trash."

Cousin Jessie started to answer her, but Mama interrupted.

"Both of you hush," she said. She sat up slowly, shifted my body slightly away from her with the movement. I could hear Billie Sue breathe hard, furiously tap her foot.

"I'm the one who needs to apologize," Mama said softly. "I spoke from my pain, from the bed jostling me so. I never meant to insult this fine girl of yours, Jessie."

"Billie Sue knows that, Aunt Evvie," said Cousin Jessie. He

sounded funny, like something was caught in his throat. "We're just sorry there's not more we can do. Ain't that right, Billie Sue?"

"Seems to me taking on Carly Hope here ought to be enough for anyone," she sniffed. "I'm sure I don't know how we'll manage. Good thing that institution over in Greensboro agreed to pick her up and check her over while we finish here." I heard her step over toward the window and push the curtains aside. "And where are they anyway? They were supposed to be here an hour ago."

The institution. I went cold all over just hearing her say it out loud. I'd overheard them fight about it. Billie Sue wanted to leave me there. Said it wasn't right for Mama to expect them to throw away their new life. That I'd be happier with my own kind. Cousin Jessie had argued back, but she wouldn't stop pestering him. He finally agreed to what Billie Sue called "an evaluation." I told Mama what I'd heard, but she told me not to worry. Cousin Jessie would always do what was best for me, she said. He'd promised her long ago that he'd take care of me. Long before he had a pretty new wife, I'd thought. Long before his green and blue colors took on red streaks that matched Billie Sue's.

Fear overwhelmed me. I struggled to control myself—to pay attention to Mama. She'd promised to protect me, but she was so weak. This was out of her control.

"They'll be here soon enough," Mama said to Billie Sue. "Come away from the window, girl. Give me your hand."

Billie Sue sighed real loud, like she was mad. She waited a few moments and then, when Cousin Jessie started to say something, moved away from the window and plopped down on the bed. I know it hurt Mama, but she kept on talking like nothing had happened.

"I don't have much time left and I can't have bad feelings go on to the next world with me." Mama shifted closer to Billie Sue. "I'm grateful to you for taking on Carly Hope. I know your life— and hers—will change in ways none of us can foretell, but I know it will all work out for the best."

"I'm glad you're so sure," muttered Billie Sue. "We'll see what the doctors at the institution think."

"And that's another thing that gives me comfort," Mama said warmly. "You're looking out for her welfare already."

"Why, that's exactly so, Miss Evvie," Billie Sue said in a triumphant voice. "I just wanted to make sure everything was fine with Carly Hope. Your nephew didn't agree."

"That's not what I said," Cousin Jessie began.

"Stop right there, Jessie," Mama scolded gently. "You've always been mighty protective of Carly Hope, but you have a good wife now who knows more about these things than you. This checkup will ease all our minds."

The whine of a laboring engine filled the room. Heavy tires ground into the dirt and gravel of the road approaching our home.

"It's the van," cried Billie Sue. "I'll go let them in." She jumped up.

"Hold on," said Mama quickly. "They're not quite here." I could feel her lean forward, stifle the pain. "It's almost a shame they came right now. We were having such a nice talk." She sighed. "But, I suppose now is as good a time as any. Will you give me a kiss, Billie Sue?"

"Of course, Miss Evvie," Billie Sue gushed with a loud smacking sound. "There. We girls have to stick together."

Mama eased back against her pillows.

"That was lovely, dear. Now, kiss Carly Hope before she has to leave."

Billie Sue didn't say anything. A car door opened outside.

"I should go see to the drivers," she said.

"That's fine, dear, but kiss Carly first," Mama insisted. "This trip will be the first time we've ever been apart. Soon there will be an even longer separation for Carly and me. I know you understand she needs to know she can count on all of us for love and support."

"The drivers—" Billie Sue began.

"The drivers can wait," said Jessie. "This is more important." I heard him walk to the bedroom doorway and slap his hand against the door. The hinges screeched in protest as it swung closed.

Billie Sue came around to my side of the bed. She'd never been this close to me before. Her perfume irritated my nose.

"I don't know why you're all making such a fuss," she said. "It will only be for a few days and then, if the doctor says it's okay, we can all be together again."

"You mean *when* the doctor says it's okay," said Cousin Jessie.

"Of course, Jessie. That's what I meant," Billie Sue said. She brushed her lips against my forehead. Both our bodies jerked, repelled by even this brief contact.

"Good," said Mama with a satisfied smile. "Now I feel we're all family. You can go ahead and get the driver if you like."

I looked in the front room mirror, barely recognizing the face staring back at me. I didn't look at all like Billie Sue. All the sharp edges and pinched features had relaxed. I looked eager. Curious. Happy. I touched the corner of my mouth, traced the upward journey of my lips as they curved into a smile. All the cloudy black colors had disappeared. A rosy haze blushed and pulsed around me, like that pretty scarf Mama kept tucked away in her treasure box.

"She's all set to go," said Cousin Jessie from the doorway.

I turned around to look at him. He stared at me for a long moment, held out his hand and winked.

"This is just for show," he whispered to me as we walked down the front steps to the van. "Act like you expect her to come back in a few days. They'll take one look at her and lock her up for the rest of her life. We'll be free."

Free. What did he know about being free? I could hear the furious howling coming from the van. My legs, weak and uncooperative, began to buckle. I stumbled and clutched his arm for support.

"Just a few more minutes, Darling," he said. "I have to get Aunt Evvie to sign these papers for the doctor. You wait here." He patted my arm and asked the driver to come into the house to finish the paperwork. The other attendant, a squat, muscular man with ugly brown colors, waited until they'd entered the house and then walked away from the van to light up a cigarette.

I stood there a minute and then bent down to look in the back seat. They'd strapped her into some kind of special carrier chair, like a large child's car seat. Tight restraints crisscrossed her, barely containing the frenzied bucking of her body. Violent flashes of black and red exploded in rhythm with her struggles.

Even though I was sure the swap was final, I was afraid to touch her—especially her face. Mama had made her kiss me, gave me my chance to escape. I knew that without all those years of linking into Mama, it would have been impossible to get into Billie Sue. But Mama was right. She remembered how strong my gift was when I was just a baby. Once in, it had been easy to push Billie Sue out of her body and close the link forever. I leaned in as close as I could.

"You'll get used to it," I whispered. She went rigid, straining her head in my direction. "They'll take real good care of you and, if the doctor says it's okay, you can come live with Cousin Jessie and me."

A warm hand closed around my arm and eased me away from the van. The terrible wailing grew louder.

"It's time for them to go," Cousin Jessie said. He glanced inside the van and shook his head. "The driver said the doctor would give her a shot when they got to the institution."

The driver honked the horn. The other attendant ground his cigarette into the dirt and strode back to the van. He reached inside the back seat, yanked the restraints tighter, slammed the door closed and climbed into the passenger seat. We watched the van turn around and pull slowly away from the house.

"Good-bye! Good-bye!" I called as I waved to the thrashing figure in the back.

Cousin Jessie put his arms around my shoulders from behind me and gently turned me toward him. My heart pained me when

I saw his face. He looked so relieved. His colors glowed greeny-blue with gold speckles—like they always did when he was happy. I guess maybe he didn't love me as much as he'd said.

"Didn't I promise?" he said as he ran his hands down my back and pulled me closer. "Didn't I promise your Mama I'd spend the rest of my life taking care of you?"

Day of the Dead

Victoria A. Brownworth

It has been a warm autumn, what used to be called Indian summer, although she never really understood what that meant. As a child, she thought it was because the leaves were red, like the skin of an Indian. Now she doesn't know. Something to do with heat, she thinks. Something to do with racism. She feels a little snarl escape her lips as she thinks about this. Involuntary. *Once I cared about these things*, she thinks. *Sometimes I still do.*

It is not warm today, though. On Hallowe'en it was like summertime—hot, steamy, a damp dust coming off the leaves as she shifted under the blanket. *She* always knew what day it was. Not like some of the others. *She* always knew where she was. And it made things that much harder. She knew right where she was today. Camped out rough between St. Louis Cathedral and the Cabildo on All Soul's Day sometime just before dawn. *The Day of the Dead.* Soon that would be her. An involuntary shudder passed through her as she struggled to stand.

I will not do this, she thought, feeling another snarl coming on, this time directed at herself. She had three more days to get through and she could do it. She had made it this far.

Maeve Dorcas was on her feet now and shivering all over. It was a chill dawn for New Orleans in early November and the fog was so thick on the small cramped streets of the French Quarter that it seemed to slink by like a long-furred beast. It made her think of that Yeats poem; it seemed fitting today of all days. The cobbled streets and slate sidewalks were slick with damp from the heavy mist. The cypress shutters that encased the long French windows along the streets of the Quarter were coated with sweat, and fog horns blew deep and throaty off the Mississippi. The alternately bitter and sweet smells of chicory and *beignets* wafted across from the Café du Monde, and the wet air kept the smells there, clinging in the back of her throat, thick enough to bite. Or to choke her.

Maeve steadied herself against the gray stone walls of the tiny alleyway. Her heart was beating very fast, like trills and grace notes—three rapid beats, then a rest, then a thud, then more quick beats. She was shaking and sweaty in the fog and she could hardly breathe. She fell hard against the wall and leaned her head back, trying to concentrate on Chloe, trying to concentrate on breathing for three more days until Chloe came back for her.

As she stood with her back against the wall she stared up into the face of a statue in a niche just across from her. She remembered being there in the Quarter with Chloe one afternoon and a mime had performed from that very niche. He had been marvelous, with his white-face and harlequin suit. She had hated mimes before that day and she still did. He had been an anomaly, she had thought then and still thought as she stared up into her memory of him. He had moved her almost to tears that day. She wondered if he was dead now. He had seemed so ethereal, so clearly moving between one world and another. *The way I am now*, she thought.

Now as she stared into the eyes of the gray stone statue, she thought of the mime, she thought of herself, silent, standing there against the wall, waiting. Words like iconography and symbology came into her head but she was trying to breathe, trying to focus on one thing at a time and that thing was remembering what time her clinic appointment was, how long till that. She still wore her watch, even though the battery had run out over a month before. She knew from the color of the sky that bled through the gauze of fog that it was nearly sunrise. At 7:30 A.M. the clinic doors would open and she could just go there. Go there and wait till they called her name. It didn't matter what time her appointment was. She would go and wait until they called for her. Until they came out to take care of her.

"Some rough beast," she whispered, "slouching toward the clinic, hoping not to die." Maeve had always been clever with words, clever with memory. But this wasn't what she wanted to be thinking. It was too early—or too late—for irony, she thought. And all she wanted to be thinking about was how many days it would be until Chloe came and rescued her.

Three more days. Another holiday—at least it was at home. It seemed such a long time since she had smelled the bonfires in London on Guy Fawkes Day. Sometimes, when she would ride on the streetcar up St. Charles to the library at Tulane she would smell that smell. The tracks down the median where the trolley ran were covered with tiny round leaves the size of a halfpenny and those leaves always held the dusky scent of fire, like they were themselves incendiary.

Maeve wished she were home. Felt like crying, suddenly, she wanted to be home so much. Wished she were there with Chloe, instead of here, alone. Here Hallowe'en had filled the streets with drink and drunkards, people spilling out all over in costumes that were sometimes just a G-string and sequins. She had slept uptown that night, in Audubon Park near the zoo and she'd been terrified all night, not really sleeping, but the Quarter had been too full of crowds, the streets running with rain and piss from the celebration. Today the celebrations would be solemn, she knew. Like a jazz funeral. The Day of the Dead brought out a different kind of reveler. Soon there would be old women lined up at the doors of the Cathedral and incense would filter out from the cypress shutters on the streets off the Quarter. But right now she yearned to walk down into the Tube and see the Guys dressed up and lying in their carts, the children with their faces painted black, a Guy on every street corner in Hackney. Instead she was here, caught in another bedeviling fog. Aching for Chloe and counting the days until she arrived. Afraid she would die before she saw Chloe again.

Maeve had been living on the streets of New Orleans for just over three weeks now. Since after Chloe had called her at the University and told her when she was flying in from France, when she would be in New Orleans to help Maeve wrap up her work and move back to London. Chloe was supposed to come and spend two weeks here with her, take her up to Lake Charles to meet some Cajun women she knew, have some alligator stew and fly back to London. Home.

Chloe didn't know what had happened to Maeve. Chloe had been on a research tour deep in the Loire Valley in France. Maeve sighed and looked up at the Cathedral spires and wondered if the churches in Lille or Rheims looked anything like this. When the French built this city what were they trying to copy, she wondered. Home or some new hybrid? Chloe was like that—a hybrid, a mix of cultures and places, an American at home only in London.

Chloe. She didn't know about any of it. She wouldn't have believed Maeve had been sleeping on the streets of the Quarter for close to a month. Chloe didn't know Maeve was dying.

It was a month to the day of her diagnosis when Maeve had gone home from the clinic to find her apartment had been padlocked, her things on the street. *Bloody, fucking Napoleonic codes*, she'd shrieked. You couldn't *do* this in London, so *bloody* uncivilized.

There wasn't much, really, sitting there on the sidewalk under a live oak on Elysian Fields three doors down from Ruby's Bar. A few boxes—her kitchen things and some of her reference books.

A bag of clothes—at least they'd had the decency to throw them in a plastic trash bag. Her suitcase had been stuffed full of her bedclothes. The radio had been stolen by the time she got there and so had most of her tapes. Her letters from Chloe were there, though, and her manuscript and her notes. Chloe had taken almost everything else back with her when she left. Maeve had assured her she would only need the basics until her research was finished.

That was before Chloe left. That was before Maeve got sick. That was before she had no money left to pay her rent because the hospital—Charity—had been so unaptly named. That was before, when she had had a life so cleanly and clearly mapped out. That was before the Day of the Dead, before, when she had a future.

Maeve had taken the bus downtown and crammed everything into two lockers at the Trailways station. She put some clothes and the blankets in her suitcase and sat at the terminal for the rest of the day watching television and drinking cans of juice from a vending machine. She had $103 until Chloe came and no place to live.

Maeve had roughed it before. After she'd finished school she'd even trekked across the Subcontinent with her Pakistani lover, Shaheen. You could do that then, the borders were still open. It had been hot and terrible, but it had also been the most marvelous thing she'd ever done up till then. It had taken three months. Now she was wondering how she would manage three days.

There wasn't really anyone she knew here in New Orleans. She was a stranger, a foreigner with a visa for research that expired at the end of the month. She knew professors at the University, knew them to speak to. Knew a curator at the Museum, also to speak to, to have a coffee with, to exchange a few tips on the best places to stay for a tourist in London. But that was all. She had been alone, except for Chloe. It was Chloe's town, where Chloe had grown up, where Chloe had fled from. Maeve had only come to do the research—her dissertation on Lillian Hellman, her declarative study on women and theatre, on women, politics and the theatre, on women and lying, on women and invented lives—all as defined by the life and work of Lillian Hellman.

Maeve didn't know what had first drawn her to the American playwright, she who came from the land of storytelling, the country of poets. Why hadn't it been Yeats, whose every poem she had once known by heart? Or Joyce, her fellow Dubliner? Or, if she needed a playwright, O'Casey, whose world was so like hers?

Sometimes she thought it was the foreignness of Hellman. But Hellman never felt foreign to her, Hellman always felt like someone she knew, someone she could sneak into the local pub with and have a cigarette and a shandy. There was a bawdiness about Hellman that enticed her, a solidness to her writing that made Maeve feel tough and strong. Hellman had reinvented herself—not just once, but again and again, the way other women changed hairstyles. Maeve had grown up in the dirtiest part of Dublin waiting for the day when she would leave for London and become the woman she wanted to be. Hellman was her model, her icon, the imaginary friend who taught her how to be brave enough to leave the tiny little backstreet house with the washing strung line by line across the scrap of sooty yard. If Hellman the Jew could brave the Nazis for her beloved Julia, then Maeve the Irish Catholic girl could brave the Church and her father for the love of knowledge, of learning, of having an independent life that didn't include squalling babies, a loveless marriage and no money as its only constants. If Hellman could stand up to McCarthy, Maeve could stand up to her mother and go off to London and reinvent herself as a woman with choices.

Without Hellman, there would not have been Chloe.

It was how she'd met Chloe, back in London. Chloe, professional expatriate. Chloe, who still had, after ten years in London, an unmistakable American accent, Southern accent.

Chloe Marchand was an expert on Lillian Hellman. Hellman, whose town was also New Orleans, who continued to live half of each year in New Orleans, had been Chloe's friend and mentor, had helped her escape New Orleans. Just as she had helped Maeve escape Dublin. Chloe said Hellman had taught her how to be herself. Maeve had been introduced to Chloe when she had begun the book she had hoped would be definitive. Chloe was an instructor at the college where Maeve was studying.

Their attraction had been immediate, mutual. They talked about the ethics of it long into the night over rich port, some Stilton and pears and six packs of Turkish cigarettes, and then they had gone to bed. Maeve had moved out of her rooms at the college and into Chloe's North London house. They had decided, without even discussing it, to stop seeing other people. Maeve had a long talk with Danielle, a French exchange student she'd been seeing; Chloe told her longtime friend Sylvia about Maeve. Sylvia had been angrier than Danielle who had shrugged, said "Okay, Chérie," and kissed Maeve on her cheeks and pinched her ass. Sylvia was very bitter and had told Chloe that Maeve was too young, that it would cause a scandal, that Chloe would jeopardize her career. "Remember you're an American," she had hissed as she shut the door after Chloe was barely through it.

But Maeve wasn't, despite the years between them, too young, and they had lived and worked well together, respectful of each other's work, passionate about each other's bodies, full of a kind of intellectual and sexual excitement that both claimed was new to them, different. Maeve thought there would be years together. It was Chloe who had sometimes worried that Maeve would tire of her as Chloe got older and Maeve was in her prime. Chloe had worried again when she left for France and Maeve stayed in New Orleans. But Maeve knew only a few people in the city, only the people at the college, at the library, where the papers were kept. She didn't like to go to the bars without Chloe, didn't want to do anything but her work, begged off politely offered invitations to dinner from professors at the university. Maeve wasn't American, she reminded Chloe; she didn't make attachments easily or readily.

"When I've done the definitive book on Hellman," Maeve had said softly to Chloe on the night before she had left for France, "you will love me as much as I love you." Chloe had laughed then, and touched her everywhere, kissed her all over, told her there was no way she could possibly love Maeve more than she did now. "Well, keep away from those French women," Maeve had admonished. But Chloe reminded her about Danielle and they had kissed again and fallen into a short, ragged sleep before Chloe left for the airport, Chloe staring back at her through the rear window of the taxi until the traffic swallowed her up.

Two months ago, that was. A literal lifetime, Maeve thought with a bitterness that caused her an almost physical pain. Now nothing was definitive except the death sentence she'd been given—could it be only a week?—after Chloe had left. She'd collapsed on the floor of the library, felt like she was suffocating. Awakened in a ward the color of a manila envelope, with tubes in her arm, bags dripping above her head, a huge mask over her face filled with a sharp, biting air.

Blood test. HIV positive. Lungs filled with fluid. A kind of disease that birds get, that birds die from, some kind of microbial thing, infecting her lungs. It meant something specific, the doctor told her as she gasped for breath, as she swam in her own sweat. It meant she had AIDS. How did she get it, the doctor asked her. *How did you get it? Do you take drugs?* he had asked her. *Are you a prostitute?* She had laughed a gagging kind of laugh through the oxygen mask, had coughed out that she was a fellow from London University, that she was in this bloody hot swamp doing research, that she wasn't a bloody prostitute but if she were, she'd charge him triple.

How did you get it? That question echoed in Maeve's head now, pounded in her ears as she shook the leaves from her blanket and folded it tight, damp dirty side in, cramming it into her case. She pulled her blue cotton sweater off, shook it out and put it back on. She walked back to the end of the alley near the rear entry to the Cabildo and peed into a pile of old newspapers. The effort made her dizzy but she couldn't sit down; she might not get up.

An ochre-pink light was breaking down the fog now as she

brushed her short, spiky black hair and tucked her shirt back into her jeans. She hefted the bag up over her left shoulder and headed toward the river, toward Camp Street and the clinic. In another half hour it would be open and she would be as close as she would get to home for the next three days. Three more days and Chloe would take care of her. Three more days. If she didn't die on the Day of the Dead.

The walk to the clinic was long. Down Decatur past all the SRO hotels and Greek bars, past sailors slumped on the sidewalk sleeping off whatever or whoever they had done the night before. Past the end of the Quarter and into the CBD, the Central Business District, and then over CL10 into the Irish Channel and into the clinic. She had to keep stopping on the way, trying to breathe. The bus would have taken her right there, but she only had nine dollars left and three more days till Chloe arrived. She couldn't afford the bus, she couldn't afford to pay for anything but a meal later, when she just had to eat. A po' boy or a muffaletta or eggs and biscuits at the Hummingbird where you had to upend waterglasses over the roaches that crawled out, brazen, onto your plate.

If she was lucky, they would feed her at the clinic. Give her coffee at least, and a bun, maybe a sandwich. Maeve knew she had a fever. She was shivering and hot, aching all over. She wanted to lie in a steamy hot tub for hours and just soak the fever and pain from her body. All along the route to the clinic there were bodies in doorways, bodies piled up against trash cans and bins, bodies strewn under newspaper and cardboard boxes and blankets. Bodies just like hers. How many of them had AIDS, too, she wondered. How many of them knew it was the Day of the Dead? How many were traveling on expired visas?

The doors were open when she reached the Camp Street Clinic and most of the orange plastic chairs that lined the reception area were full of slumped-over men and women. Noreen was behind the bulletproof glass and waved to Maeve as she came in, gesturing to the phone she spoke into and then pointing to an urn of coffee on a small table near the restroom door. Maeve went into the bathroom and brushed her teeth, blood spattering into the sink. She rinsed it and filled the sink with hot water and stuck her head into it, washing her short hair with the disinfectant soap that squirted out of the container on the wall, drying her rinsed hair with paper towels and brushing it into the black spikes Chloe loved.

Her face was paler than any Irish girl's should ever be, she thought, as she gazed into her blue bloodshot eyes. Deep gray-green circles ringed her eyes and even her lips looked white. *Day of the Dead.* She had seen the Mexican masks in a museum somewhere, or a book, or something, she couldn't remember, some Mexican woman artist, she was so dizzy, really faint now and the face in the mirror swam in front of her before she crashed to the floor.

Noreen and Rita were talking softly to her as something sharp and sickening was forced under her nose, jerking her back from the dead. Noreen's long dreadlocks fell across Maeve's breasts as she leaned into Maeve's face and asked her what day it was, if she could hear alright, if she could see okay. Maeve always expected Noreen to sound West Indian, like the women at home who looked so much like her, and the long drawn-out sounds of Alabama brought Maeve back as much as the amyl nitrate had done.

And Rita was there. Rita with her soft fuzzy red hair and her deep olive skin and a look she had never seen in London. Rita was as close to a friend as Maeve had in New Orleans. She came to the clinic on most of the same days as Maeve. She was funny and sweet and Maeve liked looking at her, talking to her. Like Chloe, Rita made Maeve feel safe, with her big breasts and her strong face. Now she had one of her warm silky hands on Maeve's forehead and she was saying, "It's alright, babe, you just been sleepin' poorly. You be okay, Noreen and Dr. Toussaint gonna give you somethin'. You gonna be alright, babe."

The women helped Maeve to her feet and took her into one of the blue-curtained examining rooms. Rita told Noreen she'd stay with Maeve until the doctor could see her. Noreen brought them both in some orange juice and Rita joked and asked if she was getting her Methadone early. Noreen gave her a little shove and said, "Giirrl—" and went back to the phones.

"Whatchu been doin', Maeve Miss?" Rita asked her, still stroking her face as Maeve lay on the examining table, her breath coming in short hot spurts. Rita always called her Maeve Miss, and it sounded like Christmas or Michaelmas and she liked it somehow, it was comforting, familiar in a way she couldn't explain.

Now Maeve could talk, could tell someone about sleeping rough, about Hallowe'en night, about the Day of the Dead and how she was afraid she'd die before she saw Chloe again.

"You ain't gonna die, girl," Rita told her, pulling the sickening orange chair closer to the examining table. "But why you been on the streets? Why you ain't come here and tell them you needs a place to stay? Y'all know they help you here. Noreen, she's a real good woman. Now y'all know you comin' home with me to my mama's after this, they say you okay to go home. You can't be living on the streets this sick. It ain't good for you. Ain't good at all. I can't believe y'all ain't been eatin' or havin' noplace to sleep. That's so bad, girl." She smoothed Maeve's hair with her strong olive hand.

Maeve lay on the table and looked up at the ceiling, tears running down the sides of her face into her ears, her breath coming in gulps and gasps. Why hadn't she come here before, why hadn't she asked them to telegraph Chloe, find her a room, anything? Why hadn't she asked Noreen or Rita or the other woman she liked, the junkie with the white-blonde hair, Melanie, for some help? Now that she had told Rita, it all seemed so simple. Rita was right. Rita would take care of her until Chloe came. Rita would make sure she didn't die. Maeve took a deep breath, tried to quiet her heartbeat, looked around for some tissues to wipe her face.

"Thank you," she whispered to Rita, "you're so very kind, so very, very kind." Maeve told her how she had woken up shrouded in fog behind the Cathedral, feeling like the ghosts of all New Orleans were stalking her. "I thought I might die," she told Rita slowly. "I thought I might die before I could even get up off the ground."

"Ghosts *is* all around there, girl. That ain't no joke," Rita said, no trace of mockery in her words. "That's why I got to get you home with me, 'cause it ain't safe out there for y'all, you so small and, don't mind me tellin' you this, but a little simple, too. My mama fix you up till your girl get here. She take me back when I get sick, don't say nothin' about it. Don't ask me how it happen, don't say nothin' about me dyin' or any such thing. She just give me some stuff, make me better, send me off down here." She leaned very close to Maeve's lips and whispered, "It weren't no Day o' the Dead, but I sure be scared when I go back there to her." She kissed Maeve lightly and put her hand gently on Maeve's left breast. "It be okay, babe. We dyin' girls got to stick together."

Maeve turned toward Rita and put both her arms tight around Rita's neck, feeling her fuzzy red hair against her cheek. "Women must really fancy you," she whispered into Rita's ear, and then lay back down, dizzy again, Chloe and Rita's faces swirling above her as the room went black.

Dr. Toussaint gave Rita pills, some cans of a liquid protein drink, and a list of things Maeve must do if she was going to live to see Chloe. Her blood sugar was low and her blood pressure even lower. She had a fever of 101 degrees and she was, he told her, "Malnourished, which is why you've been fainting. You must sleep, eat and stay away from drugs if you're going to stay out of the hospital. If your fever goes up, call me and then go right over to Charity and I'll have them admit you again and don't worry about money, they have to take care of you. You're a smart enough woman that you should have known that the last time and just not paid the bill. It would have been better for you to be worried about a bill you might never have to pay than living out of dumpsters and alleys. Now let Ms. Micheaux here take good care of you and don't take any drugs, except what I give you."

He handed some things to Rita, putting an arm around her small shoulders and whispering to her. Then he turned back to Maeve. "You need to come back here Saturday morning and let me check you out again," he said with a kind of benign sternness. "I understand you have a friend coming into the country to take you back to Britain, but you might not be well enough to travel, so please be sure to see me. Ms. Micheaux has given me her telephone number and if you aren't here by nine in the morning, I'll call you there. I really can't emphasize enough how important this is. You are a very sick young woman, Ms. Dorcas, and I don't want to be sending you back to England in a box."

With that he spoke once more to Rita and left.

Rita and her mother live in Desire, in a tiny shingled bungalow on a narrow barren street. Inside the house it is dark, beaded curtains separating the rooms that open in shotgun style from each other. Rita helps Maeve into a fat plush chair in the dusky front room. She lights some candles with writing on them that fill a table under a small mantle with figures Maeve cannot see. Rita says some words in French and puts some incense in a little green jar. The dead are everywhere, she tells Maeve, and from Hallowe'en till tomorrow, it's important to pay attention to them.

"Y'all respect the dead, the dead pass you by," she explains and goes through the red beaded curtain into the darkened space beyond. Maeve leans into the overstuffed comfort of the big chair and feels herself falling toward sleep.

In the dream, Chloe is sitting on a cane chair across from Maeve, whispering to her in French, telling her about the Loire Valley and the huge stone castles that line the river there, the Moselle. Chloe sits back in the darkened room, candlelight shimmering behind her. Her hair is longer and more steely gray than

Maeve has remembered, but her eyes are the same golden color, like a cat's, that once had been the same color as her hair—amber, glowing. But as Maeve leans forward in her chair, as Maeve tries to tell Chloe how much she has missed her, how afraid she was Chloe would never come, how sick she is, Chloe moves into the light and her face is skeletal, white outlined on green, terrifying, a death mask. She reaches her green glowing bony hand toward Maeve's face and Maeve begins to scream.

When Rita wakes her, she is tucked into a narrow white bed in a small room with a high window paned in blue-green glass. She is wearing a long lavender shirt that is not hers and the room smells strongly of gardenia and hibiscus. There is another tiny altar in the corner of the room and it is filled with low red candles. The room glows red from the lights and blue from the window glass. Maeve is sweaty and scared. On the wall directly facing the bed are seven small masks like cats' skulls, white painted on black with green and red crosses painted in the eye sockets. Maeve tries to get up but Rita pushes her back onto the bed and sits down beside her.

"The fever," she says simply. She is no longer wearing the tight green dress she wore at the clinic. Now she is in a long lavender robe and she has a string of tiny conch shells around her neck. There is a kind of humming sound coming from another room. On a small table next to the bed are the pills Dr. Toussaint prescribed for her, a red glass bowl, a small covered plate and a pitcher of water with two glasses. Rita hands her one of the glasses and three pills. She helps hold Maeve's head up while she drinks down the pills. Maeve feels dizzy again, but doesn't black out. Rita tells her she must eat.

"Beans and rice," she tells Maeve as she lifts the red bowl and spoons some into Maeve's mouth. "Protein, mama says you need protein." The food is hot and spicy and very good. Suddenly Maeve feels hungry. Rita feeds it all to her, gives her the small plate with a hot biscuit with honey drizzled over it. Maeve eats this too. She wonders if all she needs is food and a bed and she will live until Chloe gets here.

"Mama and me, we give you a bath," Rita says, smiling at her. "My Tante Renée, she take all those clothes to be washed. Whatchu been doin' in all them leaves, girl?"

Maeve laughs then, and realizes the last time she laughed was when the doctor at Charity asked her if she was a prostitute. She tells Rita this story, tells her what she does, tells her what she told the doctor. Rita laughs too.

"I been strippin' on Bourbon Street for six years," Rita says, flatly, waiting to see what Maeve will say. "I don't do men, though," she adds. But all Maeve says is how pretty Rita is, with her Creole looks and her fuzzy red hair. She doesn't ask any questions. She doesn't say to Rita, *How did you get it?*

Maeve knows now how *she* got it. The question has reverberated in her head for weeks. Fever and fear have made her forget so much since Chloe left. She has not been back to the university since the day she collapsed. She has called once to say she is ill, but she has not explained further. She has called twice more to see if Chloe has left a message for her and has found that Chloe will meet her at a restaurant in the Quarter the night her plane gets in. She will be staying at the Pontalba House. She hated Maeve's little apartment. Maeve is glad to have these details, now. Glad she will be able to have Rita meet Chloe, bring her here.

Maeve tells Rita how she got sick, how she thinks she got AIDS. She tells Rita about a long half-term party in her friend Jack's rooms at the college and how there were eight of them drinking themselves sick for two days straight. How she had done some heroin with her friends, just chipping, just trying it, feeling brazen. How she had ended up in bed with Shaheen and Jack, something that just happened because they were all so high and having such a bloody good time. How now she realized that Jack was HIV, that when he died suddenly three weeks after term ended everyone thought it was because he'd done that long bicycle trip up north in the rain. Pneumonia, his sister had told them. None of them had thought it was AIDS. Maeve didn't even think he had known it himself. He had been so healthy, such a fitness freak. Maeve had had sex with Jack and Shaheen several times over those two days, not even thinking she might get pregnant. They had done a lot of chipping, heating the needle over and over again. None of them had thought about AIDS. None of them was sick.

Rita lifted the faded blue quilt and slid into the bed beside Maeve. She leaned over her and pushed the lavender shirt up over Maeve's breasts, slipped it off over her head. Maeve didn't say how much she loved Chloe, how she had never been unfaithful. Somehow Rita was part of Chloe now, taking care of her for Chloe, keeping her safe for Chloe. But Rita was also the woman who understood everything Maeve told her, who was sick too, who had said to her at the clinic, "Us dyin' girls got to stick together."

Maeve folded herself into Rita's arms, spread her hands between Rita's legs, whispered and sang into Rita's ears, ran her tongue along Rita's long, slender neck, linked her fingers in Rita's fuzzy red hair. The sex was simple and sweet, none of the desperation of two women dying, Rita riding up and down on Maeve's skinny thigh, thrusting herself up and down onto Maeve's long fingers. Maeve pushing Rita's tiny fist deep into her, locking her legs around Rita's dark olive back.

Maeve was slick with sweat, and shivering when Rita led her, shaking, into the bathroom and lay her down in the deep, clawfoot tub, pouring gardenia oil into the hot water, sponging Maeve's shoulders and back. Telling her she would keep Maeve safe until Chloe came for her, telling her it was good to have someone to take care of, telling her Maeve made her feel she wasn't going to die.

For two days Maeve went in and out of fever, in and out of consciousness. Rita fed her, sponged her, fondled her and spoke to her in her sweet, low *patois*. She lit candles, spooned incense into a little purple jar, fanned Maeve with a gray feathered fan and talked in the doorway to a large, dark woman with fuzzy red hair like Rita's.

In Maeve's dream, the dead came for her again and again. Lillian Hellman sat at her bedside and talked to her about Julia and all the other women she had invented in her life. "Don't be afraid to make up your own life," she told Maeve intensely, smoking a long brown cigarette like the ones Maeve had smoked with Chloe the first night they had been together. "Don't be afraid to say whatever you think. They can't kill you." Hellman's voice was gravelly thick, coming to her through fog. Her accent was subtle, like Rita's, but her voice was deep and forceful, and Maeve kept trying to find a pen to write down what Hellman told her.

The dead always sat beside her on the bed and glowed green or amber in the tiny room. Hellman came many times, smoke from her brown cigarettes swirling like a green gassy fog around her amber face. Hellman talked to Maeve as she smoked, conspiratorial, chatty, the way Maeve had thought she would be when she imagined Hellman at the pub with her in Dublin. Chloe came once, her face still a skeletal mask, and Maeve remembered that she had seen that mask in a book about Frida Kahlo. She tried to have a conversation with the death-mask Chloe, but she found she couldn't talk to the dead, she could only stare and listen.

On November 5, Guy Fawkes Day, the day Chloe was coming to get her, Maeve's fever finally broke and she woke up tight against Rita's sinewy back, feeling for the first time like she might live. Rita turned toward Maeve, felt her cheek and told her the dead wouldn't come back to get her now that the fever was gone. "But the dead, y'all remember, they come up everywhere, they always about, always lookin' for friends."

Maeve sat up in the narrow bed and held Rita tight, looking deep into her smoky eyes. "I love you," she said simply, her breath hot against Rita's ear. "Women must really fancy you. You should come to London with Chloe and me. The women would go wild for you, absolutely wild. Come with us." Maeve didn't want to leave Rita, wasn't sure she *could* leave her.

The fever was gone now, but not the fear. Rita slid around Maeve and out of the bed. She reached for a silky yellow robe that had dropped from the chair to the floor. She turned back to Maeve, her smoky eyes wet. She walked slowly toward Maeve, sat on the blue quilt where Hellman had sat in Maeve's dream.

"I ain't comin' with y'all to London, babe," Rita said. "I got my own life here, what-all I got of it. Y'all was afraid of the dead and I told you me and my mama would keep you safe. Now I got to get back to my own stuff and y'all got to get back to yours. There's this girl at the club, y'know? And there's some other things I got goin' here. Y'all are a real sweet woman and this was real nice. But honey, this ain't real, y'know? We both got real things we got goin', and that's what's next, that's what you got to do."

She lay back down on the bed and pulled Maeve to her, folding the yellow silk robe across Maeve's naked back. Tears slid from Maeve's cheek onto Rita's full breast.

"You got to tell your girl about bein' sick, you got to do that book y'all been workin' on so hard. And you got to get home. *This* my home, babe, and this where I want to die, not in some strange place. That's what I been doing for you these last few days—keeping you safe so you can die at home. Y'all know what I mean? Now you get yourself ready to go. I got to call Dr. Toussaint and tell him you ain't comin' today. And I got to go get your girlfriend and bring her back here."

Maeve's chest felt hard and full, and the tears ran down her cheeks in a sharp hot rivulets. She clung to Rita like she had clung to Chloe the night before she had left for France. This was what dying was about, she thought. That was why the dead were everywhere. Rita had made her well—or at least as well as she could be. Now she had to get on with her life. Otherwise she was just using Rita, just taking and not giving anything back. She had nothing to give Rita. Nothing but her own life. Nothing but keeping the dead at bay a little longer. She had work to do, she had to explain to Chloe about the death-mask dreams, she had to remember everything Hellman had told her, she had to keep living, she had to keep the dead away as long as possible, she had to see London, maybe even Dublin, once again. She had to go home to live—or die.

Before Rita left for the Quarter, before Rita left to get Chloe, she gave Maeve a small black muslin bag, sewn tight with blood-red thread. "My mama," she told Maeve. "She says you got to keep this with you all the time." She held Maeve then, looked straight into Maeve's blue eyes with her deep smoky ones. She kissed her, this time a kiss between friends, friends who share a secret, friends walking through the land of the dead.

"Y'all stay here, now, till we get back," she said, and left the little house.

Maeve stands by the darkened window in Rita's front room, looking out onto the empty street where a scrawny orange cat slinks through a patch of chicory growing near the whitewashed fence that stands between this house and the next. Rita is right, she thinks as she sees the taxi with Chloe and Rita heading toward the house. Rita is right, she thinks, as Chloe steps out of the taxi and looks anxiously toward the window where Maeve stands behind the thick red curtain. The dead are everywhere. And we have to go on living.

About the Contributors

Meredith S. Baird is a mystery author whose short stories have appeared in many anthologies, including *Out for Blood, Out for More Blood, Night Bites, Mitternachtskuss, Death Knell 2* and *Death Knell 3*. She has participated as a mystery author on panels at the Mid-Atlantic Mystery Convention, Sisters in Crime and Rosemont College. She has won awards for her short fiction, including mystery writing, from the Philadelphia Writer's Conference and Flash Mystery at the Mid-Atlantic Mystery Convention. She is an active member of Mystery Writers of America and president of the Delaware Valley chapter of Sisters in Crime. She teaches courses in mystery fiction at Rosemont College.

Toni Brown is an African-American writer of fiction and poetry. Her work has appeared in literary journals and anthologies, including *Night Bites* and *Out for More Blood*. She is a Cavecanem Fellow in Poetry and resides in Philadelphia.

Joanne Dahme is a Philadelphia writer whose stories have been widely anthologized, appearing in *Thirteen by Seven, Night Bites, Out for Blood* and *Out for More Blood*, among other books. Her novel, *The Vampire's Baby*, is forthcoming. By day she manages the Public Affairs Division of the Philadelphia Water Department; by night she likes to write, run, read and hang out with her husband and son.

Diane DeKelb-Rittenhouse makes her home in the Philadelphia suburbs with her husband, comix writer W. E. Rittenhouse, their daughter and the cat who owns them. She has written horror, fantasy and romantic fiction and has been widely published and anthologized. The idea for "Femme Coverte" came to her while researching an editorial for the seventy-fifth anniversary of women's suffrage. Reading bell hooks's *Ain't I a Woman* added another dimension to the tale, as did her research into the history of Louisiana, voodoo, slave religions and the life of planter aristocracy. Catherine Clinton's *Plantation Mistress: Woman's World in the Old South* was particularly helpful in the latter regard.

Terri de la Peña, author of the novels *Margins* and *Latin Satins*, is taking a break from writing fiction. In the meantime she has co-written a children's book, *A is for the Americas*, with Cynthia Chin-Lee. Terri daydreams about the elusive Noche, but hasn't yet decided whether to write more about her.

Susan Raffo is a writer and community organizer and the editor of the anthology *Queerly Classed: Gay Men and Lesbians Write About Class*. The former managing editor of *The Evergreen Chronicles*, she is the recipient of a Vice Versa journalism award and a finalist for the Lambda Book Award and the American Library Association's Best GLBT Book of the Year Award.

Ruthann Robson is the author of the novels *A/K/A* and *Another Mother*, and the short fiction collections *Cecile* and *Eye of the Hurricane*, which won the 1990 Ferro-Grumley Award for Fiction.

Jean Stewart is the author of a series of feminist sci-fi fantasy books, *Return to Isis*, *Isis Rising* and *Warriors of Isis*, and a modern work, *Emerald City Blues*. She lives near Seattle with her partner Susie, two rowdy dogs and two sweet cats.

Susanna Sturgis grew up around horses and, during her city years, considered her bicycle an urban horse. Her fiction, nonfiction and poetry have appeared in an array of publications, including *Sinister Wisdom*, *Calyx* and *Trivia*; her story "Sustenance" was published in *Night Bites*. Long an avid reader of fantasy and science fiction, she edited three original anthologies of women's fantasy and science fiction in 1989–91: *Memories and Visions*, *The Women*

Who Walk Through Fire and *Tales of Magic Realism by Women*. She lives on Martha's Vineyard, Massachusetts, with her dog, Rhodry Malamutt; she makes her living as a copyeditor and sings alto in the Island Community Chorus.

Joyce Wagner is a writer and former managing editor of *Planet Vineyard Magazine*. Her short stories have appeared in *Night Bites* and *Out for More Blood*. She writes for *Planet Vineyard Magazine* and *Martha's Vineyard Times*. She has recently completed her first novel, *Gatecrasher*. She resides in West Tisbury, Massachusetts, with her fiancé, David Wilson.

Roz Warren's short stories and humorous essays have appeared in numerous magazines, including *Seventeen*, *Fantasy and Science Fiction* and *The Utne Reader*, as well as in twelve anthologies. She is the editor of fifteen collections of women's humor, including the classics *Women's Glib* and *Dyke Strippers: Lesbian Cartoonists from A to Z*. Her most recent collection is *Women's Lip: Outrageous, Irreverent and Just Plain Hilarious Quotes*. An at-home mom, Roz spends quantity time with her son, Thomas, works at the local public library and has just completed her first novel.

Mary E. Wilkins-Freeman was a well-known New England writer of the regionalist school. Her first story was published in *Harper's New Monthly* in 1884. She penned numerous volumes of short stories as well as a succession of twelve novels—all very well received critically by major literary figures of her time, among them Henry James. Wilkins-Freeman's fiction focused on issues of class, poverty and the decline of the milltowns of New England at the turn of the century. Her fiction is also notable for its highly developed feminist vantage point. Like few women of her era, Wilkins-Freeman supported herself through her writing and won several prestigious literary awards. In addition to her regional writing, Wilkins-Freeman wrote a series of gothic tales, among them "Luella Miller," first published in 1903. Wilkins-Freeman died in 1930.

Lisa D. Williamson is a features writer for *Main Line Today* magazine and a contributing editor for *Murderous Intent*. Her award-winning short fiction has appeared in numerous anthologies, including *Night Bites, Death Knell, Out for Blood, Out for More Blood* and other publications. She is the author of two novels, owns and operates a personalized interactive mystery theater company and lives with her family of male Midgetts in suburban Philadelphia.

Barbara Wilson is most recently the author of *Salt Water and Other Stories* and *The Death of a Much Travelled Woman* (stories featuring translator sleuth, Cassandra Reilly). Her memoir *Blue Windows* won the 1997 Lambda Literary Award for Best Lesbian Autobiography and was nominated for the PEN/USA West Award for Creative Nonfiction. She lives in Seattle.

Linda K. Wright's mystery fiction has appeared in several anthologies, including *Night Bites, Out for Blood, Mitternachtskuss, Death Knell 3* and *Out for More Blood*, as well as several magazines, including *Murderous Intent*. Her literary fiction has appeared in print and on-line in *The Princeton Arts Review, The Seattle Review, The Maryland Review, Cyber Oasis, Echoes* and *Slice of Life*. Her nonfiction work includes biographical sketches in *American National Biography* and articles in trade, computer and writer's journals. Awarded the 1995 Charles Johnson Award for Fiction, she is former vice-president of the Delaware Valley chapter of Sisters in Crime and regularly chairs mystery panels.

About the Editors

Victoria A. Brownworth is the author of seven books, including the Lambda Literary Award finalist *Too Queer: Essays from a Radical Life* and *Film Fatales: Independent Women Directors*. She is the editor of seven books, including the Lambda Literary Award finalist *Night Bites: Vampire Tales by Women*. She writes for many national publications, is a columnist for several magazines, including *Curve*, and has written screenplays for several award-winning short films. She lives in Philadelphia with her partner of twelve years, four cats and a dog.

Judith M. Redding is a Philadelphia-based independent filmmaker and writer. A graduate of the London International Film School, her videos include *Mondays* and *but would you take her back?* She is the film and video editor of *Curve*, co-editor with Victoria A. Brownworth of *Out For More Blood: Tales of Malice and Retaliation by Women*, and co-author with Brownworth of *Film Fatales: Independent Women Directors*.

Selected Titles from Seal Press

Night Bites: Vampire Stories by Women edited by Victoria A. Brownworth. $12.95, 1-878067-71-0. Featuring sixteen original works, this subversive collection offers gothic atmosphere with a contemporary twist, scintillating writing and enough blood and lust to satisfy even the most discriminating connoisseurs.

Film Fatales: Independent Women Directors by Judith M. Redding and Victoria A. Brownworth. $16.95, 1-878067-97-4. Includes profiles of over thirty pioneering directors, producers and distributors who have changed the face of contemporary film by delivering distinctly female images and sensibilities for the screen.

Beyond the Limbo Silence by Elizabeth Nunez. $12.95, 1-58005-013-1. A spellbinding story tracing a young woman's journey from her Caribbean home to the United States during the civil rights struggle.

The Dyke and the Dybbuk by Ellen Galford. $12.95, 1-58005-012-3. A fun, feisty, feminist romp through Jewish folklore as an ancient spirit returns to haunt a modern-day London lesbian. Winner of the Lambda Literary Award for Best Lesbian & Gay Humor.

Egalia's Daughters by Gerd Brantenberg. $12.95, 1-878067-58-3. A hilarious satire on sex roles—in which the "wim" rule and the "menwim" stay at home—by Norway's leading feminist author.

Girls, Visions and Everything by Sarah Schulman. $12.95, 1-58005-022-0. A spirited romp through Manhattan's Lower East Side featuring lesbian-at-large Lila Futuransky. By the author of *People in Trouble*, *After Delores*, *Empathy* and *Shimmer*.

If You Had a Family by Barbara Wilson. $12.00, 1-878067-82-6. A poignant novel that traces one woman's journey as she comes to terms with the memories of her Christian Science childhood and experiences a transformative new relationship.

Out of Time by Paula Martinac. $12.95, 1-58005-020-4. A delightful and thoughtful novel about lesbian history and the power of memory. Winner of the Lambda Literary Award for Best Lesbian Fiction.

Seal Press publishes a wide range of titles by women writers. To order from us directly, or to request a free catalog of our books, call us toll-free at (800) 754-0271. Visit our website at www.sealpress.com.